Ms. Shirley Erbert
504 Sunset Dr•Norton, KS 67654-1540

"A page-turner that will leave you on the edge of your seat . . . another wonderful thriller from Carlene Thompson . . . a must-read."

"An intriguing tale told in a wonderfully fresh voice. Thompson has a truly unique style that blends beautiful prose with compelling plots . . . this novel reads like lightning—and has the same effect on the reader . . . Thompson has created sharp, smart characters with motives that drive the story along. They are enough to keep the story moving at a quick pace. Her voice has a sense of rhythm and a rustic beauty that lingers in the reader's memory."

"An action-filled read with plenty of twists and turns that will keep you guessing until the very end! This story is highly detailed with an array of in-depth characters that are smart, funny, and engaging."

IF SHE SHOULD DIE
"A gripping suspense filled with romance. Ms. Thompson has the reader solving the mystery early in the novel, then changing that opinion every few chapters. [An] excellent novel."

"With engaging characters and intriguing motives, Thompson has created a smart, gripping tale of revenge, anger, and obsession."

—*RT Book Reviews*

"A riveting whodunit!" —*Road to Romance*

"In the tradition of Tami Hoag or Mary Higgins Clark, Thompson has created a gripping page-turner. The story line is engaging and the characters' lives are multidimensional. This is literally a book the reader will be unable to put down."

—*Old Book Barn Gazette*

BLACK FOR REMEMBRANCE

"Bizarre, terrifying . . . an inventive and forceful psychological thriller." —*Publishers Weekly*

"Gripped me from the first page and held on through its completely unexpected climax. Lock your doors, make sure there's no one behind you, and pick up *Black for Remembrance*."

—William Katz, author of *Double Wedding*

"Thompson's style is richly bleak, her sense of morality complex . . . Thompson is a mistress of the thriller parvenu." —*Fear*

TO THE GRAVE

CARLENE THOMPSON

**Doubleday Large Print
Home Library Edition**

St. Martin's Press

This Large Print Edition, prepared especially for Doubleday Large Print Home Library, contains the complete, unabridged text of the original Publisher's Edition.

This is a work of fiction. All of the characters, organizations, and events portrayed in this novel are either products of the author's imagination or are used fictitiously.

TO THE GRAVE

Copyright © 2012 by Carlene Thompson.

For information address St. Martin's Press, 175 Fifth Avenue, New York, NY 10010.

ISBN: 978-1-62090-257-8

Printed in the United States of America

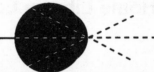

**This Large Print Book carries the
Seal of Approval of N.A.V.H.**

To Pamela Ahearn and Jennifer Weis

Thanks to Mollie Traver and Keith Biggs

PROLOGUE

Renée Eastman stared through the window at the October night. The moon shone sharp and harshly metallic against an empty black sky. She loved nights filled with bright lights, people, and revelry. Quiet nights spent alone made her uneasy.

She refused to give in to her anxiety and close the curtains. Instead, Renée shut her eyes. The area was so quiet she caught the sound of Aurora Falls. Hearing water rushing to plummet almost a hundred and fifty feet into the Orenda River thrilled her as much as it had when she'd arrived in this city named for the waterfall. Renée smiled wryly. How ironic, she thought. She was not a nature lover, but the natural wonder of the falls was the only thing she liked about the place she'd come to as a bride.

Thinking of her marriage sent Renée's spirits into a dive. Marrying James Eastman—handsome, intelligent, accomplished, a true gentleman—had been the biggest mistake of her life, Renée silently mourned. What had she been thinking?

She had been thinking of getting away from home, she reminded herself. She had been thinking of escaping her family, spiteful ex-boyfriends, jealous girlfriends, the trouble she always attracted, and, most of all, bad memories.

Marriage to James hadn't turned out as she'd expected, though, and neither had life in Aurora Falls, the city where James had grown up, the city where he had returned after law school at Tulane University in New Orleans to share his father's firm, the city where so many citizens respected and admired him. She, Renée Moreau Eastman, had been born and lived in the thrill and animation of New Orleans. Its excitement had burned itself into her soul. Here, in this lovely but quiet city of only about forty-five thousand people, she had always been an outsider.

No, worse than an outsider. She became an outcast, because before long people decided she was unworthy of James. She hadn't been hurt, but she hadn't been surprised, either. Renée had decided that James was no different from most people she'd known—people who acted honorable and earnest but in reality were full of suppressed hungers, anger, hatred, and violence. She, on the other hand, suppressed nothing, denied herself nothing, and therefore wanted for nothing. She'd shown her true colors to the world; James had not.

So she had left two years ago and never looked back. Everyone—especially James—must have thought she had just disappeared off the face of the earth.

But now she was back in this town where it all started. And she wasn't sure it had been the best idea to return.

Renée shivered. The high winds of a storm earlier in the evening had torn down power lines, cutting off electric in this area.

She'd found only two plastic flashlights, one flawed by a cracked lens. She'd been lucky to find a few candles. Candles set a sensual mood, Renée thought, but they were lousy at providing ordinary illumination. Maybe the quivering light they cast on the walls caused her edginess tonight. The rooms looked surreal and crawled with shadows. She couldn't see down the dark hall or into the oversized kitchen and she didn't like the unknown.

To make matters worse, Renée heard the repeated *whip-or-eeeo* call of a whip-poor-will. Hadn't the damned things migrated south by now? The night her beloved grandfather had been taking his last breaths, she'd first heard a whip-poor-will calling. When a heartbroken five-year-old Renée had kissed Grandpapa for the last time and been dismissed from his room, her spiteful nanny forced her outside to hear a whip-poor-will singing loudly near the house. She'd told Renée the whip-poor-will always knew when Death came to claim someone and the bird called to signal the departing soul—in this case, Grandpapa's. Renée had rolled her dark eyes and given the woman a little-girl scoff, but secretly she'd been terrified. Even now, the haunting song gave her the creeps. Tonight she couldn't bear to hear the bird's call.

Renée had found a boom box with charged batteries and her CD by Queen. She loved music and clicked to a favorite song, "Who Wants to Live Forever." For a minute, she was able to lose herself in the voice of Freddy Mercury.

But the music did nothing for the chill she felt, even though she wore a cashmere sweater. The temperature had dropped below fifty degrees and the furnace wasn't working. She'd always been overly sensitive to cold. What a night this was turning out to be, she fumed inwardly. She decided she needed a drink. Badly.

Renée snatched up one of the flashlights and went into the large kitchen, cautiously stepping around scattered boxes loaded with household junk. She'd set a bottle of single-malt Scotch on a countertop and didn't need much light to find the liquor and the glass next to it, pour a shot, and down it. She poured another shot, forced herself to take just a sip, then gave up the pretense and emptied the glass.

Renée decided to postpone sipping until her third shot.

She carried her drink back to the living room and sat on the couch. The Scotch had warmed her body, but she was frustrated at becoming too dependent on alcohol. She didn't like to be dependent on anything. Oh well, she was not an alcoholic, Renée thought reassuringly. She could cut back when she didn't need so much liquor to soothe her nerves.

What most concerned her was that her nerves didn't used to need so much soothing.

Renée took two more sips of Scotch as she sat in the silent near darkness, her anger growing. She looked at her watch. Ten ten. Their appointment had been for nine. She stood so abruptly she swayed, stalked to the window, and shone her flashlight through the slightly parted curtains.

She took another sip of her drink and peered into the night. She had no nearby neighbors, but usually she could see bulbs burning by distant front doors. No lights shone tonight, though. The absence of all electric lighting jarred her. Renée felt alone in the world and her apprehension heightened. From childhood, she'd hated solitude. She craved the company of at least one lively, admiring person. Now the craving had turned into a need.

Renée started the CD again and returned to the couch. A fat candle placed in a glass holder sat on the end table beside her, sending up a weak flame. After a minute, she sighed gustily. Music couldn't calm her. She couldn't take much more of this, but she wouldn't make a call to find out what was going on. Calling might not be wise. Besides, she was tired, she was cold, and she was getting drunk.

With abrupt anger, Renée decided to leave. In her car, she had three pieces of luggage filled with everything she needed. She longed to stay at the beautiful Larke Inn overlooking the waterfall, but the Larke Inn dining room was a focal point for Aurora Falls society and she didn't want people to spot her tonight. For days, she hadn't wanted people to see her, but she knew she'd been careless, which wasn't good. She wouldn't make things worse by checking into the inn, but she wanted to go somewhere nice, somewhere welcoming, somewhere she could cuddle up in a cozy, comfortable bed and stop this foolish waiting. Dammit, Renée Moreau Eastman didn't wait for anyone.

No matter how many times she told herself she was simply indignant, though, Renée knew that beneath her resentment lay raw fear. Something about this evening felt wrong—very wrong. Maybe it was just the Scotch, for once making her paranoid instead of mellow, but she wasn't able to shake the feeling. In fact, the whole day had felt wrong and so had the previous day. She'd never let herself give in to fear or dread or dark fancies, believing them to be the hallmarks of cowards, but now she wondered if they might possibly be warnings—warnings perhaps she had foolishly ignored.

Renée shuddered. The involuntary reaction of her own body stunned her, making her feel as if she were losing control. Badly rattled, she fumbled for the flashlight she'd left lying on the couch, and when she couldn't find it she snatched up the fat candle and headed for the bedroom. Her stiletto heels tapped smartly on the hardwood floors. She entered the room, placed the candle on a small bedside table, grabbed her light coat thrown across the bed, and froze.

One of the sliding glass doors leading to an overgrown patio stood open a couple of inches, allowing a chill breeze to creep through the room. Just over an hour ago, the door had been closed. Or had it? She'd been repelled by the dank, unwelcoming atmosphere of the empty house. The opening was so small, could she not have noticed it?

No. The mind fog created by the Scotch lifted as abruptly as it had descended. She remembered clearly that the temperature had already dropped considerably by nine o'clock when she'd been in this room. Why would she open a sizable window in an already-cold room? She wouldn't.

The window had been unlocked and somebody had opened it within the last hour—somebody who now waited in this house with her.

The certainty turned Renée's heart to

ice, froze it into skipping a beat. For a moment, she couldn't move. Then she fought the sudden desire to run. Some primal instinct told her that whoever had sneaked in *wanted* her to panic, to fall apart, to lose the essential brashness that was Renée Moreau. She wouldn't give anyone that pleasure, though. She would not crumble, no matter how much she'd begun to tremble inside.

Besides, she was prepared. She was always prepared.

Renée hadn't eaten since morning and she'd sent too much Scotch down to an empty stomach. She felt nauseated from alcohol and fear. Still, she must act calm, she told herself. If she didn't want someone to know her insides quivered, she must maintain the appearance of bravado. She slipped on her coat without rushing. When she picked up her large handbag, though, Renée's confidence shattered. The bag was too light.

Someone had removed her .22-caliber revolver.

The candle flame flickered before it died. Renée turned toward the doorway and stood still in the room lit only by moonlight filtering through the lightweight curtains.

"Something missing from your purse?"

Renée recognized the voice although she'd never heard it so toneless. She was proud that she sounded merely irritated when she asked, "What the hell are you doing?"

"I wanted to surprise you. And you *are* surprised. Drunk but surprised."

Renée's eyes had adjusted to the dimness and she saw moonlight glinting off the stainless-steel barrel of the upraised gun. "I think *you're* drunk. What idiotic behavior." She paused. "I was just leaving."

"For the night?"

"I'm leaving Aurora Falls forever. I've realized there's nothing here for me."

"You made up your mind so quickly?"

"I came on a whim, but for some time I've had my doubts. Now I know this isn't what I want. I never want to see this town or anyone in it ever again."

A beat of silence passed. Finally, the almost unrecognizable voice chuckled. "Beautiful Renée—still lying."

"I'm not lying. I'm absolutely serious. Sincere."

"You never were sincere and you aren't sincere now. You don't know the meaning of sincerity. Or faithfulness. Or simple human decency."

The voice sounded as unemotional and final as a judge delivering a death sentence. In the other room, Freddy Mercury wailed, "Who wants to live forever?" Renée did. Although she had a feeling of doom, she wouldn't stop trying to survive this horror. She decided to try another tack. She didn't have to force the quiver in her voice. "I've changed."

"Then why aren't you already gone?"

"I just wanted to explain myself. And I wanted to say good-bye."

"Here. You wanted to explain yourself *here,* in this little cottage, when you just said you never wanted to see anyone in this town again." Soft, mirthless laughter. "You can't stop lying even with a gun pointed at you."

"I mean it. I know now that coming here was a mistake and I'll *never* come back to this place or to Aurora Falls."

"We both know that's not true. You never stop pursuing what you want."

Renée hated the desperation that made

her voice shake. "Well, maybe I've changed my mind about what I want."

"No . . . you . . . haven't."

Now Renée's heart beat so hard she thought it might crack a rib. "Are you threatening to *murder* me?" Silence. A gaze burning into hers, an eerily inhuman smile, a gun pointed at her face. Inspiration struck her. "He knows where I am."

"Of course he does. Do you think I'm stupid? Do you think I don't realize things aren't always as they seem?"

"If you're so smart, you know this won't be the end." Renée's voice turned shrill. "It will only be the beginning, the beginning of a life of anxiety, of suspicion, of knowing you can't keep a secret forever—"

Renée did not have time to hear the sound of a .22-caliber gun firing with a sharp *ping*, or to feel the bullet pierce her right eye. Renée's head snapped back, then forward. She remained standing for a few seconds, blood beginning to stream down her cheek, over her lips, her chin, and onto her cashmere sweater. Finally, she fell forward, her face smashing against a rough hooked rug.

Her attacker watched until Renée went

still with a last twitch of her manicured fingers. A booted foot slid beneath Renée's shoulder and gave it a hard flip, rolling her body on its back.

Renée wasn't beautiful anymore.

CHAPTER ONE

Catherine Gray positioned herself on the front lawn, held up her camera, and called for her sister to hurry. As soon as Marissa walked out the front door, Catherine yelled, "Smile!" and snapped her picture.

"Catherine, you are driving me nuts with that camera!" Marissa spluttered. "Besides, you took me by surprise!"

Catherine looked at the LCD display of her last shot. "Not great, Marissa—you're pop-eyed and your mouth is open. I'll take another one."

"I don't want—"

"Now this time don't look like you've just

seen aliens landing. Smile and one, two, three . . ." *Click.* Catherine checked the display and nodded. "Great!"

Marissa shook her head. "Did James know he was creating a monster when he decided to buy that expensive camera for your birthday?"

Catherine grinned sheepishly. "Probably not. And the camera wasn't his inspiration—I'd dropped hints for weeks."

Marissa joined her sister and glanced at the picture. "Wonderful. Hair in a very sloppy ponytail, no makeup, and the denim jacket I sewed butterflies all over when I was sixteen. I look pathetic."

"You look great—not a day over twenty-five."

"I'm twenty-six," Marissa said dryly.

"And you look twenty-five. You're aging gracefully."

"You are, too, for a woman who's almost thirty."

"Not for another ten months, and my thirties don't scare me at all," Catherine said lightly. "After all, Mom was as beautiful at thirty-five as she was at twenty-five. I've seen her photographs. In fact, looking through family albums is what made me want to become a good photographer. I want to leave a record of our lives, just like Mom and Dad left for us. And we'll want a whole separate album for baby pictures."

Marissa raised an eyebrow. "Is there something you'd like to tell me?"

"No, but someday I will, and someday you'll have something to tell me, and then I'll take hundreds of pictures of our children."

Marissa laughed. "Pictures that will mortify them when they're teenagers and we drag out the albums and show the photos to their dates."

"*I* won't. I'll make a point of never embarrassing my children."

"Catherine, all parents embarrass their teenagers sometimes."

"I'll prove you wrong." Catherine gazed up at the crystalline blue sky, smiled, and headed for her white sedan. "It's an absolutely beautiful day. Come on before we lose the whole afternoon."

"Uh, how about taking my car?" Marissa watched her sister's smile fade. "I know you aren't crazy about convertibles, but like you said, this is a beautiful day. We won't have many more until winter." Catherine's gaze grew stubborn. Marissa walked behind her and started pushing her gently and relentlessly like a tugboat nudging a steamship into port. "This is the kind of day God made for rides in candy apple red Mustang convertibles! It'll be fun."

Catherine sighed. "Okay, but don't drive like a bat out of hell like usual."

"I won't," Marissa said solemnly. "I don't want to wreck my car and destroy your wonderful camera. I'll drive just like you do."

Marissa put on her large sunglasses and started out at a snail's pace, looking vigilant as she hunched over the steering wheel she clutched with both hands, not reaching for a CD, and braking with exaggeration at every stop sign.

Catherine finally burst into laughter. "I feel like I'm with a hundred-year-old chauffeur. I don't drive like this." Marissa said nothing. "Okay, maybe I do sometimes, but I can't stand it when *you* do. Put on some music and pick up the pace!"

Marissa grinned, slipped in a Natasha Bedingfield CD, and pressed her foot harder on the accelerator. Catherine tipped back her head, letting the wind lift her long, honey brown hair. She closed her heather green eyes, listening to "Pocketful of Sun-shine" and letting the gentle late October sun warm her face.

Catherine knew family and friends con-sidered her the sensible, cautious sister versus free-spirited Marissa, and during her late childhood she'd started trying to live up to their image. Few people realized how often Catherine had wanted to give in to her own devil-may-care impulses, but af-ter years of constant levelheaded behavior letting go was hard. Ever since she'd moved into the Gray family home left to the sisters after their mother's death, though, Cath-erine had felt her restraints loosening and a different side of her personality creeping out to greet the sun.

"I told you it would be fun!" Marissa shouted over the loud music.

Catherine merely smiled and then raised her arms, swaying them in time with the music as if she were at a rock concert. Ma-rissa laughed.

They drove south, away from the city and the Aurora waterfall. Catherine remem-bered that when Marissa was eight she'd begun telling the story of Sebastian Larke, who'd discovered the falls in 1770, which she'd called ancient times. Sebastian had named the waterfall for a Greek goddess, she'd explained. Catherine had listened patiently to Marissa's remarkably accurate lectures about the wide, horseshoe-shaped falls that measured 124 feet high and cascaded into the Orenda River, the third-largest river in the "United States of America," Marissa had always announced proudly. Then, with her brilliantly blue eyes cast down, her voice beyond sad, she'd ended, "And he never, ever got married and had kids, the poor, lonely guy."

"Remember when you used to make Mom, Dad, and me listen to your account of Sebastian Larke finding the falls?" Catherine asked suddenly. "You got so carried away one time, you announced that you were meant to be Sebastian's wife—God just got mixed-up and you were born too late."

Marissa laughed. "I was a weird kid."

"You were a smart, imaginative kid. I always felt like you could really see Sebastian Larke work during the day building the town, and then go back to his lonely cabin at night. You were wrong about one thing, though. God didn't mean for you to be with

Sebastian. He meant for you to be with Eric Montgomery."

"Oh, really? Did God tell you that in person?"

"He told me in a dream," Catherine returned in a soft, undulating voice, her eyes closed. "He said, 'Eric will become master of Sebastian's creation, the city of Aurora Falls, and rule it with Marissa by his side. It is meant to be.'"

"Have you been calling those psychic hotlines? Or do you believe *you* can see the future?" Marissa returned with mock solemnity. "You'll have to tell Eric about your dream. He's afraid he'll lose the election for sheriff and then he won't become the master of Aurora Falls. Oh, you can leave out the part about me being by his side."

Catherine's eyes snapped open. "What? Are you and Eric breaking up?"

"No, but I don't want him getting too confident." Marissa grinned. "Got to keep him on his toes, make him think he must still woo me with flowers and candy and give me an impressive engagement ring for Christmas."

"I think you're awful for plotting to get a specific gift."

"I know. I feel extremely guilty about it. I guess I'm just like my sister."

"I wanted a camera, not an engagement ring."

Marissa grinned. "Sure, Catherine. I guess if James Eastman had proposed on your birthday and given you a ring instead of a camera you'd have told him to jump over the falls."

Catherine ignored her sister and closed her eyes again, thinking that just last year at this time she couldn't have imagined herself riding in Marissa's car as they went to look at land owned by the Eastmans. When she'd left Aurora Falls at seventeen to attend the University of California at Berkeley, she'd known she wanted to be a clinical psychologist, which would require a Ph.D. Somewhere in a hazy future, Catherine had thought, she'd be married to a man she had yet to meet and have a child. She'd never dreamed she'd end up right where she started and dating a guy she'd loved for years.

"You're smiling," Marissa said. "Thinking of James?"

"Why don't you watch the road instead of staring at me?"

"Oh, I can do both," Marissa returned airily. "Were you thinking of James?"

"You'll never leave me alone until I give in and tell you." Catherine opened her eyes. "Ten years ago I would never have pictured myself coming back to Aurora Falls to live with my sister."

"I know the thought of living with me would bring a smile to anyone's face," Marissa said dryly, "but I believe you were also thinking about James."

"Okay, I was thinking of him. I remember hoping he'd notice me someday."

"And he did. Therefore, the smile."

"Yeah." Catherine's thoughts spun over all the years she'd loved James Eastman; then slowly her smile faded. "Do you ever feel like things are too good to be true?"

"Do you mean like things that happen to me are too good to be true?"

"Well, maybe sometimes." After a moment she said, "When Eric and I got back together after five years I felt at first that it was too good to be true. Maybe that's why I kept pushing him away." She paused. "Are you feeling like you being with James is too good to be true?"

"Well, being with James is wonderful. I

guess sometimes I feel it's too wonderful because he was married."

"Oh no." Marissa grimaced. "You've been thinking about Renée. Why?"

"Mrs. Paralon mentioned her to me the other day."

"Mrs. Paralon rehashes forty-year-old gossip as if it's hot off the press. No one pays any attention to her."

"Maybe. But it made me think of Renée, especially when Dad insisted that *all* of us attend James's wedding to her in New Orleans."

"Jeez, Catherine, that was years ago!"

"Yes, but I'll always remember it as one of the worst experiences of my life."

"Well, don't get mad at Dad about it now. He and James's father had been friends forever and the families were friends—we couldn't skip the wedding."

"*I* didn't have to go."

"I know Dad kept pestering you about it, but since you and I weren't little girls anymore he thought it would be our last trip as a family. And it was."

"I've never been mad at Dad for guilting me into going to the wedding. How could I be? He didn't know how I felt about James."

"No, I don't believe he had a clue. Only Mom and I knew."

Catherine's gaze snapped toward her sister. "*You* and Mom? I told her I cared about James in strictest confidence and she promised she wouldn't tell anyone else!"

"She didn't tell me, but I could tell you were crazy about James."

"Oh no," Catherine groaned. "If you could, other people probably could, too. What if guests at the wedding were laughing about the girl gazing at James with big cow eyes full of love?" Catherine could feel her face growing hot. "I shouldn't have looked at him at all!"

"Relax. You did a great job of hiding your feelings. Dad didn't notice. You were cool and composed, even when James introduced you to the bride."

"Oh God. Renée. I'll never forget all the thick, gleaming black hair cascading down her back, those huge, doe-like eyes, her porcelain skin. No wonder he married her barely three months after meeting her. She was so beautiful."

"She was striking in a flashy, sexy way. *You* are beautiful," Marissa said firmly.

Catherine went on as if Marissa hadn't spoken. "You say no one knew how I felt about James, but *she* did. I could tell when she looked at me. She was amused by my love and my misery and I hated her, Marissa. I don't think I've ever hated anyone, but I hated her."

"So did everyone who knew her in Aurora Falls by the time she vanished."

Catherine glared at her sister. "Why did you say 'vanished'?"

"I don't know. I guess because that's what so many people say."

"People who think James killed her say 'she vanished' because it sounds creepy."

"Yeah, well a lot of people love drama and Renée gave it to them. For years, she stirred up trouble in Aurora Falls, broke up at least two marriages, pushed James to what everyone thought was the breaking point; then suddenly she was gone. No one saw her leave and no one has heard from her again." Catherine sighed. "James could have saved himself a lot of grief if he'd divorced her a few months after marrying her, before she had so much time to become a . . . a legend."

"A legend! Oh, that's just great."

"It's true."

"You're certainly creative today, but your memory is terrible, Marissa. I've told you at least twenty times that in this state James couldn't divorce her on the grounds of irreconcilable differences unless she agreed and they lived apart for a year. Fat chance of her going along with that plan."

"Then he should have charged her with adultery. She didn't make a secret of her affairs."

"James is too much of a gentleman to do that!" Catherine snapped.

"There are times for being a gentleman and times to act like a man."

Catherine looked at Marissa furiously. "How dare you imply James is a . . . a . . ."

"Wimp?" Catherine's glare didn't stop Marissa. "Don't tell me you haven't thought it, too."

Catherine went silent for a moment, clenching her jaw. Then she said slowly and distinctly, "He is *not* a wimp, a coward, or a weakling, Marissa. He just should have taken action sooner to end the marriage."

"He never took *any* action to end the marriage until she . . . left."

Catherine felt her breath come faster in anger. "What are you saying?"

"That I've just never understood why he held on to Renée for so long."

After a pause, Catherine said, "I never told you this, but after James married her, he found out she was a really troubled woman. He's never gone into details, but her past wasn't what you would expect after briefly seeing her life in New Orleans. Anyway, he thought with enough time and understanding and love she'd change. When he saw that she either couldn't or didn't *want* to change, he still hesitated because divorcing her for adultery would humiliate his parents."

"He didn't think she humiliated them, too?" Marissa asked incredulously.

"I don't know exactly what he thought at the time. He just says for some reason he can't understand, she loved tormenting him and his family. He thinks that's why she left the way she did—to create suspicion about him by making it look like he'd killed her." Catherine's voice rose. "Even if I'm a psychologist, I don't give a damn if she was troubled! She was a bitch!"

"Finally we agree on something," Marissa said evenly, "but the best way she could have hurt him would have been to stay. She's been gone for ages, though, James got his divorce on the grounds of desertion, and people have moved on to new topics of gossip." After a moment of silence, Marissa said softly, "If all of the past gossip—if James's marriage to Renée—upsets you so much, Catherine, you should stop seeing him."

Catherine looked sharply at her sister. "Stop seeing James? Marissa, I *love* him!"

"Does he love you?"

"What? Of course. He tells me so all the time."

"Then concentrate on the present and stop being so touchy about the past. Stop even thinking about it."

Catherine's anger drained, leaving her feeling foolish and mean. "You're right. I should think about *now* and quit being so overly sensitive about James and Renée. They're history." She paused. "Sorry I lashed out at you. But if you ever call James a wimp again—"

"I didn't say 'wimp.' *You* did."

Oh hell, I did, Catherine thought, her mind scrambling for a quick save. "I just said what you were implying."

"Whatever."

The sisters rode in silence for a couple of minutes. Then Marissa asked as if there hadn't been a harsh word between them, "And now for the age-old child's question: 'How much farther is it?'"

"About five or six miles. Why do you care? I thought you love to drive."

"I do, but not for the whole afternoon. It's Saturday and we both have dates tonight. Last weekend you missed your dinner out with James because he went alone to that conference in Pittsburgh, so I'm sure he'll take you somewhere special tonight as compensation. Anyway, we have hair to be curled, nails to be painted, eye shadow to choose, and a dozen lipsticks and glosses to be tried before we reach perfection."

"Like teenagers?"

"Like females with the romantic spirit of teenagers and the wisdom of women."

"Yeah, sure." They'd left the city and Catherine turned her gaze to the countryside, wondering if, even at twenty-nine, she was still more romantic than wise. She was in love with a man she'd known most of her life and loved nearly half of her life. At least, she thought she'd loved him that long. She was a clinical psychologist, though, and she knew how easy it was for an adolescent to mistake attraction for love.

Then, last Christmas when she'd come home for her college break and her first Christmas at home without her mother, who'd died the previous summer, James Eastman had finally entered her life as a romantic interest, not just a family friend. That holiday had been both bizarre and wonderful, and she'd known that as a woman, not a teenager, she passionately loved James.

Afterward, they'd traveled between Aurora Falls and California to see each other and when she'd passed her tests and earned her license as a clinical psychologist in June she had made the decision to live in Aurora Falls. She'd joined the practice of an older, more established psychologist just over four months ago—not long, really, Catherine told herself. Maybe hoping that James would propose by spring was like a child's fairy-tale wish, especially after what he'd been through with Renée.

Catherine and James didn't live together. She didn't want to move into his town house, but James had never asked. Maybe he knew she'd refuse. She wondered if he thought such an arrangement in a city of around forty-five thousand would damage her new position in the psychology practice or even his established law practice. He must realize, though, this was the twenty-first century. More likely, she'd reluctantly decided, James didn't want her to become a permanent part of his life any time soon. Maybe ever. An immediate feeling of rejection hit Catherine, unnerving her. Idly guessing about James's possible feelings shouldn't affect her so much, Catherine thought in concern. She was already too emotionally dependent on him, too—

Absently looking at a browned soybean field and another field full of faded cornstalks, Catherine suddenly emerged from her reverie and almost shouted, "Turn right!"

Marissa hit the brakes, throwing them both forward against their seat belts. "What are you yelling about?" she demanded loudly. "You want me to turn right? *Right* into that cornfield?"

"I meant just past the cornfield," Catherine said meekly. "I'm sorry I startled you."

"You said the cottage was five or six miles away. We've only gone three." Marissa picked up speed again while muttering absently, "You are a driver's nightmare, Catherine. I don't know how you ever got a driver's license. Of course, at the speed you drive, you hardly need one. A horse and buggy would serve you just fine—"

"There's the road," Catherine interrupted, still embarrassed over her outburst but determined not to apologize again. "Perry Lane. Isn't that the name of a Beatles song?"

Marissa said irritably, "Not Perry Lane— 'Penny Lane' on the *Magical Mystery Tour.* We have the actual vinyl album, which you've heard a hundred times. The CD version, which we also have, was released in 1987 and . . ."

She'll go on like this for another couple of minutes, Catherine thought in relief, having known "Perry Lane" wasn't a Beatles song. She also knew her sister was nearly a walking archive of *Rolling Stone*

magazine and making a blunder to Marissa about a Beatles song was the perfect
way to change the subject.

Perry Lane curved left about twenty feet
ahead. Marissa soared around the gentle
coil and followed Perry Lane nearly a quarter of a mile. Almost twice the normal
amount of rain had fallen so far this October, and two inches had doused the area
three days earlier. The grass was greener
than usual for this time of year, and the dirt
on either side of the asphalt road looked
damp.

Catherine looked to the right in search
of the Eastman cottage. The sun shone
brightly and the air smelled fresh, as if
both had just gone through the wash, she
thought whimsically before pointing and
saying, "I think that's it!"

Marissa came to a slow stop. Catherine
stared at a small, shabby, dark gray-green
cottage with a covered porch running half
the length of the building, a wide front window, and two smaller windows toward the
southern end. Paint peeled all over the
building and a few roof shingles lay on what
passed for a front lawn. The limbs of large
trees crowded in from the sides, overhang-

ing the patchy roof and giving the little cottage an air of huddling in on itself, crouching.

Marissa frowned. "Are you certain this place belongs to James's family?"

"I'm not absolutely certain, but his mother mentioned that it's gray."

"It's not gray."

"It *is* gray. I think the green is mildew from all the moisture and shade."

"Mildew! Ugh!"

"Oh, don't be so prissy. Just pull up in that little driveway."

Marissa's hands dropped to her lap. "I can't even see a little driveway, Catherine."

"It's right there." Catherine pointed. "The evergreen branches are hanging over it. The Eastmans only have the grounds mown four or five times a year. No wonder the yard is a disgrace."

"The yard isn't the only disgrace." Marissa turned to her sister and said seriously, "Catherine, I'm getting a bad vibe from this place."

Catherine made herself smile teasingly. "I thought I was the one sensitive to 'bad vibes.' You've always said you're too smart to believe in all that illogical, sixth-sense stuff."

"I've suddenly realized I'm not as smart as I thought," Marissa returned. "I mean it."

Catherine felt a tingle of uneasiness, but she didn't want to argue. "The place is depressing because it's neglected," she said with bright determination. "It's just an old summer cottage. Don't tell me you're afraid of it."

"Only because it looks like a serial killer's lair. Even those evergreen trees look diseased."

Catherine snapped, "Marissa, you've watched too many movies. A serial killer's lair? That's—"

"True?"

Catherine looked around, surprised by feeling insulted, and softened her tone. "The place doesn't look great, but you're being silly." She forced another smile. "Pull into the front yard near the cottage."

Marissa squinted at the scrappy land in front of the cottage and sighed. "Here goes."

She drove carefully, dodging shingles and a fallen tree limb, and then stopped her Mustang near the cottage. "So much for the obstacle course. Is there a reason James's father won't take care of his property?"

"He hates the cottage," Catherine said. "He told me even though he couldn't swim and he detested fishing, when he was a kid his father used to drag him out here every weekend to fish. Even during his teenage years." Catherine stepped out of the car and glanced around. "James's great-grandfather built this place in the forties."

"That would be the seventeen-forties?" Marissa asked sarcastically as she emerged from the car.

"Right after World War Two, smart-ass, although it looks as if it's stood here abandoned for at least a century." Catherine looked at the desolate cottage and surrounding grounds. "James's mother wants to sell the property—three acres of land that could be beautiful with proper care. James's father was an only child and inherited everything, so ownership isn't a problem."

"What *is* the problem?"

"Probably Peter's guilt about selling family land to strangers. Selling the land to James would keep it in the family, though."

"Is James interested in buying it?"

"His mother usually brings up the topic of selling. James doesn't say anything."

"Then what makes you think he wants to buy the land?"

"It's only an idea."

"I see," Marissa said knowingly. "*You* think James could buy the land as a site for a new house."

"As I said, it's only an idea," Catherine evaded. "Today I just wanted to show you the land and get your thoughts about how well it would suit a nice house for James. You know how he hates living in a town house."

"Why, no, I didn't know," Marissa drawled. "He hasn't discussed the matter with me."

"Well, he does," Catherine maintained, ignoring Marissa's grin. "He sold his house after Renée left. I'm sure he wants another one."

"But he doesn't know you're looking at this place as a potential site for *his* new home," Marissa said as Catherine smiled serenely. "Okay, let explore." Marissa looked at the cottage. "Can we go inside?"

"No. I don't have the key, but we can look through the windows."

The boards of the long, uneven porch creaked as the women walked across it to the large front window with curtains parted less than a foot. They made tunnels of their hands and looked into a dim room lit only by sunlight coming through a back window to show a sagging couch, an oval coffee table, a hooked rug, and one lamp topped by a crooked shade.

Marissa made a face. "Obviously the cottage wasn't decorated to impress anyone."

"They probably kept things simple so they didn't have to worry about anyone breaking in to steal nice furnishings. It's better than I'd have expected from looking at the outside. I think someone cleans a couple of times a year and the Eastmans maintain the utilities—water, electricity, and gas for a furnace so they can keep the place warm enough in the winter that the pipes don't burst."

Catherine gazed around a large, raggedy flower bed filled with bright sunflowers, purple wild asters, and goldenrod. Several yards beyond the flower bed stretched a line of oak and maple trees shedding their brilliant, late October leaves. When she took a deep breath, she picked up the bitingly sweet scent of apples. James once told her his grandmother had planted a small grouping of apple trees, which she'd called her orchard.

"Forget the cottage," Catherine said. "Look at this three-acre lot. It could be beautiful with a little tender loving care." She grinned. "Let's go look at the river!"

The grass stood tall, some weeds as high as their knees. As they walked around the cottage, Catherine was glad she'd suggested they wear jeans and sneakers with socks. Behind the building, untrimmed trees had blocked most of the sun and the grass grew in patches. She and Marissa linked arms and began down the gentle slope to the river and the old dock.

"How far would you say it is between the house and the river?" Marissa asked.

"I'm not good with distances." Catherine frowned in thought. "Maybe eighty yards before it drops onto that steep bank leading down to the river. I'd put a fence in front of the bank."

"Especially if you don't want your toddlers rolling down into the river. How many are you planning on having? Toddlers, I mean."

"A dozen," Catherine answered, seemingly oblivious to Marissa's teasing. "I think this would make a great backyard."

"It sure would. You were right about this place. It's a nice spot for a house."

"What about your bad vibe?"

"I think it came from that dreadful cottage. The rest of this area is great. There's plenty of room for a nice, sizable house for all of those children you're planning to have, a big lawn for them and their little friends, and you'd even have room to build a large boathouse. You could keep the *Annemarie* here," Marissa said, referring to the Gray family's cabin cruiser that their father had named for his wife and the sisters now jointly owned. "And doesn't James also want a motorboat?"

"Yes."

"Well, there you go. It's perfect." Marissa raised her eyebrows. "What I wonder is why you're showing this place to your sister as if you're trying to persuade *me* it would be a great site for a new house? Why aren't you talking to James? Do you think he really doesn't want another house, a real home for a wife and children?"

Catherine sighed. "Here's my problem.

James has talked about wanting a house. He hasn't asked me to marry him, although he says he loves me. Does he never want to marry again because of the way things went with Renée? Because I won't be a live-in girlfriend who maybe gives him the couple of kids I think he wants, Marissa. I know a lot of people would consider me old-fashioned, but I want commitment."

Marissa looked at her seriously. "You should just come out and ask James if he ever plans to remarry. After all, you're the psychologist and I thought you people believed in talking about your feelings."

"We do, except—"

"Except this matter concerns *you* and also you're afraid of what you'll hear. In that case, I'll give you my opinion. I think James wants to marry you, but he's someone who plans everything and who won't move ahead with a project until he thinks he has ironed out every wrinkle. The two of you deciding where you would like to live is a wrinkle he wants gone when he asks you to marry him. He's not impetuous, which is good, because neither are you. You'd have a nervous breakdown if you were married to an impetuous man."

Catherine stood still for a moment, looking out over the Orenda River. The breeze created ripples that sparkled in the sun. The water lapped softly against the thick layer of granite riprap neatly piled along the shoreline to prevent erosion. Off to her left, she heard a robin singing and she saw a squirrel running back to the trees with a nut in its mouth, storing food for the coming winter. Yes, this place could be beautiful, Catherine thought. What a perfect place for a house to share with James and the children both Marissa and she thought James wanted.

She turned back to Marissa. "This would be a *wonderful* spot for a house!"

"So give James a little push, silly, and tell *him,* not me. Don't be shy about making suggestions to the man you love. I'm certainly not."

"I know," Catherine said drolly. "So does your Eric."

"Eric appreciates my candor." Marissa paused. "Most of the time. Occasionally he gets stubborn and I don't think he listens to me. Just because he hasn't asked for my opinion, though, doesn't mean he shouldn't hear it—" Marissa frowned. "Are *you* even listening to me?"

Catherine had wandered away and was snapping a photo of bright leaves sailing toward the river on a crisp, buoyant breeze. Whimsy swept over her and she whipped around to face Marissa. "More pictures! Just a few more pictures before we go!"

Marissa beamed. "You've made up your mind, haven't you?"

"I've decided to give it a try, but if James doesn't go for it I want memories of seeing this gorgeous spot on this gorgeous day with my gorgeous sister."

Catherine took several photographs, her smile never fading. She heard herself giggling and felt as if she were listening to someone else—Marissa or her mother, Annemarie, both with their unadulterated joie de vivre. The feeling was foreign and heady.

When they'd worked their way to the front of the cottage again, Catherine insisted Marissa shed her denim jacket and sit on the hood of her red convertible Mustang.

"You're not going to sell James on this place by showing him a picture of me sitting on the hood of a car," Marissa protested.

"This is for Eric. He can frame it and put it on his desk when he's elected sheriff next month," Catherine said as Marissa slid onto the hood. "Let down your ponytail."

Marissa pulled the rubber band from her long ash-blond hair with its sunny highlights and shook it free around her shoulders. "How's that?"

"Great. Now slip your sunglasses on top of your head for that carefree, beach-girl look."

Marissa laughed but obeyed.

"Wonderful!" Catherine crowed. "Now put your right hand slightly behind you and lean on it. I'll take a few more steps back. . . ."

"Do you have to keep backing up to make me look good?"

"No, you look great, but you could look even better. Thrust your left shoulder forward slightly and—"

Catherine's heel banged against something hard. She looked behind her and saw old, widely spaced wooden planks cut into a circular shape and set on a low, round concrete rim. She took a step up onto the planks and looked back into her viewfinder.

"Perfect! Eric will love this picture."

Marissa's eyes widened. "Be careful! You're standing on a cistern—"

Suddenly Catherine heard the boards groaning. Old wood splintered and snapped beneath her feet, and with stunning shock she plunged into a vat of cold water. Deeper, deeper, deeper she fell until her feet touched a hard surface. She'd swallowed water and fought the reflex to open her mouth and cough. Terrified, Catherine thrust upward, flailing arms weighed down by the sleeves of her sopping-wet flannel-lined corduroy jacket until she collided with something large, something soft yet with a hard core she instinctively knew was a body. She thrashed wildly, panicked, and gulped more water. Then she tried to calm herself. It's an animal, she thought. It's just a large animal—

With arms just like mine, Catherine's stunned mind registered as her own arms slipped beneath the others and slid up to where they joined a torso. She tried to shake loose, but her right hand had tangled in what seemed like thousands of long threads attached to her limp companion. She couldn't keep writhing to jerk free of them without losing the momentum of her upward surge, though. Her feet paddling frantically, her lungs nearly bursting from the struggle to hold her breath while handling the extra weight, she finally rose to the surface, gasped for air, and opened her eyes.

Catherine shrieked as she looked into the mutilated, bloated face of a dead woman.

CHAPTER TWO

1

In her shock, Catherine's feet went limp and her head slipped underwater. Then pain shot through her scalp. She rose once more to see Marissa lying on the ground and reaching forward over the cistern. Catherine realized her pain came from Marissa grasping a sizable hank of her hair and using it to pull Catherine's body back to the water's surface.

Catherine looked at the corpse she still clutched and screamed, "Oh my God!"

"Let go of it!" Marissa shouted. "Let loose of the body!"

Catherine looked at the atrocity in front of her, opened her mouth to scream again, and then raised her right hand tightly tangled in long, thick black hair. "Caught!" Water splashed into her mouth, but she managed to spew it out before swallowing. "I'm caught!"

Marissa pulled on Catherine's hair, dragging her closer to the cistern's side. "Help me, Catherine. Reach for the concrete edge!"

Concrete edge? Catherine went blank. Concrete edge of what? She couldn't see anything except for a horribly swollen face only inches from hers.

"Catherine, snap out of it!" Marissa shrieked. *"Now!"*

Catherine coughed, blinked, looked around, and finally focused on a rim of concrete. She tried to stretch her arm, but the mass of hair tangled in her fingers wouldn't allow enough extension for her to reach the rim. She sobbed and tried to propel both herself and her dark companion closer to the edge of the cistern, seeing the strain on

Marissa's face and knowing she couldn't keep her grip on Catherine much longer.

Marissa ordered, "Pull the hair out of the head!"

Catherine cringed as she tugged. "Can't! Too much hair!"

"Dammit, the skin's spongy. Just rip out the hair with all your might!" Marissa yelled with brutal desperation.

With Catherine losing her strength and panicking, her squeamishness vanished. She slid her left arm from beneath the corpse's armpit and braced her hand against the chest. She stopped paddling, raised her legs until her feet made contact with the body, and pushed backward as hard as possible until her hand jerked loose from the head.

Catherine sank for a moment until she began using her feet again. As she surfaced, the corpse lowered into the water. She moved closer to the concrete rim of the cistern, grabbed it, and then reached for her sister's grasping left hand. Marissa let go of Catherine's hair and with both hands began pulling her by the upper arms.

After what seemed like an eternity, Catherine completely emerged from the water and collapsed. Marissa lay crumpled beside her. Both women gasped loudly from exertion and Catherine shook violently. Finally, she glanced at the fingers of her right hand—fingers twined with long, black hair and pulpy roots. "Oh God," Catherine moaned, almost retching.

"Stop looking at your hand," Marissa said flatly. Then, "We have to call nine-one-one."

"I can't. Not now." Catherine shuddered. "Marissa, I think that was—" She rolled on her side, wanting to cry, but she had no tears. Instead, she emitted an agonized bleat that sounded hardly human.

After a moment, Marissa asked just above a whisper, "Are you all right?"

"No." At last, Catherine began sobbing. "Marissa, I think that's Renée."

2

After Marissa called 911 on her cell phone, time crawled for Catherine. She felt as if an hour passed before sirens shredded the cool, peaceful ambience of the October afternoon. Marissa had retrieved a blanket from the trunk of her car, and after demanding Catherine unwind from her fetal position and stand up she had removed Catherine's jacket, wrapped her in the blanket, and made her rest on a reclining bucket seat of the Mustang. As soon as the EMS ambulance stopped, two paramedics spilled out and led Catherine to the vehicle. She sat inside the open rear doors as they checked her heartbeat, blood pressure, temperature, and flipped a small, sharp light back and forth into her eyes. She felt tender and hypersensitive and didn't want to be touched. She told them three times she was fine—only cold and filthy—but they merely gave her patient, empty smiles and continued their examination.

The first police officer to arrive was Deputy Roberta "Robbie" Landers, a tall, slender young woman with a fine-boned, serious face, glossy brown hair, and steady dark blue eyes. Catherine and Marissa had met her the previous Christmas when she was a new deputy. Her father, Hank Landers, worked with Marissa at the *Aurora Falls Gazette.* While the paramedics continued checking out Catherine, Deputy

Landers approached, notebook in hand. I can't talk to her, Catherine thought, her muscles tensing. I can't answer questions sensibly. I can't tell Robbie I think someone murdered James's ex-wife and stuffed her in that cistern.

Catherine could have kissed Marissa, who intervened. "Hi, Robbie," Marissa said in a steady voice. "I'm glad you got here first. I'll give you the details while the paramedics finish examining Catherine, if that's all right."

"Of course." Robbie offered a small smile and encouraging nod to Catherine before she stepped aside with Marissa. Catherine could still hear their conversation.

"This cottage belongs to the Eastman family," Marissa explained. "Catherine and I decided to take a look at it. Even though the cistern is big, the place is so overgrown, I didn't even notice the wooden lid at first—not until Catherine stepped on it. The boards were weak, rotting, and they broke."

Robbie took notes. "Didn't the Eastmans warn you about the cistern, Miss Gray?"

"Please, Robbie, you've known me for a

year. It's 'Marissa.' And no, the Eastmans didn't warn us about the cistern because they didn't know we were coming here. Anyway, when the lid broke, Catherine fell in. There's a lot of water in the cistern because of all the rain we've had lately. She didn't surface immediately and when she finally did"—Marissa swallowed hard— "when she finally did, she'd caught the body under its arms and tangled her hand in its hair. At first she couldn't get loose and the body kept dragging her down—" Marissa's voice broke. "It was awful."

Robbie continued to write, although even from a slight distance Catherine noticed her face tensing. "Could you estimate the level of decomposition? I mean, when you say a body, I don't think you're referring to a skeleton. Is flesh clinging on the bones or—" Robbie raised her shoulders. "I don't know how to phrase this like the medical examiner would."

"The body has most or all of its flesh and hair. I only got a glimpse, but the face looked dreadful—not just bloated but also . . . damaged." After a moment, Marissa said, "It's definitely a woman."

"I see." Robbie's voice seemed carefully

toneless. "Can you tell me in what way the face is damaged?"

"Well, not really. There's something about the right side—maybe a hole where the eye should have been?"

"A hole? Like a puncture wound? Or a bullet hole?"

"I only got a glimpse, but I'd say either."

"About how old is the woman?"

"It's hard to tell because of the water damage to the body and I only got a quick look. If I had to guess, I'd say less than forty."

"Hair color?"

"Black. Long, thick, and black. I'll never forget it." Marissa drew a shaky breath. "I don't know anything else, Robbie, and I'd really like to check on Catherine."

The deputy nodded and followed Marissa to Catherine and the paramedics. "How's my sister?" Marissa asked.

"She's scared and cold, but she's not going into shock. No broken bones, no cuts, no contusions," one young, red-haired man said jauntily, addressing himself to Robbie. Catherine wondered if he was trying to flirt with the pretty deputy. "She doesn't seem confused." He stooped and looked into Catherine's eyes. "Are you confused, honey?"

"I don't think so," Catherine muttered.

The older paramedic looked at his partner, obviously annoyed. "Her name isn't *Honey.*"

The younger paramedic flushed and then flashed a tight smile. "Just tryin' to lighten things up some." He looked at Catherine. "No offense, *ma'am.*" Then he looked back at Robbie, still smiling, now engagingly.

Robbie ignored the young paramedic but lingered closely as Marissa turned to Catherine. "Are you really all right?"

Catherine nodded. "I guess I'm okay, considering."

"Dr. Gray, your sister told me the corpse is that of a woman," Robbie said. "Do you have any idea who she is?"

Catherine and Marissa exchanged quick glances. "The face was bloated and I was terrified and choking," Catherine answered, and saw Marissa's anxious expression lighten. Catherine knew her sister had been afraid she'd blurt out something about the woman being Renée. "We haven't seen another car since we've been here."

"How long is that?"

"Uh, maybe twenty minutes. Thirty at the most." Robbie nodded. "Maybe someone dropped her off or she came in a taxi, but I don't know why," Catherine went on. "The area is nearly deserted at this time of year. I can't think of anyone she would have been coming to visit, especially the Eastmans. They *never* come here. They aren't even home. They're on a trip—"

Marissa shot a warning glance and Catherine realized she was going too far in her effort to hide any suspicion that she might know the woman. Even Robbie had stopped writing, staring at her. Catherine nervously looked away from them at the sheriff's car pulling near. "Oh, thank God! Here's Eric!"

As Eric Montgomery, dressed in jeans and a heavy sweatshirt, stepped from the car, sunlight brightened his wavy blond hair and played over the planes of his young face. Less than a year ago, he'd taken over for Mitch Farrell when cancer had forced him to leave the elected position of sheriff he'd held for over twenty years. The election in two weeks would reveal if Chief Deputy Eric Montgomery would become the next official sheriff. Catherine had no doubt he was the best man for the job. Although he was only thirty, he'd had several years of exemplary experience with the police force of Pittsburgh until he resigned and came home to Aurora Falls, where he'd lived most of his life and long ago fallen in love with her sister.

Catherine watched Marissa rush toward Eric, love and relief in her expression. In fact, Marissa clearly almost hugged him before she hesitated and instead began animatedly chattering. Eric nodded solemnly, his concentration obviously intense, until Marissa finally seemed to run out of details. When she fell silent, Eric walked toward Catherine.

"Having a rough day, girl?" he asked in a relaxing, casual manner accompanied by a sympathetic smile.

"I've had better." Catherine still shivered, although the paramedics had thrown a dry blanket over her shoulders. Her soaking-wet tennis shoes felt like lead weights and tension drew her scalp so tight she thought her ears must be pulling back.

"What are you doing here?" Marissa asked. "You have the day off."

"My people knew I'd want to be here and called. I was nearby."

"I suppose Marissa has filled you in on the details of my . . . discovery," Catherine said.

Eric nodded. "She said you two were having a nice afternoon sightseeing until this happened." Eric's deep voice remained easy and his brown eyes kind yet keen. As they quickly traveled over her, they dodged away from her right hand. Catherine looked down to see long dark hairs still trapped under her fingernails and trailing from her hand. Repulsed, she immediately began rubbing her fingers against the rough weave of the blanket. "The paramedics say you're okay, physically at least." Eric smiled encouragingly.

"Yeah. They said I should go to the hospital for a more thorough checkup, but I had a feeling I was getting the standard recommendation. I think I'm just fine."

"That's good." Eric glanced at Robbie and the male deputy Jeff Beal. "You two secure the crime scene."

"We're on it," Jeff said snappily, and Catherine expected him to salute. He was three years older than Eric, but he didn't seem to resent Eric's senior position.

When Marissa joined Eric, Catherine said to him, "I'd just like for Marissa to take me home now. Please."

Marissa looked at Eric. "She's free to go, isn't she? There's nothing else she can tell you and—"

Marissa broke off as a fire truck pulled onto the lawn and two men spilled from the vehicle. Catherine knew they'd come to retrieve the body and she shrugged the blanket off her shoulders. "Oh, I *really* want to go now. Please don't make me stay for this, Eric."

"I don't want to"—Eric looked at a silver Lincoln Town Car slowing down in front of the cottage—"but James is here."

James Eastman carefully pulled his car to the side of the asphalt road, out of the way of the official vehicles, then flung open the door and hurried toward Catherine, who sat at the open rear doors of the ambulance. He wore jeans and a pale green shirt with long sleeves rolled halfway up his forearms. His black hair, short on the sides, longer on top, and brushed to the side, gleamed in the sun. As he drew near,

Catherine saw that James's dark brown eyes looked even more intense than usual.

An abrupt wave of guilt swept through Catherine, as if she'd set out to cause him trouble. She controlled it by straining to act composed. "How did you get here so fast? I thought you were playing golf."

"I had work at the office I decided was more important than golf. You know I don't even really like golf—I was supposed to play with some friends of Dad's." Suddenly, near panic washed over James's handsome face. He grasped her shoulders and peered into her eyes. "My God, Catherine. I don't think I've ever been as scared in my life as I was when Eric called me. Are you all right?"

"Y-yes."

"You don't sound sure."

"Everyone is asking me the same thing." She gave him a weak smile. "I'm going to put a sign around my neck making the announcement."

James's grip tightened. "Catherine, don't try being okay about this. Be honest. *Are you all right?*" She nodded vehemently and stared at him, unable to speak. "I know about the body and I don't want details.

You don't have to talk about *anything* now." He went silent and then suddenly burst out, "But why are you here at the cottage, for God's sake?"

Catherine's guilt returned accompanied by embarrassment. She felt like she'd done something sneaky. "Your mother talks about what a pretty place this is or could be without the cottage. I wanted to show it to Marissa."

"Show it to Marissa? Why?"

"Well . . . I don't know." Catherine hesitated. "To be honest, I thought you might want the land. For a house. A house for yourself. I know you hate living in that crappy place the owner calls a town house."

James looked at her closely. Catherine longed to shift her gaze away from his probing eyes, but she knew she'd look evasive. She forced herself to look innocent.

"I know I'm not getting the whole story about this trip to the cottage," James finally said with a touch of indulgence. "It doesn't matter now, though." He hugged her and she clung to his warm body. Then she thought of her own damp, stringy hair and filthy clothes. She quickly pulled away. He peered at her, his forehead creasing again. "You're wet and cold. Let's get you home."

"James, I'd appreciate you staying a few minutes." Catherine had forgotten Eric Montgomery still stood beside her. Eric nodded in the direction of the cistern. "I need for you to take a look at something."

The body, Catherine thought with dull, horrified inevitability. Marissa told Eric that I think the body is Renée.

James hesitated, obviously knowing why Eric wanted him to stay and just as obviously wanting to leave. James, however, never ran away from anything. "Sure, Eric." He looked at Catherine. "You sit still, sweetheart. Don't try to walk by yourself. I'll be right back."

Catherine watched James nearing the cottage, his shoulders straight but a lag in his step, and her heart wrenched. She desperately wished she hadn't come to look at the place. She wished she'd never seen it, never heard of it. She wished it didn't exist. But it did and she'd come to it with all her joyful plans—plans she hadn't even mentioned to James—and look what had happened. She'd found the body of a dead woman, for God's sake, and her nosiness had dumped a load of trouble and darkness onto the Eastman family, especially her dear James.

Catherine closed her eyes for a moment, chilled by the thought of the bloated, decaying body rescue workers were now preparing to retrieve from the cold water. James had to watch, she thought, and considering the circumstances, he shouldn't have to do it without her support. Despite his instructions, she left the safety of the ambulance and on weak legs walked to his side and linked her arm through his. He looked at her and she wanted to give him an encouraging smile, but she simply couldn't muster one.

Catherine realized a smile wouldn't matter to James, though. He'd only flicked a vague glance at her when she clasped his arm. Then his silent, intense gaze focused on an orange piece of equipment shaped like a stretcher that two men carried to the cistern.

Eric stood beside James. "That's a Skedco Sked stretcher system," he said casually. Catherine knew Eric was merely chatting, trying to calm James by diverting him. "It's an especially good transport system for rescues in confined spaces like storage tanks and manholes. It's flexible and easy to hoist with ropes and only weighs eleven pounds without its attachments, which they don't seem to need. This isn't a difficult job."

James nodded, pulling Catherine closer to him as a tall, muscular man wearing protective eye gear lowered the stretcher into the cistern and then slid into the water with the fluidity of a seal. He rose once, took a breath, and called to Eric, "Got the body partially secured!" He looked at his fellow rescue worker. "We don't need ropes. I'll be sending up the stretcher in a minute."

Catherine's breathing slowed as the sled rose from the water. One rescue worker took hold of the rails while the other clambered unaided from the tank. Together they lifted the stretcher, tilting it as much as possible to maneuver it out of the cistern, and laid it gently on the ground.

Eric glanced at James, who said firmly, "Stay here," to Catherine. He and Eric walked to the stretcher. Catherine could see the body's dark slacks, a long-sleeved sweater, a puffy, dangling white hand, and long, wet black hair. She couldn't bear to look at the face, but James stared at it for almost a full minute, his complexion turning gray beneath its remnant of a summer tan. Then he looked at Eric, not a trace of emotion on his face, and Catherine heard him say dully, "It's my wife Renée."

CHAPTER THREE

1

Torn between feeling she should stay with James and frantically wanting the safety of home, Catherine argued when Marissa told her they were leaving. Catherine was still arguing when Eric ordered her home in his most authoritative voice, but it was James giving her a quick, soft kiss on the lips and telling her he'd feel better if he knew she was safe, warm, and, he added with a weak smile, "cleaned up" that sent her homeward.

Even though the temperature had

dropped considerably since afternoon, Catherine didn't want Marissa to raise the roof of the Mustang convertible. Marissa drove her usual five miles above the speed limit and Catherine closed her eyes, letting the cool wind whip at her damp sweater and the hair she'd pulled back in a pony-tail.

"If you're cold, I'll put up the top, now," Marissa finally said.

"No. I like the air. I stink."

"You don't stink."

"Yes, I do. I'm going to burn these clothes. And my hair is—"

"Your hair will be fine after a couple of rounds with shampoo. You don't have to burn it off."

"I was going to say my hair is rank. I wasn't planning on setting fire to it."

"That's reassuring. It's been a hell of an afternoon. I'm afraid of what might come next."

"You're never afraid. I'm the timid one."

"Oh, not this again," Marissa said in the voice Catherine recognized as half-teasing, half-serious. "I'm afraid a lot. I just don't ad-mit it. And you aren't timid. You just think you are because people have told you so all your life. For God's sake, Catherine, you're a psychologist. You should know you're not timid."

"Psychologists aren't good at analyzing themselves."

"Well, take it from me that you're braver than I am."

After a pause, Catherine said, "He called her his wife."

"What?"

"James. He looked at the body and he said to Eric, 'It's my wife Renée.' Not 'my ex-wife.' 'My wife.'"

"So?"

"Maybe he still thinks of her as his wife," Catherine said drearily.

"He doesn't. He was stunned and upset."

"Maybe he was still in love with her."

Marissa let out a long sigh. "Catherine, you've had a terrible shock today and you're letting it send you into a downward spiral just because James said 'wife' instead of 'ex-wife.' Well, remember this. He's had a terrible shock, too. He misspoke because he was astounded and worried about you finding Renée's body. He doesn't think of Renée as his wife. He doesn't love Renée. He loves *you*. Period."

"If you say so," Catherine answered tonelessly.

"Cry, scream, wave your arms around, stomp your feet, put in a CD, and blast the music, but do something besides going numb."

"Will that make *you* feel better?"

"Much. And smile or I'll pick up speed. How does ninety sound?"

Catherine tilted her lips. "Like you'll get a speeding ticket on top of everything else."

"That's better. Much better. Let's keep it that way. Now, do you want to hear some music, have a normal conversation, or just remain silent?"

Catherine knew Marissa was incapable of maintaining silence after the afternoon they'd had and any conversation would involve a rehash of events, so Catherine chose music and retreated into her headache, her misery, and the songs of Coldplay.

An hour later, Catherine emerged from the steam-filled upstairs bathroom of the Gray home. She wore a floor-length terry-cloth robe over flannel pants and a long-sleeved

T-shirt and she was still cold. She wrapped a towel around her hair with fingers that had puckered from their long exposure to water. She'd scrubbed her nails so hard, the skin around them burned.

"I've built a fire!" Marissa called from downstairs. "I've also fixed you something to eat, whether you want it or not! Hurry before it gets cold!"

Catherine closed her eyes and sighed. All she really wanted to do was curl up in bed. Instead, she tightened the belt on her robe, slid into some soft scuff house slippers, and descended the stairs. Marissa stood at the foot of the steps, beaming at her, obviously having worked to make the lovely cream, cinnamon, and dusky blue family room even more comforting and welcoming than usual. Behind the grate, a fire crackled cheerfully in the large stone hearth and Marissa had turned on two brass lamps and lit three cinnamon-scented candles.

"Do you feel better?" Marissa asked.

"I feel cleaner."

"Well, you should. I think that was the longest shower on record." Marissa looked down at the medium-sized yellow dog sitting dutifully by her side holding a small stuffed tiger in her mouth. "Lindsay thought we'd have to come in and rescue you."

Catherine bent and patted the dog on the head. "I appreciate your concern, Lindsay." The dog stood and wagged her tail, keeping a firm grip on the tiger. "I always feel safer when you're around."

"You should. She's very loyal to you even though she's officially my dog." Marissa grinned. "Please sit on the couch. I've fixed a feast."

A feast, Catherine thought in dismay. God only knew what that could be. Marissa's cooking ranged from bad to merely passable. Nevertheless, Catherine sat down and tried to look eagerly at the tray of food.

"Hold out your hand." Catherine did as told and Marissa dropped a small blue pill onto her palm and handed her a glass of water. "You took aspirin for your headache when you got home. Now a Valium. I didn't insist on it earlier for fear of you getting dizzy and falling in the shower. Don't protest. You've always said there's nothing wrong with taking a tranquilizer in an emergency."

"I wasn't going to protest." Catherine swallowed the pill. "I think everything inside of me is quivering."

"No wonder."

"And I feel ridiculous for getting so upset because James called Renée his wife."

"We were both freaked out," Marissa said dismissively. "I've fixed a grilled-cheese sandwich—I used that Jarlsberg cheese you bought—and some tomato soup made with milk, and a pot of chamomile tea. Chamomile is supposed to be calming and you don't need alcohol with a tranquilizer. How does all of that sound?"

"Wonderful. You didn't need to go to such trouble."

"Of course I did. Still, don't be complimentary until you've tasted it, although it's hard even for me to mess up a grilled-cheese sandwich and soup. I'm having coffee and a piece of the German chocolate cake I bought at the bakery day before yesterday. There's plenty of cake left for you, too."

Catherine laughed as Marissa spread a napkin over Catherine's lap and poured her tea as if she were an invalid. "Don't be insulted if I can't eat everything, Marissa. I still feel a little queasy."

"Don't worry. Lindsay and I will take care of any leftovers."

Marissa kept up a steady stream of light chatter about the doings of Hollywood celebrities as if they were all family friends. While she listened to Marissa's dramatic account of an actor leaving his wife of two months for a supermodel, Catherine took the towel off her head, letting her hair fall to her shoulders and dry in the warmth from the fire. When Marissa finally exhausted her movie-star stories, Catherine looked in amazement at her empty dinnerware. "Well, how about that? I could have sworn I wasn't hungry."

"You didn't eat lunch and only had toast for breakfast. You needed food. A piece of cake now?"

"I think I've finally reached my limit. Thank you for dinner."

"It was my pleasure," Marissa said as she began gathering dishes onto the serving tray.

Catherine could have sworn Lindsay looked crestfallen at the empty plates, and smiled. "Marissa, you have to give the poor thing something special. She's breaking my heart."

"Don't kid yourself. She's practiced that heartbreaking look, but she'll get at least one dog biscuit and maybe another bacon treat."

As Marissa disappeared into the kitchen, Catherine glanced at the frisky, friendly dog she'd come to love. "I know it's only nine thirty, but I'm exhausted," she said. Lindsay tilted her head as if she could understand her while Catherine lay down, pulled the afghan over her, and reached for the phone. "Let's give James a call while I can still hold my eyes open."

2

James Eastman stood in the front yard of the little cottage. Under a sweeping panorama of glittering stars, the place looked even smaller and more forlorn than it did in the daytime. Crime-scene tape still stretched around the area of the porch and the cistern and sealed the front door.

"What did you say, sweetheart?" James asked into his cell phone. "Sorry, my attention wandered for a minute."

"I asked what you're doing," Catherine repeated. "You don't seem to be listening to me."

"I'm just sitting in my apartment reading," James said, and could have shot a whip-poor-will that decided to emit a loud call. "Got a nature show on television, but I can't concentrate on the reading or the TV. I am listening to you. I'm just tired and you sound the same way. I think we should both go to sleep."

"In different beds."

"It happens about five nights a week anyway and it's best for tonight. You can toss and kick and mumble all you want."

"You're the one who tosses and kicks and mumbles," Catherine said.

"That's not true. Tell you what. If when I see you tomorrow you tell me you haven't slept, I'll take you on a five-mile run."

"Then I promise I'll sleep."

"That's what I thought. Good night, sweetheart. I love you."

James Eastman clicked off his cell phone, wishing he could talk to Catherine longer but knowing he couldn't without getting onto the subject of Renée.

Renée who was dead. James knew many people in town thought she'd died at his hand years ago. He'd endured the innuendoes and rumors, pretending they didn't faze him, but they'd embarrassed, infuriated, and deeply hurt him, which he'd been certain that Renée had hoped would happen. When he'd finally decided she wasn't coming home on her own to get a divorce, he'd begun the formal search for her, legally necessary in order to acquire a quiet divorce on the grounds of desertion. To his relief, when she had not been found within a year the divorce proceedings began and ended quietly. He didn't have to think about her anymore. He could begin a new life.

Except that now, after what Catherine had found, he couldn't begin fresh as the memory of Renée Eastman faded from everyone's minds. When she was alive, most people who knew her had disliked or even hated her. But people's sympathy could change overnight. James knew many people would suddenly feel sorry for Renée when they knew she'd ended up dead.

Worse than just dead. She'd been shot in the head and stuffed in a cistern to rot.

James walked, drawing closer to his car in what served as a driveway, and stood a few feet closer to the wooded area. It looked dense at night, although the trees grew widely spaced in a less than two-acre grove. In the soft dusk he caught the movement of a small animal venturing toward him from the protection of the trees. Too late in the season for a groundhog, he thought. A raccoon coming to search for trash? The cottage, usually vacant, wouldn't be a usual stop on the trash-patrol circuit. More likely, a cat crept near.

And so did headlights. Oh damn, not sightseers, James thought angrily, although he knew a few had come by earlier. Perry Lane was off the beaten track and many people didn't even know the small collection of fishing cottages existed. Today that had been a blessing. Word might have spread by now, though, and people with nothing better to do on a Saturday night were hunting down the scene of a murder.

The car slowly stopped in front of the cottage and someone turned off the headlights. A sense of violation filled James.

Who in hell would be bold enough to actually approach him here after what had happened today? What did they think gave them the right? Or did they believe he was merely a fellow sightseer sharing their morbid curiosity?

The car's interior lights came on as a woman emerged and called, "Hi, James! When I couldn't reach you at home, I didn't even try your cell phone. I knew you'd be here. I wanted to see for myself that you're all right. I hope you don't mind that I came."

Patrice Greenlee. James's irritation ebbed as he saw his partner at Eastman and Greenlee Law Practice. He'd known Patrice since he was on the verge of adolescence.

"I'm glad you're here," James said loudly as she walked toward him. "I was starting to get the creeps."

When Patrice reached him, she pulled him close and hugged him. At forty, Patrice stood five-seven, with a slim, toned body, above-the-shoulder curly ash-blond hair, high cheekbones, and striking light gray eyes. Tonight she wore a full-length black cashmere coat unbuttoned over a chic blue dress and white running shoes.

"Why didn't you call me?" she demanded. "I heard on the police scanner about a body being found on Perry Lane and remembered that your family has a cottage here. I called the office, your town house, and your cell phone, but I got no answer, and I've been in a knot all day."

"You could have saved yourself all that anxiety by not always listening to the scanner."

"I can't stand not knowing what's going on around here."

"So instead you listen constantly and get worked up like today." James shook his head. "Where's your best guy tonight?"

"We were having dinner at the Larke Inn dining room when he got a call," Patrice said, referring to her fiancé of two months, Lawrence Blakethorne, owner of Blakethorne Charter Flights. "Sometimes I hate cell phones. The call was about the big merger of Blakethorne and Star Air that lately is just consuming Lawrence. He said it was an emergency, as usual, and he had to go to his office to look up some files. He dropped me off at the house on the way, and after I got there I decided to come looking for you. I didn't even bother to change clothes except for my shoes." She held up one running-shoe-clad foot. "Classy, huh?" She didn't wait for an answer. "So they did find a body at this cottage."

"Unfortunately, yes." James sighed. "I thought I'd take another look at the place and it wouldn't bother me, but . . . well . . . you always seem to know when I need a friend."

"No one should be out here alone," Patrice said briskly. She gazed at the cottage and dug her hands deep into her pockets. "They were as vague as possible on the police scanner, so they just gave the code for dead body. Was it a man or woman?"

"Woman."

"How was she killed?"

"She was shot."

"Did they find identification?"

Silence spun out before James said slowly, "No, but it's Renée."

Patrice went still for a moment before she murmured, "Renée?" Then louder, "*Your* Renée?"

"Yes."

"Hell, no!"

"Hell, yes."

"Oh, James, no!"

"Don't keep wailing. People already think I murdered her. If anyone is around, they'll think I'm murdering you, too."

Patrice pulled her hands from her pockets, raised open palms, and gave him a light thump on the chest. "Don't even say such a thing!" She huffed in frustration. "How long has the body been here?"

"The police think maybe a week."

"A *week*?" Patrice looked stunned. "She's been dead a week? Not months? Not years?"

"Definitely not years. Or even months."

"Well then, you've made a mistake," Patrice said definitely. "It can't be Renée. It's a homeless woman. Someone saw her wandering around out here, panicked, and shot her. They were too scared to report it to the police, so they hid the body."

"No one is living out here now, Patrice. Besides, I saw the body. It was Renée."

"No, you didn't!" Patrice went silent for a moment before asking grudgingly, "Even if it *was* Renée, why would she be at your family's cottage?"

"I have no idea. Catherine found her in the cistern."

"Catherine?"

"She was with Marissa, thank God. That big cistern at the end of the cottage is about seven feet deep and nearly full of water from all the rain we've had lately. Catherine stepped on the half-rotten lid, which broke. She fell in, and when she surfaced she was holding Renée's body. She's not a good swimmer, and between panicking and getting her hand twisted in Renée's hair I think she would have drowned if Marissa hadn't been here to help her."

Patrice looked appalled. "How horrible! Catherine must have been hysterical."

"Just the opposite. It was like she just shut down emotionally, but she looked awful."

"Is she hurt?"

"The paramedics said that physically she's fine except for scrapes, bruises, probably strained muscles. Marissa took her home, gave her a tranquilizer, fed her, and sent her to bed." He sighed. "She just called me. She's okay for now, but I'm certain she won't be getting over the shock any time soon."

"Don't underestimate her, James. I've always believed Catherine is far stronger and more resilient than people think," Patrice said bracingly. "Why were she and Marissa here?"

"My parents have told her about the place. Catherine said something about looking at it as a possible site as a house for me."

"The *cottage*?"

"No. Mom keeps talking about selling the land to someone who could tear down the cottage and build a nice house. Catherine's never seen it. Maybe she and Marissa came because it was a pretty day and they were curious about it. I'm just glad Catherine didn't come out here alone."

Patrice pressed her thin, well-shaped lips together as she usually did when she was thinking. After a moment, she demanded irritably, "If the body is Renée's, where has she been? My God, James, it's been over a year since she left and then she finally shows up like *this*?"

"I'm aware of how long it's been." He paused and said dryly, "I'm also certain Renée didn't intend to show up like *this*."

Patrice ignored his attempt at gallows humor. "But why is she here?"

"I have no idea."

"Maybe one of her lovers kept track of

her and lured her home to rekindle their romance. Neither of them struck me as the type to give up easily. Or one might have pretended to want her back when he really wanted to make her pay for dumping him. Or—sorry to sound cruel—who knows if there were really only two men? I mean, knowing Renée . . ."

"Knowing Renée, there could have been a dozen men. Still, after so long . . ." James fell silent for a moment and then said in a musing voice, "I guess finding her now is ironic. Our divorce just became final on Monday. Five days ago."

"Did Renée know about the divorce?"

"I haven't had any contact with her since she left me. Maybe she's in touch with her parents, but I don't know. They stopped returning my calls a few weeks after Renée left, but I sent her father a registered letter when I started divorce proceedings. I also sent one informing him of the approximate time the divorce would be finalized. I received his signature as proof of delivery for both of them." James looked fixedly at the cottage. "Anyway, I'm sure she didn't come back here about the divorce."

"No, you can't be sure. After all, the

timing is suspiciously coincidental. Maybe Renée's father told her about the divorce and at the last minute she decided she wanted to reconcile."

"After the way she treated me when we were married? After the way she left without a word then or in the years since she's been gone? Then suddenly she wanted me back?" James shook his head. "No, Patrice, she certainly did not come back for me."

Patrice was silent for a moment, then said slowly, "You sound bitter, James."

"Bitter that I know she didn't want me back?"

"Well . . ." Patrice sounded uncomfortable. "I don't know."

"She made my life a living hell, both before and after she left, and if I sound bitter it's only because I can't seem to free myself of her. I'm in love with Catherine. I was happy. And here's Renée again, tearing my life apart, tearing Catherine's apart."

"She can't tear anyone's life apart again if she's dead, James," Patrice said quietly.

"Can't she? She was murdered. There will be another investigation and again I'll be the number one suspect. And look at what happened today. Catherine could have died out here, drowned in that cistern because she was dragged down by Renée." James laughed sarcastically. "Even as a corpse the woman is dangerous."

Patrice frowned. "I'm worried about you, James. You sound . . ."

"Crazy?"

"Well . . . different. Not like the steady, rational James Eastman I've known for years."

James's smile faded. He looked away, and after a moment he answered drearily, his earlier anger seeming to slip away, "I think I'm in shock, Patrice. Finding her in Aurora Falls at my family's ratty old cottage where someone shot her in the head and crammed her body in the cistern is just . . . just . . ."

Patrice closed her hand around his upper arm. "Stop, James. Stop talking about it; stop picturing it; stop wearing yourself out with it. What you need now is to go home."

"I will. Soon. I think I'll get drunk."

"You never get drunk. You should follow Catherine's example."

"I don't have a loving sister to give me a tranquilizer, feed me, and put me to bed."

Patrice smiled. "Marissa and Catherine bicker like young girls sometimes, but they really love and take care of each other." She sighed. "My sister and I used to be just like them. I miss that kind of unconditional bond. Still, I think you're capable of taking a pill, eating, and going to bed without help." She waited a few seconds and then asked, "Have you talked to Eric Montgomery?"

James nodded. "He arrived on the scene before I did, even though it was his day off. I don't mind saying I'm relieved he's in charge of all this, although he's already started questioning me about my whereabouts last weekend."

"That's normal. The spouse is always the prime suspect."

"I'm not the spouse."

"You were last weekend. Anyway, you were at the conference in Pittsburgh. A lot of people saw you."

"Maybe not a lot. I got there Thursday afternoon and was already coming down with the flu. I skipped a few seminars on Friday and Saturday and the big dinner on Saturday night. Besides, right now they're only estimating that Renée was murdered a week ago. It could have been six days ago, on Sunday, when I'd gotten back home and gone straight to bed. Alone. Not even Catherine can vouch for me."

Patrice shook her head. "So, even dead, that damned Renée's still causing trouble for you. But at least Catherine is all right and your parents are away on a cruise. Are you going to let them know what's happened?"

James shook his head. "Do you think I'm going to interrupt their thirty-fifth wedding anniversary trip to Italy with this gruesome piece of news?"

"Your mother will be furious if you don't."

"She'll get over it. She always does."

Patrice squinted down at her slim dress watch. "Well, you seem to be okay, James, although you do need to go home." She stood on tiptoe and kissed James lightly on the cheek. "I'm sorry about all of this. Will you be taking off work next week?"

"No. I'll be in the office Monday morning, bright and early."

"Monday! Give yourself at least a couple of days to recover."

"Recover by sitting around my town house watching television? No. The best thing I can do for myself is to work."

"You're a remarkable man."

"Yeah, I'm feeling remarkable tonight."

"Go home."

"Okay."

Patrice turned her car around and started back the way she'd come, waving briefly at James as she passed him. James lingered for a couple of minutes, then went to his silver Lincoln, scooted behind the wheel, started the car, and slowly backed up a few feet. Then he stopped, planning to flip on the headlights and take one last look at the hideous old cottage crouching like a small monster in the dark.

Suddenly a pillar of bright yellow fire shot skyward at the back of the cottage. Within seconds, a second fireball lit the night. The pillars spread into a wall of flame stretching along the entire back of the cottage, dropping blazing debris onto the roof, spitting sizzling pieces of wood flying across the black night sky, and turning the small building into a raging pyre.

CHAPTER FOUR

1

Catherine bolted up on the couch, screaming. Immediately Lindsay began barking
frantically. Within seconds, Marissa was
gripping Catherine's arms.

"My God, Catherine, what's wrong?"

Catherine took hold of Marissa, shuddering, as Marissa clung to her. Catherine
drew her even closer and buried her head
in the long hair at her sister's neck.

"When I came back from the kitchen,
you'd dozed off," Marissa said. "You've been

asleep about twenty minutes. You just had a nightmare, that's all."

Catherine pulled away from Marissa and shook her head. "No! Something has happened to James! I have to call him!"

"Okay. Take a breath." Marissa picked up the handset of the phone on the coffee table and looked at Catherine's trembling fingers. "Want me to dial the number?"

"Yes. His home phone." Catherine rattled off James's landline-phone number. He'd turned off his answering machine, and Catherine groaned when he didn't answer after six rings. "Oh God."

"Don't panic. Considering what happened this afternoon, he might have turned off his landline phone. Give me his cell-phone number." After two rings, James answered.

"Hi," Marissa said in relief. "Catherine just had a nightmare about you and she's upset, so I dialed your number for her. Here she is."

Catherine snatched the handset away from Marissa and nearly shouted, "James, are you all right?"

"S-sure. I'm . . . fine," he said shakily.

"You don't sound fine. Why didn't you answer your home phone?"

"Because I'm not home," he said vaguely.

"Where are you?"

"Just . . . driving around."

Catherine snapped alert. He was obviously dodging the question and her patience cracked. "James, don't hide things from me," she said sternly. "Tell me what's wrong!"

"Well . . . I . . . I just missed being in an explosion. Well, not exactly *in* it—"

"An explosion!" Catherine felt as if a knife blade ripped her stomach and she heard Marissa gasp. "Are you hurt? Are you at the hospital?"

"Honey, calm down. I'm not hurt."

"You are and you're just not telling me."

"I'm *not.* Really. There's not a scratch on me."

Catherine drew a deep breath, desperately trying to regain her calm. "Where are you and what happened?"

"I'm at the cottage. Someone blew it up."

"The *cottage*? Oh, the police wanted you to go back about the explosion."

"Well . . ."

Catherine glanced at Marissa. "He was at the cottage. I guess someone blew it up, but he's all right."

Lindsay, always high-strung, was huffing and snorting. Marissa nodded to Catherine and took the noisy dog into another room.

Catherine turned her attention back to the phone. Then her churning thoughts slowed, reason beginning to regain its footing. "James, you said you were almost *in* an explosion. You were already there. The police didn't call you about it."

"No. I just came by myself earlier." James sighed. "I was here when you called me."

"Oh." Catherine's voice went flat. "You lied to me."

"Yes. I'm sorry."

"Why did you go there tonight?"

"I don't know. It was a mistake. I'm sorry." James quickly went on, sounding direct but awkward. "At home, I had a couple of drinks, but they didn't help. I couldn't stop thinking about how awful the scene was today—that ratty old cottage turned into a carnival horror house. I decided to drive out here and look at the place. I guess I thought it wouldn't look as terrible in the moonlight as it did in the sunlight. I was wrong."

James stopped, clearly waiting for Catherine to say something. Confusion and anger overcame her, though, and she knew maintaining silence was better than voicing her rush of boiling feelings.

James drew a deep breath, assured her again that he wasn't hurt; then he said on a painfully ashamed note, "Catherine, I'm sorry about everything that's happened today."

"I know you're sorry," she managed, keeping her voice emotionless. "You don't have to keep telling me. But I don't understand why you thought you had to lie—"

"Here's a fire truck!" James's voice rose over the sound of a siren. "Go back to sleep, Catherine," he ordered, sounding relieved. "Everything will be all right, I promise."

He abruptly hung up and Catherine stared at the handset, stunned and baffled.

An explosion. The man she loved had barely escaped an explosion, but after this surreal day she couldn't fully process the reality of another horrifying shock. As she rose from the couch, wanting the peace and solitude of her bedroom, she realized she should feel nothing except relief that James was safe. Instead, she couldn't stop thinking about his weird nighttime visit to the cottage where his ex-wife had been murdered. He'd given Catherine a reason, but it sounded flimsy and certainly not like the normal behavior of the James Eastman she knew.

Why had he really gone there?

And why had he lied to her about it?

2

Patrice Greenlee looked out a sunroom window, her gaze sweeping over the sun-drenched terrace and the rear lawn with its sprawling flagstone patio. Beyond the patio, a seven-foot-tall wall of evergreen shrubbery enclosed a large fishpond. "I hope this weather holds for a week. It's perfect for our wedding."

"Our wedding will be in a church. You know, with walls, a roof, a furnace. Why does the weather matter?"

Patrice turned and looked at her fiancé, Lawrence Blakethorne, sitting at the casual dining table. He lowered his morning paper, smiling at her. She had met him twenty-four years earlier when he'd married her older sister, Abigail, and he'd changed little except for a few wrinkles in his perpetually tanned skin, the silver lacing his thick black hair, and nearly twenty pounds of muscular bulk he'd added to his tall, once-lanky frame. Patrice thought that at fifty Lawrence was even more attractive than he'd been in his youth.

"I'm afraid a lot of people won't attend because they disapprove of you marrying your sister-in-law," Patrice said quietly.

"My *former* sister-in law. Abigail has been dead for over twelve years. I don't think as many people disapprove as you think."

"My mother would be outraged."

"I agree. If we'd married when she was around to see it, she would never have given us any peace."

"Is that why you waited until after she died last year to propose?"

"Yes." Lawrence's gaze grew distant. "The two of you never had a good relationship. She was never fair to you, but you valued her opinion more than that of almost anyone else. I never understood why.

Anyway, she would have hated the idea of us getting married, bitched at you constantly, and ruined your happiness, maybe even our marriage.

"Now she can't constantly voice her unwanted opinions, Pat," Lawrence continued. "You don't have to listen to her, even just to be polite. Your life is entirely your own to do with as you please. As for caring what people think, my own son is honestly pleased for us. He says this should have happened a long time ago." He looked at her closely. "So what's really worrying you, honey?"

Patrice moved away from one window in the dining area and wandered to another in the sitting area at the other end of the room. "Just details. I may be forty, but this is my first wedding and I want everything to be flawless. I want the weather to be perfect; I want people to be fine with our marriage." She paused and added fretfully, "And silly as it sounds, I'm also worried about the reception. I don't want to lose people in transit from the church to the Larke Inn."

Lawrence threw back his head and laughed. "We're having an evening wedding and there will be lots of excellent food and liquor at the reception. I doubt if we'll lose *anyone*." He laid down his newspaper and joined her at the window, resting an arm around her shoulders. "Pat, you're taking all the fun out of this thing."

"You think of our wedding as 'this *thing*'?"

He groaned and pulled her closer. "Poor choice of words. I'm looking forward to our *wedding*." He lowered his head and kissed her curly ash-blond hair. "I can't wait until we're husband and wife."

"Am I interrupting a beautiful moment?"

Lawrence and Patrice turned. Lawrence's son, Ian, lounged in the doorway, surveying them with the large, thickly lashed blue-gray eyes that had inspired the rapt fascination of many teenage girls and earned him the nickname Dreamy Eyes, which he hated.

"You're interrupting a small display of affection. Get used to it," Lawrence answered good-naturedly. He glanced at his watch. "You're late for Sunday brunch."

"I forgot to turn on the alarm clock."

"'Forgot to turn on the alarm clock,'" Lawrence repeated. "I remember using that line during my wild youth. Can't you come up with a better excuse for being late and looking a little ragged?"

"Maybe I had too much to drink last night. Anyway, I had to stop for gas at the convenience store and ran into Robbie Landers."

"*Deputy* Roberta Landers?" Patrice asked. "You know her?"

"Yes. We started talking and more time got away from me. Sorry."

"I'm sure she's just an acquaintance." Lawrence had turned a question into a statement. "And I'm not angry that you're late. There's not a thing wrong with a good-looking young guy sowing his wild oats on a Saturday night, although I don't want you to make a habit of it. You have responsibilities now that you're an important part of Blakethorne Charter."

"I won't." Ian glanced at the dining table covered with a light green linen cloth. "It seems late in the year to be eating in the sunroom."

Patrice nodded. "Well, it's like any other room; it's air-conditioned and heated. I know it's chilly outside, but the weather is so lovely. I thought I should take advantage of all these windows. I told your father I hope it stays nice through next weekend for the wedding."

"I'm sure it will," Ian said absently. He sauntered into the room and gazed out one of the windows overlooking the sun-drenched patio. As always, Patrice noticed the handsome twenty-two-year-old's resemblance to his mother. At six foot one, he had his father's height but Abigail's honey brown hair, fair skin, straight nose, dimples, and remarkable eyes. "At least the hedges won't have to be trimmed again this year, Dad."

"Thank God," Lawrence said. "The sound of three or four of those electric hedge trimmers roaring along at the same time drives me wild."

"Get rid of them."

"I thought you loved them," Lawrence said in surprise, but Ian merely shrugged. "Maybe it was only your mother who loved what she called her 'magic hideaway.'"

As usual, whenever Lawrence spoke of Abigail his voice turned slightly caustic. He'd never forgiven his wife for putting their ten-year-old son in the car and driving over the speed limit during a wild spring

storm after she'd taken a mixture of tranquilizers and alcohol. The resulting wreck
had killed her instantly. Ian, who'd nearly
died as well, had spent a week in a coma
and the next several months in rehab recovering from two broken legs, a broken
arm, a broken collarbone, and a severe
head injury. All the while, his remaining
family had waited in agony until the neurol-
ogists felt safe in pronouncing that his head
trauma had not resulted in permanent brain
damage.

Lawrence brushed a hand through the
air as if whisking away a pesky memory.
"Noisy hedge trimmers or not, though, I
intend to cut down on the hours I spend at
my office after next weekend." He winked
at Patrice.

Ian grinned. "Now you have a good reason not to spend more time here. You'll
have a new bride." He looked at Patrice.
"Mom."

"Oh, please, Ian, you've called me Patrice since you were three. Let's keep it
that way."

"Fine with me." Ian raised his head and
sniffed. "I smell all kinds of wonderful things
coming from the kitchen and I'm starving."

"Me, too," Lawrence said enthusiastically. He raised his voice. "Mrs. Frost, we're ready!"

They sat down at the dining table, and in less than a minute a tall, sturdy, silver-haired woman with a long, rectangular face and the beginning of jowls appeared in the doorway. Patrice remembered when her sister, Abigail, had hired the woman and introduced her as "Mrs. Frost." Nearly twenty years later, everyone in the household still called her Mrs. Frost. Patrice couldn't remember her first name, but the woman was so much a part of the Blakethorne household, Patrice had always wanted—and failed—to win her approval. Still, Patrice kept trying.

"Ah, a feast!" she exclaimed as Mrs. Frost swooped down and deftly slid dishes off a silver tray.

"Bacon and cheddar quiche, fruit salad, and spice-walnut muffins," the woman announced in a clipped voice with the trace of a British accent. "I'll be right back with crumb cake," Mrs. Frost announced. "Kona coffee for you, Mr. Lawrence?"

"Yes."

"I'll take some, too, please," Ian said.

Mrs. Frost smiled fondly at him. "Of course. I didn't forget you."

"And I'll have tea," Patrice said with a smile.

Mrs. Frost flicked mirthless, faded blue eyes at her. "I'll fetch it immediately, madam."

As soon as she left the room, Patrice leaned close to Lawrence and murmured, "She called me *madam*."

"What's wrong with that?"

"She used to call me Miss Patrice. She's never cared for me, but I think she actually dislikes me now that we're getting married."

"Nonsense, Pat," Lawrence announced loudly. "You're being paranoid. Mrs. Frost doesn't dislike you."

Inwardly Patrice cringed, knowing the woman had heard him. Lawrence never worried about whether or not people liked him, and as a result most people liked him enormously. Patrice knew her strong voice often sounded commanding and her personality frequently came across as aggressive rather than self-assured. These traits served her well as a trial lawyer, but they'd never made her socially popular. Ever since girlhood, she'd tried to monitor herself in personal situations, but flipping the switch to sweet voiced and gentle wasn't easy and she regularly failed. She wondered if Mrs. Frost accepted her for what she was or if the woman resented her for not being sweet-voiced, languid Abigail, to whom she'd been devoted.

Mrs. Frost returned with iced crumb cake, china cups and saucers, and a beautiful silver service with tea, coffee, milk, and sugar. Patrice noticed the small container holding discount tea bags. She decided not to point out Mrs. Frost's intended slight by asking for her usual expensive blend of Earl Grey tea.

"Did Roberta have anything to say about what happened at the Eastman cottage yesterday?" Lawrence asked. "You did hear about them finding the body of a dead woman in the cistern."

"Yes, I heard about it at the gallery last night," Ian said.

"Was Roberta on duty? Did she go to the cottage?"

"I'm not sure."

"But even if she wasn't there, she'd know if the police had identified the body. I only heard it was a woman's."

Patrice kept her gaze on her plate. She hadn't said anything to Lawrence about seeing James last night or of him being certain the body was Renée's. Patrice knew the information would spark a barrage of questions from Lawrence that she didn't want to dodge.

"If the police did identify the body and Robbie knew the name, she didn't tell me," Ian answered, sounding bored.

"Come on, Son. Roberta must have said something," Lawrence prodded. "This is big news. Exciting."

"This quiche is great," Ian said. "But I guess I have to sing for my supper or, rather, brunch. First off, I didn't ask Robbie about the body. I just said hello and that it was good to see her. She immediately apologized for her appearance, although I thought she looked fine. She said she was tired because she'd been up most of the night working on a case she couldn't discuss."

"How informative." Lawrence dug into his fruit. "Is that all she said?"

"No, it wasn't. She said yes when I asked her to be my date for the rehearsal dinner and the wedding reception."

"You invited Roberta Landers?" Patrice burst out.

Ian looked at her coolly. "Yes, I asked her for a date. Actually, two dates, I guess. Do you object to her?"

"No, of course not. I barely know her." Patrice didn't look at Lawrence. She'd snapped at Ian because she knew Lawrence wouldn't be pleased about his son dating a cop. "I just thought you'd ask one of the girls you've been seeing this past year."

"You mean a member of our small gaggle of Aurora Falls society girls? Last night I took one to the showing of Nicolai Arcos's paintings at the Nordine Gallery."

"You've spent quite a bit of time at that gallery."

"Dad, the owners, Ken and Dana, are friends of mine. And the gallery is fairly amazing, especially for a city of this size. You should take Patrice. I know you'd both be impressed."

"I saw it when it was new, but I'm not an art lover. Still, maybe a cultural evening wouldn't do us any harm, would it, Pat?"

"Certainly not."

"Was Arcos there last night?" Lawrence asked.

"Yes. I even introduced my date to him. I don't think he'd taken any of the drugs he claims help to free his creativity, so he was in complete control of his moody Romanian act. He gave her deep, soulful looks and nearly charmed her to death."

"You sound sarcastic for someone who admires the man."

"Dad, you haven't been really listening again," Ian said irritably. "I've never said I admire anything about him except for his talent. I think as a person he's half-insane."

"I've heard one painting of his is getting a lot of attention," Lawrence went on, ignoring Ian's assessment of Arcos. "It's called *New Orleans Girl* or something."

"*Mardi Gras Lady.* It's totally different from his usual work. I don't care for it. Anyway, after Arcos floated off to another group my date said she wanted to leave and go to a friend's party, so I took her."

"And you partied too much," Lawrence said.

"I was self-medicating to get through the evening."

"Just say it—you got drunk. I could smell

the breath mints as soon as you came in the door."

"I drank too much, but I didn't get drunk."

"Your date's father is an investor in the business—*our* business, now that you've graduated from college and come aboard. You have responsibilities, and those include social responsibilities. I hope you were nice to the young lady."

"I think you'll get a good report about my behavior. She's just not my type."

"Not like Roberta Landers."

"Marissa Gray works with Roberta's father at the *Gazette* and I've heard her mention Roberta. She says Roberta is smart and nice and that Eric is impressed with her work," Patrice offered quickly. Lawrence and Ian usually got along smoothly, but today the tension between them caused her usually steady nerves to tingle. She did not want trouble during this of all times—the week of her wedding—and she desperately cast around for something else pleasant to say. "Roberta is very pretty, Ian."

He tossed her a grateful look. "*Robbie* is very pretty, very nice, and very intelligent. I like her."

"Well, if you insist on bringing her to the

wedding, Ian, I hope she dresses appropriately," Lawrence muttered, reaching for a spice-walnut muffin and taking a large bite.

"Even though she scrapes by on a cop's salary, she might have a couple of decent dresses," Ian returned with an edge. "If not, she'll wear her uniform. Don't worry, Dad. She won't embarrass you. She looks smokin' hot in a uniform."

Lawrence angrily turned on him. "What is wrong with you this morning? You were late, you're being flippant, deliberately irritating, *rude,* and—"

Suddenly Lawrence's face froze, turned bright pink, and he barely got his hand to his mouth before he began to choke violently. Patrice's gray eyes widened and she looked at him for a moment before jumping up and rushing to his side. "What's wrong?" she asked in a high, alarmed voice while she pounded him on the back. "Are you all right?"

Ian rose from his chair, his face pale but confident, and went to his father. By now, Lawrence had stopped the loud, ragged coughing, but his face was crimson, his dark eyes watering and terrified. "Dad, can you speak?" Ian asked calmly. Lawrence shook his head no. "Can you stand up?" Again, *no.* Ian looked at Patrice. "Stop pounding on his back and be quiet. Please. You're making things worse." Patrice, still frightened but chastened, backed away.

Ian moved behind his father. "Dad, don't be scared. I'm going to do the Heimlich." Ian then leaned down, placed a fist at his father's waist, covered that fist with the other fist, and thrust-pressed three times before a walnut in a wad of dough flew out of Lawrence's mouth and onto his plate. Lawrence emitted a combination belch-bleat and then sagged in his chair.

"Are you okay?" Patrice half-asked, half-begged. "Lawrence, answer me!"

He waved her away with a weak hand and ground out, "I'm *fine.*"

"Are you sure? Ian, call nine-one-one."

"No! Dammit, I told you I'm fine!"

"You are definitely not fine. You're going to the hospital," Patrice insisted.

"Sit down and try to relax, Dad." Lawrence obeyed and began drawing in shallow, cautious breaths as Ian stood beside him like a faithful, anxious dog. In a moment, Ian glanced at Patrice with the young, vulnerable look she'd seen so often when he was in the presence of his father. "Dad has to rest for a few minutes before we make any decisions. You sit down, too, Patrice, and stop asking him questions and threatening him with a trip to the hospital," he said imploringly. "Choking is frightening enough without having some amateur medic like me literally squeeze the air out of him. He'll be okay."

Ian leaned down and looked into his father's eyes. "You're just out of breath and shocked, aren't you, Dad?"

Lawrence glanced up at Ian, and Patrice saw gratitude. She also saw resentment in Lawrence's dark eyes. She knew Lawrence was deeply embarrassed, his fierce macho pride wounded.

Mrs. Frost appeared carrying a crystal pitcher of ice water and without a word refilled everyone's glasses before vanishing to the kitchen. Patrice and Ian took their seats and began lackadaisically nibbling their food while Lawrence sat nearly immobile, sipping water.

"Patrice, will James be coming to the office this week?" Ian asked casually, his gaze fastened on the maraschino cherry she futilely chased around her plate.

"I talked to him last night and he said he was coming to work." She caught herself. "I talked to him briefly on the phone."

"This morning, a couple of guys at the convenience store were talking about a fire at the cottage last night. Know anything about it, Patrice?"

She tried to look surprised. "No! A fire? It must have happened after I talked to James or he would have mentioned it. Was it bad? How did it start?"

"I didn't get much information about it, but I believe it almost destroyed the place." Ian frowned. "Maybe someone was trying to destroy evidence."

Lawrence abruptly came to life. "Evidence of murder?" he asked, his voice gritty although his facial color had returned to normal.

"Yeah, Dad," Ian said. "The woman in the cistern *was* murdered."

Lawrence huffed. "Well, if it was Renée Eastman, she deserved it."

"What makes you think it was Renée?" Patrice asked.

Immediately Lawrence flushed deeply. "Oh, I don't know. Just a wild thought." He avoided the stares of Patrice and Ian. "I think I'll have another one of those muffins."

CHAPTER FIVE

1

Catherine awakened slowly, glanced around her tranquil ivory and sage green bedroom and finally to the sun beaming on the last red leaves clinging to the big maple tree close to her window. She yawned, stretched, and sighed in contentment. Then the memory of yesterday flashed, making her feel as if she were free-falling from a soaring jet.

She struggled to a sitting position and glanced at her bedside clock. Ten fifteen.

Always an early riser, Catherine knew she hadn't slept this late for over a year.

Catherine nearly leaped from her bed. In less than five minutes, she ran down the stairs. The smell of burned pastry hit her on the bottom step and she heard the oven fan furiously whirring. Marissa had been trying to cook again. Fleetingly Catherine hoped the burned food was so far gone she wouldn't have to eat some and pretend it wasn't too bad.

She walked into the kitchen to see Lindsay sitting near Marissa, dutifully watching her pulling a cookie sheet of steaming cinnamon rolls from the upper wall oven. Marissa smiled beatifically at the rolls and then at Catherine. "I burned the first batch to charcoal. I baked them in the lower oven and I think it's running too hot, because I'm sure I didn't leave them in too long. At least I don't think I did. Anyway, these look perfect!" Marissa's smile wavered, and her carefully cheerful tone changed to cautious. "How do you feel this morning?"

"Oh, much better! I feel great!" Catherine realized she could fool no one, least of all Marissa, with her high, chirpy voice. "I slept just fine," she said in a more natural tone, although she was lying. She hadn't fallen asleep until near morning.

"Eric called around midnight," Marissa said. "He wanted to reassure us that James is fine and he'd sent him home. I would have told you about Eric's call, but when I looked in your room you were sound asleep. I couldn't bear to wake you even for good news. You needed a full night's sleep."

Catherine nodded, although last night she had heard the bedroom door open and only pretended to be asleep. She just couldn't talk to anyone, not even her sister. "I left my cell phone down here last night. Has James called this morning?"

"Not yet. He's probably sleeping late like you did."

"I hope so. He needed sleep even more than I did. Did Eric know anything more about the explosion?"

"Not last night, but he called again an hour ago. He's meeting the fire marshal at the cottage this morning. They should be there now, in fact. He said he'd come by when they're finished and tell us what he's found out." Marissa gave her a long, patient look. "I know you're worried about

James. If we don't hear from him by eleven you can call him, but right now I want you to sit down, have some coffee and a couple of cinnamon rolls."

"I'm too worried to eat."

"I believe I heard a similar excuse last night. Now, I mean it, Catherine Faith Gray." Marissa sounded exactly like their mother when she chose to issue a rare command. "Quit pacing and sit down. You can at least drink some coffee even if you don't want a cinnamon roll."

Twenty minutes later, as Catherine swallowed the last bite of her fourth roll, she grinned. "This experience seems to have supercharged my appetite. I can't stop eating."

"Good. You're too thin."

"Well, thank you very much."

"You can't deny you've lost nearly ten pounds lately."

Catherine rose and carried her mug to the coffeemaker. "I probably have lost a few pounds, but I've been under a lot of stress the last few months. First, I moved back here, to my childhood home, and had to go through feeling fifteen again—it was a hard adjustment, no offense."

"None taken. I understand," Marissa replied, pinching off a bit of her cinnamon roll and dropping it down to Lindsay's expectantly open mouth.

"Then I had to find a psychologist with an established practice willing to take a novice. *Four* turned me down. Thank goodness for Dr. Hite."

Catherine knew she was rambling, that Marissa had heard all of this before, but she couldn't seem to stop talking. She came back to the table with her full mug of coffee. "I'm so glad Dr. Hite and his wife are in Florida until next week for the birth of their first great-grandchild. They know I'm seeing James and they'd swoop down on me, trying to get information about the body."

"You mean they'd start asking if the body is Renée's," Marissa said gently. "I know you've had a lot of big adjustments to make lately, but she is why you've lost weight. Ever since you and James really got serious, you've worried that Renée would come back."

Catherine looked gloomily at her sister. "And she has." Then a strong defensiveness surged through her. "But that's not James's fault."

"I didn't say it was." Marissa's gaze held Catherine's. "Eric told me James was at the cabin when the explosion happened. Why was he there?"

Marissa's tone was mild, but Catherine suddenly felt as if she sat in a courtroom witness chair and Marissa was a prosecutor. "He just couldn't believe what had happened earlier. It hadn't seemed real at the time. He felt a need to see the place again. I know it sounds weird—he says so, too—but that's all it was. What else could it have been? Do you think *he* blew up the cottage?"

"Whoa, Catherine," Marissa said, her eyes widening. "Chill out! I wasn't making accusations. I was just curious."

I was the one making accusations, Catherine thought. Most of the night, as she'd laid up there in her bed, she'd been furious and suspicious of James, the most steadfast, trustworthy man she'd ever known. What was wrong with her? How could she have for one moment doubted him?

"I'm sorry," she said, trying to make her voice sound as if she weren't feeling a load of guilt nearly burying her. "I was still on edge from yesterday when I heard about the explosion last night. . . ."

"That's understandable."

The doorbell rang. They both jumped and Lindsay went on a barking spree.

Marissa attempted to laugh. "No one around here is nervous! Be right back."

As soon as Marissa left the kitchen, Catherine's hands tightened around her coffee mug. Don't let this be more bad news, she thought in dread. I can't stand more bad news this morning.

In a moment, Marissa called, "James is here, Catherine!"

Catherine walked into the family room feeling tense and resolute, not knowing in what emotional shape she'd find the man she loved. After one look at him, though, she didn't think she'd ever been so glad to see James, as he stood tall and composed, his cheeks ruddy from the morning chill, his even teeth showing in a wide smile, his dark eyes twinkling beneath a shock of black hair the breeze had dragged across his forehead.

"James!" Catherine cried, every ounce of anger draining from her. She ran to him. "Why didn't you call earlier?"

"I thought I might wake you."

"You could have called Marissa's cell phone."

"And if you were sleeping she would have woken you up to speak to me."

"It wouldn't have mattered." She hugged him fiercely. "I've been so worried."

"That's why she's been sitting in the kitchen eating cinnamon rolls like she'll never be offered food again," Marissa said with teasing indulgence. "It's amazing."

"Nerves," Catherine told James quickly. "I eat everything in sight when I'm nervous."

James blinked at her. "Not that I've ever noticed."

You've never seen me in a situation like this one, Catherine almost said, then caught herself. She didn't want to say anything that might spark a thought of Renée, especially when a closer look at James's face revealed shadows beneath slightly bloodshot eyes and a tight, controlled look around his mouth. Catherine beamed at him. "You don't know how relieved I am to see you. I love you," she murmured as she pressed her lips gently against his. James kissed her tenderly but quickly, his gaze shooting over Catherine's shoulder to Marissa still standing in the room. He had a reluctance to show even small public displays of affection, which Catherine often found annoying.

She leaned back and tilted her head, gazing into James's dark eyes. "Are you hungry?"

Right on cue, James's stomach let out a long, loud growl, and he laughed. "I haven't eaten since noon yesterday."

Catherine raised her eyebrows. "You didn't even have a snack?" James shook his head. "That's awful! Your blood sugar must be dropping. You should have at least eaten some toast this morning."

"Yes, ma'am. I know I should have, but I didn't have any appetite." His stomach growled again. "Until now."

"Catherine left a couple of cinnamon rolls and I'll start another batch," Marissa said. "I think I've finally mastered baking something, if you can believe it."

James grinned. "I could eat about ten cinnamon rolls and I'm suffering from caffeine withdrawal. I need strong coffee—lots of it."

2

Eric arrived an hour later. Catherine immediately tensed, scared of what Eric would tell them about the fire. She took a breath and tried to ask steadily, "Have you been to the cottage this morning?"

Eric nodded. "The fire marshal and I just finished going over the place."

Within five minutes, Marissa had taken Eric's jacket and given him a large mug of coffee. He sat in an oversized recliner, his thick, tousled wavy blond hair at least an inch longer than advisors thought a sheriff should wear it, his dark brown eyes solemn. His face bore the shadow of stubble and he looked tired, the line between his eyebrows deeper than usual.

"I'm sure at night it looked like a bomb had gone off in your cottage, James," Eric said, rolling the smooth mug in his hands as if to warm them. "We're certain it wasn't a bomb, though. Actually, we found the remains of Molotov cocktails."

"Molotov cocktails?" James echoed in disbelief.

Eric nodded. "The fire did a lot of damage, but we were still able to retrieve enough material to be almost certain someone threw Molotovs at the cottage."

"Where would someone around here get Molotov cocktails?" Catherine asked in shock.

"People usually think of Molotovs in connection with riots, or terrorist attacks, but it only takes one person to make and launch one. That's why experts often call Molotov cocktails *makeshift* incendiary weapons, meaning they aren't manufactured in arms facilities. All it takes is one person to prepare them," Eric explained.

Catherine said, "I always imagined them as being a complicated mix of chemicals."

"Most people do, but Molotovs can be made of a few simple chemicals." He smiled at her. "With a few instructions, my grandmother could probably fix up one in her kitchen." Eric's smile faded. "But, Catherine, just because they can be simple doesn't mean they can't be deadly."

"Like the ones last night."

"Yes, I'm afraid so."

"What makes you think someone used Molotov cocktails on the cottage?" James asked.

"Evidence. We found a lot of what the

fire marshal thought was soda-lime glass and flat metal lids and screw-on rings used in home-canning jars like Mason jars or Ball jars. He said they're often used to hold Molotovs and a quart jar would be easy for even a woman to throw quite a distance."

"About how many of them were there?"

"We couldn't tell for certain, James, but we found four lids. More could have been lying in the debris. Also, the marshal used to train chemical-sniffing dogs in the Armed Forces. He has his own now. The dog led us to several pieces of wood that must have had traces of the chemicals used. The fire marshal took them in for analysis."

Catherine sat rock still, horrified. Then she leaned forward. "Have you ever come across anything like this before, Eric? I mean, do you think there's any possibility that someone just threw the Molotovs as a prank?"

"I've never seen anyone go to so much trouble for just a prank." Eric paused. "I think whoever made and threw those Molotovs did so out of pure hatred and rage."

3

"I know you're not crazy about spending the night when Marissa is here," Catherine said.

"Tonight I'd stay if fifty people were here. I should have stayed last night instead of going to the damned cottage."

They lay in Catherine's bed, their naked legs twined together, his strong arms holding her gently, pressing the side of her face against the warm skin of his chest. "You didn't tell me last night that Patrice had been at the cottage with you."

"Well, you and I didn't exactly have a long conversation. Besides, she just stopped by. She said she knew where I'd be."

"And I thought that's the last place you'd be. She must know you better than I do."

"You sound like you're implying something," James said lightly. When she didn't answer, he put his hand under her chin and raised her face, looking into her eyes. "You're not, are you?"

"Implying something about you and Patrice? Not anything romantic. Just what I said—she knows you better than I do."

"Maybe in certain ways. We've worked together for years and she could know some of my behavior patterns better than you do. Oh, and she's madly in love with me, too."

Catherine gave him a playful tap on his cheek. "With that huge ego of yours you think every woman in town is madly in love with you, but I know of two exceptions—Marissa and Patrice."

"Do you really think I have a huge ego?"

Catherine giggled. "If you did, I wouldn't be in love with you. Huge egos are a gigantic turnoff for me."

"Is *gigantic* bigger than *huge*?"

"Oh, definitely." Catherine snuggled closer to James. "I just love you so much, I'm bothered that another woman knows you better than I do."

"Patrice might know me better in a superficial way, but she doesn't know my heart." He kissed the top of Catherine's head. "You're the only woman who's known my heart, my soul."

Catherine felt as if her own heart squeezed tight as deep and passionate love for this man washed through her. She ran her open hand down the side of his face. "Oh, James, when I think of what could have happened to you last night if you'd been closer, in the cottage, if one of those Molotov cocktails had hit you—"

"But I wasn't in the cottage and nothing happened to me. You have to stop thinking *what if, what if.*"

"How can I when you came so close to being hurt or . . ."

"Or killed?" James pulled her closer. "Maybe you're right. Maybe I need to be more careful. Going to the cottage where Renée was murdered a week ago was downright stupid. I don't know what I was thinking. I *wasn't* thinking—not reasonably. But I promise you, I won't be so careless again." He paused. "And the same goes for you, Catherine. You heard Eric say he didn't think someone was throwing those cocktails as a prank. Maybe it wasn't a coincidence that I was at the cottage when they were thrown. Maybe someone has it in for me, too. And my obvious love for you—our relationship— might make you a target, too."

"But I hardly knew Renée," Catherine said vaguely, her mind focusing on his phrase "my obvious love for you."

"We don't know what's going on here, sweetheart," James said. "We don't know why Renée was murdered or why someone *might* have been trying to hurt me last night." He looked piercingly into her eyes, his jaw hardened, and his voice deepened. "You don't know what you mean to me, Catherine. I can't stand the thought of someone taking you away from me. If I lost you . . ."

"If you lost me?"

"I can't even think about it. Just promise me you'll be careful."

"I'll be careful," Catherine said gently. "I promise."

After a moment, James's face relaxed and he smiled and he pulled her on top of him, wrapped his arms around her so tightly she could hardly breathe, and pressed his lips to hers with tender, then growing, demanding passion.

Two hours later, James slept peacefully. Although Catherine had dozed after their lovemaking, she'd awakened a while ago and couldn't go back to sleep. Instead, she lay on her side, looking at the moonlight touching James's exposed chest and abdomen like a caress. He looked like the men in designer underwear ads, she thought, muscular and perfect. He could give David Beckham a run for his money, she thought. Telling him so would probably only embarrass him.

Earlier, he'd said "my obvious love for you." He'd said, "I can't stand the thought of someone taking you away from me." Playing over the words in her mind thrilled her almost as much as hearing him say them to her.

Catherine reached out and lightly ran her fingers over his chest. God, how she loved him. How she wanted to make up to him for all the hurt Renée had caused. If only she hadn't caused so much hurt he never wanted to try marriage again. Catherine knew many people found him cold and formal. Maybe she was the only person who knew just how sensitive he really was beneath the imperturbable façade. Maybe she was the only person who knew how deeply he could be hurt and how difficult it was for him to recover from hurt and disappointment. James was not a resilient man. He didn't easily forgive or forget. In fact—

Suddenly James's hand grabbed hers, nearly crushing it in an iron-like grip. "Damn you, Renée," his voice low and growl-like, unrecognizable. *"Damn you—"*

"James!" Catherine yelped, thinking any moment a bone in her hand might crack. "James, stop it! *James!*"

He moaned, shuddered, and opened his eyes. Immediately he released her hand. "What happened? I think I was dreaming." Then he saw Catherine rubbing her hand, her face white. "My God, Catherine, did I hurt you?"

"I . . . I don't think so," she said.

He took her hand in his left, gently touched it all over with his right. "I don't think anything is broken, but do you want to go to the hospital for X-rays?"

"No. It's all right."

"We'll wait a few minutes and see." He brought her hand to his mouth and kissed it several times. "I'm so sorry. I was having a nightmare."

"I know."

"I wouldn't hurt you—"

"I *know,*" she said sharply, then lowered her voice. "I'm all right, James."

But it wasn't all right. He'd been cursing Renée with such fury in his voice, he'd sounded as if he could kill her.

CHAPTER SIX

1

The next morning at eight thirty, Catherine pulled into the parking lot of the discreetly named Aurora Falls Center. The two-story brick building sat somewhat isolated on a quiet, tree-lined street and looked more like a home than an office building with its white shutters and long, roofed front porch and neat lawn. The area had been strictly rural when the building was constructed, but as Aurora Falls grew in population Catherine knew that soon the "city sprawl" would reach the area, costing the center its sense of privacy. She regretted the changes that would come but knew one had to accept the inevitable.

The beautiful weekend had been a blessing whose time had ended, Catherine thought as she hurried toward the building beneath a low, gray sky dribbling cold rain. A quick look at the weather report this morning had told her the rain would increase as the temperature dropped throughout the day. She groaned. She hated dreary days under ideal circumstances. The last few days had certainly been less than ideal.

Catherine rushed up the two porch steps, put a key in the door lock, another in the dead bolt, and swung the door open to see the thick, moss green carpet brightened by golden oak-paneled walls and matching office furniture. Behind the reception desk sat the efficient secretary Beth Harper. Catherine knew that Beth had, as always, arrived promptly at eight fifteen, although she kept the doors locked so patients wouldn't walk in until either Dr. Hite or Catherine had come. As usual, Beth had started a fresh pot of coffee. "Good morning, Dr. Gray," she said cheerfully.

Catherine poured a fresh cup of coffee

for Beth, one for herself, and then checked the appointment book. Three patients this morning, she thought with a slight sense of dismay. Only three. She had hoped for a more auspicious beginning, but she often reminded herself she'd only joined Dr. Hite's practice in the summer. Good word of mouth over time would establish her reputation and build her list of patients.

When Dr. Hite hired Catherine, he'd told her the first month might be uncomfortable because his wife insisted the office needed redecoration. The project added sour lines to his pudgy face, but he admitted she was probably right—the last redecoration had been thirty years ago. To Catherine's surprise, he had given her free reign when it came to her office, and the room reflected her personality, making her feel more comfortable and at home. Her closed office door bore a bronze nameplate reading: *Dr. Catherine Gray* in black.

She entered the room with its expanse of restful tan carpet and contemporary armchair and couch upholstered in matching vanilla and light brown tweed. A maple coffee table sat in front of the couch and an end table by the chair. Her large maple desk faced the sitting area and sat out from the wall bearing two long windows set six feet apart. Between the windows hung a large print of Renoir's *Boating on the Seine* with its vivid blue sun-dappled water and two passengers sitting in an orange-gold canoe.

A fifteen-inch-tall gilded porcelain temple jar adorned with delicately painted green vines and pink, blue, and white flowers sat toward the right side of the credenza behind her desk. Ian Blakethorne had dropped by week before last and presented her with the jar for her newly decorated office. She'd protested that the gift was far too extravagant, but he had insisted she accept it and she couldn't say no without insulting him. Besides, she loved the jar. She also loved Ian, who in his young life had gone through so much with such grace.

The two had formed a bond years ago when he'd spent weeks in the rehabilitation center of the hospital after he'd been in the car wreck that killed his mother and nearly took his life, too. That summer Catherine had been sixteen and a volunteer in the rehab unit at the hospital where her father was a surgeon. She'd taken a special interest in the ten-year-old boy who'd bravely suffered through the pain of recovery. Catherine had spent hours reading to him, watching television with him, and teaching him chess. They'd maintained a friendship ever since, in spite of the age difference and all the time Catherine had spent in California.

Now Catherine glanced at her tidy desk, adorned with only a desk pad, a gold pen set, and the tall milk-glass vase that held the dozen long-stemmed coral pink roses James sent every Monday. Then she retrieved the files of her morning patients.

At precisely 9:01, Catherine's first patient seemed to blow through the front door, slamming it behind her and demanding, "Is Dr. Gray here yet? I really need to see her *fast.*"

"Of course Dr. Gray is here, Mrs. Tate," Beth answered in a pleasant voice. "She's always early."

Catherine walked to her open office door and looked at the woman standing in the middle of the waiting room, her wrinkled beige raincoat buttoned unevenly as she flung raindrops off her large, partially open umbrella. Beth said, "I'll take that for you," as droplets of water hit her desk. The patient clung to it, and for a moment Catherine thought Mrs. Tate and Beth might battle over the contraption. The woman finally released it when Catherine diverted her by smiling as she said, "How nice to see you this morning, Mrs. Tate, but you look chilly. Would you like a cup of fresh coffee?"

"Do I look like I need caffeine?" the woman demanded as she finally released her death grip on the umbrella handle.

"I guess that's a no to the coffee," Catherine managed with a smile. "Please come in my office. I'm all ready for you."

Mrs. Tate swept into the office and thumped down on the couch, placing her ever-present huge, black vinyl tote bag beside her. Catherine had never seen such a large tote bag. Nevertheless, the woman kept it full to the point of bulging.

At thirty-four, Mrs. Tate had been married for six years, had no children, and was convinced her husband was having his third affair. Her overbleached hair frizzed to her shoulders, her iridescent purple eye shadow and slash of shocking pink lipstick glared under the overhead lights, and she glowered at Catherine. "I know I look like hell. You don't have to tell me. Those damned bright office lights of yours show every wrinkle in my face. They're also hurting my eyes."

"Then I'll fix the lighting for your comfort, not because you have wrinkles," Catherine said diplomatically as she flipped off the two bright ceiling fixtures and left on the large, soft-shaded lamp sitting by the chair. She sat, opened her notebook, and looked seriously at her patient. "You don't seem to be feeling well this morning. What's wrong?"

"I've been up half the night, that's what's wrong! My husband didn't come home!"

"All night?"

"Not until around midnight. *Midnight* when he *said* he had to be at work at eight today instead of nine!"

"Did he say where he'd been until midnight?"

"Helping his best friend fix a water heater. He said the guy couldn't get a repairman on a Sunday night and had to have hot water for family showers in the morning. I called the friend. He backed up my husband's story, but then he *would.* I asked to speak to his wife for confirmation of his story, but he said she was asleep. I think she just wouldn't come to the phone and lie. Then my husband left at seven thirty this morning—the early day at work, he claimed. I think he was meeting *her* for coffee."

"*Her* being his secretary."

"Of course. Who else?"

"I see. Are you certain he didn't go to work? Did you follow him?"

Mrs. Tate's bloodshot eyes slid away. "I tried, but he must have seen me, because he went to his office. She was probably lurking in a back room, waiting for him."

"Did you see her car?"

"Well, no, but she could have parked anywhere. I don't see so well in this damned rain."

"You would if you'd wear your glasses."

"I hate my glasses! I look awful in them! And I've told you I can't wear contact lenses! Didn't you write down all that stuff?"

Catherine suppressed an impulse to sigh. Sometimes talking to this woman was like having a conversation with a thirteen-year-old.

"Mrs. Tate, do you have any real proof that your husband is having an affair?"

"Proof is everywhere. You just have to be observant, like me. It's wearing me out, but I'm on the ball all the time! Nothing gets by me!" She sagged slightly as if in defeat. "But I think I do need a cup of coffee after all. I'm running out of steam."

No wonder, Catherine thought as she poured the coffee in a china cup. Then she motioned to a plate of candy sitting on the coffee table. "How about a snack? They're an Italian candy called Perugina Baci—*baci* means 'kisses' in Italian. They're chocolate with hazelnut filling—"

"Italian!" Mrs. Tate leaned forward, glaring at the silver-wrapped candies decorated with dark blue stars. "I don't eat foreign food. Nothing but American fare for me."

"Oh." As the woman took a couple of sips of coffee, Catherine wondered if Mrs. Tate thought the coffee beans had been grown in the United States, not Colombia. Apparently, she hadn't given the matter any thought, because she had no qualms about emptying the cup and asking for a second one.

After a few minutes, Catherine said

carefully, "Mrs. Tate, you're obviously suffering a great deal of anxiety. I'm a psychologist, not a medical practitioner, so I can't
prescribe medication. I think you'd benefit
from some mild tranquilizers to help relax
you, though. I can refer you to a family phy-
sician or even a psychiatrist who could give
you a prescription for some."

Mrs. Tate looked at her in near horror.
"That's what my husband told me to do!
Get tranquilizers. *Strong* ones, he said.
He just wants to keep me so groggy I don't
know what's going on. Well, it won't work.
I'm not taking anything except an occasional drink or two before bed. I'm not turning into some zombie. And I'll *never* divorce
him. I plan to make his life as miserable as
he's made mine!"

"I see."

"I also don't want to take medicine. He
could substitute pills and dope me, *poison*
me, make it look like suicide!"

Paranoia? At least the appearance of
paranoia. Catherine was certain Mrs. Tate
was not above acting dramatic to get sympathy. Still, better to be safe than sorry.
Better to calm the woman, she thought, to
ease the fear that might drive her away

from any professional help. "I certainly won't force you to take medication if you'd rather not," Catherine said calmly. "That is *your* choice."

"I knew after our first session you were exactly what I needed!" the woman announced triumphantly. "You don't treat me like I'm crazy. You don't bully me. You treat me with respect." She took a deep breath. "Don't you ever worry, Dr. Gray—I'll *never* stop being your patient! I'm faithful and loyal and stuck to you like a tick on a dog!" Mrs. Tate looked at her with near threat in her tired eyes. "I'll be back next week and the next and the next and maybe just forever!"

Five minutes later, Mrs. Tate marched through the waiting room, unfurling her umbrella and flinging more water drops before she'd even opened the door. After a brief struggle, woman, huge tote bag, and umbrella made it safely to the porch. Catherine had followed her, closed the front door, and tossed Beth a rueful smile. "I suppose you heard some of that."

"I always do. I don't know how you manage to keep your patience with her."

"I keep my patience because she's one of my *few* patients."

"Well, Dr. Hite always says it takes time to build a practice. Don't give up yet."

Catherine's next patient was suffering family problems because she couldn't bring herself to put her live-in, late Alzheimer's stage grandmother who'd raised her into a nursing home. Catherine needed to talk the woman out of her guilt before the elderly woman's constant needs and often dangerous behavior caused her granddaughter's husband to leave, taking their three teenage children because he worried for their safety, but Catherine could tell that today she'd made no progress with the woman.

The third patient, a sixteen-year-old girl, suffered from bulimia and refused to say anything except a vague, "I'm not sick." Her gaze never met Catherine's. Instead, it strayed almost hungrily around the room, making Catherine glad she'd remembered to remove the dish of candies.

By noon, she felt as if she'd accomplished little for half a day's work. Still, she was relieved her cases hadn't been more challenging. Distraction about the events of the weekend and James's nightmare about Renée—the hatred in his voice when he'd said the name of a woman recently murdered—had severely weakened Catherine's focus. She touched her hand, slightly bruised and sore from James's grasp last night. What exactly had he been dreaming about Renée? When Catherine had asked, he'd said he didn't remember. She wasn't sure she believed him.

In a weak effort to fight the dreariness of the day, Catherine had chosen to wear her cheerful, new red trench coat. She'd brought a sandwich and pudding cup to eat for lunch, but suddenly she knew she had to get out of the office for a little while. She pulled the bright coat from the closet, grabbed her purse and red umbrella, and hurried into the waiting room. "I'm going out to lunch," she told Beth. "I think I'll try that new café on Foster Street."

"I've never seen you wear so much color! You look great! Good idea about the café, too. I've heard the food is good and I'm sure you could use a break."

"So could you. It's so gloomy and quiet

today. We have a window of freedom while Dr. Hite's not here. Why don't you join me?"

Beth smiled, reaching for the sack lunch she always brought to the office. "A secretary's work is never done. I need to be here to make appointments, which reminds me, your one o'clock canceled half an hour ago. He said he broke a tooth and has an emergency appointment at the dentist in a couple of hours. He sounded like he was in pain."

"Poor thing. I'm glad he could get in to see a dentist so soon." Catherine reached in her pocket, pulled out a red flowered chiffon scarf, and tied it around her head. "I don't want my hair to get wet in the rain. I hate having damp hair." She almost flushed at her lie. Damp hair hadn't bothered her until the last two days, when she couldn't stop thinking of Renée's wet hair wrapped tenaciously around her fingers. "Marissa talked me into all of this red, but I have to admit the coat, umbrella, and scarf make me look downright festive."

Catherine, usually bad with directions, used her GPS system and drove directly to the Café Divine. The place had a cozy, old-fashioned atmosphere with hardwood floors, exposed brick walls painted creamy beige, dark green booths, pots of lush, healthy plants hanging above the mirror-backed bar, and a large vintage jukebox sitting at the back playing songs from the fifties and sixties. The place was nearly empty. She quickly chose a booth halfway down the length of the narrow room, and a smiling waitress immediately appeared with a tray holding a tall glass of ice water and a menu.

As soon as Catherine looked at the menu, her nervous appetite kicked into gear again. She ordered a garden salad, a "Double-Thick Hamburger," a piece of coconut cream pie, and an iced tea. She wanted French fries, too, but decided the hamburger would provide enough fat for one meal.

Catherine had finished her salad and begun eating her hamburger when over a dozen people arrived within ten minutes. They occupied nearly every stool at the bar, and she heard the voices of two women scooting into the booth behind her. Catherine lingered over her meal, enjoying the hum of conversation rising over the music pouring from the jukebox. For the first time that day, she was able to put the events of the weekend out of her mind and pretend this was just an ordinary day as she concentrated on the simple pleasure of good food.

She was finishing the hamburger when the song "Runaround Sue" ended. Apparently, no one had selected more music, because the jukebox went silent and Catherine clearly heard the women behind her talking.

"Did you hear about the dead body found at the Eastman cottage on Saturday afternoon?"

"Sure I heard!" answered the other in a loud, authoritative voice. "Someone told my husband it was a woman. The police claim they can't give out the name of the victim until there has been next-of-kin identification, but everyone knows it's James Eastman's wife, Renée."

Catherine went rigid. Was the woman exaggerating, or had identification of Renée as the deceased woman been leaked to the public? How many people in Aurora Falls knew Renée was dead?

"Who's James Eastman?" the woman's companion asked.

"The lawyer whose family owns the cottage. You *must* remember the flap a few years ago when his wife Renée disappeared."

"Well, not really—"

"Renée came from New Orleans and she didn't like it here," the loud-voiced one began excitedly. "I'm not surprised. She wasn't the type to be an Eastman— they're very classy, but she was awful, brash, flashy, drank *way* too much, never saw a man she didn't like. She and James were married about a year before they started arguing in public.

"Then they had a really bad fight at a party, and the next day Renée vanished." The woman halted dramatically before saying slowly, "The police suspected foul play. They investigated, but they *never* found Renée."

Catherine took a bite of her coconut cream pie and had trouble swallowing. At that moment, the waitress stopped by and Catherine ordered a cup of coffee, trying to smile casually. "Iced tea doesn't really go with pie," she explained unnecessarily. "I want coffee."

"Certainly, ma'am," the waitress said. "I like coffee with dessert, too. Is the pie good?"

"Delicious. Just . . . yummy."

The waitress hurried away and Catherine hoped no one put on more music for a few minutes. She knew she should leave, but leaving felt almost physically impossible. She had to know what else people were saying about James and Renée.

"You know, some of it is coming back to me now," the softer-voiced woman said.

"Well, I should think it would unless you've had your head in the sand!"

"I seem to remember something about a fight at a housewarming party?"

"That's the party I was talking about—the one where they had the real blowout!" The loud one's voice rose a notch. "Renée was immoral as all get-out, but at first she had the sense to try being secretive. Then she got more open with her shenanigans and then just brazen. At that housewarming party, she'd gone into a bedroom to get her coat. Someone went in and caught her lying on top of a pile of coats kissing the host! I heard that James was so furious he nearly dragged her out of the house. Well, he didn't *drag* her—he's sort of a gentleman— but everyone knew she was going to catch hell on the way home. Still, she left the house laughing. Laughing, for God's sake!"

The waitress stopped at their booth and they both ordered coffee refills before the loud one picked up the subject of Renée again. "It was right after that party when she vanished. *Immediately,* like the next day."

Catherine's coffee arrived and she took a large, scalding gulp. The coffee burned her tongue, but she took another bracing sip nevertheless.

Meanwhile, the woman who seemed to know all about Renée took a deep breath and asked loudly, "Have you been to Nicolai Arcos's exhibit at the Nordine Gallery?"

"Who's Nicolai Arcos?"

"Don't you keep up with any local news? He's a local artist. At least he's the only one who's getting any real attention from the art experts. Anyway, I heard that Renée had an affair with him before she left. Now he has a big exhibit at the gallery. Didn't you read about it in the *Gazette*?"

"I only read hard news, not society stuff."

"Oh, you do not! Don't try putting on airs with me. Anyway, the showpiece of the exhibit is a portrait called *Mardi Gras Lady.* Ken Nordine, who owns the gallery, didn't invite my husband and me to the opening exhibit, so my husband got mad and wouldn't go see it later. The mayor's wife—we're very good friends— told me that although the woman in *Mardi Gras Lady* is wearing a mask and Nicolai Arcos won't admit that woman in the painting is even anyone he knows, she's certain it's a portrait of Renée Eastman. She says no one who'd ever seen Renée would be fooled and Arcos *meant* for everyone to know it was her. He was *crazy* about her."

"Really?"

"Really."

"So this Arcos person actually painted her when he was having an affair with her? Or was it after she disappeared?"

"I don't know when he painted it. He just did."

"Is he married?"

"No. Never has been."

"But Renée was and he didn't care even

though everyone knew about the affair. My goodness, what nerve!"

"I'll say he has nerve! But he's an artist, and we all know how eccentric and arrogant they are," the loud woman pronounced with confidence. "I don't know him except by sight. He's tall and thin—all angles and penetrating eyes—and has black wavy hair. He wears crazy jewelry—always the same, a hoop earring with what I swear is a real diamond, a huge tiger's-eye ring—and these long leather coats. He must be in his early thirties or so. You'd never forget him if you've seen him. I've heard that the exhibit might put him on the map in the art world, but the painting *Mardi Gras Lady* is the one that has everyone talking." She hesitated and then added excitedly, "We should go see it! Maybe tomorrow—I'm too busy today, but I really want to go! My husband would be furious, but I won't tell him if you won't tell yours."

"It's a deal," the other woman answered. "Now I can't miss seeing that painting for the world!"

And neither can I, Catherine thought guiltily as she drained her coffee cup. Neither can I.

2

Catherine glanced at her watch. Quarter of one. Her next patient would not arrive until two o'clock. She quickly ate her last bite of pie, finished her coffee, left a generous tip, and walked to the register before the waitress had returned with Catherine's check. While she waited to pay her bill, someone put more money in the jukebox. She left the café to the sound of Petula Clark singing "Downtown."

It was almost like Petula knew where she was going, Catherine thought as she left the Café Divine, walked hurriedly in the rain to her car, and drove four blocks to the Nordine Gallery, located in what had once been the center of the city. She remembered almost five years ago when a new Aurora Falls citizen—thirty-year-old Ken Nordine— bought the remains of a long-vacant three-story building in the now-neglected part of the town, razed it, and built a beautiful four-story art gallery.

The *Gazette* had assigned Marissa the story and she hadn't been able to resist researching the new owner in greater depth than needed for the newspaper article. Marissa had learned that Ken Nordine's father—a talented artist of temporary fame named Guy (pronounced "Gē") Nordine who'd been born and lived in Aurora Falls—moved to the Midwest in his late thirties. Shortly afterward, Guy's wife deserted him and their young son, Ken. Guy had fallen into depression and drinking and never fully recovered. His career dwindled and then completely failed. He'd died young, barely earning a living as a housepainter. His son, Ken, however, had vowed that the people of Aurora Falls—as well as the world—would never forget his beloved father's early, excellent artistic works.

Marissa had known Guy's estate could not have paid for the gallery and she'd discovered Ken's numerous business ventures had not been successful. She learned he'd married Dana Hanson, whose father owned a successful chain of home-improvement outlets in Utah, Nebraska, and Iowa. Dana had grown up privileged and even in adulthood seemed to be denied nothing by her doting, wealthy father.

In true reporter fashion, Marissa had immediately dispatched her research about the enigmatic Mr. Nordine to Catherine, whom Marissa considered cut off from the exciting activities of home while she attended graduate school in Berkeley, California. Catherine had devoured the information with the gusto of a champion Aurora Falls gossip and had been looking forward to visiting the gallery when she returned home. Before she'd had a chance, though, she'd heard from several people that Ken Nordine also had been one of Renée's lovers. Catherine's curiosity about the gallery hadn't died, but she'd been determined not to set foot in the place. Until today.

As usual, Catherine felt awe as she drove past the pale stucco gallery whose contemporary circular lines seemed to spiral skyward like a dove rising gracefully amid a stand of dingy dark-brick towers. Luckily, she found a parking space nearby and rushed to the door of the gallery just as a man unlocked the front door and swung it open, smiling.

"What luck for me! My first visitor of the day is a beautiful lady! Hello. I'm Ken Nordine."

Catherine fell silent, for the first time

coming face-to-face with the gallery's strikingly handsome owner. His well-cut, honey brown hair waved back from a classic face that showed intelligence and humor, punctuated by electric blue eyes that were both serious and rakish. For a moment, she stood mute before she found her voice. "Hi. Catherine Gray. I'm afraid I've never visited the gallery before today."

"What a shame, but we've gotten you here at last. Please come in." He flashed a self-deprecating grin. "You've beaten the afternoon crowd."

"I'm glad." Catherine started to shake rain from her umbrella, but he gently took it from her and vibrated away the rain before closing it.

"Sorry about the water," Catherine said.

"Don't worry. The floor is granite," he said, looking at the tan ceramic flooring punctuated here and there with dark brown and blue mosaic-patterned tiles. "Second-hardest stone to a diamond. We don't care about some water on the floor. It's also micro-etched, so don't be afraid of slipping."

"Ken, you're bragging again."

Catherine looked up to see a woman descending the wide, four-floor curving staircase leading to the pointed skylight on the roof. From above, the woman looked slender, glamorous, and about thirty years old. As she reached the first floor and approached her, though, Catherine could see she was bone thin and she bore the tightly stretched face of a woman who'd had too much plastic surgery. She had glossy, shoulder-length mahogany brown hair with blunt-cut, eyebrow-length bangs and not a strand of gray. Her careworn dark eyes and the slight lines circling her thin lips, though, put her age at early forties.

"Hello, I'm Dana Nordine." She smiled to show perfect teeth, obviously veneers, and extended a thin right hand with prominent veins. "Welcome to the gallery. Escaping the weather?"

"Not at all," Catherine said easily. "I have a long lunch break today and thought I'd take advantage of my extra time. I was near, and I've never been here before, although I've certainly been curious."

Ken gave her a natural and pleased

smile, then a slowly dawning look of not-so-genuine puzzlement. "You're *Catherine* Gray? Marissa's sister?"

Catherine nodded.

"Marissa did a wonderfully thorough and *long* article about the place!" Dana exclaimed. "We were so elated I think we bought about fifty copies of that issue of the newspaper."

Ken gave Catherine an admiring smile. "I saw your picture in the paper when you opened your counseling practice, but the photo didn't do you justice." He paused. She stared. "I thought you'd visit the gallery before now since you're Marissa's sister and she seemed impressed with the place."

"She was—is—but when you opened I was still in California finishing my psychology degree. When my mother died, she left the family home to Marissa and me, and I've moved back in with her for now, but I still haven't managed to get completely settled." Catherine knew she was talking too much, but she felt awkward and slightly guilty for being here. She could have kicked herself for going on. "I've also been establishing my practice with Dr. Jacob Hite. But then you know that if you saw the article in the newspaper."

Dana tried to frown, but Catherine could see the woman had obviously paralyzed the muscles around her forehead and eyes with Botox. She asked without facial expression, "So you're seeing patients now, Dr. Gray?"

"Yes. Since August."

"How enterprising to begin so soon. Don't you agree, Ken?"

Dana's husband merely gazed at Catherine. Dana gave him a long, wearily knowing look before he finally swung into action. "Well, Dr. Gray, we're just standing here like we've never had a visitor, leaving you in your wet coat and scarf. Shed some of those wet clothes and I'll offer you something to drink before we show you around."

Catherine was not as outgoing as Marissa, but she'd never been shy or socially awkward. She felt reticent and guarded in spite of the Nordines' welcoming warmth, though. Her unusual stiffness made her self-conscious, and she wondered if they were being extra-friendly because she was so clearly ill at ease.

Then she looked up and met the shrewd

gaze of Ken Nordine, who was staring at her with the knowledge of someone who was not a stranger. Although James rarely talked to her about his ex-wife, Renée, after Catherine started seeing him a few people couldn't resist the oh-so-well-meaning impulse to tell her that art lover Renée Moreau Eastman had had an affair with the handsome, charming, married Ken Nordine. James had chosen to ignore the rumors, in public at least, but then that was the way of James Eastman. It didn't mean he didn't believe the affair existed.

With a sudden tingle like a small electric shock, Catherine thought Ken Nordine had recognized her the minute she arrived and he knew she was involved with James, which was why she and James had never visited the gallery. Worst of all, she had the distinct sense Ken was being overly charming because he was maliciously amused by her obvious discomfort and excuses for not visiting the gallery sooner.

Catherine realized she might have been overanalyzing, but she felt oddly certain she was correct. She tried to give Ken an "I don't give a damn what you think of me" smile, but she knew it wasn't successful when his expression didn't change. She hadn't a clue as to what Dana thought of her or her visit. The woman with her frozen-muscled face was a cipher. Catherine wished she could immediately leave, but she couldn't think of a graceful exit. With an inward sigh, she decided her only option was to get through her ill-advised tour of the gallery with as much composure as possible.

"Your sister seems to be our muse," Ken told Catherine as they circled the first floor of the gallery. "She did another excellent newspaper piece on our latest exhibit—the work of Nicolai Arcos. I'm sure you've heard of him."

"Yes, I have. He's supposed to be very talented."

"He's remarkable," Ken said. "He was already well-known by his mid-twenties. I don't remember seeing you at his opening exhibit, though."

"No, I couldn't make it that night. I was coming down with the flu," Catherine lied again, and this time didn't care if she sounded as if she was lying. After all, she had no doubt Ken Nordine knew Arcos's relationship with Renée was the real reason Catherine hadn't attended the Arcos exhibit opening.

"What a shame! It turned into an even bigger night than we expected, didn't it, Dana?" Dana had not left Catherine and Ken alone for a moment, keeping close behind them, as if they would forget she existed. Ken rarely acknowledged her, but Catherine made a point of glancing back at Dana's narrow, searching eyes. Catherine recognized and sympathized with insecurity when she saw it. "We think the success of the showing was partly because of Marissa's newspaper article." Ken added.

"She likes writing hard news, but I think she's best at feature writing," Catherine said. "They always seem pleased with her features at the *Gazette*."

"No wonder! She's an excellent writer." Ken gave Catherine another dazzling smile. "Let's begin by showing you some of Nicolai's work."

He started swiftly across the gallery toward a painting. Dana raced to keep up, no small feat in her skintight black designer jeans and turquoise platform pumps with what Catherine guessed were four-inch heels. Dana had tightly cinched her turquoise silk blouse with a wide silver belt. She looked as stylish and whip slim as a model. She also looked winded.

Catherine slowed slightly and Dana dropped back with her. Ken didn't appear to notice either of them. He stopped about four feet from the painting and stared at it. 'This is *Eternal Wait.* It's one of Nicolai's earlier paintings. What do you think?"

Catherine gazed at the oil portrait of a boy sitting on a boulder under a sky the color of smoke, gazing at a restless dark gray sea with a film of hovering fog. The child appeared around ten years old, his pale face shown in bleak profile, his near-shoulder-length black hair blowing back from high cheekbones and large dark eyes.

Although far from being an art expert, Catherine had seen portraits of this style before—sad, misty studies painted mainly in shades of gray and usually featuring a lonely-looking child. She recognized that in *Eternal Wait* Nicolai Arcos had captured a true melancholy with the child's rounded shoulders and hopeless eyes gazing at the slightly silvery mist above the intemperate sea.

"The boy is Arcos, isn't it?" she asked.

"Yes, it is," Ken said. "He was born in Romania in a small village on the coast of the Black Sea. He never knew his father and his mother ran away before his first birthday. He lived with his grandparents. Thank God they considered him a gift from God and he adored them." Ken sighed. "It could so easily have worked out just the opposite, since the daughter gave birth only four months after her marriage and her parents were very religious.

"Nicolai's grandfather worked on a fishing ship that traveled the Black Sea," Ken continued. "When Nicolai was twelve, the ship never returned. People in the town thought well of his grandparents and of Nicolai. He'd sketched before then, but I believe that's when sympathetic townspeople managed to give him some canvas, brushes, paints, and he began his work in earnest. His grandmother died when he was fifteen, and that's when he made his way illegally to the United States."

Catherine nodded, thinking the narrative sounded as if Ken had told it word for word many times. She didn't blame him for perfecting the story of Nicolai's background that made the painting even more poignant.

"The style seems mature," Catherine said. "You said it was one of Arcos's early works. How old was he when he painted it?"

"Oh, about eighteen," Dana piped up. "After he came to the United States and began formally studying painting."

"Where did he study?" Catherine asked.

"The University of Arizona," Ken answered quickly, "but he attended only for a couple of years and received an associate's degree. He didn't like Albuquerque. He taught for a while at the local community college just to earn a living. Then someone brought him to *my* attention."

Ken couldn't seem to suppress a slightly smug smile. He turned and quickly pointed to another painting. "This is one of my favorites, *Cathedral.* I particularly like the play of light on the towering boulders. Nicolai painted it a couple of years after *Eternal Wait* and I think you can see the growth of his style."

Catherine cordially agreed that she could see Arcos's growth of style, although she really couldn't see much difference. Ken showed her four more paintings resembling *Cathedral.* She "oohed" and "aahed" appropriately, although she felt certain Dana sensed her lack of sincerity. Catherine knew enough about art to recognize Arcos's impressive talent, but at this time works like *Cathedral* didn't affect her. She hadn't come to the gallery to see a Nicolai Arcos collection—she had come to see only one painting. As a result, her restlessness and distraction grew with every minute until the fingers of her left hand began twitching, a lifelong sign of nervousness.

Finally, they took several steps to the right and Catherine felt Dana tense and draw a sharp breath before Ken announced grandly, "And here is *Mardi Gras Lady*, the painting everyone is talking about! I never dreamed it would cause such a sensation, did you, Dana?"

The painting hung with at least ten feet of empty, light bisque wall space on each side, making it a showpiece, and it was twice as large as any others on display. The portrait bloomed with so much vivid color, depth, seemingly inherent life, vivacity, and motion that for Catherine the other works of Nicolai Arcos seemed to disappear, banished to obscurity by the image of a woman.

Catherine thought she'd prepared herself for what she might see by smiling casually at Ken before looking at the painting. To her shock, the image seemed to fill her vision, to overwhelm her, and she couldn't stifle a gasp.

Mardi Gras Lady gleamed in rich though refined shades of gold. Although the lady was poised at a slight left angle, the viewer could still see at least a foot of her wide, horizontally hooped skirt cinched dramatically at the waist. A corset flattened her bodice, pushing her breasts into creamy, full orbs above the low, square neck of silk damask elaborately embroidered with deeper gold metallic thread and topped by a thin row of ivory lace. A wide, ivy-patterned gold choker embedded with pearls and diamonds circled her neck, and long teardrop pearls hung from gold bezel-set diamonds on her earlobes.

Tight sleeves stretched to her elbows, where below a wide band two layers of ruffles cascaded to her mid-forearms, the second ruffle swooping lower at the back than the first, elongating the arm. The Mardi Gras Lady obviously wore a wig—glossy, black hair upswept nearly six inches in front with long shining coils draped over her shoulder and running nearly to her waist, a slender string of milky pearls gracefully winding their way through the elaborate hairstyle. Her raised left hand held a delicate, unfurled ivory silk fan constructed with what looked like mother-of-pearl gilded sticks. Sequins highlighted the carefully arranged figures of women and men, fully naked and caught in the act of sex in a lush garden setting. Obviously, the vintage fan had been made for the private view of a connoisseur of erotica, not to be flaunted in a formal painting.

Catherine felt every detail of *Mardi Gras Lady* etching itself on her brain, including its delicate brushstrokes, the textured quality of the oil paint giving the painting a sense of depth, the seemingly flickering light in the background, and the overall haunting quality of the piece.

Most of all, she was entranced by the life Arcos had infused in his subject, especially her graceful, ethereal quality. Catherine had not seen Renée up close since the wedding, but she would never forget that perfect, oval face, the porcelain skin, the delicately curved nose, and the perfectly shaped lips. Especially, she would always remember Renée's eyes—those dark eyes with tiny burnished gold rings around the pupils and set at a slight, beguiling tilt—haunting eyes with a trace of vulnerability and hurt beneath their blatantly magnetic, enticing siren song of sexual invitation and risqué self-confidence. At the wedding, Renée had sent the full power of those eyes into Catherine's gentle heather green gaze.

Now, Renée once again directed the full power of them into Catherine, only this time the unmistakable eyes looked out from behind an elegant white and gold half mask with a thin, delicate band of lace around the edges, the mask bathed with a light sprinkle of gold glitter. The most striking aspect of the beautiful mask, though, was the black five-pointed star painted around the right eye.

The eye through which someone had shot a bullet, sending Renée to her death.

CHAPTER SEVEN

1

James Eastman unlocked the door to his small town house, walked inside, flipped on a bright overhead light, winced, and looked at a towering grandfather clock he'd brought from his former home to see that it was only 6:32. He felt as if it were midnight and he'd been digging ditches all day.

James ambled to the kitchen and fixed a double shot of bourbon. He took a sizable sip and carried the drink to the sparsely furnished living room, where he flung himself on the couch. He'd turned out the entry light, and the only illumination came from the halogen lamp across the street shining through the front window with its open draperies. He lay in the near darkness, rubbing the cool glass over his aching forehead and trying to blot out the image that seemed burned into his brain. How many drinks did it take to wipe out a memory? More than he could stand if he planned on going to the law office tomorrow. Maybe he should have taken off a week as Patrice advised.

James took another sip of bourbon and groaned. No. A week of idleness, a week without business to occupy his thoughts, would be unbearably depressing and give him far too much time to think. He wished he'd taken off today, though, instead of working even harder than usual. He felt almost weak with fatigue.

Earlier in the day, Chief Deputy Eric Montgomery had called James to tell him the dead woman's fingerprints were not on record and as yet police had located no official identification of her from the cottage—no purse with driver's license or Social Security card, and no car with license plate, vehicle identification number, insurance, or rental papers. The police could not reach the Moreaus in New Orleans. Otherwise, they could have come to Aurora Falls for next-of-kin identification. The autopsy had been completed by the medical examiner, and now the body lay at the morgue, unofficially identified but with no one to claim it.

Eric asked if James would consider visiting the morgue to take another look at the body. "I hate to ask you to do this, James, but I have a feeling the Moreaus aren't unreachable—they're just dodging us. If *you* can get hold of the Moreaus, they might come here and identify her."

"I've tried," James had told Eric with a mixture of dullness and anger. "If they're just dodging you, they're just dodging me, too."

"Well, that's unfortunate."

"Unfortunate?"

"I could use more colorful language, but I'm at the office. Anyway, you've only been her ex-husband for about a week. A formal identification by you might carry some weight. Also, you signing a few forms could expedite the release of the body when we're finally able to notify her family," Eric had said. "You're under no obligation to put yourself through this ordeal, though. I don't know that I would do under the circumstances. I just wanted to let you know the choice is yours."

James had told Eric he'd think about it, certain he would be calling back in a couple of hours to decline seeing Renée again. Four hours later, though, he realized he was having trouble concentrating on anything else. The situation troubled James. He knew he could just let the matter drift— Renée was no longer his responsibility— but she had once been his wife and he couldn't stop thinking about her lying unclaimed in the impersonal coldness of a morgue. If viewing her body again and signing release forms could help free her remains from the place, he would do it. If nothing else, she deserved to be laid to rest in New Orleans with family, he thought.

Finally, he'd told Patrice he would be leaving work half an hour early so he could go to the morgue. She hadn't asked if he wanted her to go with him or even mentioned that he might prefer to go with someone else. She had simply announced she would be accompanying him—an act he knew she would loathe, but one she would do without thought for a friend she thought needed her.

At first, James had protested, telling Patrice he was capable of making quick work of the task and not letting it bother him; after all, he'd seen the body Saturday. Still, she'd insisted. Later, he was secretly glad not to be alone as the drizzling rain of the day stopped, followed by an unusually foggy dusk as they pulled up to the old morgue sitting on a damp, dreary piece of land nearly a quarter of a mile away from the new hospital on its beautiful, well-lighted grounds. The construction company promised they would finish the new morgue attached to the hospital by spring, but for now construction conditions were not optimum. In other words, the dead could wait.

Inside, the morgue showed every one of its sixty years with dark green and yellowish white tile floors, chipped institution green walls, and loudly buzzing, bluish fluorescent lights. A creeping chilliness pervaded the building—a chilliness James thought the mechanical efforts of a furnace could not dispel. The damp cold lingered stubbornly, as if it belonged to the place and heat did not. Chemical smells tingled in James's nose and all he could think of was the intoxicating, exotic perfume Renée wore on special occasions—the perfume she'd worn on the night he met her. She never wore too much. She never wore the wrong kind of perfume for an event. She'd always known exactly how to lure and attract, even with scent.

But no longer. A young, dull-eyed lab assistant had slid open a drawer and unzipped a body bag. There lay the face and shoulders of a naked, bloated, cold, medicinal-smelling Renée Moreau Eastman, her glorious dark hair skinned back from her expressionless face, her lips white, her eyes mercifully closed. James heard Patrice draw in her breath. He managed to remain quiet and motionless. They simultaneously nodded to the lab assistant, and then each said aloud that the body was that of Renée Eastman. The cold little man had slid the cold drawer holding the cold body back into its place, firmly twisted a cold handle sealing the drawer, and turned away from them to do paperwork.

They'd barely spoken on the way back to the law firm, where Patrice had left her car. Before emerging from his, she'd asked if he'd like to come to the Blakethorne home for a while or even just go some-place quiet and get a drink with her. James had declined both invitations, thanked her for accompanying him to the morgue, told her he'd see her in the morning, and prom-ised to call her if he was having a bad night. They'd both known he wouldn't call no matter how miserable the next twelve hours were for him. Nevertheless, they each kept up the pretense of honesty and said a quiet, friendly good night.

James sat up straighter on the couch, took another sip of bourbon, and forced himself to focus on the business of what would have to be done for and to Renée rather than the horror of what had hap-pened to her. It was time to be her attorney, not the man who had married her and thought they would be husband and wife forever. They now had a business arrange-ment, which he would honor. As far as he knew, the Moreaus were still unaware that their daughter was dead. At the moment, he considered informing them his most important obligation to his ex-wife.

He had tried to call Gaston Moreau on

Saturday night but had been told by a servant that Mr. and Mrs. Moreau were "out somewhere." The servant had sounded so vague James had not left details but instead just asked that they return his call as soon as possible. The Moreaus hadn't called before he went back to the cottage prior to the fire, and he found no messages afterward. He had called several times Sunday and always been told they were not available. By Monday, he'd still been reluctant to announce Renée's death to a servant over the phone, but he'd underscored the importance of at least one of the Moreaus returning his call. Now, over forty-eight hours after the body's discovery, he'd still not heard a word from her parents.

James finished his drink and then once again called the Moreau home in New Orleans. Luckily for them, their large and historic house had not sustained irreparable damage when Hurricane Katrina ravaged New Orleans. He and Renée had not seen the home following the storm. After their impetuous marriage, James had been shocked to learn the Moreaus had carefully hidden a bad relationship with their only daughter. Later the three rarely even spoke on the phone. Renée refused to tell him what the trouble had been, but that didn't change the fact that her parents had to be told she was dead. After all, they were her family. His own familial relationship with Renée had started at what he'd considered an ecstatic wedding and had ended with the emotionless signing of court documents.

When they were able to reach the Moreaus, the police department would inform them of their daughter's murder. He could stay out of this completely, not speak to either parent. But he had been Renée's husband. As far as he knew, she hadn't remarried in the few days since the court had finalized their divorce. If she had any other family members who knew of her death, they hadn't come forward. No matter how elusive the Moreaus were trying to be, he had to get in touch with them.

James sat up, emptied his drink, thought about having another one before trying to call New Orleans, and then decided he'd only be stalling. One more drink wouldn't make the phone call easier, he thought tiredly as he reached for the phone and dialed the number he'd memorized since Sunday. The same vacant, middle-aged female voice he'd heard several times over the last three days said, "Moreau residence."

"This is James Eastman from Aurora Falls calling *again.* I'd like to speak to Mr. or Mrs. Moreau."

"I'm sorry, sir, but they aren't home. They haven't been home since Thursday. They've gone on a trip with friends."

"Where?"

"Where? Uh . . . somewhere in California."

"Yesterday you said they'd gone to Mexico."

"I'm sorry, sir. You must have spoken to someone besides me."

"I need to tell the Moreaus that their daughter has been murdered. If you don't believe I'm who I say I am I'll give you the number of the Aurora Falls Police Department, although I know they've tried to contact the Moreaus, too."

After a pause, the maid said wearily, "I don't need proof, at least of who you say you are. I can't keep playing this game even if I lose my job. It just isn't right." She paused, and when she spoke again it was with spirit. "Mrs. Moreau is home. She has been ever since you started calling. She just didn't want to talk to you. But I'll *make* her talk to you. You can count on it!"

She sounded as if she'd enjoy the opportunity to *make* Audrey Moreau do anything, James thought. One of the few things Renée and he had agreed on was their disdain for the beautiful, haughty woman who had given birth to Renée at twenty-three, turned her over to nannies, and lived a hectic, aimless life of socializing, shopping, and travel. Audrey's only halfway serious pursuit was acting, which she did very badly.

Renée, an only child, had spent most of her very young years with servants and a few socially acceptable little friends and her older years mostly in private schools. Her somber, humorless father, Gaston, almost old enough to be her grandfather, sometimes took her with him on his world travels concerning vague legal business he never liked to discuss because he considered the actual making of money to be crass. He found acquiring dated objets d'art much more to his liking and taught his young daughter, when he had the time, to do the same.

Reserved, intellectual Gaston and a gaggle of aging nannies raised a beautiful, introverted, almost psychologically shy girl who at sixteen abruptly returned to the family home in New Orleans and never again traveled with her father. By the time James had met her in his third year of Tulane Law School, she had turned from a wallflower into a beautiful, flamboyant, exciting woman who, to her family's disgrace, lived on the edge of scandal.

In spite of her personality, or maybe because of it, James quickly had become enamored of Renée, and the Moreaus had provided them with a lavish marriage ceremony in a hasty two months. Over the next few years, the Moreaus invited James and Renée to visit the family home only three times, all stays cut short because of Gaston's "unexpected" business demands abroad and only one visit including a social event—an extremely small dinner party made up mostly of relatives.

Nearly five minutes passed before Audrey Moreau's annoyed voice said without so much as a greeting, "Why do you keep calling, James?" She still spoke with her fake southern drawl. "You've been told several times Renée isn't here."

Familiar irritation swept through James at the mere sound of Audrey's voice. "I never asked to speak to Renée and I've been told several times that *you* weren't home."

"I simply didn't want to talk to you," Audrey returned without a touch of remorse or embarrassment. "You will not stop calling, though, and I'm getting extremely annoyed. You're being a pest. What do you want?"

James wished he could make himself say something cutting and cruel, but he held in his anger. After all, Audrey was Renée's mother. He turned down both his volume and the edge in his voice. "Something has happened to Renée."

"I knew it when your local police called."

"You didn't speak with them, did you?"

"Of course not. They left a message with one of the maids asking me to call back, but I didn't. I don't consider Renèe part of this family anymore."

"She's your daughter, Audrey, whether

you like it or not. Or she *was* your daughter. Renée is dead."

James heard a sharply drawn breath before Audrey returned hotly, "Oh, she is not! The police would have said so."

"They wouldn't tell your maid and you didn't talk to them. Neither did Gaston, I suppose."

"No, he didn't. I didn't even tell him the police had called. I don't want him bothered with her nonsense. I know she's just gotten herself in trouble again, and we don't want to hear about it. We have nothing to do with her."

James inhaled and said evenly, "Audrey, Renée's body was found Saturday afternoon here in Aurora Falls." He paused. "The police have no doubt that her death wasn't an accident. She'd been murdered, probably just over a week ago."

Silence spun out and James could almost see Audrey marshaling her ability not to believe anything she didn't care to believe. "That can't be true. Why would Renée be in Aurora Falls? She hated it there. She ran away from that place and from you." Audrey's voice picked up its tone and pace.

"I know you're convinced she's been living with us off and on ever since she left you, but I told her we wouldn't take her back. She's tried to come home three times, but I have literally turned her away at the door.

"Frankly, I think she is getting desperate for money," Audrey continued. "Whatever the case, I'm certain she has *not* been murdered, and this is not funny. It's a trick concocted by you or her, or both of you, and if you're involved I can't be shocked that you would stoop so low to either help her or find her, James. I know you loved her, God knows why, but I swear on my Bible that she isn't here."

"I doubt if you own a Bible, Audrey, although you claim to be a devout Christian, so that statement doesn't mean a thing to me."

Audrey sighed. "I don't care what you believe about my religious beliefs."

"I know and you're right. I don't give a damn about you or your religious beliefs. I want to speak to Gaston."

"Gaston isn't here, and I don't know when he'll be back."

"Why don't you know when he'll be back? Has he finally left you?"

The knife stabbed exactly where James had aimed. Indignation rang in Audrey's tone. "Of course he hasn't left me! Gaston would *never* leave me."

"Then why are you getting so upset?"

"Because the very idea of him leaving me is . . . is . . ."

"Ludicrous?" James asked, trying to goad her into blurting out information. "Or would him leaving you merely be too socially embarrassing for him to stand?"

"Oh, you are so—" She broke off and he heard her take a deep breath. "Gaston has been in Paris and London for over a week."

"Where can I reach him?"

"You *can't.* I won't let you upset him. He has a lot on his mind."

"How considerate of you, Audrey. I guess I never realized you're such a sweet, loving, protective wife."

James could picture her scouring her mind for a scathing retort and she finally came out with, "I won't have him bothered."

"You'd rather he not be bothered while he's out making money. But I repeat, Audrey—his daughter is *dead.* Someone has to tell him. He of all people should know. Or maybe I'll talk to some of his friends."

"Is that a threat?"

"What do you think?" James took a deep breath. "Audrey, he has to claim her body and make burial arrangements. Renée would want to be placed in the family mausoleum in New Orleans."

"She's not part of this family and she will *not* be placed in the family mausoleum."

"She's a Moreau, for God's sake."

"No, she's an Eastman. Look, James, I don't know whose body you've found. If it *is* Renée's, she's your responsibility. She's your next of kin, after all."

"Have you forgotten that I sent a letter when I started divorce proceedings? I sent another letter telling Gaston when the divorce would be finalized. As soon as I got the divorce decree, I sent a copy."

"I've never seen any of those things."

"I sent everything registered mail. Gaston signed for them."

"Well, he didn't tell me."

"I'm certain that he did. He wouldn't keep something like that from you." James drew a deep breath. "I don't know why you're bothering to go through all of this feinting and dodging when you know it won't work.

I'm capable of tracking down Gaston my-self, if I have to, and you know I will. Renée is *your* responsibility, no matter how you felt about her." He surprised himself by hav-ing to swallow to open a tightening throat. "You wouldn't love and protect her when she was alive, but I'll see that you take a few days to look after her now that she's dead. You owe her that much. So good night, Audrey. Sleep well knowing that Renée will never bother you again."

He slammed down the phone handset and felt sick. He'd known Audrey Moreau almost as long as he'd known Renée, and he knew the type of person she was—selfish, grasping, shallow, conniving, per-haps even incapable of love. She'd married for money. She had no love for children and often joked with an edge of truth that she'd agreed to give birth only to satisfy Gaston.

Audrey was a seriously damaged per-son, James thought grudgingly. In so many ways she needed as much sympathy as her daughter.

But he couldn't feel sympathy for Au-drey Moreau, he realized. All he could feel for her was contempt.

2

"I can drive to James's by myself!" Catherine nearly shouted into her cell phone as she descended the front steps of the Gray home and headed for her car, tightening her clasp on her umbrella. The wind had picked up force as if it were trying to carry her voice away. "I don't need a bodyguard, much less my little sister."

"It's nearly dark and starting to rain again and there's a murderer on the loose. Why can't you just wait for James to call you? He will any minute."

"It's after seven, Marissa. He should have called half an hour ago. How much time can you spend in a morgue identifying a body?"

"You said his home phone line is busy," Marissa reminded her, sounding frustrated. "He hasn't called you because he's talking to someone else."

"Then why doesn't he answer his cell phone?"

"It's turned off?"

"Nice try." Catherine dropped her car keys and stooped, fumbling in the wet grass to retrieve them. "I should have been the first person he called when he got home from the morgue. I wanted to go with him, but he wouldn't let me. He said it would be too upsetting for me. Patrice was going with him, though. I guess he thinks I have about as much strength as a crystal figurine."

"Oh, he does not. It wouldn't be as upsetting for Patrice because she didn't find the body and the body didn't happen to be that of her boyfriend's ex-wife. You're making a mountain out of a molehill."

"I'm not. I just believe James taking Patrice instead of taking me with him for support is an indication of something wrong in our relationship. Anyway, I can't reach Patrice, either, which just makes me worry even more. Something else—something bad—has happened."

"Catherine, will you please go back inside and have a glass of wine and settle down? Nothing has happened."

"You don't know that," Catherine said, picking up her keys from the rain-slicked grass. "Stop talking to me like I'm a child!"

"I will when you stop acting like one!" Almost immediately Marissa followed up with, "I'm sorry. It drives me crazy that you're so rational about everyone except James. I have to remember that you're in love with him, though. He's not just *anyone* to you." Marissa sighed. "I'm going to try one more time. I'll leave work right now—not in half an hour like I said earlier—and I'll be home in twenty minutes. If you haven't heard from him by then, we'll go together to his place."

"You said you have to finish your story before you leave. You do what you have to do and I'll do what I have to do." As Catherine neared her car sitting in the driveway, another gust of wind pulled her umbrella sideways, blocking her view of the street, and she staggered, trying to keep a firm grip on the wet handle. "I'll call you when I know anything. Bye."

Catherine knew her sister felt only love and concern for her, but Marissa simply didn't understand the situation. When James had told Catherine on the phone this afternoon that he'd decided to go to the morgue, she'd immediately volunteered to go with him. He'd said no. He'd tried to soften his flat refusal by saying putting her through such an unsavory task was unnecessary, he didn't want her to get upset, on and on. Besides, Patrice would be with him. Catherine didn't need to worry.

Catherine realized James was trying to protect her feelings, but she also knew he needed help getting through this night-mare. He was just so stubbornly indepen-dent and so unwilling to show her his vulnerability. She had to make him let her in, she'd thought after their unhappy phone call. She had to be more forceful, just as she knew Patrice must have been to make him let her go with him. Catherine had to make him see that she wasn't a little girl in need of shielding. She loved him, he loved her, and they needed to lean on each other in times of trouble. That's what she'd planned to tell him when he called her after the identification at the morgue.

Except that he'd never called.

Now, when she should have heard from him nearly two hours ago, Catherine had decided to take action. Maybe he'd been upset, gone back to his father's law office to work, and not bothered to call her, ex-cept that such self-involvement was totally unlike James. Maybe he'd gone some-where for a drink with Patrice, except that once again he wouldn't have left Catherine waiting for a phone call. If for some reason he couldn't phone, Patrice would have called her. At least, she thought Patrice would have called her. . . .

Abruptly the growing wind turned her umbrella sideways, blocking her view of the street. More darkness and rain accompanied the wind. Catherine felt like running back to the warmth and comfort of the house, but she knew she couldn't find real comfort until she found James. No doubt, most people would think her concern ridiculous—after all, he was a man in his early thirties, smart, strong, capable. Today, though, he'd had to look again at the murdered body of his ex-wife, Renée—

"Miss Gray? Miss Catherine Gray?"

Catherine righted her umbrella and saw a large form hurrying toward her from the street before a swath of her hair blew across her eyes. She grabbed at it, missed, and jerked when she felt someone else's fingertips brush against her forehead, moving the hair, while another hand closed over her shoulder. Startled, she dropped her cell phone.

"Don't be afraid." Blinking away rainwater from her eyes, she could blurrily see a tall man standing uncomfortably close to her. "I was on my way to your door when the wind blew up. You were struggling with your umbrella and didn't see me. We almost collided!" He smiled and made a movement that resembled a slight bow. "I am Nicolai Arcos. I apologize for frightening you."

He extended a hand to shake. Catherine blinked twice, clearing her vision, and looked up at a man who was at least six foot four with heavy black hair falling almost to his shoulders, deep-set dark brown eyes, a long, narrow nose, extremely high cheekbones, and sensual lips above a square chin. He was handsome in an unusual way, almost slightly unreal, like a character in a movie. And his name. Nicolai Arcos? Also slightly unreal. Yet familiar. He also smelled strongly of liquor and he was standing too close to her.

Catherine took a quick, firm step away from him. He'd done nothing except invade her personal space, but she sensed menace. She moved backward but decided she would not act afraid. She might not be armed, but many people lived on this street, people who looked out their windows, people who could hear a scream. "What do you want?" she asked with semi-calm.

"Only to talk."

"I don't have time to talk. I'm going somewhere." She took a step to the right, planning to walk past him to her car, but he moved, too, blocking her. Then he stood still, grinning at her. "I don't have time to talk to you, Mr. Arcos. I'm in a hurry." He continued to grin. "Get out of my way, Mr. Arcos."

He held up his large hands in a gesture of surrender. "You are offended because I touched you. Once again, I am *so* sorry. I should not have touched you, but you would have been more frightened if you'd simply run into a big, hulking man like me. Still, I mean you no harm. I only came here to talk to you." He nodded vaguely toward a black car sitting at the curb. "See? That is my automobile. I pulled up just before you came out of the house. You are too intelligent to think I would park my car in front of your home if I meant to come in and hurt you."

Catherine glanced at the cell phone lying on the wet autumn grass. She knew the connection between her and Marissa had been broken when she'd dropped the phone, jarring the battery, and she wouldn't take her eyes off this man long enough to reach down for it, even if Marissa called her back.

He wore a long, black raincoat, and an extremely large tiger's-eye ring glittered on the middle finger of his left hand. Squinting through the rain, she saw dark troughs beneath his eyes along with deep lines etched into his forehead and around his mouth. His skin was almost frighteningly pale. The man looked exhausted and sick. She could also tell he was drunk.

"Mr. Arcos, I told you that I have somewhere to go now," she said stiffly.

Their gazes locked. He looked sincere yet amused. In his near-black eyes, though, Catherine detected an impishness that had nothing to do with the glitter of alcohol. Also, his Eastern European accent seemed practiced and exaggerated. He was trying to act charmingly innocent, even slightly buffoonish, because he'd had too much to drink, but his act wasn't convincing. He was neither innocent nor a buffoon, and

Catherine's scrutiny of his eyes revealed dilated pupils. He'd had more than alcohol. He'd taken a drug or maybe more than one. The man was operating on alcohol mixed with God-knew-what chemicals. She wouldn't underestimate him.

"I heard you visited the Nordine Gallery to see my paintings today. Ken Nordine described your strange reaction to *Lady.*" Nicolai raised an already-arched eyebrow. "May we not go into your home and talk about it?" He looked up at the lowering slate sky. "We can't keep standing here in this weather."

Catherine fought an urge to turn and run for her front door, but she knew he'd just follow her, and he was so big and strong. For a moment she panicked. Then she glanced across the street and saw alert, athletic Steve Crown's face watching them intently from behind his front window. Steve and his wife maintained a deep concern for the safety of this street where they raised their three young children. Both kept close eyes on the activities. Catherine knew Steve already saw that she needed help. No doubt, his wife stood right behind him, calling 911, while Steve was pulling away from the window. Their presence gave Catherine courage.

"No matter how bad the weather gets, I'm not taking you into my house," she said. "You need to leave."

Arcos raised his shoulders. "Would you like to go someplace quiet to talk? A bar? Or perhaps my place. It isn't far from here. You could look at more of my work while we have a drink, get warm, talk . . . art."

"Get away from me." Catherine made her voice cold and hard. "The police are coming."

"The police?" He looked around and then laughed. "I don't see the police. I think you're drunk. Or delusional. Isn't that one of the words you doctors of the mind use? 'Delusional'?"

Catherine thought of running toward her house, but she stood firm. "Don't play this stupid game with me. If you stop right now, nothing will happen to you. If you don't—"

"What will you do, Miss Gray? Hit me? Or do you have something worse in mind? Are you capable of violence?" He leaned closer to her. "Are you capable of killing if someone stands in the way of what you want? I think you are. I think you already *have*."

Deep inside her, nearly overwhelming alarm rose in Catherine. The fixed smile had vanished from Nicolai's face, leaving it sharp edged and menacing. Even his lips drew back from the teeth in the near-feral position of a snarl. He was a big man charged on alcohol and drugs and he was someone to be feared—

Suddenly Nicolai's large hands closed over Catherine's shoulders and jerked her toward him. He held her so close they almost touched and she could feel his hot, sweet-sour alcohol breath on her face as he spoke just above an agonized whisper.

"What did you think when you looked at the portrait of my lady? She was *my* lady, you know. No matter what anyone else thought. No matter what she *let* them think or *made* them think or what she *did,* she was mine. I could have it no other way because it couldn't be any other way. She didn't always understand how it had to be, but I understood." He nodded slowly, absently. "Yes, I understood."

Catherine kicked with all her might, but he stood just an inch too far away for her boot to connect with his leg.

He glared at her. "She didn't want *him,* you stupid woman. She never really wanted him, even in the beginning. She made a mistake, that's all. And now—" A deep, strangling sound came from his throat before he jerked Catherine closer and said viciously, "But she will always be mine. Death cannot separate us. We were for each other. We were *of* each other. Renée and Nicolai— one person. Always. No matter how things looked. Didn't you understand? Didn't *he* understand? Is that why you killed her and then went to the gallery to get another look at what you destroyed?"

Steve Crown had appeared behind Arcos. Bent at the waist, Crown charged the artist. Crown's shoulder drove into Arcos's midsection, breaking his hold on Catherine and knocking him flat on the slick ground. Catherine barely had time to move before Arcos's right leg rose and snapped out at his attacker. Crown's left leg buckled and he fell to his knees, groaning. With almost unbelievable speed, Arcos jumped up and stalked toward Crown. Catherine screamed as Arcos kicked Crown in the ribs. He fell flat and rolled onto his back. Before he could cross his arms across his rib section, though, Arcos kicked Crown again, this time even harder.

As Steve Crown moaned and rolled into a fetal position, Catherine burst into an instinctive run for her house. She'd only managed a few steps before she slid. Arcos caught her before she fell flat. He jerked her to a standing position and then closed his hands around her throat.

"No, you will not escape me," Nicolai Arcos hissed into her ear. "And you will not escape her. *Renée* will follow you to the grave."

Arcos tightened his grip on Catherine's neck. He held her at arm's length. Again she kicked wildly, but she couldn't make contact with his legs. She flailed her arms uselessly. She couldn't scream—she had no air as Arcos's hands tightened. In the background, she heard Steve Crown moaning, moaning. . . .

Then the sound of a police siren cut through the wet night air. Someone had called the police. Crown's wife, Catherine thought dully.

Suddenly the pressure on Catherine's neck loosened and she tumbled, limp as a rag doll. Blinking against the raindrops, she watched as Arcos dashed to his car. In what seemed one smooth motion, he'd climbed inside and begun speeding down the street.

Meanwhile, Catherine's gaze had switched from Arcos's car back to the patrol car just as in horror she saw a little boy run from his lawn into the street, directly in front of the police car. He froze and Catherine froze at the sight of the patrol car swerving violently, the sound of tires screeching audibly above the siren's wail.

Miraculously, the car stopped about a foot from the little boy. A woman came shrieking into the street to clutch the child, both of them standing rigidly in front of the patrol vehicle, as Nicolai Arcos's car disappeared around a corner.

CHAPTER EIGHT

1

Catherine clambered to her feet as the patrol car pulled to the curb in front of her house. In a minute, Robbie Landers helped her stand steady while her partner rushed to Steve Crown. Although Robbie breathed hard, her voice remained calm. "Who was that man?"

"Nicolai Arcos. He's an artist. I've never met him before. He was high on drugs and alcohol and—" Catherine moved closer to Steve. "Oh, Steve, I'm so sorry!" she called to him, and then turned to Robbie. "You should be chasing Arcos!"

Robbie held Catherine's arm firmly. "The woman who called nine-one-one got the license number of the other car. My partner Jeff alerted all patrol cars in this area to be on the lookout for the vehicle when we lost sight of it. He also called the paramedics."

"I'm okay, but I'm worried about Steve," Catherine said. "Steve Crown. He was looking out his front window when Arcos grabbed me in the yard."

"This man didn't come to your door and then grab you?"

"No, I was outside headed for my car and talking to Marissa on my cell phone. The wind caught my umbrella, and between trying to hold on to it and the phone I didn't see him pull up. He just seemed to appear."

Steve's wife was already running across the street toward her husband, who was trying to stand in spite of the deputy's efforts to hold him still. Mrs. Crown commanded, "Steve, lie still this instant," and he immediately subsided. She turned on Catherine. "Who was that man?"

"Someone I've never seen before." Catherine felt ridiculously guilty, as if the attack by Arcos were her fault. "The police will get him."

"They'd better," Mrs. Crown answered grimly.

"Or else she will, and then God help him," Robbie muttered close to Catherine's ear, managing to make her smile. Robbie was right—the big-boned, taut-muscled Mrs. Crown looked like she could take down a grizzly bear. Gently Robbie began leading Catherine toward the house. "Let's get you inside out of this rain."

Twenty minutes later, paramedics had pronounced Catherine's neck bruised, but they'd detected no sign of serious trauma. Still, they advised that she go to the hospital for X-rays. She promised she would, although she had no intention of leaving her house unless her pain worsened.

Steve Crown was a different matter. He had at least one broken rib and a second that was either badly cracked or broken. The paramedics loaded him into the ambulance, his wife barking orders nonstop, and sped off to the hospital.

Robbie and her partner, Jeff Beal, took

Catherine into the house, where she gave them a full report about the incident and the little she knew of Nicolai Arcos. They were leaving when James arrived, surprised to see them and nearly speechless when they told him what had happened. After Robbie and Jeff left, James took Catherine in his arms. "When I think of what that maniac could have done to you . . ." He trailed off, tightening his hold on her. "You weren't going to let him in the house, were you? Because I've told you about him. He's crazy."

"Do you think *I'm* crazy? Of course I wasn't going to let him in the house."

"Then how—"

"He caught me on my way to my car. I was coming to check on you because you never called me after you got back from the morgue," Catherine interrupted sharply.

James's embrace loosened. "Oh. I'm sorry." She stared at him. "I called the Moreaus again."

"You called them before you called me."

"When I got back, I was furious. All I thought of was that they still didn't know Renée is dead. I acted on impulse."

"Okay. Did you reach them this time?"

"Yeah. I spoke to her mother, but I don't want to talk about that conversation right now. She wouldn't let me talk to Reneé's father, Gaston."

"Did she say she'd tell him?"

"She said she wouldn't, that she doesn't believe me."

"Do you think she does?"

"I'm not sure, but I think so."

"But she still won't let you talk to Gaston." James shook his head. "She won't let you tell the man who sexually abused his daughter for years that she's dead."

James's face paled and his mouth opened slightly. "Sexually abused?"

"Oh, come on, James. Did you think I didn't guess? I *am* a psychologist, you know. What man travels for years all over Europe with his little girl? You told me he did. She only came back to New Orleans when she was sixteen. No doubt she was too old to interest him then. And even if I hadn't known about all the years she spent with *Daddy,* I would have been almost positive of abuse by her behavior—the hypersexuality, alcoholism, lack of friendships, inability to trust, mood swings, I could go on and on."

She stopped, seeing James's eyes almost burning holes through her. "Don't look at me that way. You said she had a rough past. That was putting it mildly. I'm right about him, aren't I? If I'm wrong, you don't want me to keep thinking something so awful about the man."

"Yes, dammit, you're right!" James's voice lowered. "She never admitted it until we'd been married over a year. I've never seen Gaston since then. I should have done something."

"To Gaston? What could you do? The damage was done. As for Renée, you stayed with her so long because you thought you could help her with your love and your kindness. That's certainly nothing to be ashamed of, James. I also know you didn't tell me about the abuse because you were protecting her privacy, even after everything she'd done to you." Catherine paused. "Sometimes I hate her and I feel like shaking you for not realizing Renée needed professional help and divorcing her before she nearly ruined your life. Other times, I feel sorry for her and your attempt to help her only makes me love you more."

"She always promised to change."

"I'm sure she did and I can't tell you whether or not she really *meant* those promises to change. If she did, she needed a psychiatrist." Catherine paused. "Enough talk about Renée. Why didn't you call me as soon as you finished at the morgue?"

"I told you, when I got home I called the Moreau home."

"You could have called me first. A five-minute call to let me know it was over and you were all right emotionally would have put my mind at rest. Instead, I imagined all kinds of awful things."

James said a bit impatiently, "Catherine, I tried to call you right after I spoke to Renée's mother, but I couldn't get an answer on your cell or home phone. That's why I came here. If I'd been sooner—"

"You should have called *me* as soon as you got home from the morgue," Catherine bridled. "If you had, I wouldn't have been certain something had happened to you, I wouldn't have been outside in the rain, and I wouldn't have been a prime target for Arcos. Why didn't you call?"

James stood and walked slowly to the fireplace, propping his arm on the mantle. He gave her a long look. "Catherine, this

afternoon two people called me and one
client informed me of your noon-hour ac-
tivity. If you want to sneak into the Nordine Gallery to see *Mardi Gras Lady,* you
shouldn't wear a red raincoat and carry a
big red umbrella."

Catherine flushed. "Oh! So you didn't
call because you were mad at me."

"I wasn't mad."

"Yes, you were. And for your information, I wasn't *sneaking.*"

"Were you going to tell me you'd been
to the gallery?"

"Of course." James continued to stare
at her until her gaze dropped. "I don't
know. I hope I would have even though
you wouldn't have been happy about it."

"I wouldn't have been and you know
why."

"Because Arcos had an affair with
Renée."

"Because you were supposed to be
careful, not parade into the Nordine Gallery in a red coat for all the world to see!"

"I didn't *parade* and I hardly think a
couple of people in Aurora Falls constitutes
all the world!" Catherine took a deep breath.
"Okay, I wasn't careful. I realize that now.

I'm just not used to being careful around here. But what's the rest of the reason you got mad about me going to the gallery?"

James looked away for a moment, almost childishly, as if he were going to refuse to talk. Then he started speaking fast and loud. "Because Arcos had the gall to paint her portrait and put it out for public consumption with his intriguing, totally unbelievable denials that the picture was of Renée. Then that slimy Ken Nordine, another one of her lovers, hung it in his art gallery! Made it the showpiece of the exhibition, for God's sake! I didn't want to go there and I didn't want you to go there, either."

Catherine said nothing in her defense. She waited until James's expression visibly calmed.

"I have no right to dictate your actions, though. I'm not your master, your boss, your dictator. I never told you *not* to go because what Arcos and Nordine had done humiliated me; you should have told me to go to hell and that you'd do what you pleased." He paused. "I know you'd never do that, though. Instead, you constantly tiptoe around my feelings. It makes me feel like you think I'm some emotionally unstable patient you might send over the edge, and yes, it annoys the hell out of me. I was embarrassed and irritated this afternoon because you'd gone to the gallery without telling me you were going and because I was certain you wouldn't have told me you did go." He sighed. "Why would you do that, Catherine?"

"Because I don't want to hurt you. Renée showed you no respect. Worse. I've tried very hard to do just the opposite." To her surprise, tears rose in her eyes. "Maybe I'm just as bad for you as she was if I'm stirring up gossip and people are actually calling you at your office to report on me. I'm sorry."

James looked at her solemnly. Then the right side of his mouth twitched. Finally, he burst into loud laughter, bending slightly at the waist. Surprised, Lindsay, who'd been watching quietly from a corner, burst into a volley of barks before snatching up her stuffed tiger for protection.

"What's wrong?" Catherine shouted above the din, indignant at his laughter. "What's so damned funny, James?"

"You," James managed before striding

toward her, grabbing her hands, and pulling her up from where she sat on the couch. He hugged her so tightly she could hardly breathe. "Darling girl, don't you think there's a happy medium between treating me the way Renée did and treating me like I either am too fragile to hear the truth or will get furious with you when I do? I'm *not* fragile and I know I can be stubborn and over-bearing at times, but I'm not an ogre!"

"I don't think you're an ogre." Between her desire to cry some more and the pres-sure of James's hug, Catherine had trouble squeezing out words. "But maybe I see something you don't. James, Renée's be-havior didn't just anger you—it trauma-tized you."

James stopped hugging her and took a step back, keeping his hands on her shoul-ders. "I'm not traumatized. I never was."

"Yes, James, you were. You're just be-ginning to recover. Trust me—I've spent years learning to recognize the signs. I may go overboard trying to protect your feelings, but you've been hurt more severely than even you realize."

Finally, he said carefully, "All right, Renée did hurt me badly. I think saying it traumatized me is going too far, but if that's the word you want to use, then go ahead. However, Catherine, keep in mind that she left me years ago."

"Yes. She just disappeared one day and a lot of people, including the police, suspected you of murdering her. Now she's back. Dead. Murdered. And you're the prime suspect—again. So don't insult my intelligence by trying to convince me you're just fine in spite of everything that's happened the last few years, especially the last three days. I can't let myself love a man who thinks I'm weak *and* stupid!"

James looked at her disbelievingly at first, then with a flash of fear in his eyes. "Catherine, you can't believe I think you're either weak *or* stupid. My God! Are you telling me you don't love me, you *won't* love me, if I refuse to wear my heart on my sleeve, to let everyone, especially you, know how I feel—"

Abruptly the front door opened and Marissa rushed in, full of apologies and questions because she'd heard at the newspaper office about the 911 call. Catherine saw James swallow hard a couple of times and then rapidly compose his expression.

Before Marissa had shaken the rain off her coat and hung it up, Eric Montgomery arrived, also because of the emergency call. Marissa spent the next ten minutes checking Catherine's neck where Arcos's hands had squeezed; scolding her for not going to the hospital; getting everyone seated; fixing refreshments; and settling Lindsay.

When she finally sat down, Eric leaned forward, looked at Catherine, and said in a low but authoritative voice, "I hate to make you go over this now, but I'd like to hear from you about the incident."

James had sat down beside Catherine on the couch and he took one of her still-trembling hands, holding it tightly as she gave Eric a concise account of Arcos's approach to her and his subsequent attack. "I smelled alcohol on his breath and I'm sure he'd taken some drug—I could tell by the dilated pupils in his eyes. He was polite at first, and then he got more aggressive and grabbed me. He clutched my neck—not hard, more as if he were trying to scare me rather than strangle me. He was babbling—not making a lot of sense—when Steve Crown came. I didn't see exactly what Steve did, but it broke the hold Arcos had on my neck."

Everyone in the room went motionless. Even Lindsay grew stock-still, focusing on Catherine.

"What was Arcos babbling?" Eric asked gently.

Here it was—the one question she'd dreaded, the one question she'd hoped Eric wouldn't ask. Eric never avoided details, though. She should have known she couldn't slide anything about her encounter with Arcos past him.

For once, Catherine wished James weren't with her. Earlier he'd been offended, saying she always tiptoed around his feelings, but when it came to all he'd been through with Renée—including her murder—Catherine knew for now she had to be extra-careful when it came to protecting his emotions. She couldn't bear doing or saying anything that might cause him further pain.

But Eric's gaze bore into hers. He wanted to know what Arcos had said and for some reason seemed determined to hear it in James's presence. Catherine knew stalling would be useless. She might as well tell Eric the truth and be done with it, no matter what the outcome.

Catherine took a sip of Coke to ease the roughness in her throat. "Earlier in the day, I had a cancellation of my one o'clock appointment, which gave me a two-hour lunch break," she began slowly. "I used the extra time to visit the Nordine Gallery."

Catherine glanced at Marissa to see her eyes widen and could tell she wanted to demand why Catherine had gone alone, without her sister's company. Fortunately, Marissa firmly closed her mouth without saying a word. "When Arcos got here, he said he just wanted to talk to me about my visit to the gallery. Then he began to seem somehow . . . menacing. I told him to leave me alone. He asked what I'd do if he didn't—hit him? Or was I capable of violence? Was I capable of murder if someone stood in the way of what I want?"

"Murder!" Marissa burst out. "*You?* That is the most absurd thing I've ever heard. How dare he—"

"Go on, Catherine," Eric interrupted, earning him a glare from Marissa.

"He started asking me about what I

thought of the portrait of *his lady.* I'm sure he meant *Mardi Gras Lady.* Then he rattled on about how she was *his* no matter what she let them think or made them think—"

"Made *who* think?"

"I don't know, Eric. He just said she was his, it couldn't be any other way, and even though she didn't always understand that, he did. Then he said I was stupid for thinking she wanted *him*—it was obvious he meant someone besides himself—and that she'd *never* really wanted him, this other man." James's grip on Catherine's hand tightened. "He said I'd killed Renée and gone to the gallery earlier today to look at the portrait of the woman I'd destroyed. And then . . . well, he was just babbling."

Eric gave her a look that made her feel like a bug pinned on a wall and wriggling but unable to free itself. "What did he say, Catherine?"

"He said I couldn't escape him or her." Eric kept staring at her and Catherine knew he wasn't going to let her off easily. She might as well give up, she thought as she drew a deep breath and added reluctantly,

"He said Renée would follow me to the grave."

2

Nicolai Arcos slowly turned his car into the morgue parking lot, turned off his head-lights, and pulled parallel to the brick build-ing where the shadows hovered deepest. For the last four hours, after escaping from the Gray home, he'd cruised backstreets and alleys, navigating by using only his parking lights and sometimes only the glow of the moon. He hadn't returned home—the small warehouse with plenty of room for his art supplies, canvases, frames, and finished paintings.

Heady with the success of his showings at the Nordine Gallery, he'd holed up in his warehouse to celebrate with vodka, some drugs of choice, and a CD marathon. He didn't even own a radio or television and never saw the news. Not until this after-noon—Monday—had Ken Nordine called and told him about the dead woman found on the Eastman property and that every-one thought she was Renée. Ken had also given Nicolai a detailed account of James Eastman's girlfriend, Dr. Catherine Gray, her visit to the gallery, and her agitated reaction to *Mardi Gras Lady.*

As soon as Ken left, Nicolai had sent three shots of vodka into his slightly clearing mind and thought. Within what seemed moments, he decided exactly what had happened. Renée had been at the cottage and waiting for him—her *pishiskurja,* the Romanian word for "darling" she'd called him in intimate moments. Renée who had cared enough about him to learn the word without a hint from him. He shook his head, clearing it as the vodka hit his empty stomach with a dizzying slap. He must concentrate, he told himself.

Ken said maybe she had returned to Aurora Falls because she'd heard about his exhibition. She'd come back because she wanted to see the exhibit. Nicolai knew immediately she had come back to see him. After all, Ken had claimed reluctantly, although without malice, she'd cared about Nicolai more than she'd cared about him. After all, Nicolai told himself, he was the artist, the genius, the one with the tender soul. He had been her true love. Still,

Nicolai had been stunned that a man with Ken Nordine's ego could admit such truth.

Ken had also suggested that Renée had been killed somewhere else and her body dumped in the cistern of the Eastman cottage just to throw suspicion on James. Nicolai knew Ken was wrong, though. He pictured the scene. Renée had sent him a message on one of the technological gadgets she'd given him telling him she'd returned and would be waiting at the cottage. For some reason—probably because he was not good with the gadgets that he didn't trust—he had not received her message. Someone else had, though. and while she'd waited innocently, eagerly, for Nicolai, the person who had intercepted her message had murdered her at the cottage. The cottage—old, shabby, but *theirs* because the Eastmans had cast it off; because it sat isolated in the winter and early spring when their affair had reached its zenith.

Before she began to pull away from him.

Nicolai was certain the fear had caused her desertion of him years ago. He knew Renée had panicked at the overwhelming love she felt for him. She hadn't understood this—she didn't understand so many things about herself—but he knew. He was an artist, which meant he had the sensitivity to understand so much other people did not. A lawyer like James Eastman? He could never come close to comprehending the complexity that was Renée. A businessman like Ken Nordine, with whom she'd had a short fling? She'd only done it to hurt Nicolai, to turn him against her, to drive him away. The performance had not worked. He'd seen right through her and he'd kept on loving her, maybe more than ever for going to such lengths to escape their love. Yes, even throughout the years, during the many times his thoughts had been fogged with drugs, he had always been certain of this one truth.

For the last couple of years, Nicolai's drug of choice tended to be the mind-expanding Ecstasy. Today, though, he had fallen back on his old favorite—cocaine— and he now snorted some of what he'd brought with him. As it tingled through him, he threw back his head and laughed, tossing the hair he kept long because it complemented his image. Renée had loved to run her hands through it—her exquisite, gentle hands never marred by her wedding and engagement rings. During their times together, she'd only worn the narrow platinum band he had given her. Earlier, he'd realized she must have been wearing it the night she was murdered.

Over the last few hours, while he'd hidden from the police, he'd become obsessed with that ring. Where was it now? Nicolai knew they stripped corpses. He shuddered at the thought of Renée as a *corpse* lying naked in a cold metal drawer. Trapped. Alone.

He lowered his head, snorting his last, small line of cocaine and wishing he'd brought more with him earlier today. The small amount had to be enough, though. It had to give him the strength to get him through what he knew he must do: free Renée.

Power surged through Nicolai. He could do this. He could take her away from James, from her family—from the people who hated her. He would take her physical remains someplace safe, someplace sacred, and keep her hidden until their souls met on a different plane.

Nicolai peered around the parking lot

again and then stepped from his car. The rain had stopped, but the night felt heavy. He was already sweating from the cocaine, so he shrugged out of his coat and tossed it on the seat. Then he took a deep breath, trying to slow his rapid heart rate and cool his overheated body.

The air smelled dank. He held his breath, uncertain, repulsed. The smell couldn't be leaking from the morgue, he told himself. Calming down, he closed his eyes and smiled. He did *not* smell decomposing bodies. He was merely letting his imagination take control. Sometimes having an imagination as powerful as his was not a blessing. The combination of vodka and cocaine wasn't helping to keep it in check, either.

Nicolai crept to the back door of the morgue. He was sure the hospital didn't pay for a security guard. They probably didn't even have a security system. All he would have to contend with would be some weak, substandard creep. Who else would work in a morgue? Nicolai knew he would have no trouble overpowering such a pathetic being. Then he would find her. . . .

He shook his head to clear it. The quick movement made him feel slightly nauseated, but he held still and took deep breaths. He still crouched by his car with the door he'd left open only a crack so the interior lights wouldn't glow. Swiftly he opened the door, grabbed his lock-picking kit, and gently pushed the door to its former position. The police might still be looking for him, even here. Completely shutting the door would make unnecessary noise.

Nicolai crept to the back door of the morgue. For a moment, he hesitated again, wondering if he was doing the right thing or if grief and drugs were controlling his actions. What would his grandparents think of this? They were distant memories but still lingered in his mind. Would his grandfather have let someone take away the remains of the one true love of his life if he hadn't been lost at sea before she died?

No. His grandfather would never have let such a travesty happen. He'd been a strong man, a man of principle and of passion, and he would have done anything to protect his mate for life, Nicolai's kind and devoted grandmother, Iona. Yes, Nicolai reasoned in his churning thoughts. Taking Renée to safety was the only right and just thing to do.

His mind settling, Nicolai stooped down and looked closely at the doorknob. He let out a snort of derision when he didn't see a dead-bolt lock—only the relatively simple doorknob lock. No one had wasted any money on this building, he thought, almost laughing until he abruptly wondered if administrators had spent much money on modernizing, or even maintaining, the inside.

The inside, where bodies lay.

Nicolai no longer felt like speculating or wasting time on scorn and ridicule. He merely wanted to rescue Renée and never see this awful place again.

He opened his lock-pick set, pulled a small penlight from his pocket, and shined its narrow beam on the utensils. He picked one and withdrew it from the kit, quickly inserting it into the cylinder running through the center of the doorknob. Abruptly he stopped as fear passed through him like a cold wind. Shocked, he froze into immobility, unable to move anything except his eyes. He saw no one.

Still, he knew he was not alone.

Someone had come into the parking lot. They could not have driven—he would have heard a car. They had walked, cautiously, stealthily—

From behind him came a smooth voice. "Good evening."

Nicolai, agile even in a drugged state, had shot halfway to his feet before the muscles of his back cramped violently, sending shock waves of pain through his midsection. In a moment, another flare of excruciating pain sent him facedown to the ground.

A foot rolled him onto his back. Nicolai, fully conscious, squinted upward. His vision wasn't as keen as usual, but he saw expressionless eyes and a gun pointed steadily at his face. He muttered a pitiful "no" before the bullet hit.

And for Nicolai Arcos, the world ended.

CHAPTER NINE

1

Eric Montgomery pulled into the morgue parking lot, stopped the patrol car, and looked out the windshield at the second murder scene he'd witnessed in less than a week. He took a sip of coffee from an extra-large Styrofoam cup and sighed. "Here we go again," he said to Deputy Jeff Beal.

"When I was a teenager, I always thought going to murder scenes would be exciting, but they aren't," Jeff said morosely. "I guess I'd watched too much TV."

Eric took another sip of coffee. "At least I've never seen you vomiting into the shrubbery at the sight of a dead body. That's a plus."

"I guess." Jeff frowned, his eyes narrowing into a sharp stare. "Isn't that Marissa?"

"Damn!" Eric threw open the car door and made a beeline for her. "What are *you* doing here? It's seven thirty!"

"Good morning to you, too, and it's seven thirty-five to be exact," she said calmly, glancing at her watch. "I'm here because I got a call on my cell phone over half an hour ago telling me Nicolai Arcos was here. Murdered."

"Nicolai Arcos? The artist?"

"The voice said only, 'Nicolai Arcos.' Nothing about him being an artist."

Eric gaped at her. "Why didn't you call me? Who called *you*? What else did he say? Or was it a she? Are any other reporters here? Does Catherine know?"

Marissa took a deep breath. "I did call you. I got no answer on your landline phone and your cell phone was busy. I don't know who called me. Whoever it was used a voice distorter and only said, 'Last night Nicolai Arcos was murdered trying to break into the back door of the morgue. He's still lying there.' I couldn't tell if it was a man or a woman. When I couldn't get hold of you, I called nine-one-one. They said they'd already been notified and I knew they'd called you—that's why your cell phone was busy. I left a note for Catherine saying only that I needed to go into work early—that's all. Any other questions?"

"No, but I wish you weren't here."

Marissa lifted her right eyebrow. "Thank you, Eric. I love you, too."

"You know what I mean. You're a reporter."

"I'm a reporter who cooperates with the police, which is why, under usual circumstances, I wouldn't be here. This time my editor had no say in the matter, though. Even *he* doesn't know about this murder unless he was my anonymous caller." Marissa looked closely at Eric. "You're tired and you have a headache."

"How did you deduce that information?"

"You're carrying a twenty-four-ounce cup of black coffee from Starbucks—you only drink that much black coffee in the morning when you need extra caffeine.

Your eyes are slightly bloodshot, indicating you either went on a bender last night or didn't get much sleep—I'd rather it was the latter reason—and the crease between your eyebrows is deeper than usual. All of that adds up to you having a headache."

Eric's mouth twitched in a suppressed smile. "Marissa Gray, you *are* a wonder."

"I'm merely observant. In fact, I'm observant enough to notice that people are beginning to stare at us. Time to get down to business, Chief Deputy."

"I know." He hesitated. "Everything you see and hear is off-the-record unless I say so. Okay?"

"Do you even have to tell me that? You know you can trust me with sensitive information."

And so did your anonymous caller, Eric thought. But then why alert a reporter at all?

He turned away from Marissa and walked purposefully toward the first officer on the scene, a dark-haired young deputy named Tom. "What do we have under that sheet, Tom?"

"A tall man lying on his back who is, to

quote a very shaky morgue attendant, 'dead as a doornail.'"

"Was he found with a sheet over him?" Eric asked as he pulled on latex gloves.

"No. The attendant said he's just getting over the flu and he felt bad. He only had an hour to wait before the day-shift attendants came, so he came out here to 'get some air.' That's when he found the victim. *He* covered the vic, which he shouldn't have done."

"No, he should have known to leave the scene exactly the way he found it," Eric said crossly. He pulled back a corner of the sheet. "But I think I know why he covered the body."

"Is it bad?"

"It's not good," Eric said, tossing back the sheet to reveal the chalky face of a man with a gaping hole where his right eye should have been.

2

"Thank you for working me in on such short notice and so early."

"It was no problem. I had a cancellation."

It was a little after ten o'clock. Catherine motioned to her office couch, glad a cool morning sun lit up the room to its best advantage. "Would you like a cup of coffee, Mrs. Nordine?"

"Call me Dana. And thank you, but I was up most of the night. I was so tired this morning I had to drink more than enough coffee for the whole day to get myself in gear at six thirty. That's when Ken wakes up. Always exactly six thirty. He likes it when I serve him coffee and a pastry in bed." She smiled tightly. "You probably think that's hopelessly old-fashioned or subservient of me."

"I think it's fine if you both enjoy the ritual."

Dana Nordine, dressed in a tight gray pencil skirt, a black silk charmeuse blouse, and sky-high black suede heels, walked with practiced grace from the doorway to the couch and sat down, carefully crossing her bare, spray-tanned legs. Another one of those women who would endure cold legs even in winter to be fashionable, thought Catherine, who refused to abandon panty hose in chilly weather.

"You must think it's odd that I wanted to

see you after we just met yesterday," Dana said.

Catherine smiled. "I'm pleased." She hesitated. "I enjoyed my tour of the gallery."

Dana gave her a wry look from her dark eyes. "Really? You seemed like you couldn't leave fast enough."

"I did leave in a hurry." Catherine felt herself blushing and was annoyed. "I—"

Dana held up a slender hand. "You don't need to make polite excuses. I was furious with Ken for going on and on about Nicolai Arcos, although clearly you came to see his work. I know you're very close to James Eastman and everyone thinks *Mardi Gras Lady* is a portrait of James's wife, one of Nicolai's sex partners. Some say she was the only one—the great love of his life. I must admit, that portrait just brims with life. Seeing it must have been upsetting for you."

Dana paused. "And that is the last remark I'll ever make about your private life, because this isn't a social call. Dr. Gray, I want you to be my therapist."

"I knew that when you filled out the patient form," Catherine said quietly.

"I have to be certain our sessions will be confidential."

"That goes without saying," Catherine replied, offended. Did Dana assume because Catherine was young she was also unprofessional?

"I can tell I insulted you. I'm sorry, Dr. Gray. My comment about confidentiality was no reflection on you. It's a symptom of my problem—trust. My *inability* to trust, to be more specific." Dana gave Catherine a self-deprecating smile. "You aren't the first therapist I've seen in the last few years. They've all given me essentially the same diagnosis, but I've found that I still need someone I can talk to frequently—someone I can depend on for complete discretion."

Catherine nodded. "I understand and you're wise to continue therapy if it helps you maintain an even keel. As for me"—Catherine managed to grin—"discretion is my business."

Dana laughed. "You should put that on a business card!"

Catherine picked up her pen and notebook. "What would you like to talk about today, Dana?"

The woman's fingers began to fidget

and she glanced at the coffee table. She wants a cigarette, Catherine thought, but seeing no ashtray, Dana realized smoking was not encouraged. "Well, I have a daughter."

"How old is she?"

"Five. I named her Mary for my mother." Catherine nodded. "Ken wants another child."

"And you don't?"

Dana stared out the window for nearly a minute. "You probably noticed that Ken is younger than I am. We were married for four years before I conceived Mary with the help of in vitro fertilization. She was our fourth try. I had a very difficult pregnancy—I was confined to bed at six months—but still Mary was born almost seven weeks premature." Dana looked away and sighed. "I'm forty-three now, and frankly, I don't look forward to going through the whole process again. In fact, I dread it."

"Does Ken know how you feel?"

"Yes."

"Does he care?"

"Well . . ."

Catherine waited.

"No." Dana pressed her perfect lips thin

for a moment, then blurted, "And I don't want to do it, but I would if . . . if Ken loved children."

"Doesn't he love Mary?"

"I suppose he does in a way—after all, she is a part of him—but he pays so little attention to her that sometimes I wonder how he really feels about her."

"Yet he wants another child."

"He wants a boy," Dana announced sharply. "He's trying to reproduce his father, whom he adored. He wants me to go through another course of in vitro, another pregnancy. Four gynecologists have told me another pregnancy wouldn't be a good idea for *my* health. And if the baby isn't a boy . . . well, I don't know what Ken will do."

Dana's right foot began to jiggle nervously. Her eyes narrowed. Her fingers tapped the top of her Chanel handbag.

"Dana, would you like to have a cigarette?"

"*God*, yes!" The tapping fingers dived into her bag as Catherine retrieved an ashtray from her desk drawer. In a moment, Dana clamped a long cigarette between none-too-steady red glossed lips and lit it. Almost immediately, she blew out a thin, loud stream of smoke. "I've been smoking since I was thirteen. I can't seem to stop. Thank you."

"I see no sense in making you miserable to enforce a rule. Besides, it's Dr. Hite's rule, not mine, and he's on vacation." She winked. "He'll never know."

Dana laughed. "I like you. You make me relax a bit."

"Only a bit?"

"I never entirely relax, even when I'm drunk. And I haven't been drunk or even *tipsy*, as my father used to say, for many years."

"Then alcohol isn't a problem for you."

Dana took another ferocious drag from her cigarette. "I can't stand to lose control of myself." She glanced sharply at Catherine and announced, "My husband had an affair with Renée Eastman." Catherine stared at her. "I wanted to take you by surprise with that statement, catch you off guard. I did, but I can see by your expression you already knew about Ken and Renée." Catherine said nothing. "Ken and Arcos both had her. They were like two puppies fighting over an old slipper, not that it's easy to picture Renée as an old slipper. Still, it was pathetic—even laughable to anyone except me, and James, I would guess."

Catherine always tried to avoid the cliché question "How did that make you feel?" Instead, Mrs. Tate's preoccupation with spousal philandering flashing through her mind, she asked, "Are you sure Ken had an affair?"

"Oh yes," Dana returned casually. "He tried to hide it at first. Then he did everything except come right out and tell me." Dana's foot began jiggling again. "Then Renée disappeared."

Catherine longed to ask if the affair had ended before Renée vanished, but she couldn't. "How did Ken act when Renée left town?"

"Left town? Are you certain she simply left town?"

"I thought you weren't going to ask me personal questions."

"I didn't think that was personal. But of course it would be, because so many people thought James murdered her." Catherine fought to keep her expression unreadable. She remained silent as Dana

looked across the room. "That's a beautiful temple jar."

Catherine found Dana's swift changes
of subject unsettling. "Thank you."

"May I take a closer look?"

"Of course."

Dana rose and walked to the temple
jar. She didn't lift it, obviously with an
expert's respect for not leaving skin oil
on a piece of art. She bent over, her
glossy, precision-cut dark hair gleaming
in the sunlight, and she closely inspected
the jar. "Expensive gold veneer—not the
cheap stuff you so often see." She shifted
position. "A lovely, well-executed flower
and vine pattern." She stood up and
looked at Catherine. "You have excellent
taste."

"It was a gift."

"From James?"

"No personal questions, Dana. Remember?"

"Yes." Dana returned to the couch. "I'm
certain it didn't come from my husband.
He didn't meet you until yesterday. He
didn't know how beautiful you are."

Catherine let a beat of silence pass. "Do

you want to talk more about the possibility of you having another child?"

"Not really, although it's why I came." Dana took another cigarette from her handbag, glanced at Catherine, and tried to raise her eyebrows in her Botox-frozen forehead, and waited to light it until Catherine nodded permission. "I think my mother was born wanting children," Dana said. "She was a kindergarten teacher, a Sunday school teacher, a Girl Scout leader. She got pregnant four times and lost three of the children—two miscarriages and one stillbirth. I'm the only one that lived. What a shame, because I couldn't let her get close. I've never been able to connect to women. I was a daddy's girl, first and always. I'm not heartless, though. I care about my daughter. When I see how uninterested Ken is in her, it hurts me. I don't want to bring another little girl into the world just to watch the same thing happen."

"I certainly understand your concern."

After a moment, Dana emitted a loud bark of laughter. "As long as we're talking in the sanctity of your office where my confidences will remain, I might as well be completely honest. I'm afraid if I have another girl, Ken will leave me for a younger woman who has plenty of time to give him a son."

"Has he ever threatened to?"

"No, but I know him. He'd do it to me and to Mary without a backward glance or a touch of remorse." Her features seemed to sharpen. "And I'll tell you something else. I won't allow it. I will *never* let him leave me, because I've been obsessed with Ken Nordine since the first week I met him." Dana leaned forward and looked deep into Catherine's eyes. "I'm still obsessed with him and I will do *anything* to keep him."

CHAPTER TEN

1

"Did I tell you I'm staying at James's to-night?" Catherine asked.

"Three times," Marissa answered. "Are you going out to dinner?"

"No. A home-cooked meal tonight."

Marissa grinned. "Then I'm sure he's glad *I'm* not the one staying over."

Twenty minutes later, James arrived. Usually Catherine drove to his town house when she spent the night, but tonight James had insisted on doing the driving and Catherine was relieved. After the incident with Arcos on the front lawn, not to mention Arcos's murder during the night, Marissa would have been more comfortable if her sister were never alone.

"Come in, James," Marissa said warmly at the door. "Would you like a drink? Catherine's still gathering up a few things."

"No drink, thanks anyway." He sat down still wearing his coat and looking appallingly pale. "I don't know why Catherine won't leave more stuff at my place."

Because she's determined not to make any gestures that could be interpreted as her moving in with you, Marissa thought. "Oh, you know how organized she is," she said as an excuse. "Everything must be in the right dresser drawers—*her* dresser drawers." Marissa hoped James would get that small hint, but he looked blank.

"I'm ready!" Catherine said as she walked into the kitchen carrying an overnight bag and a bag of groceries.

Marissa smiled. "No morbid talk, no morbid thoughts, tonight. Just have fun, you two. That's an order!"

2

"I ordered pizza. Is that all right for to-night?" Marissa asked an hour later when Eric arrived.

"Absolutely not. I expected you to fix coq au vin and a chocolate mousse."

"You've lost your mind."

Eric pulled her close, kissed her slowly and passionately, then continued to hold her so tightly she could barely breathe. "My goodness, what's all this about?" Marissa gasped.

"I missed you today. I miss you every day but today in particular. I could hardly wait until I was sure James had left with Catherine before I came by."

Marissa pulled back slightly and looked at him closely. "You didn't want to talk to him about Arcos."

"No. I've already questioned him briefly and I'll have to do a more thorough job of it tomorrow, but not tonight."

"Let me guess—he didn't have an alibi for last night when Arcos was murdered."

"Home alone. No visitors, no calls on his landline phone that we've been able to trace. I haven't asked for his cell phone, but I guess I'll have to if I'm going to do a thorough job of this investigation. After all, after what Arcos had done to Catherine just hours before someone killed him . . ." Eric shook his head. "It looks bad, Marissa, especially after Renée's—"

She put a finger over his mouth. "Don't say it. We will not say the word 'murder' in this house tonight. Two people *died*—that's it."

"Two people *died* by being shot through their right eyes. Their *right* eyes, Marissa. *We* never released the information that Renée was shot in her right eye."

Marissa gave him a hard look. "Are you insinuating that I leaked that information?"

"What? No!"

"Because I wasn't the only person who saw the body on Saturday, Eric. What about other cops—"

"Robbie? Jeff Beal? Are you accusing them?"

"No!"

"And we still haven't figured out who called you this morning telling you to come to the Arcos murder scene."

"You haven't even had twelve hours to discover who it was, Eric."

"But why did someone call *you*? You didn't have anything to do with Arcos."

"I'm a reporter. Maybe they thought I'd scoop the news—"

Eric looked at her unbelievingly. "This is not a big city, Marissa. A lot of people know about our relationship. Other reporters on the *Gazette* might leak the news, but not you." He sighed. "What I'm trying to say is that Renée and Arcos were not killed the same way by coincidence. I think the same person killed each of them. And I think that person called you this morning. Hell, for all I know you were meant to arrive earlier than you did and be the killer's third victim."

"But that person isn't James Eastman. He is *not* a murderer."

"How do you know? My God, Marissa, you sound like a naïve little kid!" Eric's face tightened. "He married Renée and no matter how slutty she acted, how she humiliated him, he didn't start divorce proceedings until she'd vanished and he'd supposedly spent a whole year looking for her!"

"Supposedly?"

"Okay. I talked to the private detective

he hired who swore he worked for a full year doing everything he could to find Renée. I haven't had time to fully check this private detective's records, though. His firm has a good reputation, but . . ."

"But?"

"But maybe James paid him off *not* to find her. After all, does James's putting up with Renée's shenanigans for years sound like normal behavior? Not to me. Then she *apparently* just left one day without a word. Then, Catherine accidentally finds her—murdered—in a place James didn't think Catherine would ever go."

"Catherine found her less than a week ago. Renée had been dead for around a week, not years. Certainly not since she left James. She hadn't even been in Aurora Falls until right before she was murdered."

"That's an assumption."

"Oh, you think she's been sneaking back here? Do you have proof?"

Eric sighed. "One man told me he thought he saw her downtown on Wednesday, two days earlier than the medical examiner places her time of death. I don't put much faith in that particular guy's opinion, but a woman reported today that she'd seen Renée up close on Wednesday afternoon—the same day the man told me he'd spotted her."

"Both of them could have been mistaken."

"Yes, the man could have been, but I believe the woman. I've known her for years. She's levelheaded and not the least excitable or the type to want attention. Besides . . . well, she said she saw Renée in the Nordine Gallery. Renée made an attempt at a disguise wearing a heavy dark coat and her hair tucked under a crocheted hat like the girl wore in that movie *Twilight*—"

"That's detail for you."

"This witness was *very* detailed. It's part of what made her so convincing. Anyway, she said Renée's visit to the gallery was brief and discreet. She only looked at one thing: *Mardi Gras Lady.*"

"Oh," Marissa said faintly.

"Yeah. *Oh.* That pulled me up short, too."

"Eric, a young woman who looks a lot like Renée works at the gallery. Maybe that's who the woman saw."

"And this young woman wore a heavy coat and tucked her hair under a hat to stand looking at a portrait she sees every day?"

"Oh," Marissa said again. "I see your point."

"I'm telling you—again off-the-record— that Renée probably arrived in Aurora Falls at least two or three days before she was murdered. She made the mistake of going out in public. People saw her. Maybe James saw her. And if he did, considering how much pent-up rage he must have felt for her—"

"Don't say it."

"Then *you* stop saying James Eastman isn't capable of murder, Marissa, because maybe there's something terribly wrong with him that we know nothing about."

She clutched Eric's strong forearms. "No, there just can't be something wrong with James. My sister is deeply in love with him!"

"And that's what scares me most, Marissa. Exactly who does your sister love? The man most people think he is? Or the man he *really* is?"

3

James gave Catherine a quick squeeze and a kiss on the cheek. "That was a great dinner, sweetheart."

"Thanks. Steak, baked potato, and salad aren't exactly hard to fix. And I bought the cherry pie."

"I wonder if they serve meals like that in prison."

"You aren't going to prison," Catherine said briskly, gathering dirty dishes. "Stop talking nonsense."

"It isn't nonsense, Catherine. First Renée, then Arcos, and here I am with motives to kill both of them."

Catherine poured hot water over the plates, waited for a moment, and then said, "Maybe you had a motive to kill Renée, but you didn't have opportunity. You were at a conference in Pittsburgh when she was murdered. The medical examiner said she was probably killed late Friday or early Saturday. You were gone then."

"I also had the flu and mainly stayed in my hotel room. I wasn't visible at all times."

Catherine looked at him. "You wouldn't

have been visible at all times even without the flu unless you'd shared a room with someone—someone who never slept."

James smiled again. "Good point. I'll have to bring it up next time Eric questions me."

Catherine frowned and asked tentatively, "Eric isn't like those cops on television, is he? He doesn't take you into an interrogation room, yell at you, slam the table with his fist, and make threats."

"God, no. He's businesslike. Completely professional. Calm and even tempered." James stared ahead, his dark eyes seeming to mask dark thoughts. "He might not stay that way, though. Police treatment might become a little less civil, particularly if people keep getting murdered. But I'm whining and it's time to stop. I want to wipe all of this from my mind."

"Me, too."

"So how would you like to spend our evening?"

"Obviously not going out to visit with those nice folks on the front lawn."

"No, and we can't leave here without them plunging at us with questions or following us."

"Then I guess we'll just have to occupy ourselves inside."

"You want to watch television?"

"No. I want to listen to music."

"Fine with me." James went into the living room. Catherine opened the refrigerator, grabbed a can of beer, and followed him, watching as he began inspecting his CD collection. "I have Tchaikovsky's Ballet Suite from *The Sleeping Beauty,* Handel's *Water Music,* Delibes's *Lakmé* (I know that's one of your favorites), or—"

Catherine had pulled a CD from her tote bag. "I want this."

James took the case from her and peered at it. "Barry White!"

"Yes."

"This is Marissa's, isn't it?"

"Yes, but I want to hear it tonight."

"Catherine, *you* want 'Can't Get Enough of Your Love, Babe' and 'Never, Never Gonna Give You Up'?"

"Yes. Definitely. And we're going to dance."

"I can't dance."

"All you need to do is a little bumping and grinding. Certainly you can master that much."

James held the CD for a moment and then nearly doubled over laughing. "My sophisticated, refined Catherine who loves opera tonight wants to *bump* and *grind* to Barry White?"

"More than anything," she returned seriously. "Are you just going to sit there and laugh or are we going to get to it?"

James finally stopped laughing, wiped the tears from his face, and looked at her adoringly. "We're gonna get to it, baby!"

"From now on, I'm only listening to Barry White," James said in a soft, deep voice as he pulled Catherine's naked body closer to him under the down comforter. Catherine giggled and buried her head in a pillow. James tickled her until she came up for air. "He was *your* choice, Catherine."

"I know, but I didn't think I'd get quite so carried away with his music. Jeez! I'm embarrassed."

"Are you sure you didn't work your way through college in strip clubs? Do you have a stripper pole stashed somewhere in your house?"

"Oh yeah, with my figure I was in constant demand. I would have needed serious breast implants to even get an audition."

"You would have been if anyone saw your bumping and grinding." James ran his hands lightly over her breasts. "Besides, I hate the look of those things. Your breasts are perfect."

"You must need glasses. And my bumping and grinding was sedate."

"Not after you'd downed a few beers, darling girl."

"I guess I didn't know I have so much rhythm in me."

"*Rhythm?* Is that what they're calling it these days?" James rolled onto his back and laughed uproariously.

"Well, I had no idea you have so much rhythm, either."

"You're the only person in the world who does."

"I'm very glad about that." He began snickering again, louder and louder.

"James, you're starting to cackle."

"I'm sorry, babe. It's just that if you'd told me this afternoon that tonight I'd be lying in bed *cackling* I'd have thought you were crazy." He turned his head and kissed the top of hers, which she'd laid in the hollow below his shoulder.

"Are you going to start calling me 'babe' now?" she asked.

"Only in private. I'm also going to request more performances of that dancing."

"Only in private."

"Not the office Christmas party?"

"Definitely not." Catherine waited a beat. "Just make certain I don't drink too much at Patrice and Lawrence's wedding reception. Everyone might get a surprise when the music starts."

"I don't think Patrice has any Barry White songs planned for the musical entertainment. You're safe." James laughed again, put his hand under her chin, and tilted her head so he could look into her eyes. "I love you *so* much, Catherine."

"I love you, too. I have for years. Even when—" Catherine broke off, flushing in the shadowy bedroom. Too much beer had loosened her tongue, she thought regretfully.

"You loved me even when I married Renée?" She nodded. "After the reception, she told me you were in love with me."

"Damn. I knew she could see it."

"I didn't take her seriously. I thought she believed I was so irresistible that all women were in love with me." This time his laugh was harsh. "Irresistible. Ha! I sure wasn't good at reading her mind, was I?"

"You were young."

"I was arrogant and stupid. I didn't know the woman for me was Bernard Gray's beautiful eldest daughter, the one I thought was so painfully shy and inhibited."

Catherine began to laugh. "Tonight, Barry White and I put an end to that illusion!"

"Thank you, Barry! You and Catherine gave me the greatest show of my life."

"Barry, me, *and* beer."

"Beer never tasted so good as it did tonight."

"I bought the most expensive kind."

"There's just no holding you back when it comes to spending money, Catherine Gray. However, now I'm craving a soft drink," James said. "How about you? Can I get you a Coke? Seven Up? Tonic water?"

"Not right now, thanks. Maybe later."

James slid out of bed and into a white terry-cloth robe. "Sure you don't want another beer?" he asked, grinning.

"I'm absolutely sure, but I'd love to have a couple of aspirins."

"Hangover coming on?" James shook his head. "Pleasure has its price, Catherine."

How good hearing him snickering as he left the room, Catherine thought. His mood had certainly improved in the last four hours. She considered getting a headache from drinking too much beer had been well worth it.

Catherine shivered slightly and drew the down comforter over her. Still, she wasn't comfortable—she'd never liked sleeping naked. With a huff of exasperation, she tossed back the comforter and sheet and walked to the one dresser drawer where she kept a few items at James's. She reached for a pair of bikini panties, hurriedly pulled them on, and fumbled for one of her long-sleeved satin sleep shirts. The fragrance of her sweet, flowery cologne wafted from the drawer. Just as she withdrew a sleep shirt, though, she caught a whiff of a perfume different from her own—something faint but with a definite hint of the exotic. She drew in a deep breath and smelled mandarin and coriander.

Guided by the soft light from the bedside lamp, Catherine reached into the corner between the dresser and the chest of drawers. She retrieved two bits of delicate material—black silk tulle bikini pants and a lace-detailed baby-doll top. Her brows drew together as she focused on the La Perla label. *La Perla*? These pieces of fluff must have cost between two and three hundred dollars, Catherine thought in vague shock as she glanced under the La Perla label to find a tag reading:

La Belle Boutique
New Orleans

Shaking, she clutched the expensive nightwear that she'd never worn in her life.

CHAPTER ELEVEN

1

"Robbie and I located Renée Eastman's car, sir," Deputy Jeff Beal said as he sat across from Eric Montgomery on Wednesday morning.

Eric looked up from his paperwork. "Where?"

"In the garage of the vacant cottage to the south of the Eastman place. The lock on the manual door had been broken recently, I'd say within the last couple of weeks." Jeff shook his head. "It shouldn't have taken us so long to find it."

"Sometimes the most obvious place is the best spot to hide something," Eric said. "Sounds to me like right next door to the crime scene was a fairly clever hiding place. What did you find in it?"

"In the glove compartment was registration, car insurance documentation, car keys, and what Robbie called a 'cosmetics case' loaded with lipsticks and mascara and other whatnots women use. A couple of coats were hanging in the back. We took a quick look in the trunk and found a couple of suitcases and something Robbie called an 'urban weekender.' Looked like a big duffel bag to me. We didn't open them, of course."

"You didn't find a .22-caliber revolver in the car?"

"I would have told you that first thing, sir."

"So we still don't have the murder weapon."

"No, but the car is at Forensics now. Maybe they'll find it. It could be in one of the suitcases," Jeff added hopefully.

"Right." Eric glanced down at the papers he'd been reading. "This is the Nicolai Arcos autopsy report. He had four puncture marks on his back. They were cauterized, so they must have come from a Taser."

"So he was hit twice."

Eric nodded. "He was a big man, and from the amount of drugs in his system one hit might not have been enough. Scratches on his nose and forehead indicate he probably landed on his face. Then the murderer flipped him over and shot him through the right eye at close range. But here's the really interesting part. Ballistics show that the gun used to kill Renée Eastman wasn't the same one used to kill Arcos. The bullets don't match."

"But they were both .22s," Jeff said slowly. "You'd expect someone to use a .38 to be certain of a kill." Eric nodded again. "So someone knew Renée Eastman had been shot with a .22."

"Yes. They also knew she'd been shot in the right eye. And they found something else unusual."

"I'm almost afraid to ask," Jeff admitted.

"Arcos dressed flamboyantly—all part of the exotic-artist image according to Ken Nordine. Arcos also liked jewelry, especially a platinum hoop earring with a half-carat diamond and an heirloom tiger's-eye ring. Nordine said Arcos had other stuff, too, but those two pieces seemed to be his favorites and any jewelry he wore was expensive."

Eric continued, "When Arcos was found, he had his wallet with over two hundred dollars in it and the earring and ring—he wasn't killed during a robbery." Jeff nodded. "What I didn't tell Nordine was that Arcos was also wearing four long strings of purple metallic Mardi Gras throw beads."

"Throw beads?" Jeff echoed.

"I've never been to Mardi Gras, but I've read about it, so I did a little more research. The beads are just cheap decorations people throw off the floats to the crowds lining the streets."

"Well now, isn't that interesting," Jeff said seriously with a slightly befuddled look on his face.

"Beal, my point is that they're *cheap.* You can order five dozen from the Internet for less than ten dollars." Jeff raised his eyebrows. "I also learned that there are usually three bead colors—green, gold, and purple—that have meaning. Green is for faith. Gold is for power." Eric waited a second before saying with significance, "And purple is for *justice*."

2

Ian Blakethorne stood watching a gleaming white Learjet 45 as it taxied, accelerated, then rushed down the sixty-foot runway. It lifted off, the white of the jet contrasting with the background of a clear, cerulean blue sky and the crystalline, rainbow colors refracting through the mist of Aurora Falls. Ian closed his eyes for a moment, wondering where the jet was headed—to the Caribbean, he hoped, not knowing why. Today, he simply had a desire to visit Jamaica. Instead, he would be having lunch with his father at Blakethorne Charter Flights.

Ian walked back to the terminal. He remembered the original building, which had been small and intimate. As the business grew, his father had expanded the terminal to over twice the original size when Ian was barely twelve. He recalled preferring the old, small version, perhaps because it reminded him of what life had been like before the car wreck, when his father sometimes brought him to the airport to see an incoming or outgoing flight, then take him into the terminal to Cici's Café, where he always had a banana split.

Five years ago, his father had decided to expand the business, adding rentals of high-end recreational vehicles as well as lavish medium-to-large tour buses. Everyone had told him he was overextending himself, but the venture had taken off with a speed that seemed to astonish even Lawrence. Ian remembered his father boasting about renting buses to rock bands like the Dave Matthews Band and The Pretenders, although Lawrence had only the vaguest knowledge of their music or history. He'd only known they were rich and famous.

Shortly afterward, Lawrence had demolished the old terminal and built a new one that had impressed the locals, who said it looked like a commercial airport. It featured wide corridors, tastefully decorated waiting areas, three fast-food outlets, two casual bistros, a formal restaurant, and a myriad of stores, including drugstores, bookshops, a discount store, a luggage shop, and five bars. Lawrence Blakethorne always laughed when he recalled architects hotly telling him five bars were far too many. Years later, he could boast that they accounted for more income than all the restaurants put together.

Ian took the escalator to the second floor and strode to the wide double doors at the end leading into his father's office. Lawrence gave Ian a quick wave with one hand while holding a phone set in the other, talking loud and fast. Ian nodded, but rather than sitting down, he wandered around the office.

Naturally, his father had designed his own office, not leaving it to the more modest tastes of the architects. The room occupied the entire space at the back of the corridor. He'd picked a deep royal blue for the rich carpet that contrasted with the much lighter, steel blue walls decorated with large, beautifully framed photographs of jets, impressive twin-engine airplanes, and his own first plane: a used single-engine red and white Piper, which was still carefully maintained and sitting at the rear of a hangar. A huge mahogany desk dominated the room, with a heavy, beautiful mother-of-pearl gemstone globe mounted in gold, sitting near the left corner. It had been given to him by Patrice last Christmas. The globe's luminescent colors sparkled in the light flowing through bay windows completely covering the wall behind the desk and overlooking the runway where the Learjet had just ascended.

On the credenza sat an eighteen-inch-long mahogany model of the Bell XS-1, the first aircraft to exceed the speed of sound at Mach 1.06 on October 14, 1947. The plane had been flown by West Virginian Charles Yeager and christened *Glamorous Glennis* after Yeager's wife. Ian had given his father the model four years ago, just after Lawrence had finally met the now-retired Major General Yeager. Ian remembered with pride that Lawrence had never acted more pleased with a gift.

"It's a deal, then," Lawrence said firmly. "We'll talk about it later this evening, but right now I have an important lunch guest waiting. Good doing business with you."

Lawrence beamed at Ian. "Sorry I didn't have time to go out to lunch with you, Son," he said, hanging up the phone.

"You never go out to lunch."

"Well, I intended to make an exception today. I ordered something good brought in from one of the best terminal restaurants, though. Should be here in about twenty minutes. Have a seat. You're giving me the jitters walking around here like you've never seen my office."

"Sorry." Ian sat down in a plush chair across from his father's desk. "You look tired, Dad."

Lawrence shook his head and rubbed a spot in the middle of his forehead. "It's this damned Star Air merger. They're making it about five times harder than it needs to be. Trying to show how important they are, I guess."

"Are they that important?"

"Not as important as they think they are, but we need them." He winked. "Not that we'll let them know."

"I wasn't planning on announcing it."

Lawrence laughed. "I'm sure you weren't." His smile faded slightly. "You know, a few of our executives have expressed some worry about how quiet you are. They seem to think because you're not walking around here like a big shot, letting everyone know your old man owns Blakethorne and you'll soon officially be joining the company, you're not . . . well . . . dynamic enough."

"In other words, I'm too shy to be an asset," Ian said calmly.

"That's exactly what they mean." Lawrence leaned back in his chair and looked appraisingly at his handsome, composed son. "You want to know what I think?"

"Of course."

"I think people respond to a friendly but reserved man of intelligence who actually *listens* to them and gives them a response indicating that he's really listened, not a cliché line he's repeated ten times already that day, nor a man who is so hearty and full of practiced charm he makes your teeth hurt." Lawrence leaned forward. "You, Ian, are the first man. You are the man to whom people will respond. And you are *my* son, my heir. You are exactly the person we need to be second-in-command here at Blakethorne Charter Flights."

Ian swallowed. "Well, Dad, I'm overwhelmed."

"I'm not flattering you. I'm simply telling you that if I could have *chosen* a son, he would be you."

"That's high praise, but I'm afraid you're giving it to me because the Star people have expressed reservations about me."

"Not at all."

"Because I don't want to spoil this deal for you, Dad," Ian went on. "I know how important it is to you."

Lawrence's dark eyes narrowed, a small twitch starting beside the left one. "You're not to listen to a word of criticism from them. You don't have to be rude to them—that's not your way—but I want you to take their 'suggestions for improvement' with a grain of salt. Ignore them. This is *our* business, Ian. They're lucky we're even considering a merger, and I don't want you to forget it—not for one damned minute!"

"All right, Dad. Don't get so wound up." Ian smiled. "I'll just keep on being attentive, diplomatic, unflappable me."

"You're damned right you will! And if they don't show you the proper respect . . ."

"By God, we'll blow them off the face of the map!"

Lawrence looked startled at his son's ferocious face and then laughed when he saw Ian beginning to grin. "That's not a bad idea considering the way I'm feeling this morning. I've been on the phone all morning about the two new hangars we're building. You can get one hell of a headache from talking about hydraulic doors and lift straps and auto latches and riding arenas and—"

"Stop! You're giving *me* a headache."

Lawrence quieted abruptly and studied Ian. "You do look a little pale today." As usual, his gaze went directly to the thin scar on his son's forehead that disappeared into his dark hair. "You're not getting those headaches again, are you?"

"They started going away when I was seventeen and I haven't had a hint of one for over two years," Ian said seriously, referring to the headaches he'd suffered after the car wreck that nearly killed him when he was ten.

"That's the best news I've heard in . . ." Lawrence lifted his arms. "God, I don't know how long. You know, Sunday morning when you seemed a little off . . ."

"You thought I was losing ground. Dad, I'd just had too much to drink the night before. You know I rarely drink—I'm not used to it. Anyway, I'm sorry for being such a buzzkill at brunch."

"Well, I don't know what a *buzzkill* is, but apparently it's bad if you have to apologize for being one. I need to apologize, too. It's this damned merger that's got me going. I work at it seven days a week; I get irritable."

"I know," Ian said softly. "I understand."

"Good. Well, what I want from you now is honesty. Brutal honesty." Lawrence watched his son sit absolutely motionless, his face almost frozen. "Are you *really* okay with my marriage to Patrice?"

Ian continued to stare at his father for a moment and then smiled broadly. "Yes, Dad. I'm glad for both of you. This is way overdue."

"That's not how everyone feels."

"You mean Grandmother."

"Well, I was thinking of her in particular. I mean, she's dead, but you know how she'd react to this marriage, and the two of you were so close, you must be bothered by how she would have felt."

"I did love Grandmother, but I didn't think she was right about everything. Besides, as she would say, the dead are beyond earthly cares."

"I suppose she would." Lawrence smiled.

"She and I didn't have many religious discussions."

"She didn't have many religious discussions with anyone until she passed her seventieth birthday. Then she wanted me to start going to church with her."

"And like a good grandson, you did to please Abigail. You idolized your mother. You would have gone with her anywhere, anytime. That's what almost caused your death."

Silence spun out for a minute before Ian said quietly, "I didn't idolize Mom. Actually, I felt as if I barely knew her."

Lawrence sat bolt upright. "Son, you *did* idolize her. You spent most of your time with her. You read stories to each other, you played games together—"

"No, we didn't. And it's not just that I forgot about those things after the accident. They never happened."

"But your grandmother said—"

"Grandmother said that's what life was like for Mom and me. Did Patrice ever say so?"

"No, but then I never questioned her about what went on in our house. She had her own life. She wasn't around constantly."

"Well, sometimes Mom went flying around the house, cleaning although we had people to do that. Or she'd get all wound up about how the grounds looked and plant more flowers—*lots* of flowers, When I got older, she spent most of her time in her room, lying down, or listening to music, or staring in the mirror or out of the window. In the summer, she sat at her fishpond in the hedges, reading or smoking cigarettes. When I tried to talk to her, she hardly answered.. She didn't ask what I'd been up to or if I was behaving myself or even get mad at me for doing something I knew I shouldn't have done. You see, sometimes I'd test her, just to see if I could make her angry. But I couldn't. I didn't have many friends, but she didn't act at all like their mothers did." Ian's blue-gray gaze grew troubled. "Was it me? Was I a disappointment to her?"

Lawrence slowly shook his head, picked up a gold pen, and began turning it nervously between his strong fingers. "I've never told you this, but your mother had a form of what they call bipolar disorder now. Back then, medications weren't as effective at treating it."

"She had bipolar disorder?" Lawrence nodded. "But I don't remember her ever being in a hospital or going away to rehab."

"As I said, Abigail's case wasn't serious." Lawrence halted. "Well, I'll just be honest. Your grandmother wouldn't hear of her being sent away, even to a rehab facility for a few weeks."

"She was ashamed of Mom?" Ian asked in angry dismay.

"No! Not at all. She just thought of Abigail's problem as being an illness, not a condition that could easily be treated by drugs. Your grandmother adored Abigail. I think she was terrified of hearing that there was something seriously wrong with her mind, something that doctors couldn't cure, something that would only get worse with age." Lawrence looked down at his desk. "I should have told you long ago. *I* should have done something, in spite of what Abigail's mother thought." Lawrence dropped his pen, reached for it but couldn't seem to close his hand around its narrow length. He ignored it and looked at Ian. "I'm sorry, Son. I didn't know how much Abigail shut you out of her life."

"You were never home to see it," Ian

said without reproach. "You left early in the mornings and didn't come home when most of the other dads did. You were always working."

Lawrence held his son's gaze. "I started this place from nothing. I devoted myself to Blakethorne Charter."

"Grandmother always told me your parents were poor." Ian hesitated. "She told me you married Mom for her money."

"Goddammit!" Lawrence shouted. "I knew she told other people that, but to fill my own son's head with that crap was unforgivable! That woman—" Lawrence broke off, his tanned face suffused with fury.

"She said your only attraction to my mother was the money Grandfather had left her when he died."

"Well, I hope I don't have to tell you that's not true. Your mother was gentle, kind, warmhearted, and beautiful in that pale, delicate way of hers." He finally managed a grin. "She even passed on her most beautiful feature to her son, Dreamy Eyes."

Ian rolled his long-lashed blue-gray eyes. "Please don't tell me you started that nickname."

"Me? You think I'd call my *son* Dreamy

Eyes?" Lawrence scoffed. "Blame that one on the little girl in rehab that had a crush on you. The nurses picked it up and it went around town."

Ian laughed. "I remember that girl. Mostly I remember Catherine Gray, though. I had a crush on her."

"I remember."

"She was working in the rehabilitation unit that summer—volunteering," Ian said almost idly. "She spent so much time with me. *She's* the one who read with me and played games with me." He laughed. "We even watched soap operas together. And she didn't forget me after I went home. She visited me every two or three weeks for the next year. After she went to school in California, she always stopped by when she was home on holidays."

"Good lord, Son, you sound like you're in love with her."

Ian's gaze grew more alert. "Do I?" He smiled. "Catherine's just a great person. I wish she hadn't gotten involved with James Eastman."

"A lot of people think *he's* a great person. At least they did until he got involved with that trash."

"Renée?"

"Who else? You met her."

"She was nice to me."

"Oh God, Ian, you look at the world through rose-colored glasses. Of course she was nice to you—you're handsome and young. You didn't have much contact with her, though, and you're not a gossip. Take my word for it—she was beautiful and charming and a whore. I don't know why James didn't divorce her within the first year of their marriage. What a fool he was when it came to Renée! Even your grandmother, who thought the Eastmans walked on water, lost respect for him."

"Well, that must have been a blow to him," Ian said sarcastically. "Dad, did Patrice resent that Grandmother left all of her money to me and none to her? You can be honest. Don't try to shield my feelings."

Lawrence stared at Ian, his dark gaze candid. "No, Son, I can honestly say that your inheritance didn't bother Patrice. I would know if it had." He tapped his fingers on the table. His parents had been excellent business partners. They had made a great deal of money together and his father decided, maybe urged by his mother, that he wanted to leave most of his fortune to Abigail. "Your mother was gentle and frail. I also think your grandfather knew she wasn't emotionally stable. He didn't want her to have the pressures of a career, but he did want her to be very comfortable. He'd already died and when I met her she was a wealthy woman, but she had no goals in life except being a wife and mother.

"Patrice was different," Lawrence went on. "Even when I met her when she was thirteen, she was driven. Her father left her a very generous trust, which she used wisely for law school and investments of her own. After your grandfather's death, your grandmother continued successfully with her own business ventures.

"She told Patrice she intended to leave her fortune to you—not to both of you. Patrice always suspected this was because of the accident that almost killed you. No one could convince your grandmother that you'd completely recovered. She wanted you to have a substantial nest egg in case your health failed because of your injuries. Patrice learned to accept her mother's peculiarities a long time ago. She didn't resent the inheritance being left solely to you. She was doing fine on her own. Besides, now she's marrying me. She'll never have to worry about money."

"I'm glad. It's bothered me, but I was afraid if I asked her, she'd . . . well . . ."

"Lie to you to make you feel better?" Ian nodded. "She would have told you being left out of the will didn't bother her, but she wouldn't have been lying."

"I feel so much better."

"I wish I'd known you were worried. I could have put your mind at ease." Lawrence smiled easily. "Anyway, since your grandmother's will was probated a couple of months ago, you'll have your own money to invest in *our* business. You'll be my partner, legally and financially, so unless you have doubts or unhappiness about my marrying Patrice, I'd say this situation is just about perfect."

"I guess it is," Ian agreed.

"You *guess*? Is something troubling you, Son?"

"Only that I promised Grandmother I wouldn't invest my inheritance in Blakethorne Charter." Ian waited a moment and then shook his head. "But Grandmother didn't always know what was best. And as *she* herself said, the dead are beyond earthly cares."

3

"Good afternoon. Nordine Gallery. May I help you?"

"Bridget, it's Mrs. Nordine. I need to speak to Mr. Nordine."

"Oh, *Dana*!" The twenty-six-year-old manager could not see Dana Nordine's grimace at Bridget's use of her first name. "You sound so tense that I hardly recognized your voice."

"I really need to speak with my husband."

"Oh well, we had to open early and we're packed with people wanting to see Nicolai Arcos's work. You know how the value of an artist's work soars after his death."

"Yes, I know that, Bridget."

"And Arcos was *murdered*!" Bridget Fenmore's excitement resonated loudly before she seemed to come to herself. "I mean, it's awful. I didn't know him very well, but he was young and talented and . . . well, what happened to him is just terrible!"

"Yes, it was. Everyone is shocked." And some people are elated, Dana thought. "Bridget, I need to speak to Mr. Nordine."

"Well, Ken's talking with some customers right now. I don't think he wants to be interrupted. Could I have him call you back?"

Dana tried to make herself sound halfway pleasant. "I'm at the hospital with our daughter. She's very sick. She needs to be admitted and I want to speak to my husband."

"Mary's sick? What's wrong?"

Dana fought to hold on to her patience. "I don't have a definitive diagnosis yet, but I will in a few minutes. Please get Ken."

"He's talking with Mr. and Mrs. Addison and I think he's just about to make a sale."

"Ken can explain to the mayor and his wife that his daughter is very ill—which she is—he needs to speak to his wife, and he'll get back to them as soon as possible. In the meantime, you take over. After all, technically you *are* the business manager of the gallery, not just a glorified receptionist."

"Of course I'm not a glorified receptionist!" Bridget returned hotly, just as Dana had known she would. Bridget Fenmore made certain everyone knew the importance of her position at the Nordine Gallery. "It's just that Ken told me not to disturb him for *anything,* especially when he looks like he's getting close to making a sizable sale."

Dana's small bit of remaining patience snapped. "Bridget, I have the Addison's cell-phone number in my directory. I will call them, explain that our daughter is sick, tell them that Ken knew she was ill when I took her to the doctor's earlier, and that we are now at the hospital waiting for him. I'll also include the information that Ken has asked not to be bothered for *anything* if he thinks he has a couple of fish on the line."

Dana smiled tightly in satisfaction at Bridget's gasp at her crude reference to the mayor and his wife, potential buyers, as "fish on the line." "The Addisons would be horrified to think Ken would put selling a painting before his own child's health," Dana continued. "I guarantee, Bridget, *that* information would quash any sales from them and also that Evelyn Addison will spread the news over half of Aurora Falls by bedtime, in which case I wouldn't expect the gallery to be packed tomorrow."

"You needn't make threats, Dana," Bridget answered sharply.

"It seems that I must. Now, get Mr. Nordine. Immediately."

Dana heard the phone handset thump down on a desktop before Bridget muttered, "God, what a bitch! No wonder he gets so pissed off. . . ."

Idiot, Dana thought savagely. But Bridget had a voluptuous body, large dark brown eyes, and long, thick, near-black hair, unlike Dana's light ash brown that for years she'd been dying as close to Renée's shade as possible. Bridget looked like Renée—not quite as beautiful, but close. If Dana had not been gone the day Bridget Fenmore applied for the manager job, the young woman would have been out the door before Ken ever got a look at her. Unfortunately, Ken had hired Bridget two months ago and he looked at her frequently—far too frequently. And he intended to keep her as an employee until . . . Dana closed her eyes. Until when?

"What do you want?" Ken asked abruptly.

Dana took a deep breath. "I want to tell you that the pediatrician sent Mary to the hospital."

"Why?"

"Why? Ken, don't you remember how bad she felt this morning?"

"No, not really," he said vaguely.

"She barely ate and she said her stomach hurt. We sent her to school anyway. They called me two hours ago saying Mary was really in pain and feverish. The pediatrician saw her immediately and sent me directly to the hospital. He thinks she has appendicitis."

"Appendicitis!"

"Yes, Ken. She told me her tummy has hurt since the middle of the night. If this has been going on for a while, there's a danger of her appendix rupturing, so she'll need an appendectomy soon. You have to meet me here now."

"At the hospital?" Ken asked distractedly. "You want me to come to the hospital *now*?"

"Of course *now*."

"Dana, people were lined up outside the gallery at ten this morning because of the Arcos exhibit. This place is full of people. I can't leave now. Besides, you have all the insurance information and her birth certificate and—"

"What would I need her birth certificate for?"

"I don't know." He spoke away from the phone, telling someone he'd be with them in just an instant. "Dana, Bridget and I are too busy to even think straight. This is the biggest day we've ever had. You can handle this thing with Mary. I don't know why you're even calling me. You and Dr. What's-his-name know more about Mary's condition than I do. Besides, he's such an alarmist—she's probably just fine. The other doctors will see that and there won't even be an operation. Anyway, I'm busy as hell, so get a handle on things and get back here as soon as possible. I need you."

"Oh, you need me, do you?"

"Sure I do. I told you we're crowded as hell. I tell you, I can get double, maybe even triple the asking price for some of Arcos's work." He muttered to someone else again and then spoke distractedly to Dana. "Give Mary a kiss for me. Get back soon. I tell you, Dana, this is *the* great time for me!"

For you, Dana thought furiously after he'd hung up. Not for Mary, not for me. For *you*. He used to think when he married a woman from a well-heeled background, that had been great for him. Since he'd bought the rights to all of Arcos's work, though, *now* had become the great time for him—maybe the greatest.

Dana looked blindly down the busy hospital hall, her gaze hardening as her mind focused on the handsome, self-involved, unethical man to whom she'd given so much for so long. She didn't even realize she spoke her single thought aloud: "Well, Ken Nordine, we'll just see how long your latest great time lasts."

CHAPTER TWELVE

1

Black silk tulle and lace. La Perla. Opium perfume. She'd discovered the perfume was Opium. . . .

"Dr. Gray, are you even listening to me?"

"Of course I am."

"Because if I'm *boring* you, I can just leave!"

"You're not boring me, Mrs. Tate," Catherine said patiently.

"I know this is Wednesday and I just saw you on Monday," Mrs. Tate went on with embarrassed irritability, "but I thought you'd want to hear this news as soon as possible." She gave Catherine a hard look. "*If* you're interested, that is!"

"I'm very interested."

"You don't act like it. You're not saying much of anything."

"Mrs. Tate, how can I react when you haven't told me your news?" Catherine heard the edge in her voice and tried to look fascinated. "Please tell me what's happened to upset you so much this afternoon."

"My husband—I caught him in the act!" the woman announced triumphantly.

Catherine blinked at her, wondering how she could sound elated at this news. "You caught him having sex with his secretary?"

Mrs. Tate scowled. "Having sex? No! Having lunch!"

"They were having lunch together?"

"In his office. Just the two of them. With *wine*!" She made the wine sound like a third guest. "What more proof would I need?"

"Did they have a whole bottle of wine?" Catherine asked, feeling stupid but at a loss for anything intelligent to say to this earth-shattering news.

"Well, not sitting there on the desk. But

they had full glasses. Fancy glasses, not those cheap tumblers we have at home. I'll bet those glasses were real crystal he keeps hidden away for their secret meals." Mrs. Tate squirmed on the couch and Catherine briefly worried that the woman's glee might cause her to lose control and have an accident. "Oh, I've got him now!"

"What did they say when you walked in on them?" Catherine asked.

"They said 'hello' normal as can be and asked me if I'd like a glass of apple juice."

"Apple juice?"

"They were trying to fool me. I can certainly see the difference between apple juice and a fine white wine!" Mrs. Tate peered at her. "Can't you?"

"Well, maybe, in the right light . . ."

"Maybe? A lady like you? You'd damned well know the difference. They couldn't fool you. And they couldn't fool me, either! I'm no country hick that doesn't know anything about wine and such and can be outfoxed by the likes of them!" Mrs. Tate gleamed at her perceptiveness. "You would have been proud of me, Dr. Gray. I stayed cool as a cucumber. I acted casual and I was pleasant and . . ."

While Mrs. Tate rattled on about her astonishingly polished performance in front of the damning evidence of her husband having a sandwich lunch with his secretary, Catherine's mind wandered back to last night. When James had returned from the kitchen with drinks and aspirins, Catherine had sat rigid on the bed.

"This is Renée's," she'd accused, holding out the black baby-doll night set to an amazed James. "It's La Perla. Do you know how expensive La Perla lingerie is? Well, I do. This little number must have cost hundreds of dollars. *And* it smells like Opium perfume. Opium. I remember that once Renée said she only wore Opium. Perfume, not cologne. I found the lingerie in the corner between your dresser and chest of drawers."

"Then it isn't Renée's," James said firmly. "It can't be Renée's."

"It belongs to another woman?"

"Of course not!" James walked toward her, gazing at the lingerie set as if it were a poisonous snake. "The only other woman who's been here since I moved in is you."

"Renée bragged to someone I know that she only wore La Perla lingerie. And the tag inside says it's from New Orleans. Did you sleep with *her* week before last?" Catherine asked furiously.

James had looked indignant. "Catherine! How could you even *think*—" James broke into near laughter, making her angrier. "This is ridiculous!"

"Oh?" She held up the lingerie again. "Is *this* ridiculous?"

"I don't know how that got here! Where did you find it?"

"On the floor in the corner between the dresser and the chest of drawers."

James stalked toward the spot and peered down into the shadows. "Here?"

"Yes."

"Why would *that*"—he gestured toward the lingerie—"be lying in this corner?"

"Uh, let's see. A woman dropped it?"

"I see. No doubt it was the woman who cleans this place once a week."

"James Eastman, if you *dare* start making jokes I will leave right this minute."

"In what? Your nightshirt?"

Catherine looked at the delicate, expensive La Perla lingerie, then her own knee-length, long-sleeved nightshirt and burst into tears.

In an instant, James sat down beside her, holding her tightly. "Catherine, darling girl, what are you thinking?"

"I'm thinking what any woman would be thinking." Catherine snuffled. "I know I'm not oozing with sex appeal like Renée, but to think that you'd turn to her the minute she comes back to town is just . . . is just . . ."

James held her away from him, his expression darkening. "What the hell are you saying?"

"That she let you know when she came back to Aurora Falls. That you must have—"

"That I must have what? Invited her here and gone to bed with that tramp that almost ruined my life? Is that what you think of me?"

"Well, no, but you have to admit that the evidence is fairly damning."

"*The* evidence? Some kind of skimpy nightgown lying in a corner of my bedroom is evidence that I slept with my ex-wife? And what makes you so sure it's hers?"

"Oh, there have been other women?"

James grimaced. "I swear, I'm going to shake you if you don't stop accusing me of being with other women," he said with a shade of amused exasperation in his voice. "How could you think I'd even *look* at another woman when I have you? You're smart, and tender, and kind, and generous, and funny, and beautiful, and—" He broke off and drew a deep breath. "Have you been suspecting me of making love, or even just having sex, with other women?"

"Well . . ." Catherine sniffled. "No."

"You haven't wondered if I might be tempted to have sex with another woman?"

"I never thought about it. Does that sound egotistical?"

James looked at her intensely, then smiled and kissed her forehead. "No. It sounds like the woman who knows I love her more than anyone in the world—the woman who knows I would *never* intentionally jeopardize our relationship. Doing such a thing would never cross my mind."

Catherine was so touched by his words, she lowered her gaze. "Then I'm sorry I suspected you, even for a moment. I don't know what made me fly off the handle like that."

"Love," James said softly. "Love isn't casual, Catherine, and people in love don't take each other for granted. Occasionally their passion makes them jump to conclusions." He paused as if thinking. "My God, I don't think I've ever sounded so pompous in my life."

Catherine grinned. "That's all right. We're both emotional right now."

"Pronouncements on the nature of love aside, though, what makes you so certain that night-thing belongs to Renée?"

"It's the kind of *night-thing* she would wear. And I told you, it was bought at a shop in New Orleans. It smells of her favorite perfume and the perfume isn't stale and old. It could be leftover from a couple of weeks ago when she was in Aurora Falls."

James finally took the lingerie in his hands and held it to his nose. Then he nodded. "I remember this perfume. Frankly, I was never crazy about it, but Renée loved it. You're right, though. I'm not a perfume expert, but I can tell this scent isn't old. It's not fresh, like what you put on every day, but it's not old, either." His eyebrows drew together. "Catherine, the lady who cleans this place is meticulous. She's worked for me for five, maybe six years. She was here last week and if she'd found it—which she would have—she would have left it on the bed. This thing was *not* in the corner of my bedroom last week."

"Then . . ."

"Then someone planted it here," James said easily, his voice calm. "Someone broke into the town house and left this for one of us to find."

Catherine came back to the present with a jolt. It was mid-afternoon the next day and she was in her office listening to Mrs. Tate grow loud with pride as she recounted a nonstop narrative of today's events.

"I sat there like a lady through the rest of their *lunch.* I kept thinking how proud you'd be of me for throwing such a scare into them without saying *one mean word,* and it's all because of you. I did what I thought you'd want me to do, Dr. Gray." Mrs. Tate was beaming at Catherine. Then her smile wavered slightly. "You are proud of me, aren't you?"

I haven't heard a word the woman said for the last ten minutes, Catherine thought, feeling regret and shame. Mrs. Tate's situation could have degenerated into one of chaos, even violence. Instead, the woman had held on to her feelings and acted reasonably because of *her* influence. Wasn't that the effect she'd hoped to have on her patients? And here she was, thinking about her problems with James and not even listening to Mrs. Tate's drama.

"I think you acted wisely."

Catherine realized her voice was flat, her praise tepid. The woman looked understandably disappointed. Catherine knew it was vitally important for her to encourage more of this moderate, reasonable behavior on her patient's part, and she'd just failed badly. Determined immediately to correct her mistake, she threw at Mrs. Tate a gleaming smile. "In fact, I think you did wonderfully!"

2

"Someone left a present at my town house."

James opened his briefcase, removed a clear, sealed plastic bag, and leaned forward to lay it on Eric Montgomery's desk. Eric picked up the clear ziplock bag, looking closely at its folded contents. "What is it?"

"A sexy nightie."

"A nightie? A little kid's sleeper?"

"Hell, no!" James said hotly. "You can see that it's black and I said it was sexy!" He glared at Eric and then relaxed slightly. "You were joking."

"Just a little. I was trying to calm you down, James. You're talking so loud everyone can hear you, even though my office door is closed. Also, you look like you want to hit someone."

"I do. Catherine found it."

"Bummer."

"Is that cop lingo?"

"It is at this moment, particularly since you described the outfit as 'sexy.' By the way, Marissa calls this kind of thing 'lingerie.' I'm glad you put it in that ziplock bag so we didn't lose any trace evidence. Can you describe it?"

"It's black, as you can see. There are bikini underpants and what Catherine called a baby-doll top—both pieces transparent. The brand is La Perla, which she also told me is very expensive. I already knew that, although I didn't tell her. You see, Renée had some La Perla lingerie. Also, it has a tag with the name of a store in New Orleans. It smells like the perfume

Renée used to wear. Opium. I bought so many bottles of it for her I'll never forget the name. The smell isn't fresh, like it was just put on a day or two ago, but it isn't stale and musty, either." James looked earnestly at Eric. "Did you find this in the cottage?"

"I haven't publicly released information about what we found in the cottage, but I'll tell only you—please don't spread around the news yet—that we found Renée's car in the garage of another cottage. There were suitcases in the trunk. This thing could have been in one of those suitcases."

"Don't you have a list of what was in the suitcases?"

Eric looked at James for a moment and then said slowly, "Yes, but it's filed away. I'll look it over later, but I think you're right. I remember a few pieces of sexy lingerie were found, and although the guys who did the forensics work on the car said everything smelled like perfume, it was Robbie who came out for a look at the suitcase contents, took one whiff, and immediately said, 'That's Opium by Yves Saint Laurent.'"

"These women really know their perfumes."

Eric smiled. "Well, some of them. My mother has worn one scent my whole life. I don't think she knows anything else exists." His smile disappeared. "Where did Catherine find this?"

"In my bedroom. It's small. The dresser is against one wall, the chest of drawers against the other, but there's a corner space between them. The nightie was lying in the corner."

"And Catherine just happened to look in that corner?"

"Catherine will only keep one dresser drawer with a few things in it at my town house. That drawer is right beside the corner. I guess she was looking for something in it, smelled the perfume, and looked into the corner."

"Ohhh," Eric said slowly. "Only *one* drawer and it happens to be beside that corner?" James nodded. "Then I'd say whoever put this 'gift' in the corner had gone through all the drawers and seen that one contained Catherine's things—one right next to that corner, where she could hardly miss either seeing it or catching the scent."

"My God, you're right," James said slowly. "We ate at my place, but we didn't get there until around six thirty. We were getting ready for bed around ten—early for us, but we were both tired. That means someone could have been in the town house as late as five thirty or six. It's already dark by then." James frowned. "But who knew Catherine was going to stay at my place Tuesday night?"

Eric shrugged. "Can you think of anyone you told?"

"No. I don't remember telling anyone. It's not the kind of thing I broadcast."

"Maybe Catherine mentioned it to someone. I'll ask her." Eric picked up a pencil, then laid it down. "I assume you've checked your locks."

"This morning I looked and saw no sign of a break-in, but then I'm not an expert. I called a locksmith to change the locks by early this afternoon."

"Good. I'd like for our forensics people to go over the place before the locksmith comes, though." James nodded. "I wish we had a team like the ones on television."

James grinned. "I doubt if there are *any* teams like the ones on television. They're magicians. In real life, test results don't come back within a couple of hours.

Criminalists don't interrogate 'persons of interest' and they sure as hell don't make arrests."

"But that's what a lot of the general public has come to expect of police departments and people think we're being lazy or don't know our jobs just because we can't work the miracles they see on TV. Oh well." Eric suddenly gave James a penetrating look. "You said Renée wore this Pearl—La Perla lingerie and that this piece came from a shop in New Orleans. Was it familiar to you? Do you remember her ever wearing it?"

James's cheeks colored. "I don't know. I don't really pay attention to stuff like that. . . ." Eric's sharp gaze remained fixed. "Okay. I recall something that looked like it. She's been gone a long time. We stopped sleeping together months before she left, but . . . well, I remember her catching her engagement ring on it and it made a little tear in the lace at the top. It was hardly noticeable, but she got so upset . . . otherwise it wouldn't stick in my mind. So many of those lace and satin or chiffon or whatever things look alike, you know." Eric's stare could have pierced stone and James sighed in defeat. "Yeah, Eric, it has the tear. I remember the damned thing all too well."

Eric nodded and said in a slow, cynical tone, "Then I guess if we go with the theory that it was planted, we just have to figure out who got hold of a piece of Renée's lingerie and sprayed it with her favorite cologne several days ago so it wouldn't smell too fresh. No problem."

CHAPTER THIRTEEN

1

"Well, well, how's my little girl tonight?" A dashing Ken Nordine sailed into the room, rushing to Mary and presenting her with droopy-petaled carnations cradled in a petite, round plastic vase. "I've been *so* worried about you!"

So worried you haven't called all day? Dana wondered furiously. She almost burst out with a scathing remark about his vast concern when she saw Mary smiling as she delightedly reached small hands for the flower arrangement. Then Dana saw

Bridget Fenmore—glowing, svelte, perfectly made up and coiffed—gliding close behind Ken. Dana wore only lotion on her dry face, and she hadn't even combed her hair for hours.

"Look who I've brought with me!" Ken continued to boom, ignoring Dana. "Bridget! She just wouldn't let me come see you without bringing her. She's been worried, too!"

I'll bet, Dana fumed as Bridget kissed Mary's pale cheek, then giggled as she wiped away lip gloss. "Why, you look beautiful, Mary! Not like you've been sick at all!"

"She almost died," Dana snapped.

It was a lie. Mary looked at her mother, horrified, and Dana could have bitten off her tongue. "I mean, if we hadn't gotten her to the hospital in time. The operation went just fine, though. The doctor is very pleased." She smiled at her five-year-old daughter, who still clutched the pitifully small collection of carnations. Dana raced on. "The doctor said she's making a miraculous recovery. She'll be good as new in no time. *Better* than new! She'll be perfect! Not that she wasn't always perfect. Why, she's just—"

Everyone stared at Dana in shocked expectancy, obviously wondering what would come out of her mouth next. But Dana had no words left. She'd stayed at the hospital all night, sleeping fitfully in the uncomfortable chair in Mary's room, frequently awakening to gaze at the delicate five-year-old she'd so often pushed aside, overlooked, occasionally resented in her desperation for the freedom to always keep an eye on her husband, whom she'd made the most important person in her life.

Ken Nordine—what a fool she'd been to sacrifice herself and her daughter for a man like him, Dana had thought in belated comprehension as the shadows of the seemingly endless night had surrounded her. Her sweet, innocent, defenseless daughter should have been her focus, her cherished reason for living, not an uncaring egomaniac like Ken.

Dana realized Ken and Bridget were still staring at her and she could have kissed Mary, who announced importantly, "I got more flowers! The blue . . . blue . . ." She looked at her mother.

"Irises," Dana supplied.

"The blue irises are from my teacher.

The orange tulips are from Grandma and Grandpa 'cause pun'kins are orange and Halloween's almost here. All the yellow roses are from my real boyfriend, even though he doesn't know he's my boyfriend. He visited me today." Mary's voice softened. "He's lots older than me but real handsome. He has dark hair like Prince Charming in my fairy-tale book. That's what I call him."

"Who is this Prince Charming?" Ken asked.

"He's a secret." Mary grinned.

Ken looked at Dana, who innocently lifted her shoulders. "I was down the hall talking to the doctor. I missed the Prince's visit."

Ken walked over and looked at the card on the roses, reading aloud, "'To my very brave girl. P.C.'"

"'P. C.' is for 'Prince Charming,'" Mary explained, beginning to look wary.

"What would *I* call him?" Ken asked cannily.

"Not Prince Charming. I'm not sayin' what you'd call him. Then you'd know who he is and he's my *secret* boyfriend. No one else can know."

"Did he tell you he's your boyfriend and to keep him a secret?"

"No, Daddy. *I* decided he's my boy-friend."

He's trying to play the concerned father in front of Bridget, Dana thought. Normally, he wouldn't even be listening to Mary.

"Oh. Are you sure he doesn't know he's your *older* boyfriend?"

"I'm sure. I didn't tell him." Dana could tell Mary sensed something different about her father tonight. "I didn't tell him 'cause I can have a secret if I want to." Her smile had disappeared and her voice had turned truculent. She'd been in some pain, found confinement in the hospital frightening, and overall had had a fretful day. This eve-ning, though, the child had calmed. Ten minutes ago, she'd been serene, even drowsy. Ken had ruined her evening, Dana thought with a wave of anger.

"Ken, it doesn't matter. Quit badgering her."

Mary, obviously sensing another argu-ment brewing between her parents, soft-ened her tone and tried smiling at Ken. "He's real, real nice, Daddy. You like him—"

"So I know him."

"Yeah."

Dana glared at Ken. "I said to stop it! What are you so worked up about, anyway?"

"I don't like my own child keeping secrets from me."

Dana stood up. "Soften your tone. You're upsetting Mary."

"Yeah, you're upsetting me," Mary said in her mother's same tone of voice, rallying at the sight of her father's defeat. "And my grown-up boyfriend is nice. And he must love me, too, 'cause Mommy said roses are real 'spensive. *And* yellow is my favorite color." She looked defiantly at her father. "I'm going to marry him."

"Is that so?"

Mary suddenly began to look uncertain as her father scowled at her. Dana realized the child's defiance had been temporary. "I think maybe you're just mad 'cause I said yellow is my favorite color, and it is . . ."—her little hands tightened on Ken's offering—"except for pink!" she exclaimed, looking with inspiration at her carnations. "Really, pink is my very, very favorite color, Daddy. Oh, thank you so much for the flowers!"

He relented and gave her a small smile. "That's why Bridget got pink flowers. I knew pink was your favorite color, sugar pie."

You did not, Dana thought, barely able to contain her herself. You only bought the pink carnations because they're wilting and they were cheap.

Ken leaned over and ruffled his daughter's blond bangs. "Later you can tell me who Prince Charming is or you'll hurt my feelings. You don't want to hurt my feelings, do you?"

"No," Mary said reluctantly. "But I made a promise."

"Sometimes promises are made to be broken."

Dana glowered at Ken, but his gaze was locked on Bridget, who sat down on the bed and patted Mary's shoulder. "Such a little angel," she said fondly, then glanced at Dana. "Haven't I always said she looked just like a little angel?"

"Not to me. Besides, how would *you* know what an angel looks like?" Dana snapped, once again horrified by her lack of control.

Bridget, however, paid no attention to her. She peered deep into Mary's eyes. "*I* know what they look like because I saw one when I was a little girl just about your age. The angel was in church. She had long, blond hair just like yours and big blue eyes like yours and freckles on her nose just like yours. She floated above the congregation, sprinkling blessings and angel dust on all of us."

Oh God, Dana thought in disgust, but Mary was enchanted. "Really, Bridget? Did you really see an angel?"

"Would I tell you I had if I hadn't?" Bridget asked, all wide-eyed and sweet voiced.

Dana rolled her eyes, but only Ken saw her before he turned his attention back to his daughter. "Isn't that wonderful, Mary? Bridget saw an angel that looked just like you." He gave Dana a long, cold stare. "I'm sure Mommy *never* saw an angel."

"Did you, Mommy?" Mary asked. "Did you ever see an angel?"

"No," Dana said flatly. "I don't hallucinate."

Mary looked puzzled. "Huh? Hal . . . hal—"

"Well, visiting hours are over," Ken interrupted, managing to sound regretful.

"Not for an hour," Dana pointed out.

Ken didn't even glance at her but kept

his electric blue eyes on Mary. "You need to get rest, honey. That's what the doctor would say. Besides, Bridget and I had a very hard day. That's why we closed the gallery early. We have to rest and get ready for tomorrow." He leaned down and once again barely brushed a kiss on Mary's forehead. "See ya later, alligator!"

"After while, crocatile," Mary answered as always.

Ken barely glanced at Dana. "G'night."

"Good night, *Mrs*. Nordine. It was lovely to see you," Bridget simpered, looking as if she might curtsy.

For nearly five minutes Mary chattered about her carnations, how handsome and nice Daddy was, how pretty and nice Bridget was, how nice it was to have so much comp'ny, and wondering if she'd have a *huge* scar from her operation. If she did, maybe she could show it at school, even if it was on her tummy. Meanwhile, Dana sat staring fixedly at the doorway through which Ken and Bridget had vanished, wondering what they were doing, what they were saying. Dana was certain they weren't discussing Mary's health.

Finally, a nurse shook her shoulder. "Mrs.

Nordine? Did you go to sleep with your eyes open?"

Dana looked up into the middle-aged nurse's gentle brown eyes. "I think so," she lied again. "I guess I'm tired."

"Well, you certainly are, dear." The nurse smiled at her. "You've been here since yesterday afternoon—over twenty-four hours! You must be exhausted. Mary is doing just fine, so why don't you go home?" She looked at Mary. "You don't mind if your mommy leaves you tonight, do you? I'll be here watching over you."

"Like my guardian angel?"

You're more like an angel than Bridget's version of one, Dana thought before she asked Mary, "You won't be scared if Mommy leaves, will you?"

Mary shook her head vehemently. "My guardian angel is here. She'll prob'ly glow in the dark so I won't be scared."

"Please, Mrs. Nordine," the nurse almost implored. "It's twenty till eight and you look ready to collapse, no offense intended. You should have some decent food, watch a little television, and go to bed. You'll have to get your little one out of this place and settled back in her own bedroom at home. Then she'll need lots of love and attention." She frowned and said rather insistently, "You really do need to leave, dear."

Dana thought of her husband and Bridget Fenmore sailing out of the room looking like they were ready for a photo shoot, both astonishingly attractive, both full of smiles and good cheer, both acting almost as if they had a shared secret. "You're right," Dana said, standing up determinedly. "I really *do* need to leave."

2

"I'm so glad we came here tonight," Catherine said, looking around at the warm interior of the Reddick restaurant. The knotty-pine walls, amber lighting, large tables decorated with fat yellow candles glowing in hurricane glasses, and soft rock music playing in the background gave Catherine a cozy, comfortable feeling. "I know I'm being wise, staying inside and under the eye of the surveillance patrolmen Eric assigned to me, but it's driving me nuts," she said. "Besides, we haven't eaten here for months. I'd forgotten how much I like the place."

"Me, too. Especially the food." He looked down at his empty plate, "Do you realize how much lasagna I ate?"

"Why, no, I didn't notice," Catherine said innocently. "Or how much bread or the *two* large pieces of cheesecake with strawberry sauce."

"Did you happen to calculate the amount of cholesterol I consumed?"

"About enough for a whole week."

"Well, you're running a close second."

"I don't care. I wouldn't mind putting on ten pounds. More."

James smiled. "Neither would I. Let's get old and fat together."

"That would suit me just fine," Catherine said airily, trying not to place too much importance on his use of the word "together."

"More coffee?" a handsome young waiter asked.

Neither of them had noticed him approaching the table. Catherine looked at James. "Is it too late?"

"No, I'm beginning to relax for the first time today. I'd love another cup." He glanced at the waiter. "It'll have to be decaffein-ated at this hour, though. Do you have any made?"

"The owner and his wife always brew a pot an hour before we close." He smiled. "That's their bedtime drink of choice. There's plenty."

"Then I'll have a cup, too," Catherine said.

The waiter looked at James and asked seriously, "Another piece of cheesecake, sir? We have *one* left."

"Ha, ha," James said dourly, although Catherine could tell he was amused. "I'll have to report that sarcasm to the owner. He'll probably fire you."

"I don't think so," the waiter replied blithely. "He's my father. Be right back with that coffee."

Catherine broke into giggles as he stepped away from the table. "Are you cer-tain you don't want that last, lonely piece of cheesecake?"

James leaned forward and whispered, "Actually, I do, but I won't let that young stud know it. Jeez, he's built like a matador!"

"Or a flamenco dancer, not that I no-ticed," Catherine returned naïvely.

"Yeah, sure." James reached across the table and clasped her hand. "Are you having a good time tonight?"

"I'm having a wonderful time," she said, realizing she felt more lighthearted than she had since the awful day at the cottage. "Why? Do I look or sound insincere?"

"You look and sound like *my* Catherine, whom I haven't seen for a while. I've missed her, although it's my fault she went away."

"She didn't go away—just on hiatus."

"After the La Perla incident?"

"My nerves have been on edge. I overreacted. Eric told us they'd found a couple of other 'fancy night-things' in her suitcase and they all smelled of the same perfume." Catherine looked at James seriously. "He said someone came into your town house and planted the lingerie."

James nodded, then added, "I got the feeling he didn't believe that theory, though. In fact, I'm not sure he doesn't suspect me of even worse."

"Like what? Murdering Renée?" James simply looked at her. "Oh, honey, that's crazy."

"Maybe."

"Definitely."

"Whatever you say."

"That's the attitude I like. Now, you did have your locks changed, didn't you?"

"Yesterday afternoon. There are only two door locks, though. You're the only person beside me with keys to my town house. Do you still have them?"

"They're locked in my spare jewelry box, which hasn't been touched. I checked and I'd know if the keys had been moved. Besides, Lindsay raises the roof barking if a stranger comes into our house."

James shrugged. "Then someone could have bribed a staff member or maintenance person of the town-house complex to get a key. If so, we'll probably never find out who. God, I hate this communal living. I like having my own house."

And you could have it so easily, Catherine thought, but said nothing.

"Anyway, the Catherine accusing me of sleeping with other women and crying is gone and *my* Catherine is back," James said tenderly. "She's the light of my life."

Fifteen minutes later, they walked briskly arm in arm from the restaurant into the unusually cold night. While James talked casually, a strange, almost primitive fear filled

Catherine as restless shadows and shifting shapes seemed to surround them. She mentally told herself it was her imagination or the result of too much wine. Then she remembered she hadn't drunk anything except water and coffee.

I'm being ridiculous, Catherine thought. She looked around the near-empty parking lot and saw nothing unusual. Halogen lights glowed softly, a light breeze rattled stiff leaves stubbornly clinging to shrubbery near the building, and somewhere in the distance a dog barked monotonously. Catherine saw nothing in the least frightening. Still, she couldn't shake the feeling that a presence hovered near, watching, waiting.

Catherine's heart began to thump and her stomach tightened. Something wasn't right. No, worse than "not right." She had no idea what it was, but she *knew.* She began to tremble, clutched James's arm tighter, and said shakily, "Something's wrong."

"Wrong?" James looked down at her. "What do you mean?"

"I can't explain it. I just have a feeling that someone is watching us, that we're in danger—"

The shot burst through the darkness, quick and crisp. James stiffened, staring straight ahead. Catherine froze, then asked in a tiny, frightened voice, "James, are you all right?"

After a moment, he murmured, "I'm . . . fine . . . just a bee sting . . ."

James's voice seemed to float away into the night. Suddenly he let loose of her arm, fumbled at his upper chest, and pulled away a bloody hand. "Well . . . what . . . ?" he slurred before slowly sinking to the concrete parking lot.

CHAPTER FOURTEEN

1

Catherine didn't scream. She didn't collapse. She didn't dive for cover beside one of the cars. She merely stood, looking at the fallen man she loved, her body turned to ice. After a few moments, she murmured, "James?" His eyelids flickered. Then a second shot tore through the darkness.

Catherine dropped beside James, huddling against him. She didn't know if she'd been shot—she felt only shock, cold, and the stillness of James. Trembling, she awaited a third shot, but the night remained hauntingly quiet. She reached toward James's chest and felt the warm blood soaking his coat. He's dying, she thought distantly. "I love you," she murmured brokenly. "I love you more than anyone in the world. Please, James. Please don't leave me. . . ."

His eyelids fluttered. She reached behind her, scrabbling for her purse, her cell phone. James's eyes closed and his breath slowed. Catherine buried her head against him. "James, don't die! Don't go. Oh God, please don't go. . . ."

Then the darkness grew even greater as a form approached and stood over them. Before Catherine could look up, a blow cracked against her skull.

2

"Marissa, it's Eric," he said with composure into his cell phone, forgetting that she always recognized his carefully modulated "Brace yourself. I have bad news" timbre. "Honey, I'm in the parking lot of the Reddick restaurant and—"

"What's wrong?" she demanded immediately. "It's Catherine and James, isn't it? They were going out to dinner—"

"Calm down and listen to me." He turned away from the chatter of deputies and paramedics who had responded to the 911 call and were now tending to the crime scene. "They had dinner. Most guests had left as they were walking back to James's car. That's when someone opened fire on them."

"What?" Marissa's voice was barely above a whisper. Then she almost shouted, "*What?* Opened fire? Someone *shot* at them? Were they hit? How badly are they hurt? Eric, are they *dead*?"

"No. They are *not* dead," he said firmly. "Take a deep breath and repeat that to me."

He heard Marissa take a slightly choking but fairly deep breath before she said woodenly, "They are not dead."

"Good."

"But Eric—"

Eric heard Lindsay barking. She always reacted to anxiety in Marissa's voice or manner. He knew she wouldn't take time to drag the dog out of the room before hearing what else he had to say, so he spoke louder. "Keep breathing and let me do the talking. Catherine is not hurt at all. She's scared, but she wasn't shot. She's fine."

"Thank God. Oh, Catherine, is she—"

"I told you to stop talking. You can't listen and talk, too." Eric hated speaking sternly to Marissa at a time like this, but he knew it was the only way to make her calm down enough to get details. "James was shot in the chest."

"In the *chest*! You mean the *heart*?"

"If you don't stop interrupting I'm going to hang up!" Eric himself took a deep breath, realizing his pulse was racing and his breath rapid. "If he'd been shot in the heart, he'd be dead. He's hurt, but they don't know how bad." A siren began roaring in the background as a red light splashed garishly in the night. "The ambulance is just now leaving the parking lot with him. Catherine is with him."

"But she's not hurt."

"She wasn't wounded, I swear."

"Lindsay, shush," Marissa finally said, and then, "Okay, I'm getting ahold of myself. Just tell me what happened. Did the surveillance officer catch whoever shot them?"

"No, but it wasn't his fault. As for what

happened to Catherine and James, do you want to hear now or would you rather go straight to the hospital?"

"The hospital, of course," Marissa said with steel in her voice. "My sister needs me."

3

Marissa's newfound steel abruptly vanished when she put down the handset and lost the strong, bolstering sound of Eric's voice. Later, she remembered only grabbing her coat, mindlessly telling Lindsay, standing stiffly with a stuffed deer in her mouth, that everything would be fine, and running for the kitchen door leading into the garage. In her car, she fumbled through her large tote bag for the car keys and started the Mustang, luckily remembered to push the automatic garage door closer to OPEN before putting the car in reverse, and mumbled curses as the door seemed to take an eternity to rise. Then she roared off into the night.

Every parking space near the hospital emergency entrance was taken. Marissa finally found only one place—five rows away where cars on either side had parked over the lines. Furious, she maneuvered her sports car into the small area, which left barely enough room for her to get her door open and squeeze out of the Mustang. She rushed for the emergency entrance and, once inside, barged into a gaggle of people standing near the doors discussing their various, minor injuries. Tossing an insincere "'scuse me" over her shoulder as a woman squealed as if in terrible pain and a refined-looking elderly man called Marissa a definitely unrefined name, she came to a sliding halt at the reception desk.

"Gray," she said breathlessly to a pretty young woman in scrubs, who was already looking at her wide-eyed. "I'm here for Catherine Gray. Or James Eastman. Yes, he's the one who was hurt. Someone shot him. Catherine will be with him. Where are they?"

"Miss, we're very busy tonight as you can see. If you'll just take a seat in the waiting room, I'll check on those patients for you." The nurse picked up a pen. "You said a James Easton was shot?"

"James *Eastman.* He was with my sister, Catherine Gray. I'm Marissa Gray." The woman dutifully wrote down all the names. "Chief Deputy Eric Montgomery called me about them about fifteen minutes ago. James was just shot in the parking lot of the Reddick restaurant. I'm sure he'll be here as soon as he can. Eric, I mean." The woman nodded and gave her a sympathetic smile that sent Marissa into an unexpected shower of tears. "I don't mean to be demanding, but please hurry. My sister needs to know I'm here. Please. . . ."

"I'll hurry." The young woman turned, handed the paper to another young nurse while firing off information. Then she looked again at Marissa. "Please don't cry. I'll let you know something just as soon as possible."

"Okay." Marissa sniffled, rooting in her tote bag for the packet of tissues Catherine always made certain she loaded in with at least a dozen other essential things like lipstick and a Snickers candy bar. "I appreciate your help."

A large, flat-screen television had been mounted on the wall of the waiting room, the sound turned off as closed-captioning text ran along the bottom of the screen. Marissa stared blindly at a show as her tears refused to stop flowing. A heavy, middle-aged woman in fuchsia stretch pants beside her continually emitted loud, rattling coughs without covering her mouth; an ancient lady crumpled like a sack of potatoes into the corner of her chair sang a loud, vibrato version of "Amazing Grace"; a teenage boy across from Marissa leaned forward, staring fixedly at her, his mouth hanging partially open.

Nurses summoned in four people for what seemed to Marissa like an hour before one appeared at the door asking for Miss Gray. Marissa leaped up, nearly dropping her heavy tote bag, and dashed toward the nurse, who led her down a crowded yet immaculate hallway. "Your sister is in here." The nurse gestured to an examination room. "She's still badly shaken up, so I'll go in with you."

Catherine sat at the foot of an examining table looking small, fragile, and ashen. Someone had wrapped a white blanket around her, but Marissa could still see her trembling beneath the fleece cloth as she looked blankly at the tile floor.

"Catherine!" Marissa ran to her, clutching her in a bear hug. "Oh my God, I've been so scared. Are you all right? Has a doctor examined you?" Catherine slowly lifted her gaze to her sister. Her heather green eyes were bloodshot, her eyelids puffy, and she didn't seem to recognize Marissa. "Catherine?" Marissa asked in alarm. Then she used the childhood name Catherine had always hated. "Chatty Cathy?"

Almost immediately, some life shone in Catherine's eyes. "Mom!"

A chill ran through Marissa. "No, honey, it's me—Marissa. *Marissa.* Your favorite sister!"

Catherine peered at her. "Marissa? My . . . sister?" Suddenly awareness flashed in the beautiful, bloodshot eyes. "Marissa! Oh . . . oh—"

With the blanket wrapped so tightly around Catherine, she couldn't move. Marissa hugged her again. She could feel Catherine's arms moving uselessly beneath the cloth and the nurse moved toward the table, reaching for the blanket and beginning to loosen it. "I guess someone thought you needed a straightjacket," the nurse mumbled crossly, then gave Marissa an apologetic smile. "Sorry. It's been a long, busy night."

"I know. So many people are here. Anyway, Catherine didn't seem to mind." Catherine didn't seem to mind anything right now, Marissa thought in distress. "Has she seen a doctor?"

"Oh yes," the nurse said as Marissa moved back and began unwinding Catherine. "I was with him."

"He said I'm fine and I should go see James," Catherine said distinctly, her voice high-pitched, almost childish. "James needs me."

The nurse removed the blanket and began to drape it more comfortably over Catherine. She winked at Marissa. Then she spoke to Catherine. "You misunderstood. The doctor wants you to stay here while he helps James."

"No, I don't think that's what he wants—"

"Yes, you do," Marissa said crisply, knowing Catherine always responded to a sharp tone of voice. "Now give me a hug."

Catherine clasped her hands around Marissa's neck and pulled her close. "I'm so glad to see you."

"Probably not half as glad as I am to see you."

"I'm sorry to interrupt." Marissa turned to see Deputy Robbie Landers at the examining-room door. "I have to take a few more notes and Eric thought it might be better for me to do the questioning than Jeff, although he's down the hall."

"Robbie, will you make them let me see James?" Catherine asked pitifully, then announced to the nurse, "*She's* the law!"

"Robbie can't help," Marissa said gently. "We have to wait for the doctor. Just try to calm down."

"I can't."

Marissa ignored Catherine. "Robbie, you're not interrupting," Marissa assured the tall, pretty girl whose blue eyes looked slightly larger than usual. She was shaken by what she'd seen earlier, Marissa thought, and it was important to keep everything as calm as possible for Catherine's sake.

"I know we questioned you at the scene, but you were still shocked and a bit vague," Robbie said to Catherine. "I know you're exhausted and I hate doing this, but I need to go over your story, Dr. Gray."

"Please call me Catherine, Robbie."

"All right," Robbie said, looking slightly uncomfortable. After all, she worked for Marissa's lover. "Catherine."

The nurse gestured to the one chair in the small room. "I don't know which one of you wants this."

Marissa spoke up. "You take it, Robbie. You've probably been standing ever since you got to the Reddick." She felt a small shiver pass through Catherine. "I'll sit on the bed beside my sister and keep her warm."

The nurse was already slipping toward the door. "Wait!" Catherine called. "I need to know how James is doing."

"And we'll let you know just as soon as we do. I promise. Now I'll give you some privacy. If you need anything, just yell. We're so busy, someone's bound to be just a few feet away." With one last smile at Catherine, she quickly closed the door.

"She didn't *want* me to know about James because the news is bad," Catherine said vacantly.

"She simply doesn't know anything yet," Marissa said firmly. "They aren't going to let you sit in here and suffer rather than telling you what's going on." She looked at Robbie. "Go ahead with your questions."

Robbie nodded, sat down, opened her notebook, and began questioning Catherine in a businesslike voice. "About what time did you arrive at the restaurant?"

Catherine looked down and swallowed. Marissa jumped up, poured her a plastic cup of cold water, and scooted onto the table again, wrapping an arm around her sister as Catherine took a couple of sips. "Well, James was supposed to pick me up around seven thirty. Then he called and said he'd be a little late—maybe ten minutes or a little more." She took another drink of water. "He didn't show up until around . . . um . . . seven forty-five or seven fifty."

"Okay," Robbie said, still writing. "Who knew you were having dinner at the Reddick?"

"No one. Earlier in the day we planned to go out to dinner, but I don't think we picked a restaurant." She looked at Marissa as if for confirmation. "Did we say anything about the Reddick before we left the house?"

"Nothing, but I didn't ask where you were going."

"Do you know if Mr. Eastman told anyone earlier in the day?" Robbie asked.

Catherine shook her head. "I don't think so, because he didn't even mention the Reddick until we were in the car."

"So someone—several people—could have known you had plans to go out to dinner, but not where. You must have been followed. Did James pick you up at your house?"

"Yes. He always does in the evenings."

"But you didn't notice anyone following you."

"No. Of course, we had the surveillance deputy following us, so I felt safe and wasn't paying much attention." She paused. "Is the deputy all right?"

"Well, your attacker got to him first—"

Catherine gasped, "Oh no!"

"He wasn't badly hurt," Robbie said quickly. "Just knocked unconscious."

"That's all?"

"Yes. He's already conscious again."

"Good. Do you know anything about James? Please be honest."

"I am. I don't know anything about Mr. Eastman's condition." Robbie looked down at her notebook. "Next question. Do you recall exactly when you left the restaurant?"

Catherine took a deep breath, obviously thinking. "Well, it took us about twenty minutes to get to the Reddick. Then we spent a long time at dinner. We were having so much fun. . . ." She sighed. "I don't think we left until around nine thirty." She frowned. "Is that what James says?"

"The waiter says you left around nine forty." James can't say anything, Marissa thought with a flutter of fright. James is unconscious, maybe dying. Or dead. Marissa felt Catherine tensing, but Robbie quickly defused the moment by smiling radiantly at Catherine. "He said you were, I quote, '*trés belle*' and that James left a *very* generous tip."

"He was a very good waiter."

Robbie again lifted her pen to her notebook. "All right, we've established that you left the restaurant between nine thirty and nine forty. Was the restaurant crowded?"

"Even when we got there, it was only about a third full. When we left, there were fewer people."

"Any leaving at the same time?"

"I don't think so."

"So no one else except you and James was in the parking lot when you headed for his car."

"I saw the patrol car and I assumed the officer was in there. No one else was walking to their car."

"Exactly where was the car?"

Marissa knew Robbie had seen the car. She was testing Catherine's memory.

Catherine didn't hesitate. "There were only four or five other cars in the lot. None of them was near James's, which was parked in the middle of the . . . let's see . . . second row."

"Did you see or hear *anything* as you walked toward the car?"

"James was talking—I can't remember about what right now." Catherine hesitated, opened her mouth, and then abruptly closed it.

Robbie's head jerked up at the hesitation. "What?"

"Nothing, really. It's just silly. . . ."

"Catherine, please be completely open with me. Otherwise, we might miss something *very* important."

"Yes. I understand. I wasn't trying to hide anything except what I'm afraid was my overactive imagination."

"Catherine, tell her," Marissa urged. "I'm sure you didn't imagine—"

"Okay!" Catherine snapped uncharacteristically. "That parking lot didn't feel right. It seemed to me like shadows were moving, but there were no clouds floating over a full moon or any scary-movie things. I just sensed something bad. A presence."

"A presence?" Robbie repeated.

"Yes," Catherine said firmly. "At the time it seemed like I'd had too much to drink, but all I'd had with dinner was water and coffee. I know I sound like a nut, but I felt something *wrong*."

Robbie looked at her seriously. "From the moment you walked out of the restaurant or when you got near James's car?"

Catherine took another sip of water. "When we were about halfway to James's car. I remember holding his arm tighter. I remember looking around. I didn't see anything. I didn't hear anything."

Catherine took a deep breath. "When I was certain I wasn't imagining things, I told James something was wrong. He asked what I meant. Then there was a shot. He pressed his hand to his chest and pulled it away. It was covered with blood. He said something else and then just sank down. He didn't crash to the concrete; he simply sank." Catherine suddenly burst into tears. "And I just stood there, useless."

CHAPTER FIFTEEN

1

"You couldn't do anything;" Robbie said.

I just dropped down to him. He grabbed his shoulder, and when he pulled it away there was so much blood. I couldn't stop looking at all the blood. . . ." Catherine gave Robbie a lost, wandering look. "I thought he was dying or dead. I kept asking him to come back. I didn't think of anything else—not who was shooting—and then I knew someone was standing over us and I tried to raise my head, but before I could, I went blank."

"The shooter knocked you unconscious. Are you sure you didn't see who it was?"

"I didn't see anyone. I'm sorry."

"Don't be sorry. If you'd seen his face, he might have killed you."

Catherine blinked, stiffening.

"Who found them?" Marissa asked.

"A couple going to their car saw them lying in the parking lot. They rushed back into the restaurant and called nine-one-one. They didn't see anyone else in the lot. No one in the restaurant heard anything, so we don't know how many shots were fired."

"I'm sure the police care how many shots someone fired, but I don't," Catherine said with startling vehemence. "All I can think of is James." Her lips began to tremble. "Oh God, I *still* don't know if he's is alive. It's been *so* long. . . ."

"No, it hasn't," Marissa said. "It just seems like it's been a long time. I'm sure he's in surgery. You know how long surgery takes."

"Not long if someone dies quickly."

"Then the longer it takes, the better." Marissa hoped that sounded logical. She couldn't think of anything else to say.

"James is young and strong and healthy. He's *not* dead. I'd know it."

Catherine looked at her quizzically. "You'd *know*? How?"

"I just would." Catherine was opening her mouth to argue. "I think I'll go out to one of those vending machines and get coffee. Catherine, Robbie, either of you brave enough to drink what those awful contraptions pass off as coffee?"

"Not me," Catherine said dully while Robbie wisely shook her head.

Just as Marissa began scooting off the table, the examining room door opened. Eric looked first at Catherine and then at Marissa, asking, "All right if I come in?"

"More than all right!" Marissa exclaimed. "I didn't think we'd see you here tonight."

Eric entered slowly, smiling at Catherine. "How are you doing?"

"All right, considering the circumstances." Her voice sounded thin and falsely calm. "Have you found out anything else about the shooting?"

"No. At least nothing important." Eric said. Marissa knew he wasn't being completely truthful, but Catherine was in no shape to absorb anything technical about

gunshot angles or distances. "We're certainly not finished investigating yet, though.
I'll be going back to the restaurant soon. I
just wanted to come by and check on
James."

"Well, if he's dead, no one has told me,"
Catherine said dully.

Marissa gave her another hug as Eric
and Robbie spoke at once, both telling
Catherine she was doing fine, James would
be fine, she just had to have faith, on and
on until Marissa felt like shouting for silence.

And then the doctor walked in.

2

Marissa and Catherine had known the
woman since they were teenagers, when
she'd joined the staff of the hospital where
their father had been a cardiologist for over
twenty years. She was tall, slender, and
fortyish, with short blond hair and a face
pale with fatigue and lack of makeup. On
television, female surgeons always wore
makeup, Marissa thought distantly, often
including false eyelashes they fluttered frequently above their surgical masks.

"Hello, Catherine, Marissa," she said. "I haven't seen you since your mother's funeral. I'm sorry I haven't seen you again until now, under these circumstances."

"I'm glad you were here to take care of James," Marissa managed, although all Catherine did was nod, her eyes huge.

"Mr. Eastman came through surgery well," the doctor immediately began. "He had a gunshot wound through the left scapula. That's the shoulder blade, as I'm sure you all know. When a bullet hits a bone, the bone may be shattered or may deflect the bullet to another part of the body, causing further problems. This was a perforating wound, meaning the bullet passed through the body. There appears to be no joint involvement and very little soft-tissue involvement. These are good things. The exit of the bullet caused a great deal of blood loss, but we got it under control. Also, he suffered some damage to tendons or ligaments, though not severe." She finally smiled. "I know it doesn't seem like it now, but considering what he's been through, I'd say Mr. Eastman is a very lucky man."

"Oh yes, lucky," Catherine said tremulously. "Lucky. . . ." She suddenly bent her head and buried her face in her hands. "Oh, thank God." Her voice was soft and tearful. "Thank God. It could have been so much worse—"

"But it wasn't. So far, he's doing well and I see no reason why he shouldn't keep doing well," the doctor interrupted. Then she looked at Eric. "You're Chief Deputy Montgomery."

"Yes."

"They told me you'd come. I'd like to speak with you in the hall." Marissa heard the serious note in the doctor's voice before she flashed them another smile, this one more cheerful. "After all, these people need some time to celebrate without listening to me droning on about surgery details."

There's more, Marissa thought, but she didn't want to hear it and Catherine didn't need to hear it. All Catherine needed to know was that James was not only alive but also holding his own.

Marissa closed her eyes and gave her sister another hug. Although Marissa was not traditionally religious, she surprised herself by saying a short, silent prayer, because she couldn't help thinking that a higher power had been watching over Catherine and James tonight.

3

"First let me start off by reminding you that I'm not a pathologist," the doctor told Eric as they strolled down the hall with Robbie, who still held her notebook and pen. "However, I can give you some information about the bullet."

"I knew that's why you wanted to talk to me," Eric said. "I'd appreciate any information you can give me."

"As I said, the bullet passed through the body, so I can't give it to you for ballistics. I can tell you that I'm sure the shooter didn't use a shotgun at short range—there wasn't enough tissue damage. In fact, my guess would be that Mr. Eastman was shot with a .22 rifle—even a .22 handgun would have left more of a tattoo pattern on the skin."

"But aren't most .22 rifles used for shooting small game?" Robbie asked.

"Yes, they are," Eric said slowly.

"But I just didn't see enough soft-tissue

damage to make me think the shooter used a high-velocity rifle. In fact, little as I know about guns, I'm surprised Mr. Eastman sustained as much damage as he did." She paused. "If I'm right and he used a .22-caliber rifle."

"Even if he used a .22, he could have shot as bad as he did if he was at very short range," Eric said.

"We're getting into an area I can't help with, so I'll stop with the gun information and leave that to the experts," the doctor said pleasantly. "I didn't want to go into a lot of details about Mr. Eastman's condition because Catherine is doing so much better than when they brought her in. I also know you're very close to her sister, Chief Deputy Montgomery, and whatever I tell you, you'll convey to Marissa and she'll tell her sister later."

Eric nodded. "I will, and I want to tell you again that I appreciate your sensitivity. What else should I tell Marissa?"

"The fracture of Mr. Eastman's scapula is not severe and doesn't look unstable, but the bone *is* fractured and will take quite a while to heal. In the meantime, there's danger of infection or the formation of a *fistula*"—she looked at Robbie's frown—"a pocket of blood or pus, which would have to be drained. I know that look. As my teenage daughter would say, 'Oh, *gross.*'"

Robbie grinned at her.

"I've heard that Mr. Eastman is a workaholic, but at least he's a lawyer, not a construction worker. I also know he's right-handed. He was shot on the left side. That will make it easier for him to keep his left side still. Nevertheless, he'll have to take it easy and get plenty of rest. You must emphasize this to Catherine. James Eastman needs to lead a less hectic life and get plenty of rest. I'm sure if anyone can make him slow down, she will be the one."

"I hope so," Eric said. "James isn't good at taking orders."

"She doesn't have to give orders," the doctor returned crisply, then smiled. "As I'm sure you know because of Marissa, beautiful women have other ways of convincing men to do what's good for them, no matter how stubborn they are."

Robbie burst out laughing and then turned bright red. "Sorry," she said meekly to a surprised-looking Eric.

"Don't be." The doctor looked at Eric.

"And don't you make her feel bad. It's the only time all day I've made someone laugh. Any other questions, Chief Deputy?"

"No, ma'am, not right now," he said with a bit less authority in his voice. "Thank you for the information, especially about the gunshot. I have a feeling I'm going to need all the help I can get."

After she left them, Eric turned to Robbie. "Well, we know someone is fond of .22-caliber guns."

"Renée and Arcos were killed with handguns. Someone used a rifle on Eastman."

"But the gun that killed Arcos isn't the one used on Renée. The ballistics don't match."

"Maybe all three guns being .22 calibers is a coincidence."

"I don't buy it," Eric said. "There's a connection."

"Yes, sir."

"You don't have to humor me. I'm not mad at you for laughing."

"I know or you would have said something by now. I truly think there's a connection."

"Okay. What did Catherine tell you about the actual moments of the shots?"

Robbie flipped back through her notebook. "She said she and James were alone in the parking lot. He was shot and fell immediately. She just stood in shock and then she heard a second shot. That's when she ducked. *After* the second shot. When she hit the ground, she passed out." Robbie looked up from her notes. "It doesn't appear the shooter was near Mr. Eastman's car."

"Not during the shooting, but he had been," Eric said grimly. "Beneath the passenger's door we found three strings of purple Mardi Gras beads."

CHAPTER SIXTEEN

1

"No one can say I don't know how to show a girl a lovely evening."

"Oh, James, don't be so modest," Catherine said earnestly as she sat by his hospital bed. "It *was* lovely right up until the sniper opened fire on us."

James's tired eyes still managed to sparkle. "Talk about looking at the glass half-full! I'd laugh if it didn't hurt."

"Then definitely don't laugh. I want you well and out of here."

"I won't be well for a few weeks. I also

won't be released for a couple of days. I'll miss Patrice's wedding."

"I hope you're not worrying about the wedding!" Catherine exclaimed.

"I'm kidding. Patrice will have to get along without both of us."

"Well, not both of us."

James gave Catherine a startled look.

"I *have* to go."

"What the hell are you talking about?"

"James, I'm the maid of honor. Patrice doesn't have any relatives or close friends who can stand in for me."

"You're being crazy," James said grimly. "Did that concussion you got make you forget what happened last night?"

"I'll have surveillance."

"We had surveillance last night."

"Eric told me the guy had been on the force for a couple of months and was so inexperienced, when he heard a rear tire blow he jumped out of the patrol car. The tire didn't blow without help, which he didn't think of. Anyway, he's on suspension."

"Well, boo-hoo for him, but that doesn't change what happened to us or what could happen to you."

"I'm not going to let Patrice down," Catherine said stubbornly, then leaned forward and gently kissed James on the cheek. "I'm not worried about going to the wedding—I'm only worried about you."

"You're talking to me like I'm a kid. You can't act like going to this rehearsal dinner and the wedding isn't dangerous because you don't want me to freak out. I'm already freaked out. Someone followed us to that restaurant and almost killed me."

"You, not me. I'm not his target."

"What makes you so sure?"

"He was close enough to bash me on the head last night, but he didn't kill me."

"Maybe he just wasn't ready to kill you, honey. Maybe he has some twisted reason for waiting to kill you."

A chill rushed through Catherine, but she didn't think James saw it. "Who could be doing this, James, and why?"

He shook his head. "Someone murdered Renée. Arcos came after you because he thought you'd killed her, but then someone got him instead."

"If Arcos wanted to kill me because he thought I'd murdered Renée, he didn't kill her. Did someone kill him because they thought *he'd* killed her?"

"Or because he had tried to hurt you. He *would* have hurt you if he hadn't been killed." He paused. "I think Eric believed I killed Renée because I hated her and then I killed Arcos to protect you."

"I . . . I don't think so."

"Yes, you do. Maybe you didn't admit it to yourself, but you felt it just like I did."

"Even if he did think you were the murderer, he has to know better now."

"Maybe," James said slowly. "Maybe."

2

Bridget Fenmore walked toward a woman wandering aimlessly around the gallery. Normally she would have ignored a "looky-loo," but Bridget knew a Burberry leather coat when she saw one. And wasn't the woman carrying a Prada handbag?

Bridget tempered her desire to rush toward the woman. Instead, she walked sedately and tried not to look at the clothes. "Hello. Welcome to the gallery. May I show you anything in particular?"

"No, thank you."

Up close, Bridget saw that the woman

was middle-aged and had a bored, blue-eyed gaze. Her makeup, though, was perfection. "Right here on the first floor we have the Arcos exhibit. It's extremely popular."

"I've seen it. Not my style."

"What style do you like?"

"Something pretty." The woman gave her a self-deprecating smile. "I don't know about particular styles. I just know what I like."

"On the second floor we have a room devoted to the work of Guy Nordine, the father of the gallery owner. He was a brilliant artist. His style is quite different from that of Arcos. Perhaps you'd enjoy looking at his paintings."

"Ummm, I've looked at them, too. We just had the house redecorated and I don't think any of them would look good with my new furniture."

What a shame, Bridget thought. The woman obviously had money—a new Mercedes was parked in front of the gallery and Bridget was certain the car belonged to her—but she had no knowledge or appreciation of art. "I'll just let you look around by yourself then. You might see something that you think would look well with your new furniture."

"Yes. Thank you." The woman was obviously relieved not to have an "art expert" tagging along with her. "That would be fine. Actually, I don't know much about art, but this is a really pretty place. I'd like to just study the lines and . . . well, the style of the building. I might get some ideas for doing a little house renovation."

"What a brilliant idea!" You numbskull, Bridget thought. You want your house to look like an art museum? "Spend all the time you like. If you'd like to ask about any of the . . . architecture, I'll be glad to answer as best I can. And I have fresh coffee and hot water brewing for tea. If you'd care for any, just let me know."

"Well, aren't you sweet?" The woman smiled, showing crow's-feet and nasal-labial folds. "I'll be sure to tell my husband how nice you are." She frowned, showing a badly wrinkled forehead. "Well, maybe I won't tell him about you. You're too young and pretty."

"Oh, thank you." Bridget had perfected her diffident look as well as a slight blush. "I'm sure your husband wouldn't trade you for anyone, though. Enjoy your trip to the gallery."

Well, Ken would be proud of that performance, Bridget thought as she headed back toward a long table where she'd been pretending to organize pamphlets for the last hour. She was alone for the time being. Dana had suddenly decided she was crazy about her kid and had spent the last three days with her in the hospital, and Ken had gone out to lunch with the potential buyer of two above-average paintings. In terms of price, they weren't close to the Arcos paintings, but two would bring a nice profit.

Glancing around for visitors she'd not already approached, Bridget noticed a man who must have quietly entered while she was talking to the well-dressed airhead, as she now thought of the woman staring in befuddlement at an excellent piece of modern art. He was tall and lean, wearing a charcoal-colored suit and full-length black coat, both of which fit him so perfectly that Bridget guessed they'd been custom-made. He was looking at *Mardi Gras Lady,* and even at a distance, Bridget could see he scrutinized the painting with the discerning gaze of an expert. Art galleries were familiar to this man, Bridget decided as she walked toward him at a leisurely pace. She wanted to impress him, which wouldn't happen if she pounced on him like an eager salesperson.

When she neared him, she came to a near stop, waited a beat, and then said, "Hello, sir," in the warm yet professional voice Ken had taught her. "I'm Bridget Fenmore, manager of the gallery. Welcome."

He glanced at her and blinked rapidly three times, looking startled. Then he made a visible effort to regain his composure. "How do you do, Ms. Fenmore?" he said somewhat stiffly in a low, heavy voice. "John . . . Jones."

John Jones my ass, Bridget thought. The guy needed acting lessons, but if he wanted to be anonymous that was fine with her. She smiled prettily. "I see that you're looking at *Mardi Gras Lady*. It's by Nicolai Arcos. Unfortunately, Mr. Arcos . . . died this week."

"Yes, I heard about his death," Jones returned slowly.

"Such a tragedy. He had so much talent."

"Really?"

The man's question and harsh tone took Bridget by surprise. She looked at his dark eyes, surrounded by deep wrinkles and staring piercingly into hers, the horizontal lines in his strong forehead beneath thick, silver-touched black hair brushed to the side, the creases running deeply from his aquiline nose to his narrow, hard-lipped mouth.

"Was his death a tragedy? Of course. I knew him. I liked him." Bridget felt stumbling and foolish. She was also lying. She had not liked Nicolai Arcos, but she certainly would never admit to it. "And *I* thought he was talented." A bit of spirit bridled in her. "So did a great many art critics."

"Well-respected critics?"

"Yes. J. Philip Ransworth, for instance."

"I've never heard of J. Philip Ransworth."

"Oh. Well, he's famous." At least Ken had told her Ransworth was famous. "He wrote a glowing review of the Arcos exhibit."

Bridget tried to dazzle John Jones with a smile. The man merely gave her a forbearing look. Oh God, where was Ken? He would know how to handle *Mr. Jones,* she thought, suddenly furious with the handsome Ken Nordine whom she'd been kissing passionately just last night. No matter what their personal relationship, though, he should be here. After all, this was his damned art gallery. Nevertheless, today she was in charge and she mustn't let this strange visitor know he was making her feel a fool. "But beauty is in the eye of the beholder," she blurted lamely.

John Jones laughed. The sound was rusty, as if he didn't laugh often. "Forgive me, Ms. Fenmore. I've made you uncomfortable."

"Not at all."

"Oh yes, I have. Please overlook my bad manners."

"Your manners are—"

"Often unfortunate. My wife has told me so a hundred times."

Bridget glanced at his hands clasped loosely just below his waist. They were pale, with veins showing prominently through soft, thin skin. He wore a simple platinum wedding band on one of his long, well-manicured fingers and she saw a platinum Rolex watch showing beneath a sleeve. He had a smooth grace that hinted at excellent coordination, but he

also tended to move a bit stiffly. Bridget
was trying to guess whether he was around
fifty-nine or sixty when he quickly turned
and looked at her as if he knew exactly
what she was thinking.

"Do you like to dance, Ms. Fenmore?"

"Dance? Yes."

"Have you ever been to a ball?"

"Well, no, I don't think so."

"Wouldn't you remember?"

"Well, sure. I mean, of course I would.
And no, unfortunately I've never been to a
ball." Or anything resembling a ball, Bridget
thought. She couldn't ballroom-dance, but
suddenly she was filled with regret, for
both her lack of classic dance skills and
the fact that she'd never been to anything
fancier than a Christmas dance in a Holiday Inn.

"That is too bad. I can just picture you
doing the quadrille."

"Oh, thank you!" Bridget glowed, although she had no idea what a quadrille
looked like.

"And if I say so myself, about a hundred
years ago I was quite good at the tango. If
I were younger, we could tango together."
He seemed to drift away, his eyes growing

dreamy. "I used to have a beautiful tango partner. My God . . . how I miss her."

Bridget imagined Jones's partner as his lover. The deepening of his voice, the saddening of his expression, almost made Bridget ask if the girl was dead. Then Bridget caught herself and said merely, "I'm sorry that you miss her."

"Yes, I miss her every day and every night." John Jones turned his gaze back to the painting. "You greatly resemble the subject of this portrait."

"Why, thank you."

"Do you think *she* is beautiful?" Bridget hesitated, suddenly feeling as if the remark was a challenge. Her palms had begun to sweat. She wished she could escape John Jones, but she couldn't do so now without seeming rude. Finally, she decided not to let his odd manner frighten her. "I think she's beautiful," she said stoutly.

He looked at Bridget again. "Do you know who she was?"

"I don't know if she really existed or if she was merely imaginary." Ken had instructed Bridget to say this and she never failed to follow his instructions about the matter. "She does look like someone I've seen, but it's hard to tell with the mask she's wearing."

"Holding," Jones corrected, looking at the gold-trimmed white mask. "It's a hand-held half mask mounted to a gold stick. Attractively stylized. And the black penta-gram around the right eye is . . . striking."

"Yes, the mask she's *holding* is lovely. But the star on the mask—you called it a pentagram. Doesn't that have something to do with witchcraft?"

"There is a small difference between the five-pointed star and the pentagram. The pentagram has lines through the middle. If you look very closely, you can see the lines on this mask."

Bridget stood on tiptoe, squinted, and for the first time saw thread-thin lines painted in a brown so dark it was hardly discernible from the surrounding black. "I see them!"

"I knew you would. So the 'star' is really a 'pentagram' and a symbol of Wicca." He paused. "Do you still like the lady's mask, even if the star is really a pentagram?"

"I'm just crazy about that mask." Bridget could have kicked herself for her exuber-ant language. Nerves had turned her into a not-too-smart babbling adolescent, she thought, and she was glad Ken hadn't heard her. Maybe Mr. Jones hadn't been listening. She rushed on, "Anyway, whether or not she's real or imaginary, the Mardi Gras Lady is beautiful."

"Yes." John Jones's eyes narrowed as he leaned closer to the painting. "Ahhh, the fan."

"The fan she's holding? It's beautiful, too. Unusual. Maybe it would have been better if it hadn't been unfurled—we've had mixed reactions to the erotic painting on it—but I like it."

He nodded. "It's exquisite."

"Yes. There's a difference between trash and erotica. Some people can't tell the difference."

John Jones looked at her and lifted one heavy salt-and-pepper eyebrow. "Obviously, you can."

"Well, I'm trained. But even if I weren't . . . well, the true artist and the sensitive viewer can tell the difference between the merely lascivious and the artfully sensuous."

Bridget was proud of that statement until John Jones looked at her with his faintly amused, superior expression again. Her discomfort with the decorous Mr. Jones and her anger with Ken grew. Jones kept staring at her, obviously waiting for her to say something else. "I wonder if such fans really exist?"

"They do. I've seen them." His gaze gentled. "Do you like this portrait, Ms. Fenmore?"

"I like the painting," Bridget said carefully. "Portrait" implied the painting was that of a real person. "I think it's . . . magnificent."

"I'm sure the lady did, too."

"If she really existed."

John Jones's expression grew half-humorous, half-sad. "I think she did." He looked back at *Mardi Gras Lady.* "Oh yes, I think this woman—this vision of a woman—did exist."

3

"Hope I didn't miss lunch."

James looked away from the television as Eric walked into the room.

"Yes, you've missed lunch by at least an hour and you should thank your lucky stars you did. I thought my mother was the only person in the world who could make bad Jell-O, but I was wrong. This place has her beat hands down."

"I wouldn't be so sure. You should taste Marissa's." Eric sat down on the vinyl-covered chair near the window, glanced up at the television, and started laughing. "Please don't tell me that in less than twenty-four hours in here you're already watching soap operas."

"The television remote is broken."

"Yeah, sure."

"It *is.* I was just ready to call for a nurse—"

Eric picked up the remote and flipped off the television. "Guess you don't need to bother anyone now, although I probably interrupted a heart-wrenching moment."

"I *was* going to vote for you for sheriff," James said coolly. "I'm already reconsidering."

"That's a shame. It was just my luck to have a murder spree break out two weeks before the election."

"Don't think that hasn't crossed my mind, and believe it or not, I feel responsible for the spot I've put you in," James said, his voice a tad less cool. "I know you're not

here campaigning, though. Is this a con-
dolence call, Chief Deputy Montgomery?"

"Partly. How do you feel?"

"Not great."

"I'm not surprised. From what the doctor
told me, you won't be up to par for two or
three months."

"Came to cheer me up, did you? You
could have at least brought flowers with all
your concern."

"You'll be getting a huge bouquet of
long-stemmed roses from me this afternoon. Red roses—red means love."

"Thanks. I didn't know you cared so
much."

Eric laughed mildly and then let his
face return to its usual serious lines. "You
were damned lucky last night, James. You
have no idea who might have done this?"

"I would have told you if I did."

Eric nodded. "Maybe this will help. After
you were shot, we found three strands of
Mardi Gras beads under the edge of your
car."

"Mardi Gras beads?"

"Yes. Cheap metal Mardi Gras beads."
Eric hesitated. "I don't like giving out information about an ongoing investigation, but

I think you should know we found the same on the body of Nicolai Arcos. Three strands of beads. The ones on him and the ones under your car were purple. I know the Mardi Gras colors are green, gold, and purple and purple symbolizes justice. I'm not certain if whoever placed the beads knew what purple means."

"In other words, if leaving beads symbolizing *justice* has significance or if whoever killed Arcos and shot me just happened to have purple beads lying around." Eric nodded. "Purple *Mardi Gras* beads." The color had slowly faded from James's face. "Purple for *justice.* Someone seems to be sending the message that justice is being served."

"I agree," Eric said softly, not wanting to break the mood. James still had the speculative expression that could be important.

"But why did someone kill Arcos and try to kill me?"

"Because Renée abandoned both of you and the killer thinks you murdered her out of revenge?"

"Revenge?" James gave him a serious look. "Eric, I've never even spoken to Arcos. I have no idea if he felt vengeful because Renée left him. For all I know, he broke off the affair with her. But I can tell you for certain that *I* didn't feel vengeful because she left me."

"You didn't? Not even a little?"

"No, I didn't." James looked reflective. "I was embarrassed, especially when the police thought I killed her and put me through that investigation. But even then, my primary feeling was . . . well, relief."

"Relief?"

"Relief that she was gone. We had some terrible fights, but I certainly didn't kill her. I didn't think anyone else had, either. I *never* believed she'd come to harm. I thought maybe she'd pushed things too far with someone and became afraid of them—that's why she left so fast without a clue as to where she was going. She was also drinking more than usual at that time—not enough to be a danger to herself or someone else, but more than usual. Drinking was sometimes a sign of nervousness with her, but it was also a sign of boredom.

"I thought this time she was just bored," James went on. "Causing scandals in this 'nothing little town,' as she called Aurora

Falls, had lost its fun for her, and she'd decided to have some fun by doing something dramatic—she set the scene for causing trouble, this time creating trouble for me by vanishing the day after we'd had a near-violent public argument at a party.

"I was certain that's what she'd done, Eric. I was furious with her, but I was also a little worried in spite of myself. I knew she wasn't stable, and as much as I wanted to be free of her, I didn't want anything bad to happen to her. I knew the police would be suspicious of me when she just disappeared, but I thought considering Renée's character and her past outrageous behavior, they wouldn't consider me a suspect in her possible *murder.*" He smiled bitterly. "When the police investigation seemed to be getting a little too serious, I stopped worrying about Renée and started worrying about myself. I got scared, Eric. Really scared, even though I hadn't done a thing to Renée. I'd never even slapped her, no matter what she did."

"Mitch Farrell was still sheriff then, James, and he was getting a lot of pressure to not let things appear to be sliding because you're an Eastman."

"I know. Still, I'm sure you can understand how I felt."

"Of course I can. Frankly, I would have been scared, too." Eric, a naturally restless man who never held still for long, got up from the chair and began pacing the small room. "So you felt *relieved* that Renée had left you."

"Yes."

"Happy or just sort of released?"

"At first, released, like I'd gotten rid of an unbearable weight."

"But you did bear it, James," Eric said sharply. "You bore the weight of your wife's public humiliation of you for over two years. I've always wondered why. What hold did she have on you? Love?"

"Love? No, definitely not. And she didn't have a hold on me the way I think you mean. She didn't know something damaging she'd tell if I sued her for divorce."

"Then what the hell was it? Why did you put up with her for so long? Why did you wait until she left you and then feel *relieved*? Why didn't you divorce her? That's what a real man would have done."

Anger flashed in James's eyes. "Oh, you're an expert on how a real man acts,

Eric? You're daring to tell me what a *real* man should have done?"

"I'm telling you what a man who isn't timid or browbeaten or a . . . a milquetoast would have done."

James glared at him for a moment. Then he started laughing. "A *milquetoast*? I haven't heard that word since my grand-mother used to say it."

"Well, mine did, too." Eric drew a deep breath. He didn't know why the old-fashioned word had popped out of his mouth, but at least it had lessened the tension in the room. "Look, I'm not trying to make you mad or upset you. I just don't understand you, James. The way you han-dled, or didn't handle, the situation with Renée frustrates me. Hell, it enrages me because it led up to all of this mess."

"Are you sure about that?"

"Yes. Aren't you?"

James looked at him steadily. "I believe Renée's return to Aurora Falls led up to all of *this mess,* as you put it."

"Why did she come back?"

"I feel like I've answered that question fifty times. I . . . don't . . . know!"

"Could it have had something to do with your divorce being finalized?"

"You're asking if she came here to stop it?" James snorted. "Give me a break, Eric. Do you honestly think she wanted to stay married to me?"

"Well . . . I don't mean to be insulting, but no. I'm fairly certain she didn't want to stay married to you."

"No insult taken. I think she hated me by the time she left." He paused and after a moment spoke thoughtfully. "The last time I talked to her mother, though, she said she thought Renée was getting desperate for money. Renée had even gone home. Audrey said she'd turned her away, which I believe, but considering how Renée felt about her mother, she *must* have been desperate if she went back to the family home. If she was that broke, she *might* have come back to me as a last resort." James's forehead puckered again, and eventually he shook his head. "No. Renée wasn't stupid. She would have known I wouldn't take her back."

"Are you sure you wouldn't have? The way you just accepted her behavior while you were married to her wouldn't lead me to believe she didn't have a chance with you."

Eric had been trying to get a rise from James, hoping he might say more about the strange marriage, but all he got was a hard stare. James took two deep breaths and Eric could almost feel the man composing himself. Eric wasn't surprised. He knew James Eastman was extremely bright and savvy. He wouldn't easily fall into a verbal trap.

"The only reason I can think of that Renée might have come back was because she heard about the success of the Arcos exhibit."

"You think she loved him enough to want to see it?"

"Love him? Eric, she didn't love him. She didn't love anyone—I don't think she was capable of it. But that exhibit features *Mardi Gras Lady.* In fact, it's the painting getting all the attention. Still . . ."

"Still?"

"Still, news of a successful art exhibit in Aurora Falls has hardly made the papers or been splashed all over the Internet. Either she was close by and heard about it or she has a connection here in town who told her."

"I was told she was spotted at the gallery looking at her portrait. If the person was correct that Renée visited the gallery, I'm not surprised."

"Of course not. She couldn't bear *not* seeing a painting of herself in an art gallery. You know she was crazy about art."

"No, I didn't know."

"Well, she was. She met Arcos when she took one of his classes. She began talking about him immediately and incessantly. Less than a month later, she never mentioned him. That's when I knew something was going on between them."

"Do you think Arcos killed her for leaving him?"

"I don't think he would have if he was in his right mind, but from everything I've heard about him, he did a lot of drugs. But that doesn't explain why Arcos was murdered."

"Revenge? Someone thought Arcos killed Renée, so he had to die, too."

"And what about me? Did the shooter also think I killed Renée?"

"Maybe Arcos and you were just possibilities."

"Have you forgotten I was at a conference in Pittsburgh at the time someone murdered Renée?"

"James, Pittsburgh is less than three hundred miles from here. You could have driven to Aurora Falls, killed Renée, and been back in Pittsburgh in nine hours. If you'd taken a plane to Pittsburgh and rented a car there, the odometer on the car could have helped clear you. It would have shown how little you used the car. But you drove your own car to Pittsburgh. We have no idea how much mileage you had on it when you left for the conference. Of course, even if we did know how many miles you had on *your* car when you left here, you could have rented one in Pittsburgh, but so far, we haven't found any car-rental agencies there with a record of you renting a car. Unless you used fake identification—"

"Stop!" James nearly shouted, holding up his hand. "God, this is driving me crazy. I was *sick* in Pittsburgh. I didn't go anywhere!"

"So you've said." They glowered at each

other, and then Eric said evenly, "Come on, James. Don't act like you know nothing about how criminal investigations are conducted."

A male nurse opened the door and glanced in the room. As they both looked at James, Eric noticed his paleness and the lines that had deepened around his eyes.

"I know it's still visiting hours," the nurse said to Eric, "but Mr. Eastman needs to rest. I'm sorry, sir, but I'm afraid I have to ask you to leave now."

"Okay," Eric said quietly, knowing he'd pushed James almost as far as he could. "May I stay long enough to ask Mr. Eastman two more questions, though?"

The nurse looked doubtful, but James said, "Yes. I'm not dying. I can certainly answer a couple of questions." As soon as the nurse backed out and closed the door, James asked, "So what do you want to know?"

"First, have you gotten a chance to tell Renée's parents that she's dead?"

"I talked to Audrey, Renée's mother, on Monday and told her Renée had been murdered. She claimed not to believe me. "Finally, I demanded to talk to Gaston, Renée's father. Audrey said he was in Europe and she wouldn't let me disturb him," James continued. "I didn't believe her. I don't think Gaston was in Europe then or now. Still, I haven't heard a word from him and I would have expected *something* from him. Maybe he doesn't know Renée is dead. All I know for certain is that he must be found and told that his only child has been murdered. Considering my condition, I'll leave finding him to you, whether he really is in Europe or if he's in the United States. I am not Renée's husband anymore. I'm not going to act like I am by tracking down her father. That's your department." He waited an instant. "Second question?"

Eric paused for a moment, wondering if he should just let things go for now. But he couldn't. In a soft, emotionless voice, he asked, "Why didn't you divorce Renée when she was still in Aurora Falls?"

James lowered his gaze. "Mostly arrogance, Eric. When I married her, I was young and full of myself. I thought I was damned great, to put it bluntly. I wouldn't listen to anybody because I thought I knew more than anybody." He laughed ruefully. "God, was I wrong. I knew it less than a year after our marriage. Sooner. Still, I just couldn't admit it."

"Finally, I started acting with some guts, like I should have from the beginning, and told her I'd charge her with adultery. And I had proof—not a lot, because Renée could be covert when she wanted—but I had enough proof to win a divorce."

"And that's when she left?"

"No. She thought I wouldn't do it—the humiliation factor again. She said she'd fight me, start rumors about my family, claim I'd physically and emotionally abused her—" James sighed. "I probably wouldn't have gone through with it, even though my parents had told me they didn't care about a little embarrassment. After all, both their families had lived and been respected in Aurora Falls for over a hundred years, while Renée was . . . well, hardly admired."

"That's putting it lightly."

"Still, I procrastinated. I told myself I just couldn't bear to put my family through such mortification, but looking back, I realize that was only partly true. I couldn't bear to put *myself* through such mortification." James looked at Eric, shame in his eyes. "That's the truth, hard as it is to admit."

Eric nodded. "I know it must have been hard for you to admit."

"Then you understand."

"I understand, but . . ."

"But?"

Eric remained quiet for a few moments. Then he said, "My grandfather used to quote a passage from Proverbs:

" 'Pride *goes* before destruction,
And a haughty spirit before a fall.'

"In this case, James, I'd say the pride you had in the past has caused a lot of destruction in the present and that's just not easy to forget or excuse."

4

Bridget blinked twice and cast a blurry look at her bedside clock: 11:45. She yawned.

Earlier, she'd asked Ken to spend the night at her house, but he'd been afraid Dana would find out. "But she said she was staying all night at the hospital again," Bridget had argued.

"Maybe she will, and maybe she just

said that so she could come back to the gallery at two in the morning and find me gone," he'd told her. "Dana's clever and I know she already suspects this affair."

"*This* affair?" Bridget had asked. "How many have there been?"

After a moment, Ken said softly, "Bridget, I've been married to Dana for a long time. It hasn't been easy. In fact, at times it's been pretty damned miserable. There have been other women. Casual affairs."

"Oh. Well, I guess it was silly of me to think . . . I mean, a man like you trapped with a woman like her . . ." Her voice had started to waver. "But I know about Renée Eastman. People say you loved her."

Ken emitted a harsh laugh. "Love? Renée? She was nothing to me. Nothing."

"And me?"

"I love you. I wish there had only been you—*ever*. You know that. Why do you sound so insecure tonight?"

"You've been acting strange lately—it's so different than you've ever acted with me before now. Ken, tell me the truth. Have you changed your mind about being with me?"

"After all we've been planning these last

few months? After all we've already started doing to secure our future? Would I go through all of that with some woman who meant nothing to me?" His voice grew more intense. "I intend to get rid of Dana and make you my wife just as soon as possible."

"Then what's wrong?"

"I guess the tension of this situation is getting to me. I have to be so careful, Bridget. The Nordine Gallery isn't mine—it belongs to both Dana and me.. I don't want to lose half of it."

"I know you don't, but when you sell the Arcos paintings—"

"Shhh. Let's not even talk about them yet. We have to be patient, sweetheart. Everything is too new, too tentative."

"You mean our relationship?"

"No, I mean the business angle," he said sharply, then more softly, "If Dana divorces me on the grounds of adultery, I'll lose half the value of the gallery, and I will not lose this place!" He sighed. "I feel a migraine coming on."

"Maybe all this worrying you're doing about the gallery brought on the migraine,"

Bridget said softly. "I know you're tired of talking about this, but can't you just buy Dana's half of the place?"

"Well . . . not right away. I'm not a rich man, Bridget."

"Not yet. You will be after you sell Arcos's paintings. You've arranged everything so Dana won't get a penny from them. You'll be rich then."

"Well-off, but not rich. And things can always go wrong."

Anxiety touched Bridget's voice. "You mean they might? You may not get *any* money from the paintings?"

"That doesn't matter to you, does it?"

"Well . . . no, of course not."

"You love me for *me,* don't you? You're not pretending to love me because you think I have a lot of money or I *will* have a lot of money."

"Ken, you *know* I'm not pretending. I've always known you aren't rich. And the Arcos thing was a fluke. We didn't know he'd become such a success. "

"But when we got involved, you thought I was well-off."

"Yes, but . . ."

"Do you love me at all? Or are you just attracted to me? Or worse, are you just entertaining yourself? Is that it, Bridget? Am I just entertainment?"

"Entertainment? What are you talking about? I *love* you!"

"It's easy to say you love someone."

Bridget, for the first time during her affair with Ken, was becoming uneasy about him. So far, he'd been the kindest, gentlest man she'd ever known. She'd felt so safe with him, so loved. But now?

"*She* said she loved me, too, but *she* left," Ken snarled.

"She?" Bridget asked carefully. "Who are you talking about?"

After a moment, Ken said in his normal voice, "Bridget, please forgive me for tonight. I sound crazy."

"No, just different," she said without conviction. "You've been acting different all week."

"I think the Arcos murder threw me. There's so much to arrange for you and me, and Dana is such a harpy but so damned smart. I have to be alert twenty-four/seven. I'm just tired. I'm going to take my migraine medicine and go straight to bed."

"I think that's exactly what you should do."

"Once again, sorry for being so weird tonight. I have a lot on my mind. Soon it will be nothing but caviar and roses and wonderful times for Ken and Bridget *Nordine*." She smiled. He knew calling her Bridget Nordine pleased her. "Call me in the morning—not too early—to let me know you're not sick. I'll worry about you all night."

"I'll be fine, Ken, really."

"I won't be able to relax until I know that for sure. You're too precious to me. See you tomorrow at the gallery."

Bridget lay in the dark, thinking. What had sent Ken into a tailspin tonight? Maybe it had something to do with these murders. After all, one had been of Renée Eastman. But he hadn't loved that woman. She hadn't meant anything to him. Or so he said.

Bridget sighed and tried to reason herself into calmness. It had been a hard day. Lots of people had visited the gallery and Dana hadn't been around to help. Ken was

only suffering from a bad headache probably triggered by exhaustion. Bridget felt
beat, too. All she wanted was to lie down
on a white velvet chaise longue with soft
music in the background and someone to
rub her feet.

Oh well, it was late—or very early in the
morning—and Bridget's energy was wan-
ing. She didn't want to worry about Ken
anymore tonight. He would be all right. And
he *did* love her. She was certain he loved
her. Maybe it wasn't the "death do us part"
kind of love, but it was enough love to suf-
fice for now. Later, it would grow . . . and
grow . . . and grow. . . .

Bridget dozed off, then awakened an
hour later. She was hanging on the edge
of sleep again when she heard a floorboard creak. It seemed to her nearly every
floorboard in this little old house creaked.
Temperature changes, she thought dully.
Another creak. The temperature must be
dropping. Late October, an unusually chilly
night, her being awake at this time when
she was usually in a deep sleep and didn't
hear anything . . .

Creak. This one closer. *Creak.*

Bridget sat up in bed. Although the room

temperature was comfortable, she felt tiny chill bumps popping up on her arms.

I am not alone in this room, she thought abruptly.

Then she looked toward the curtains hanging over the bedroom windows. Cheap cotton curtains with not much more than gauze for a lining, they allowed a bit of light from a nearby streetlamp to seep in. Silhouetted against them, she saw a shadow. No, not just a shadow—a human shape.

Stealthily, she reached toward her nightstand. In the drawer she kept a .22 revolver given to her by a past lover to keep her safe. He'd even taught her how to use it, and she was a good shot.

The drawer barely made a sound as she slid it open. Her fingers touched the cool metal of the gun—

Before she could close her hand around the gun barrel, the silhouette shot across the small room, pressed a cloth over her nose and mouth, and pushed her head against the pillow. She kicked and twisted uselessly beneath the bedclothes, but she couldn't move her head. She also couldn't hold her breath any longer. She let in a tiny whiff of something cloying and sweet. She tried kicking some more, but that only made her more breathless. Into her mouth, her throat, her lungs, flowed the sweet scent.

And then Bridget finally went to sleep.

CHAPTER SEVENTEEN

1

"The private-duty nurse will be arriving there at ten o'clock tomorrow to get everything ready." Dana held the phone handset, waiting for her husband to reply. "Ken, did you hear me?"

"A private-duty nurse?" he replied vaguely.

"Yes. They're releasing Mary tomorrow around eleven. Don't tell me you forgot."

"No, I didn't forget." Pause. "A nurse?"

"I told you yesterday that I don't feel competent taking care of Mary as soon as she comes home. They gave me a list of private-duty nurses and I hired one to stay with us for a couple of days. Maybe three. Frankly, I'd feel better if she'd stay all week." Silence. "Ken, are you listening to me?"

"Huh? Oh yes. A nurse. For Mary."

"Ken, what's wrong?"

"Bridget didn't come to work today."

"Why?"

"I don't know. She didn't call. When she was an hour late, I called her. I only got her voice mail."

"Oh. Well, maybe something came up—family troubles or something."

"She doesn't have any family here. Besides, she would have called me. I tried getting her again. Three times. Still just voice mail." His voice rose slightly. "Dana, she's over three hours late!"

Bridget had been late twice over the last year, but she'd always called to explain her tardiness. Still, annoyance rushed through Dana that Ken didn't sound frustrated or even a bit angry—he sounded upset. "I'm sure Bridget is fine."

"You don't know that she's fine!"

"The Bridgets of the world are usually fine, Ken." Normally he would have snapped back at her sarcasm, but today he didn't seem to notice. Silence spun out. "Ken, please stop worrying about Bridget. She'll have a great excuse both for being late and for not calling you."

"Do you really think so?"

Damn him! Dana fumed inwardly. Couldn't he try to hide his feelings for the woman, even when talking to his wife?

"Yes, Ken. I'm absolutely certain. Now can we get back to the subject of your daughter?"

2

As Catherine drove home, she looked out the car window at the beautiful, clear autumn afternoon. She knew that after getting only three hours of fitful sleep last night and suffering from a crashing headache she should have canceled all of her appointments and taken off the whole day; however, she'd had two patients—one at one o'clock and another scheduled for two thirty—whom she felt she must see today. Both had reached serious points in their therapy, and her sense of responsibility far outweighed her fatigue. The sessions had gone well—especially one in which she believed her patient had accomplished a crucial breakthrough—and Catherine was extremely glad she hadn't skipped, or even delayed, the appointments. Next to Marissa and James, Catherine's patients were her priority.

But now it was almost four o'clock, and as she pulled into the garage Catherine felt almost too tired to exit the car and go into the house. All she wanted was to close the automatic garage door behind her, lie down on the front car seat, and go to sleep for about eight hours.

Wouldn't that cause an uproar? she thought, and couldn't help smiling. The surveillance cop would assume Catherine had gone inside the house. Marissa would arrive home, pull into the garage, see Catherine stretched out like a corpse in the car, and go berserk. As she climbed from the car and headed for the door leading into the kitchen, she let her thoughts run free, imagining official vehicles with sirens blaring and lights blazing converging at the Gray home. Eric would come, of course. And Robbie. Paramedics. Other deputies would be stringing a ton of crime-scene tape around the place. If the news shows got wind of it, television vans might be parked out front, reporters with microphones and camerapeople covering the lawn. The ever-vigilant Steve Crown and his wife would be stationed at their front window, Steve itching to come over and get involved, even though he hadn't completely recovered from Nicolai Arcos's attack. . . .

Lindsay barked, startling Catherine out of her dramatic daydream. The dog rushed into the kitchen and barked again, tail wagging. "Hello, Lindsay," Catherine said. "Sorry it's not Marissa, but she'll be home soon."

Lindsay laid her stuffed penguin at Catherine's feet and looked up expectantly. "Well, maybe you're as glad to see me as you would be to see Marissa." Catherine stooped and rubbed the dog's ears, feeling her stomach clench at the dog's display of affection. She'd felt so much horror, fear, and doubt the last few days, she felt as if it might not take much to tip her over the edge.

"Gosh, Lindsay, I think I'm on the verge

of a crying jag." She laughed shakily. "How about taking a nap with me?"

Two hours later, Marissa arrived home from work to find Catherine on her bed curled up in her bra and panties, partially covered by a down comforter, and Lindsay lying on the bed with her back against Catherine. They're spooning, Marissa thought, smiling as Lindsay gently thumped her tail but clearly had no intention of getting off the bed.

Marissa crept near the bed. "Sorry, Lindsay, but your Catherine has somewhere to go and I'm her date. I promise we'll both come back safe and sound." She placed her hand on Catherine's shoulder, gently shaking her. "Wake up, Sleeping Beauty. We have a wedding rehearsal to attend."

Catherine whimpered slightly.

"Sorry, honey. You promised and you never break a promise if you can help it. You have to wake up now."

Catherine moaned, her eyes remaining firmly shut.

"Catherine, we have to be at the church in an hour. Wake *up*."

Catherine's heather green eyes flared

open and she burst out, "Oh shit, dammit, hell!"

Marissa took a step back, then dissolved into giggles. Her sister rarely used "bad" language, much less shouted. Even Lindsay jumped up and fled the room. "Does that mean you don't want to get up or that I should get out of the area while I'm still on two feet?"

Slowly, Catherine's eyes focused. "Oh. Marissa." Then her eyes widened. "Oh, I'm so sorry!"

"No harm done. Except maybe to your relationship with Lindsay. She took off like a rocket."

Catherine threw off the comforter and sat up, looking mournful. "I scared her and she was really beginning to accept me."

"She'll get over it. She doesn't hold grudges."

Catherine sagged and said in a voice verging on pitiful, "Are you sure we have to be at the wedding rehearsal in an *hour*?"

"Yes."

Catherine groaned. She looked and sounded so tired, Marissa felt a wave of sympathy. "Look, Catherine, you're worn-out. Let me take your place tonight. You show me exactly what to do, which is very little, and you go back to sleep."

"No," Catherine said reluctantly. "Patrice will be expecting me, and tomorrow is her big day. I don't want to disappoint her. Besides, it's the rehearsal *dinner* she's excited about, not the rehearsal itself. I can't miss it after all the planning she's done to make it as perfect as the wedding." She clambered out of bed. "After a quick shower, I'll be a new woman."

After exactly fifty minutes, Catherine descended the steps to the family room wearing a shimmering pomegranate-colored silk knit jersey dress with long sleeves, a wide burnished-gold belt around her slim waist, a two-strand diamond-cut gold necklace, and matching earrings. Marissa, who sat in the lounge chair directly across from the stairs, blinked twice, raised her eyebrows, and said, "My God, you look beautiful! I wish James could see you in that dress!"

"Oh, he will." Catherine walked into the family room and looked at herself in the mirror hanging over the hearth, fluffing her long hair and touching a smudge of lip gloss at the corner of her mouth. "I'm not the kind of woman who can wear a dress once and throw it away. Considering what I paid for this, I'll still be wearing it in twenty years."

"Providing you don't put on twenty pounds," Marissa teased. "The way you've been eating this week just astounds me!"

"I have a nervous appetite right now. When all of this trouble is settled, I'll go back to eating normally."

"Which isn't enough. A woman *can* be too thin, you know, no matter what the Duchess of Windsor so famously said, and I'd say people getting murdered and attacked right and left constitutes more than *trouble.*"

Catherine turned to look at Marissa. "I'm trying to put on a happy face tonight for Patrice's sake. And for Ian's. I think he's glad his father is finally remarrying and settling down after all of these years. In spite of everything—even James nearly being killed—I want this wedding to be as joyful as possible."

"Catherine, you're a saint."

"I know," Catherine said dryly. "Now, I

want you to smile, be charming, and live up to the fine example set by your big sister."

Catherine and Marissa arrived at the church only ten minutes late. Patrice seemed nervous, frequently tweaking and twisting pieces of her curly blond hair, expressing horror over the attack on James, following the sympathy by saying she'd been afraid Catherine had changed her mind about attending. Lawrence—calm and handsome—asked questions about James, cursed the person who'd shot him, and thanked Catherine for deciding to fulfill her duty as maid of honor after what had happened.

Ian, who was Lawrence's best man, acted calmly charming. Catherine was glad he kept a suddenly slightly shy-acting Robbie close by his side instead of depositing her in a pew while visiting with his father and three of Lawrence's friends, who would be groomsmen. Robbie wore a simple blue-gray sheath with a strand of seed pearls and matching earrings with her hair pulled up in its usual French twist. She had the prettiness of good bone structure and smooth-skinned youth, but Catherine longed to take the pins out of Robbie's hair, to let down the shining mahogany brown mane and play up her large, dark blue eyes. In a few minutes, she could turn from pretty to beautiful.

Catherine also saw Tom, one of the deputies Eric had assigned to provide protection for her after the attack on James and her. Tom did a good job of being inconspicuous, but Catherine noticed his sharp gaze constantly shooting around the room and back to her. She trusted Jeff and she felt so much safer having him near. She couldn't stop thinking that if someone like Arcos was seeking revenge for Renée's murder, she was a likely candidate for their rage. After all, everyone knew she loved James and if they thought Renée posed a threat to her relationship with James—

Suddenly the minister appeared and announced magisterially that they were ready to begin the rehearsal. For a moment Robbie looked uncertain, and Catherine realized that besides herself, the young woman knew only Ian and Marissa. Catherine watched Robbie begin sidling toward the back of the church before Marissa caught her arm, murmured something to her, and then walked with her to a pew closer to the front. They settled side by side, and within moments Marissa had Robbie giggling. Dear Marissa, Catherine thought. Sometimes she drove Catherine crazy with her headstrong, stubborn impulsiveness; usually, though, Catherine was impressed by Marissa's strength, her perceptiveness, and her consideration for others. Tonight Catherine wanted to hug her for so quickly sensing Robbie's insecurity and putting her at ease with humor and comradeship.

The rehearsal went off so effortlessly, Catherine felt as if she'd practiced it a hundred times. Only a slight quaver in Patrice's voice betrayed her nervousness. Lawrence was in good spirits—even making a couple of humorous remarks to the slightly stiff young minister—while Ian acted relaxed and happy, often smiling at Patrice and his father and even casting a couple of grins at Robbie.

For the rehearsal dinner Lawrence had rented one of the smaller dining rooms at the luxurious Larke Inn. "Lawrence is handling the rehearsal dinner, and I'm in charge of the wedding and the reception. Neither of us is asking the help of friends and certainly not one of those wedding planners.

That's what happens when two control freaks get married!" Patrice had laughed to Catherine a few weeks earlier.

"I think that's wonderful," Catherine had told her sincerely. "This way, the entire wedding will reflect the taste of only you and Lawrence. That's what I hope to have . . . someday."

She'd blushed, accidentally having said enough to make her meaning clear, but Patrice had merely smiled, not winked, or teasingly mentioned James, or in any way tried to embarrass her. Many people called Patrice brash, but Catherine had always thought the woman showed a great deal of sensitivity at just the right times.

Within an hour, the rehearsal was so polished that the wedding party was headed for the Larke Inn. Although Patrice had kept the wedding party small, she and Lawrence had invited family members of the wedding participants as well as friends to the dinner. After they'd been seated in the dining room, Catherine estimated the number of guests at around forty.

Lawrence had reserved one of the Larke Inn's smaller dining rooms. It faced west, allowing a magnificent view of Aurora Falls through a glass wall. The water looked almost magical as it cascaded in front of strategically placed white lights, and out-of-town guests went straight to the windows, exclaiming over the beauty of the falls.

Although the outside temperature had dropped to an unusually low forty degrees, the room felt warm with its walnut wainscoting and amber carriage lights. The golden linen–covered tables were topped with fat, yellow candles surrounded by circlets of dark red and orange silk maple leaves. Inside the door stood a round glass table with a large floral masterpiece of burgundy and orange tiger lilies, gold and brown sunflowers, purple asters, and bronze and red snapdragons. Colored silk maple leaves lay scattered artfully around the arrangement as if they'd just tumbled from a towering tree. From the ceiling hung around twenty small, gold iridescent stars, obviously representing Star Air—tributes to the Star Air executives whom Lawrence had invited.

"Really striking," Marissa murmured in awe to Catherine as they entered the room. "I know Patrice told you they weren't using professionals to plan the wedding, but are

you sure Lawrence came up with this decorating scheme by himself?"

"Are you joking?" Catherine asked Marissa before looking at Lawrence standing
by Patrice's side and holding a drink,
laughing casually, the picture of the relaxed professional socializing with the
ease and sophistication of long years of
practice. Then Catherine glanced at Ian,
seeing his smile, his hand tightly holding
Robbie's, and the glow in Robbie's dark
blue eyes. They make a great couple, she
thought. Robbie would be *so* right for Ian:
capable, intelligent, pretty, refined yet fun,
totally lacking the egotistical demeanor of
most of the girls Lawrence pushed Ian to
date—

"You're Cathy Gray, aren't you?"

Catherine jumped slightly as a short
woman touched her arm with a hot pudgy
hand. "Yes, I'm Catherine Gray."

"Maud Webster," the woman announced
with the familiar air of someone who'd never
met a stranger. "My husband, Ed, is senior
vice president of Star Air."

"Hello. So nice to meet you, Mrs. Webster."

"Oh, it's Maud. Ed told me you're the

maid of honor. I know Patrice's sister is dead and she doesn't have any other close relatives. That's why she's only having a maid of honor—no bridesmaids."

"Actually, no. Patrice does have relatives—a couple of great-aunts—"

"Oh, neither of them would do at all for a maid of honor. Too old," the woman rushed on, less-than-subtly pushing Ian and Robbie out of her way in order to draw closer to Catherine. The young couple smiled in sympathy at Catherine before heading toward a group of other young people. Maud held a martini in her hand and Catherine had a feeling it wasn't her first. "Lawrence told my husband, Ed, that Patrice had picked what he called *a real looker* for her maid of honor, although he didn't think that was such a good idea," Maud said loudly, although Patrice stood near them. "After all, Lawrence said, you don't want the maid of honor outshining the bride, and *you'll* certainly outshine *Patrice.*"

Catherine's cheeks grew warm with a blush. "Well, I don't know about that, but—"

"Oh, no false modesty with me, Cathy," Maud said with a wink. "Say, wasn't it you who found a body a week ago?" Maud tried to sound as if the memory had just returned. "Yeah, it was you. Ed told me. He said there was a woman's body and she'd been the wife of a man you're dating! *And* she'd been murdered!"

Stunned at Maud's blatant bad manners, Catherine saw Marissa's eyes widen for a moment, then narrow before she quickly spoke. "My sister is seeing James East-man, who is *divorced—*"

"But the body Cathy found was East-man's wife's. Or *ex*-wife's, if you want to get technical." Maud dismissed Marissa with a flick of a plump hand and frowned ferociously up at Catherine. "By golly that must have been a shock for you! Why, I wouldn't know what to do if I found a dead body! Probably scream and carry on. I scare easily."

"Catherine, you look absolutely beautiful tonight." Patrice appeared, nearly elbowing herself protectively between Catherine and Mrs. Webster.

The woman drew a breath. "Cathy and I were just talking about—"

"I'm sorry James couldn't be here," Patrice said to Catherine without a glance at Maud Webster.

"He's sorry, too," Catherine managed. "He would have enjoyed tonight."

"Have you talked with him this evening?" Patrice asked.

"Yes. I called as we were driving here from the church," Catherine told her.

"How is he feeling tonight?"

"Fairly well."

"Oh, that's wonderful! James simply amazes me. He's *such* a remarkable man!" Patrice sounded as if James had just won the Olympic decathlon. She stepped closer to Catherine, gracefully but forcefully pushing the egregious Mrs. Webster even farther away, and asked in a lighthearted voice, "What's he up to tonight? Having a party in his room?"

"Oh, I don't think he's quite up to a party," Catherine said faintly, noticing Mrs. Webster trying to push her way back to her former position, a determined look in her small eyes. Catherine relaxed and started talking to Patrice with easy humor. "James said he's going to watch something educational on TV, but I'll bet anything it's a Lifetime romantic suspense movie."

Patrice laughed. "He'll never admit to that, Catherine!"

"I know. I also know what movie they're showing tonight. I've seen it and liked it. I have a trick question all ready to spring on him tomorrow. He'll give himself away."

"I wouldn't be too sure of that. After all, James is an excellent courtroom lawyer."

"Ah, so he's cagy, huh?" Mrs. Webster pounced with loud verbal aggression.

"Maud, there you are!" A pleasant-faced man with lips stretched into an unnatural-looking smile approached them and firmly took the plump woman's arm. "I've been looking all over for you."

"I've been right here! Ed, this is Cathy Gray. Cathy is the one who—"

"Nice to meet you, Catherine," Ed Webster interrupted loudly, linking his arm through his wife's and beginning to pull her away from the group. "Harold Sutpin and his wife are right over there, dear," he said to Maud. "Let's go say hello."

"I don't like Adele Sutpin! What I'm trying to tell you is—"

"Harold! Adele!" Ed called, and waved to a couple who had the unhappily surprised look of people who'd been caught when trying to hide. "Great night, isn't it?"

"Ed, what's wrong with you?" Maud

snapped. "Cathy Gray found that dead woman last week. I wanted you to talk to her." Ed Webster ignored his wife's protests as he guided her toward the hapless Sutpins, who seemed poised for a quick escape out the main door. They didn't make it.

"Do you think she was like that when Ed married her?" Catherine asked dryly.

Marissa and Patrice burst into laughter. "Isn't she awful? But Ed's nice and a very big deal with Star Air, so I have instructions from Lawrence to be extra-nice to him, which isn't hard," Patrice told Catherine and Marissa. "He didn't say I have to be nice to Maud, though. I think I'll cut her off at the bar."

"If Ed is important to Lawrence, I hope she doesn't report to him that I was rude," Catherine said.

Patrice smiled. "You weren't rude and I don't think Ed would care if you were. According to Lawrence, Ed thinks you're an *absolute dream.* He's besotted."

"He's just shell-shocked from living with Maud."

Patrice laughed again. "Dear, self-deprecating Catherine. No wonder James loves you so much." She peered over at

Lawrence. "Oh, he's motioning to me. Someone else important to meet. Don't worry—fifteen more minutes of socializing and then we get to eat. I'm starving."

Catherine looked at Marissa. "So far *too* bad?"

"I want to sit beside Maud," Marissa said in a humorless, demanding voice. "I want her to be my new best friend."

Catherine didn't crack a smile. "Monday morning I'm calling the best psychiatrist I know and setting up an appointment for you. Obviously, tonight has been too much for you and you've finally experienced a psychological break."

The sisters looked seriously at each other before falling into another giggling fit. Catherine had dreaded having to come to the dinner without James, dragging poor Marissa along in his stead, certain she would be able only to worry about him through the festivities. She hadn't even counted on being put through the wringer by Maud Webster. Still, thanks to Marissa, as the evening wore on Catherine found herself having fun with her little sister as her "date."

The next two hours were a whirl of

excellent food, toasts, and best wishes to the bride and groom. Catherine had been nervous about her speech. She was maid of honor, but she was neither a relative nor a longtime friend of Patrice. Nevertheless, she delivered a brief address Marissa later pronounced "genial and warm without being sentimental." Catherine was beyond pleased, considering her sister was the family expert at writing and hadn't contributed a word to the piece. Ian gave a longer, eloquent speech, full of affection for his father and Patrice and joy that they would be "wife and husband." As Ian raised his glass of champagne to the couple, his father smiled and Catherine spotted a tear slipping down Patrice's cheek.

"Eric and James would have enjoyed this," Catherine said wistfully to Marissa halfway through the dinner.

"Not as much as they would have at another time." Catherine knew Marissa was referring to all that had happened in the past week. "I know I'm being selfish, but I worry about how all of this will affect Eric's campaign."

"He's doing a fine job of investigating," Catherine said.

Marissa smiled. "All most people know is that he hasn't found—" She broke off, coloring slightly.

"The killer." Catherine smiled. "You don't have to walk on eggshells with me."

"I know. I just didn't want to bring up anything unpleasant tonight."

"Unpleasant?"

"Okay. Gruesome." Marissa laughed and Catherine went on. "Maybe recent *events* might hurt Eric's chances of being elected sheriff, although he doesn't have a stellar opponent, but everyone knows about his great performance on the Philadelphia police force and that he was the person Mitch Farrell hoped would succeed him as sheriff. Mitch was highly respected and, sometimes I think more importantly, *liked* in Aurora Falls." Catherine paused. "Besides, Eric is young, and if he doesn't win this election I think he has time to try running again."

"First that great speech to the bride and groom, and now this pep talk to me," Marissa said, grinning. "Catherine, you're on fire tonight!"

Catherine looked around, pleased to see that everyone seemed to be enjoying themselves. As the evening wore on, they seemed to be enjoying themselves more and more. She saw Lawrence knock over a glass of wine. So smoothly most people wouldn't have noticed, Patrice righted the glass and laid her napkin over the wet tablecloth, then went on talking and laughing without the slightest change in her happy expression. Although Lawrence didn't act as if he'd drunk too much, he didn't seem aware of what he'd done. In the years Catherine had known Lawrence Blakethorne, she'd never seen him have more than a couple of drinks. Tonight, though, was a very special occasion and both his color and his spirits were obviously running high.

Shortly afterward, though, Patrice yawned and then drew attention to her sleepiness by laughing and acting as if she were trying to swallow yet another yawn. "Pardon me!" she said loudly. "I'm usually able to hold my own later than this, but I have a big day tomorrow."

"The wedding isn't until tomorrow evening," someone called good-naturedly. "You can sleep late!"

"Oh, I never sleep late." She looked

fondly at Lawrence. "And I'm sure I won't be able to sleep late on my wedding day!"

People took the hint. A few glanced at watches to see that it was nearly eleven o'clock. The food and drink had made them drowsy, and Patrice's remark about her wedding day had reminded them that they would be attending a much bigger celebration tomorrow. Almost as if a gong had sounded signaling "leaving time," people began to shift in their chairs, leave the dining room for what Catherine guessed to be one last stop at the restroom, and approach Patrice and Lawrence to say good night and make assurances that they could hardly wait for the wedding, which they knew would be beautiful.

Catherine and Marissa were slowly making their way toward Patrice and Lawrence when Marissa suddenly grabbed Catherine's arm. "Oh my God, there's Maud Webster." Catherine looked at the woman whose small, drooping eyes widened at the sight of them. "She's going to ask more questions about Renée," Catherine hissed.

"What will we do?"

"We will be rude and simply run for the

door. Patrice and Lawrence won't be offended. Lawrence is so tired he looks ready to drop on the floor." Marissa signaled to Tom, pointing to the door, and pulled on Catherine's arm. "Come on! She's gaining on us!"

By the time they reached the door of the dining room, Catherine felt giddy from Marissa's hurried, giggling flight toward the main entrance to the Larke Inn. The three of them burst out the front doors and hurried down the five steps leading from the sweeping veranda to the wide sidewalk.

"It's freezing," Catherine complained.

"So you're glad we didn't bring my convertible."

"If we had, I think you would have sense enough to put up the top and turn on the heater. Still, I like my cozy white sedan."

"Which I see about twenty feet ahead of us. Gosh, Catherine, you have a midsize car, but the rear end is sticking out past any of the big cars."

"You know I'm not good at judging distance," Catherine said edgily. "Besides, I'm not blocking anyone."

"But you've had that car for three years. Haven't you learned to park correctly *yet*?"

Catherine turned on her. "Do you want to walk home?"

"No."

"Then for *once* be quiet about my bad driving."

"Okay. Sorry." Marissa paused. "And sorry for being *sorry.* I just can't suit you tonight."

"I'm worn-out and my head is killing me."

"You always get fussy when you're tired," Marissa said as if Catherine were a little child. "Besides, if you'd left me, I would have had Tom drive me home."

Catherine shook her head. "I don't know how Eric puts up with you."

"Oh, but he does."

Catherine had not locked her car and she swung open the driver's side door, blinking as the interior lights snapped to life. "Well, it's a miracle, that's all I have to say—" She went stone still. "Tom?"

"What is it, Dr. Gray?" the young deputy asked immediately, reaching for his gun.

"The seat. Look at my seat."

As Tom bent to look in, Marissa stepped

back from the car. "What?" she demanded. "What's on your seat?"

Catherine shuddered. "I think it's the mask Renée was wearing in *Mardi Gras Lady.*"

CHAPTER EIGHTEEN

1

"That *woman* has been clattering around in Mary's room for the last two hours! I can't stand it!"

Dana Nordine stared at her handsome if frazzled-looking husband for almost a full minute before she answered in a soft, even voice. "That *woman's* name is Ms. Greene. She's the nurse I hired. Mary is coming home after major surgery today, in case you've forgotten. Ms. Greene is preparing Mary's room."

"Will she leave as soon as Mary gets home?"

"No, Ken, she will be staying for at least three days. Full-time."

"Three days *and* nights?"

Dana took a deep breath, trying to hold on to her patience. "Mary could have problems in the night as well as in the day."

"Well, if she has problems at night can't you just call an ambulance?"

"I could, but that's not what I want to do." Dana and Ken stood outside Mary's hospital room. A nurse was talking to her, asking the five-year-old for suggestions as to how her panties, robe, house slippers, stuffed dog, and precious though wilting "get well" flowers were to be arranged for the trip home. Dana could hear the little girl's voice, louder than usual with excitement, but still took Ken's arm and pulled him a few feet farther down the corridor out of Mary's earshot. "Mary is your child, Ken. I hope you feel the same way I do—that she deserves the very best care. After all, it isn't as if we can't afford to have a private-duty nurse for three days." She paused. "Or is she already coming on to you?"

"Coming on to me!" Ken looked horrified. "She's at least seventy and she has a nose like a pig's. I've never seen such big nostrils in my life!"

Dana glared at him for a moment before her lips began to twitch and she bent over, laughing. "Honestly, Ken, you are the only man I know who is more concerned with a medical person's looks than her expertise." Ken glared at her indignantly until she wiped the tears of laughter from her face and managed to look at him halfway seriously. "Ms. Greene will only be with us for three days and you don't even have to look at her if you find her so physically repugnant. The doctor highly recommended her; she has excellent credentials; she's supposed to be a regular pied piper with children—they love her."

"Oh, I don't care about her credentials. I mean, I'm sure they're fine. She must be good enough at her job to look after a kid getting over a simple appendectomy."

"Then what is your problem today? You look like you found out someone stole one of your father's paintings."

"Actually, I sold a painting this morning. A very expensive painting, but . . ." The indignant look faded from Ken's face to be replaced with one of near despair. "Bridget *still* hasn't turned up! No call, no text."

No sex, Dana almost said, but now was not the time for an argument. "Have you driven past her house?"

Dana knew he would have, but she'd decided to play along as if she gave a damn about Bridget Fenmore, at least until she could get Mary home and settled.

"Yes. A couple of times." More like twenty, Dana thought. "There's no sign of her. The mail and newspapers are piling up."

"What about her car?"

"What about it?"

"Is her car around?"

"Yes. It's in the garage." His eyes shifted away guiltily. "I looked in the garage window and saw it."

Dana had been to Bridget's tiny house once and knew the garage had no window. Ken had a key to the house and he'd used it, going inside to search for Bridget or any sign of her, Dana thought. In order to see Bridget's car, he must have glanced through the door leading from the house to the garage. "Have you called her parents?"

"I don't know where her parents live.

They might even be dead. She never mentions them."

"The information might be on her application form. However, after you got a look at her during the interview, I don't suppose you spent much time studying her application."

Ken's jaw tightened. "It seems to me you've gotten damned cocky lately, Dana. What's behind this new tone of yours?"

"Nothing I care to discuss with you."

"Oh, really?"

"Yes, really. What about her friends?" Ken looked blank. "Have you talked to any of Bridget's friends?"

"What makes you think I'd know who her friends are?" Ken asked defensively. "She's just our employee. We don't socialize with her."

Talk about protesting too much, Dana thought sarcastically. "She mentioned a friend to me once." She told him the woman's name. "If she has an unlisted phone number, I guess you'll have to call the police."

"The police!"

"To report Bridget missing, if you're so certain something has happened to her and she hasn't just decided to take a long weekend."

"She's been gone since Friday. You call that a long weekend? And where would she go? Who with?"

"With whom. I have no idea. You know her a *lot* better than I do." Dana waited for Ken to give her a spluttering denial of knowing Bridget better than Dana did, but he was obviously too tired. "Ken, I want you to be here when our daughter is released."

"I came here to sign papers. That's all taken care of. Now I need to be at the gallery. You and what's-her-name, the nurse, can get Mary home."

Dana took a deep breath, trying to smother her anger. Finally, she was able to talk instead of shout. "Ken, you can at least *act* like you care. After all, bad publicity wouldn't be good for the gallery," she added acidly. "I expect you to be here within the next hour. If you aren't, I will make sure half the hospital staff knows how unconcerned you are about your daughter."

"Don't threaten me."

"Don't disappoint me."

"You mean 'don't *disobey* me.'"

Dana, to her own bafflement, smiled.

"Your vocabulary has improved since you were a stock boy at one of my father's stores, Ken, although I'm aware of the occasional grammatical gaffe."

Ken looked furious. "Dammit, Dana—"

"You either stay here now or you come back within an hour. Mary can barely wait to see her father. And don't forget—people are watching you far more than they did before Arcos's murder." Dana leaned closer and hissed, "For your own sake, don't screw up because of Bridget Fenmore."

2

Eric Montgomery stood on the porch of the Gray home, hat in hand. Before he'd had a chance to ring the bell, an exhausted-looking Catherine swung open the door and demanded, "Do you know where that *thing* came from?"

"The mask."

"Yes."

"No." She frowned at him. "No, I don't know where it came from yet." He waited a moment and then asked, "May I come in?"

"Oh, I'm sorry." She moved backward

and Eric saw Lindsay peeping out from behind her. "That's quite a scary guard dog you have."

"She's Marissa's dog, remember? Give me your coat and hat." She turned and loudly yelled, "Marissa, Eric's here!"

Eric had never heard ladylike Catherine yell. *Never.* This was a definite sign that her nerves were shot, he decided, and was glad when Marissa rushed out of the kitchen and flung herself in his arms. "Our knight in shining armor! Tell us all about that awful mask!"

"I called you earlier—"

"James had a setback," Catherine announced harshly. "Apparently he got out of bed in the night—he was sleepwalking, I suppose—and . . . and . . ."

"He didn't do much damage to his shoulder." Marissa didn't even look at Catherine, whose eyes were beginning to drip. "He had to go back into surgery, but the doctor said they only needed a few more stitches to close a few that had torn. The original incision had enlarged, but four stitches—"

"Five!" Catherine snapped.

"Five stitches fixed him right up. He's snoozing away on painkillers right now.

The doctor says this will only delay his recovery for a day or two."

Catherine looked defiant. "She was just trying to make me feel better."

"No, she wasn't. Did she look like one of those doctors who pat you on the back and tell you everything's fine when it isn't? She *knew* Dad, for God's sake."

"What does that have to do with us?"

"Well, I'm sure it has something to do with respect and professionalism and . . . oh hell, I don't know."

"I'm sorry about James," Eric said. "Does he sleepwalk?"

"Not that I know of," Catherine replied.

"It might have been a reaction to his injury or the medicine," Eric replied.

"Catherine, calm down," Marissa said kindly. "Go upstairs, cry some more, and get this anxiety out of your system."

"I'm not going anywhere until I hear about the mask."

Marissa sighed. She looked almost as tired as Catherine and twice as frustrated. Nevertheless, Marissa was obviously working at keeping up her spirits. "You might as well spill all the details about the mask or there will be no peace this afternoon, and *someone* needs a nap before the wedding tonight."

"What have you found out about the mask?" Catherine urged.

"The mask was plastic," Eric said. "We didn't find any prints. However, the glue on the gold lace edging wasn't completely dry and neither was the black paint used to make the star around the right eye."

"The paint was fresh?" Catherine asked.

"I don't know. It was latex paint," Eric said. "Sometimes latex paint can dry on plastic in an hour. It's often used on stuff like model cars or ships."

"But you can't tell exactly how long ago the star was painted."

"No, Catherine, I'm sorry, but I can't. The glue used to attach it is completely dry. It could have been Krazy Glue. We'll be testing the paint and the glue Monday, but today all I can tell you is that I think the mask was decorated yesterday."

"But you know what that mask looks like." Eric remained silent while Catherine stared at him. "It looks exactly like the mask Renée is wearing in *Mardi Gras Lady.*"

"I've only seen that painting once, but as

I remember it, the mask does look like the one the woman in the painting is wearing."

"Where would someone get a mask like that around here?"

"In Aurora Falls?" Eric shrugged. "I don't know. It's near Halloween, though. A few shops around here sell costumes. We're already checking on them to see if anyone bought a full costume with a plastic half mask or just a white plastic mask that could be decorated any way the buyer wanted. I have a feeling the person who left that mask on your seat wouldn't take the chance on being recognized as someone who recently bought a mask like that, though, so I looked on the Internet. You can order plain white plastic masks and have them delivered overnight. If I were going to pull a stunt like someone did on you last night, I'd be safe and order a mask, not buy one locally."

"Do you think it could be the mask Renée wore in the portrait?"

"If she actually wore that mask and posed for the painting, Arcos could have kept the mask out of sentiment," Eric said. "After his murder, we went over his warehouse thoroughly, though, and we didn't find it. Of

428   Carlene Thompson

course, if it really existed, she let him keep it and then left him, he could have destroyed it out of anger or grief or . . . hell, I didn't know Arcos. I don't know how his mind worked, what he might have done with it. If the painting is just a product of his imagination, the mask in your car could simply be one made to look like the one in the portrait."

"So the important question is who would do something like this," Marissa said.

Eric nodded. "We have a list of people invited to the dinner. Catherine, did you know all of them?"

"Heavens, no! A lot were business associates of Lawrence. I met them, but I don't remember most of their names."

"Except for Maud," Marissa said.

Catherine rolled her eyes. "Oh lord, I'll never forget Maud."

Eric looked at her. "Maud?"

"Maud Webster," Catherine said. "Her husband, Ed, is senior vice president of Star Air. He seemed very nice. She was another matter. Pushy, nosy, no manners. Of course, she'd had too much to drink, but I have a feeling she's not much better when she's sober. She knew about my relationship with James and what happened last Saturday. She kept asking me what it felt like to discover his wife's body. She would *not* shut up and she was talking loudly. People were pretending not to hear her, but I knew they could hear every word. Marissa kept trying to interrupt, but it didn't do any good. Maud's husband, Ed, must have finally seen what was happening. He hurried over and started nearly dragging her toward a couple named the Suskins or Sutpins. I can't remember their exact names." For the first time, Catherine smiled. "I do remember that they looked like they were ready to bolt for the door when they saw her coming!"

"They must know her," Marissa said dryly. "When even *I* can't get someone to shut up, you know you're in trouble."

"I'll talk to the Suskins or Sutpins about Maud," Eric said. "Maybe she had a reason for being so tenacious."

"I think she's one of those people who just lives for gossip, but there might be something else," Catherine said.

Eric frowned. "You said a lot of people heard her."

"At least half the room."

"Did anyone look surprised?"

"Surprised?" Catherine echoed.

"Yes, like they hadn't already heard about you finding the body."

"Well, honestly, I was thinking more about how embarrassed I was than watching for other people's reactions," Catherine answered. "Why are you asking?"

"Because not everyone at the rehearsal dinner was from Aurora Falls. Some of the Star people were from at least a hundred miles away. They probably would have heard about the body being found, but they wouldn't have known what Catherine Gray looked like."

"Oh," Catherine said. "So Maud might as well have pointed me out to the whole group."

"Exactly."

"But how would whoever did this know which car was mine?"

"It would probably be easy to slip in a seemingly casual question to Patrice or Lawrence about your car."

"What if we'd taken Marissa's instead of mine?"

"I doubt if there were too many convertible red Mustangs in the parking lot that night. You're sure you didn't lock your car last night, Catherine?"

"Fairly sure. I was nervous about giving my speech and afraid I didn't look right in my new dress—it's not my usual style. But how could someone know I'd leave the door unlocked?"

"Maybe it didn't matter." Catherine looked at Eric quizzically. "Maybe someone brought along a lockout kit for opening locked car doors."

"This person came to the rehearsal dinner and brought along a mask *and* a lockout kit?"

"Both of which they could have left in their own car," Eric said. "Did either of you notice someone being away from the dinner for fifteen or twenty minutes?"

The sisters looked at each other. Finally, Marissa said, "There was a social hour before we ate. I think it lasted about twenty minutes—maybe a little more. And I counted. Forty-one guests attended the dinner."

Catherine looked at her. "You *counted*?"

"I got bored during those long-winded toasts Lawrence's friends made. Anyway, Eric, there were forty-one guests and before the dinner actually started there was plenty of time for someone to leave for a few minutes. Even longer."

Eric frowned, chewing on his bottom lip. "Maybe whoever left the stuff wasn't a guest at the rehearsal dinner. The Larke Inn has three dining rooms and a very large parking area. Someone could have just waited until they saw the two of you arrive and go inside the inn. Then they went to work." Eric looked at Catherine's bleak expression. "This might not be as serious as it seems," he said. "Remember, we're near Halloween. It could have been done as a prank by someone who doesn't even know you. They just know who you are, what happened, what kind of car you drive. After all, the car is parked five days a week where you work. They didn't have to do much research *or* much work to give you a good scare."

"Which they did. Give me a good scare, that is." Catherine seemed to be thinking over this possibility. Then she shook her head. "No, Eric, it just doesn't feel right. They would have had to order the mask and the decorations, copy the mask on *Mardi Gras Lady* perfectly, not leave any fingerprints, know the time of the rehearsal dinner—it just seems like too much trouble for a simple, harmless scare."

Which was exactly what Eric thought, although he'd hoped to sell the "harmless scare" theory to Catherine to give her at least one calm day. "Well, I'm not ruling it out," he said firmly.

He exchanged looks with Marissa. He could tell by the expression in her gaze that she knew exactly what he was doing. They been together too long, loved each other too long, for her not to understand how his mind worked and every nuance of his voice. Sometimes this made him feel so close to her, it was almost as if they were one person and the reassurance of not feeling alone was beyond joy. And then sometimes it was a colossal pain.

"And how did they know I'd be at the rehearsal dinner last night?"

"Lawrence Blakethorne is well-known in this city. A lot of people know he's getting married today. People also know that the woman who found the dead body is Patrice's maid of honor."

"That sounds like a lot of 'ifs' to me," Catherine said disparagingly.

"It sounds like a lot of 'ifs' to me, too," Eric admitted. "I was just throwing it out there as a possibility."

"Any other flimsy possibilities, Sheriff?"

"Chief Deputy," Eric said, and failed at a grin. "Okay, Catherine, this one isn't so flimsy. I realize you can't break client-patient confidentiality, but I have to know if you have a patient you believe might be capable of this," he asked uncomfortably.

Catherine looked incensed. "A patient? Absolutely not!"

"I'm not talking about a real nut job." Catherine glared at him. "Well, that was the wrong term. But you know what I mean. Not someone who's really mentally ill, dangerous, anything like that. Just someone you might have insulted lately. Not that you'd purposely insult anyone, but you might tell them something they don't want to hear."

Catherine's glare had died. "I know what you mean, Eric. I can't think of anyone who would do such a thing." Except for Mrs. Tate, she thought, but Mrs. Tate certainly wasn't angry with her. At their last session, the woman had said she was trying to act more like Catherine, and Catherine had sensed her sincerity. "None of my patients put the mask in my car."

"Great," Marissa said glumly. "So if we consider someone at the rehearsal dinner or just someone who has too much time on their hands and went to all the trouble of making that mask to scare Catherine because she's become a great target for a scare during the last two weeks we have an endless supply of people as suspects."

"I'm afraid so," Eric said.

Catherine shook her head. "I'm convinced this wasn't just a harmless attempt to frighten me. Someone went to a lot of trouble to make that mask, put it in the right car, et cetera. But why?" She looked at Eric. "Please don't try to make me feel better, even though I know you mean well. I'm not stupid, Eric. Tell me why *you* think someone did it. And be absolutely truthful."

"Okay." Eric's imagination had run dry. He couldn't come up with any more lame theories to toss out just because he thought they'd make Catherine feel less worried for a few hours, at least so she could enjoy the wedding tonight.

"This may not be New York City, but

that doesn't mean everyone knew about Renée and James's awful marriage, her disappearance, or the police investigation of James. Also, probably even fewer people knew you and James now have a relationship. However, because of all the news after you found her body, I'd say the number of people who learned about the whole saga increased by thousands."

Eric could feel Marissa glowering at him, but he couldn't soft-pedal the situation, even for her. He knew how protective she was of Catherine, but Catherine wasn't a little girl, her told himself. She was a highly intelligent twenty-nine-year-old woman who deserved the truth.

Eric began in a slow, calm voice. "Maybe the person who did this knew *Mardi Gras Lady* was a portrait of Renée and wanted to hurt you by reminding you that she had been James's wife whereas after all this time you're . . . well, you're—"

"Just his girlfriend," Catherine said tonelessly. "Not his new wife, not his fiancée, just his girlfriend."

"Well . . . yes. But the fact that you aren't either of the others doesn't mean James isn't in love with you. I mean, after all he's been through—"

"You don't have to soothe my wounded ego, Eric." Catherine managed a small smile. "I've accepted the situation and I'm fine with it for now."

"Okay. Good." Eric realized his palms had begun to sweat. For some reason, he'd been afraid Catherine would burst into tears. Marissa definitely had him brainwashed about Catherine's easily wounded feelings, Eric thought, and felt a sudden, irrational wave of anger toward her. Then came frustration with himself for letting Marissa's protectiveness of her sister influence his honesty with the person who *should* concern him—Catherine.

"And the second 'maybe'?"

"What?"

"Eric, you said maybe the person who put the mask in the car did it to hurt me," Catherine reminded him. "I can see by your face you have at least one more 'maybe' as to why someone placed the mask on my seat of the car."

"Okay." Eric drew a deep breath. "Those who do know you, or have done research about you and James, know how serious he is about you. Maybe the mask was put there as a warning of what happened to the first woman James loved."

"A warning that James might kill me just like he supposedly killed her?"

"Yes."

"But he *didn't,*" Marissa burst out.

Catherine held her hand up, quelling her sister's vehement defense of James. "I know he didn't kill her, Marissa. Thanks for your belief in him, but let's hear Eric's third 'maybe.'"

"Oh, you guessed there was a third. Okay. Maybe this person doesn't know who murdered Renée but is killing the possibilities. He killed Arcos because he thought Arcos could have killed Renée for leaving him. He thought James might have killed her because she left him."

"And what about me?"

"Maybe the murderer thinks you killed Renée because he believes you knew she returned to Aurora Falls just before the divorce was finalized and would manage to lure James back." Eric hesitated, then plowed on. "*Maybe* this person thinks *you* killed Renée."

"Then why didn't he kill me the night James was shot!"

"Maybe he had trouble killing a *woman* he wasn't certain was guilty." As Catherine looked at Eric in shock, he went on relentlessly. "The mask could have been a threat. Something to scare you enough to make you leave James, leave Aurora Falls—a threat from the killer of Arcos because maybe he's losing his reluctance to murder a woman."

"I feel like you're going in circles to protect me from something." Catherine gave Eric a hard look. "Just say it."

"Okay. Because of James, you're part of this whole group—Renée, Arcos, and James. Most people in this town have loved and respected your parents and now you. Maybe the killer is just drawing out what he feels will be his last, most shocking, and most tragic murder."

CHAPTER NINETEEN

1

"I can't believe you took a room at the Larke yesterday when you're getting married here tonight, Ms. Greenlee," Mitzi said. She was a new receptionist at the law firm of Eastman and Greenlee, a short, blond woman with a round face and red cheeks. "You live with Mr. Blakethorne anyway. You could have stayed at his house for free."

Patrice, fluffing at her wedding dress, which hung on a rack in the middle of the room, turned and gave the young woman a smile. "Mitzi, it's bad luck to see your groom on your wedding day. I didn't want to see Lawrence this morning. I didn't want to see him all day. I want to wait until tonight when I become his wife. After all, I've loved him for a long time. I didn't want us to get up and eat breakfast together as if it was just any other day. *This* day is special to me."

"Well, I think that's just about the most romantic thing I ever heard," Mitzi said, her big blue eyes filling with tears.

"Don't cry, Mitzi," Patrice ordered. "Your eye makeup is perfect and you'll ruin it."

"Oh! Oh, gosh!" Mitzi began blinking so fast her eyelids were a blur. "And you paid for this professional makeup job. I'm sorry." She took a quick look in the dresser mirror. "No damage done."

Patrice's cool gray eyes met Catherine's gaze. Mitzi had been hired because she was the daughter of one of Mrs. Eastman's friends, but Catherine could already see she wouldn't last long. Now Mitzi was in the "honeymoon phase" with Patrice, whom she admired almost to the point of worship. "It's embarrassing," Patrice had told Catherine, "but it's also sweet. Of course, in two more months she'll think I'm a bitch, just like the rest of the staff does because I'm impatient and sharp-tongued, and intolerant of mistakes. For now, though, I'm her ideal. She's asked so many questions about the wedding, I've decided to let her participate. She'll stand at the guest book, beaming at everyone coming into the wedding. The guests will think she's adorable, and she'll think I've entrusted her with an important duty when Marissa's dog could probably handle the job just as well. Do you think I'm awful?"

"I think you're being extremely considerate," Catherine had answered. "Even if later Mitzi decides she doesn't like you, she'll always remember your wedding as one of her big nights."

"Well, I just think it's an awful shame that you and Mr. Blakethorne don't get to go on a honeymoon," Mitzi now continued, still inspecting her eye makeup. "Honeymoons are supposed to come *right* after the wedding, not weeks later. It's just so sad—"

"Don't start crying again, Mitzi. Lawrence has business to take care of now, but in two weeks we'll be walking on the Champs-Élysées," Patrice said gaily. "Think of it—the specialty shops, the cafés, the cinemas . . ."

Mitzi clapped her hands. "Oh, I've always wanted to go there!"

"I know Lawrence needs to talk to the people at Star Air before the deal is sealed in mid-December, but hasn't he heard of telephones?" Catherine asked, smiling. "Business can be discussed over the phone."

"Oh, he doesn't trust foreign operators to get United States phone numbers correct," Patrice said airily.

He should get together with Mrs. Tate, who doesn't eat "foreign" food, Catherine thought. "Can't he take his cell phone? That way he'd be making the call himself."

"Oh, he's always losing cell phones. So is Ian, only he's even worse. Honestly, between the two of them, they must spend three or four thousand dollars a year just on cell phones." Dressed in a long slip, she whirled around to Catherine. "Want to help me put on my wedding dress, Maid of Honor?"

Catherine slipped the ivory silk gown off the padded hanger, holding it high while the other women in the room gasped as if they'd never seen anything so beautiful. Actually, Catherine thought Patrice had made a wise decision to wear a relatively simple gown without frills and ruffles and a long train. "I'm forty, not twenty-five," she'd told Catherine at least ten times. "I don't want people to think I'm trying to look at least ten years younger than I am. Women who do that are just pathetic!"

Patrice stood almost inhumanly still in front of a cheval mirror as Catherine slid the sheath gown over her tall, slender body. A layer of lace formed a jewel neckline and cap sleeves above the ruched silk bodice, the lace highlighted with a delicate sprinkling of rhinestones. At Patrice's neck a narrow diamond necklace sparkled, matching the diamond tennis bracelet shimmering on her wrist and one-carat, radiant-cut stud earrings—Lawrence's wedding gift to his new wife. In order to show off the earrings, Patrice wore her blond hair upswept with only a few ringlets left to dangle strategically on her neck.

"You look beautiful!" the two women cried simultaneously.

"The gown is lovely—I really like the way

the hem dips lower in back than in front so you have the illusion of a train. The dress is just perfect for your figure. Lawrence will love it, just as he loves you," Catherine said.

"You don't think I need a veil?"

"The silk rose clips match the real roses in your bouquet."

Patrice held up the beautiful cascade of ivory roses and small ivory accent flowers entwined with English ivy. "Not too long?"

"Okay, Patrice, quit soliciting compliments." Catherine laughed. "You know you look wonderful."

Patrice's smile wavered slightly. "When Lawrence married my sister Abigail, she was so young, so beautiful. She looked like the women you see on the cover of bridal magazines."

"The *airbrushed models* you see on the cover of bridal magazines," Catherine corrected. "Real women don't look like them. Besides, I've seen wedding pictures of Abigail and Lawrence. Abigail was pretty, Patrice, but she wasn't beautiful. Your mother never stopped talking about how gorgeous she was—how much prettier than you—and you started believing her. She brainwashed you into thinking you weren't a match for Abigail in any way, including looks." Patrice gave Catherine a long look, her light, silvery eyes narrowing. "Don't get mad. You just got half an hour's worth of therapy for free."

The room quieted, the other women tensing as if afraid Patrice was going to leap on Catherine. Then Patrice laughed. "Thank you, Dr. Gray. You know how I love a bargain." She paused. "And maybe Abigail wasn't *quite* as lovely as Mother always said."

"You really do look beautiful, Patrice." Everyone in the room looked at Beth Harper. For years, she had worked at Eastman and Greenlee as a legal secretary. After she'd married, she'd taken the less time-consuming position as secretary for Dr. Hite—and now Catherine—at the Aurora Falls Center. The job provided a nice salary—although less than Beth had earned at Eastman and Greenlee—but required around five hours fewer a week and no overtime.

Two weeks before the wedding, Beth told Catherine that Patrice had asked if she would sing. "I've barely seen Patrice for over a year and didn't guess she remembered that I do sing at some local events." Beth had shaken her head. "That's Patrice for you, though. You think she doesn't know you're alive and suddenly she appears back in your life knowing everything you've done and everything you're doing now."

"Did you agree to sing?" Catherine had asked.

"Of course. She wants me to do 'We've Only Just Begun.'"

"The song the Carpenters did?"

"Yes. And fortunately, one I've sung before. I won't need much practice." Beth had looked slightly dubious. "Actually, I don't think it's the right song for Patrice and Mr. Blakethorne. It seems like a song for a young couple's wedding."

"I agree," Catherine said. "Oh lord, please say you didn't tell her what you think."

"I'm not in the hospital with a concussion, am I?" Beth and Catherine had broken into giggles. "I'd never imply that something else might be more appropriate, especially to *her.* Besides, she told me that when she was fourteen she decided she wanted that song sung at her wedding, so just because she had to wait awhile on the wedding doesn't mean I'm going to take the joy out of it for her."

Now, Beth smiled, then said, "You look beautiful, Catherine."

Catherine inspected herself in the cheval mirror. Her sheath gown with its short sleeves and unadorned square neckline was far from an attention grabber. Patrice had selected it. When Catherine got it home, she put it on, looking at it critically in her full-length mirror as she modeled it for her sister.

"Well? What do you think?"

Marissa, nearly always blunt, had commented, "It borders on plain, Catherine."

"It fits well. The lines are nice—classic," Catherine had offered halfheartedly.

"True." Marissa had frowned, her gaze traveling over the gown as if she were looking for a tiny flaw in a gem. "I think Patrice meant to cast you into the shadows, but with the right makeup and accessories, *you'll* be stunning."

"But it's *her* day."

"Hey, Sis, she chose the dress. Is it my fault a few changes can make you look more than just acceptably attractive?"

"Marissa, are you planning something?"

"Don't worry. I'll be subtle as always."

"'Subtle' is not a word I'd ever apply to you!" Catherine had called after Marissa as she left the bedroom.

Now Catherine stood in front of the pier-glass mirror, looking at herself wearily, glad James wasn't here to see her looking just "acceptably attractive" in the pretty dress and the sweet, small silver locket and tiny stud earrings Patrice had given her to wear as her only accessories. She didn't want to outshine the bride, but she'd hoped to look a bit more striking.

At that moment, someone knocked on the door and then opened it before anyone had time to say a word. Catherine's eyes brightened when Marissa whisked through the doorway, full of smiles and giggles and exaggerated movements, all of which Catherine recognized as tactics to divert Patrice's attention.

"I'm sorry to burst in uninvited," Marissa said loudly, although nearly everyone was already exclaiming over her rose-colored sleeveless dress with a deep-cut cross-over neckline. Catherine was glad Eric had been able to accompany her sister to the wedding to see how beautiful she looked. "Patrice, I *just* thought about this today," Marissa raced on. "I know you picked that lovely locket for Catherine, but I remembered a set of jewelry we have that would be spectacular with that elegant dress you chose. Marissa flipped open a black, felt-covered box to reveal a silver chain from which dangled six teardrop-shaped, filigreed charms, along with a matching set of dangle earrings. "Don't you think this would be just stunning with the dress?"

Patrice neared, looking at the high-polished jewelry glittering against the black background. "Well, it wasn't really what I'd pictured. . . ."

Marissa's wide smile trembled a bit. "I know, but this set was our mother's—you know she just passed away less than a year ago—and she always thought it would look lovely on Catherine. I thought if it suited Catherine and of *course* was all right with you, Patrice, my sister might wear it tonight?"

Marissa should have been an actress, Catherine thought, trying not to smile as she realized Marissa had remembered the silver filigree jewelry set days ago. She's been planning this all along, having sense enough not to mention it to me because I might have asked Patrice about substituting it for the locket and Patrice would have probably said *no.* Now here's Mitzi, already unfastening the locket and reaching for the filigree necklace to try on "just to see how it looks."

Twenty minutes later, Catherine walked slowly down the aisle, knowing the soft church lighting picked up the glow of the silver jewelry and heightened the silvery sheen of the gown.

For the reception, Lawrence had booked the largest dining room of the Larke Inn, the one with sliding walls that could be opened to expose a smaller dining area, making one large venue. Patrice, in charge of decorating for the reception, had chosen white with accents of the same darkly vivid steel blue that covered the walls of Lawrence's office. "It's his favorite color!" she announced when some of the guests— obviously expecting pink—gasped at the sharp color contrast. "Blue for the sky!"

"That'd be one helluva blue sky!" someone exclaimed, eliciting laughter and a guffaw from Lawrence, who answered, "When

I'm behind the wheel of a plane, the sky turns this color from pure joy!"

Catherine caught sight of Marissa, diligently taking pictures with and talking into her cell phone, no doubt preparing material for the article covering the wedding that would appear in Monday's *Gazette.* She knew the article had been assigned to a reporter whose work experience consisted of three months on the weekly five-page bulletin of a tiny town forty miles away. "The editor doesn't like her and wants to give himself an excuse to get rid of her. Messing up coverage of a wedding as important as this one will do the trick, but I'm not going to let him get away with it. The poor girl just needs a little more experience."

"And an undercover agent with a top-notch cell phone to help her," Catherine had said, as usual touched by the deep, quiet kindness and altruism she so often saw in the Marissa other people thought was too brash and self-absorbed. "Good luck, Mrs. Bond."

"You don't need luck when you have skill," Marissa returned.

"Missing James tonight?" Eric asked as

he turned away from a man Catherine quickly recognized as the mayor.

"Oh, Eric, I didn't even see you! Yes, I miss James. I just called him and told him the wedding went off without a hitch."

"Now we have the reception to get through." Eric leaned toward her and lowered his voice. "Jeff is here. He, Marissa, and I will be watching you all evening. Please don't wander out of this room—we're your protection."

All through the wedding, Catherine had been telling herself she wasn't nervous or uneasy. Hearing Eric reassure her that she was under so much surveillance, though, made her muscles immediately relax a notch. James had been right—coming tonight had been taking a risk. Still, she knew she couldn't hide indefinitely. She had to dig up the courage to face the world. Thank God she had help, though.

"Thank you, Eric." She smiled. "I promise to behave myself tonight and not try to dodge you and Jeff."

Eric pretended to wipe sweat from his forehead. "Well, that's a relief."

Catherine looked around the large room where a band played "I Will Always Love

You." She saw Ian dancing with Robbie, whom she hardly recognized in a dark and light blue satin dress with a crossover halter neck. She'd let down her heavy brown hair to hang in tousled ringlets pulled toward the right and exposing most of her taut, smooth back. Catherine had never seen her look so glamorous, and from the look in Ian's eyes as he gazed fixedly at Robbie neither had he.

Catherine drank a glass of champagne. She hated champagne, but she didn't want to seem rude when an eager and obviously inexperienced young waiter offered it to her, a man she recognized as a headwaiter looking on. She danced once with Eric while Marissa was off inconspicuously conversing with the photographer from the *Gazette.* "She thinks the editor gave him bad advice about what pictures to take," Eric told Catherine. "She's setting him straight."

"I wasn't aware she knew so much about photography."

Eric grinned. "She doesn't. She's determined to help out that new girl on staff, though. Don't worry—the photographer knows what he's doing. He'll pretend to do what she's telling him, and then do what he pleases. The pictures will turn out great." He paused. "She's also taking pictures of all the guests to help us with the case, you know. If the killer is here, at least she'll probably get a photo of him."

If the killer is here. The phrase tolled in Catherine's head. What if he was here? What if James had been right and the murderer had merely spared her earlier because he wanted to kill her later? What if—

As soon as the dance ended, Catherine turned and stumbled into the grip of a thrice-married local lothario. He immediately swept her away from Eric and launched into a speech about her grace, her beauty, how when she'd "floated" down the aisle she'd nearly taken away his breath. I wish I had taken it away, she thought, then felt a flicker of shame. Only a flicker. Some men should know when to give up or at least get new seduction material. He'd probably been using the same tired lines for forty years.

Nearby, Patrice held tightly to Lawrence's arm as he talked to a couple Catherine didn't recognize. While Lawrence's attention was fastened on the man, who tended to speak using grand gestures to illustrate his meanings, Patrice rarely stopped beaming at her groom. She's loved him so much for so long, Catherine thought. I wonder if when he married Abigail she felt like I did when James married Renée.

Renée. Why did her image always flash in front of her at what should be the happiest times? Catherine thought in annoyance. What if *she* were here tonight? She certainly wouldn't let Patrice shine—she'd try to steal all the attention for herself, no matter what means it took. Poor James. How he must have dreaded attending occasions such as this one with her.

Would he have enjoyed it with me? Catherine wondered, suddenly missing him so much she knew she had to talk to him. Soon. She automatically reached for her cell phone and realized she didn't even have a clutch purse with her. She'd left it upstairs and she'd told Eric she wouldn't leave the main room. She couldn't go get it.

She looked around for Marissa. She'd memorized the number of the landline phone beside James's hospital bed. If his cell wasn't close by, answering the phone wouldn't entail his fumbling around look-ing for it. But Catherine didn't see Marissa. She didn't see Eric, either. However, she did see Robbie dancing with Lawrence while Ian watched.

She walked toward Ian. "Do you hap-pen to have your cell phone with you?"

"My cell phone?" He frowned. "Honestly, I've heard about adolescent girls who can't stop calling and texting every ten minutes, but I thought someone your age might have outgrown the compulsion."

"Well, you were wrong. Actually, I just got an urge to call James and I left my cell phone upstairs. Or I forgot it. *Or* I lost it."

"Lost it? According to Marissa, you're the most organized person in the world. I never thought you lost anything."

"Marissa tends to exaggerate my strong points."

"I wish not losing my cell phone was one of mine. I think I should tie mine onto my wrist."

"I'm sure you're not that absentminded."

"You'd be surprised." Ian smiled at her. Then, slowly, his smile faded and his gaze grew slightly distant. He looked toward the band, playing a fervent version of U2's

"Beautiful Day," and his inner presence seemed to drift away from them. Catherine turned and followed his line of vision to his father, whose flushed face grimaced as he tried to swing Robbie in a smooth turn and almost fell. With Robbie's help, he caught himself, and she guided him sideways, slowing the pace, subtly helping him find his center again.

"Dad had better get control of himself," Ian mumbled. "Patrice won't like it if he falls down in the middle of the dance floor while he's dancing with *my* pretty young date."

That's an understatement, Catherine thought as she saw Patrice, watching with her laser eyes, from the sidelines. She immediately started talking and laughing with the woman beside her, as if taking the scene in stride, but Catherine could tell Patrice was inwardly angry, maybe even worse.

"I don't think too many people noticed," Catherine said softly to Ian. "I guess he's not used to champagne."

"He drinks a lot and you know it."

"But champagne might have a different effect." The only way out of this one seemed to be a change of subject. "Anyway, naturally all of this romantic stuff makes me think of my guy and I wanted to give him a call to say good night, but I can't find my cell phone, so if you have yours, I'd appreciate—"

Someone bumped into Catherine so hard she would have fallen if Ian hadn't reached out to catch her. While she was still trying to regain her balance, she heard a man's voice: "Well, I can't turn around without running into a pretty girl!"

Catherine stiffened as Lawrence boomed the comment loud enough for one whole area of the room to hear. People turned to see what drunken lout was making such a commotion, saw it was the groom and their host, and quickly looked away.

Lawrence nearly pushed Robbie toward Ian, who caught her gently, then wrapped a protective arm around her waist. "God, I'm sorry, Robbie—"

"Know what you saw in her now, boy. A real good-looker. Definitely put her name in that little black book you keep locked away in your apartment." Lawrence looked conspiratorially at Robbie. "He never lets *anyone* in his apartment, but with your skills as a cop, I'm sure you could pull off a break-in without getting caught." His right arm snaked around Catherine's waist. "How about a dance, Maid of Honor?"

"Oh, I don't know, Lawrence. I was just about to call James—"

"That stick-in-the-mud? He can't hold a candle to me." He winked. "And I don't mean just on the dance floor."

Oh God, what should I do now? Catherine thought, horrified, when she suddenly felt trembling in the arm Lawrence had wrapped around her waist—a deep trembling that might not even be noticeable on the surface. Alarm shot through her just as Ian, anger in his blue eyes, reached roughly for his father. But as his hand clamped on Lawrence's arm Catherine caught Ian's gaze and quickly shook her head "no."

Ian, not letting go of his father's arm in spite of Lawrence's protests, leaned close to Catherine.

"He's not drunk," she murmured. Ian looked at her in disbelief. "He may have had too much to drink, but I don't think that's all that's wrong. Don't make a fuss— just make him sit down. I'll get Patrice."

"But Catherine—"

"Just get him off his feet," she hissed,

headed toward Patrice, who'd turned her very straight back to the scene.

And that's when Catherine saw him.

The tall, slender man stood with a natural elegance near one of the huge windowed walls overlooking the Aurora waterfall, two fingers of his left hand pressed against the glass as if he could reach through it and touch the water, his slender, high-cheekboned face directed at hers. When she looked at him, he made no attempt to glance away, as would most men simply looking at a pretty young woman. Instead, he openly stared, his expression seemingly meant to grip her attention, almost as if she owed it to acknowledge him.

A tiny thrill of tension ran through Catherine. Although she did not know this man, she couldn't look away. She felt as if he was studying her, measuring her not in a sexual way but almost as he would an adversary. A small, tight smile curved his narrow lips and she suddenly felt a touch of danger in that slightly scornful smile. Still, she could not look away from him. The relatively smooth, pale skin of his face and the mere dusting of silver in his obviously natural thick, black hair told her he was in his late fifties, possibly in his early sixties. His large dark eyes, though, were sunken in hollows and surrounded by deep lines. Grief, Catherine thought. This handsome, genteel-looking man could have been a nineteenth-century aristocrat, somehow dropped into the wrong time and place, yet somehow looking recognizable to her, somehow . . .

A hot, humid day sweet with the smell of white flowers. A wedding. Champagne. A beautiful raven-haired bride in white—a bride with knowing, amused eyes smiling triumphantly, mockingly into hers.

Catherine turned and stumbled away, desperately looking for Eric.

2

Dana opened heavy eyes and looked at the digital bedside clock. One twenty-four. It had been a long day and she had gone to bed around eleven thirty, exhausted. Yet here she lay, wide awake, less than two hours later.

Without turning her head, she slid a hand across the ivory silk sheet. No Ken in the king-size bed. The down pillow didn't bear the slightest depression of a head and the upper sheet and blanket were still tucked beneath the mattress. Ken hadn't yet come to bed.

Earlier this afternoon they had settled Mary in her yellow and white bedroom. Dana planned for the nurse, Ms. Greene, to stay in the guest room next to Mary's, but the woman insisted on sleeping in Mary's room. Luckily, the Nordines owned a twin rollaway bed and, although Dana knew it wasn't comfortable, the nurse had pronounced it perfect and immediately set about making it up, demonstrating to Mary how to do a "hospital corner" with the top sheet. Ms. Greene had then unpacked her small suitcase and finally placed her bag of medical equipment in a corner far away from Mary's bed.

Shortly afterward, the nurse had listened with seeming fascination as Mary introduced her seven stuffed animals (a different one to sleep with every night—nobody should be left out). They'd then played a computer game, eaten from trays in Mary's bedroom, pretending they were having room service in a fancy hotel, and watched a couple of hours of television before the child agreed she'd "try" to sleep. When Dana had last checked on them at nine o'clock, Mary looked blissfully asleep. Ms. Greene sat in a comfortable rocking chair in the corner, reading in the glow of a Tiffany lamp, the chair and lamp Dana had insisted be moved into the room for the nurse's comfort.

"Murder mystery," Ms. Greene had whispered, tucking away a paperback book when Dana peeked into the bedroom. I'm addicted to them—can't sleep unless I've read a few pages."

"I used to read them incessantly, too. I can't remember when I stopped. I might start again, though. This week in Aurora Falls has certainly sparked my interest in the subject again."

"Terrible. Just terrible, what's gone on around here." Ms. Greene shook her head and made a sound like a chicken's cluck. Then she glanced over at the lamp. "I'm stealing this when I leave."

"It *is* pretty."

"Pretty? It's the most beautiful lamp I've ever seen. I've always admired Tiffany lamps. Couldn't afford one, of course, but if I had one, I'd probably wrap it in yards of tissue paper and hide it away so it wouldn't get broken. And what fun would that be?" She'd grinned, her prominent teeth gleaming in the light. "You've made me very comfortable and Mary is doing wonderfully."

"I'm glad on both counts."

As Dana had begun to withdraw and shut the door, the nurse had said, "Mrs. Nordine?"

"Dana."

"Okay. Dana. I just wanted to tell you, Dana, you're one of the best mothers I've ever seen. The other nurses at the hospital have commented on it. Mary adores you. She loves her father, but you are Mommy, the one she knows will always protect her."

Dana's throat tightened and she felt tears in her eyes. She couldn't even manage a "thank you." She'd just shut the door, leaned again the wall, and let the tears flow. Her? A good mother? The idea stunned her. She hadn't been a good mother in the past, but she would be from now on, she silently vowed. She *would* be.

Dana trailed slowly down the circular steps from the fourth-floor living quarters to the main floor of the gallery. Between moonlight and the streetlights, she didn't have to turn on the gallery lights. Instead, she wandered around, looking almost blindly at paintings she'd seen every day for months. She did pull up short when she saw the discreet *Sold* sign on *Mardi Gras Lady* and wondered briefly who had bought it. She really didn't care, though. She just wanted the piece out of here.

Dana went into the kitchenette off the main gallery and fixed a cup of hot chocolate. When she began touring the lower floor for the second time, she realized she hadn't put on her slippers, but the cool tiles felt good on her narrow feet, especially as she sipped the warm drink. She walked to the front windows and looked out on Foster Street.

They had gotten Mary home by two o'clock with Ken grouching about having to delay the daily gallery opening for over an hour when Dana and the nurse could have gotten Mary home just fine by themselves. Dana had ignored him, Mary's good spirits had sunk into quiet conversation with Ms. Greene, and the nurse's lips had narrowed with barely concealed dislike whenever she caught sight of Ken.

For the rest of the afternoon, Dana and Ms. Greene tended to Mary. Gallery traffic had been light, which frustrated Ken but Dana had found to be lucky. She wasn't called upon to act cordial and give her memorized spiels about the artwork, and Ken couldn't conjure up his usual charm. Instead, he had paced, made phone calls, complained constantly, lost his temper over a ten-minute electric failure, and paid only minimal attention to Mary.

As Dana now stood at the front window, she saw their black Mercedes Cabriolet with Ken behind the wheel. He was headed south—south, toward Bridget's house. Less than twelve hours after his daughter had been brought home from the hospital, he was going in search of Renée's replacement, the woman Dana knew he planned to leave her for, the woman he thought would give him a son along with endless hours of passion in the bedroom.

Dana smiled slightly, sardonically,

almost cruelly. He could spend the whole night driving, calling, searching, pining.

She didn't care. And neither would Bridget.

CHAPTER TWENTY

1

Ms. Greene sat bolt upright in bed, certain something was wrong. Glad for the strong night-light, she did a quick scan of the rectangular room, white dressers, a rocking chair, a canopied bed on which lay an evenly breathing child. She sighed. She did not possess ESP, always knowing when things weren't right. She was not special. She was just Ms. Greene, Registered Nurse, watching over five-year-old Mary Nordine, who had recently undergone an appendectomy.

Ms. Greene climbed quietly from her bed, which was remarkably comfortable for a rollaway. Mrs. Nordine had wanted her to sleep in the room next door, but Ms. Greene liked to be close to her patient, even when she'd had to sleep on a few folded blankets on the floor. Compared to that arrangement, the rollaway was a dream.

Mary lay on her back, her blond hair spread beneath her head like a golden halo, her little pink mouth slightly open, her arms closed around a stuffed lion named Dandelion. "It's his turn," she'd explained seriously to her nurse at bedtime. "I have seven stuffed animals and every one gets to sleep one night a week in the bed with me. Daddy says that someday I'll get to have a *live* animal," she'd said with excitement. "But I don't think it'll be a lion."

"I doubt not, but puppies and kittens are just as good for a young lady like yourself," Ms. Greene had answered earnestly. "After all, a lion would be bigger than you. He'd be dragging you all over the place. Now wouldn't *that* be a sight!"

Mary had laughed and hugged Dandelion closer while the nurse gently tucked her in and smoothed the child's bangs back from her forehead. "You have sweet dreams, little Mary. You're home with your mother and father and both Dandelion and me to look after you. You couldn't be safer!"

Now, Ms. Greene stared at her patient, sleeping peacefully and breathing normally, the picture of a child on her way back to health. But while Mary might be sleeping peacefully, Ms. Greene felt wide awake. She looked at the clock. Three forty-five! Hours would pass before she needed to be at her duties. She couldn't just lie on the rollaway bed forever. She didn't want to turn on a light to read. Besides, if she didn't get her rest now, she'd be groggy tomorrow.

Warm milk. She'd been in this predicament before and warm milk had never failed to make her drowsy. This was her first night with the Nordines, though, and she was unfamiliar with the kitchen. She didn't want to turn on the big, glaring lights instead of the small ones or bang around looking for the proper pan. She didn't like Mr. Nordine one little bit and she could tell he had no patience. If she woke him up, he'd make a terrible fuss and awaken Mary, maybe even upset her.

Downstairs! Ms. Greene suddenly remembered seeing a small kitchenette almost hidden on the first floor of the gallery. Three stories down from here, she could probably even drop a pan and he wouldn't hear it. Certainly, they kept milk in the small refrigerator. That would be the answer. She'd creep down, fix her milk, and be back in twenty minutes without disturbing a soul.

Ms. Greene put on her fleece robe and house slippers and slipped out the door, closing it almost completely. If Mary happened to wake up in distress, the nurse wanted someone to be able to hear the child call out. Then Ms. Greene started down the wide, curving hall of the circular gallery, glad for the small lights placed every few feet at floor level. Good heavens, she thought, people in town went on and on about how beautiful this gallery was, but Ms. Greene certainly wouldn't want to live here on the fourth floor of a building that went round and round and round. . . .

Although she'd held tightly to the handrail and the tiny floor lights continued all the way down the stairs, by the time Ms.

Greene reached the bottom she felt dizzy, which was unusual for her. She'd always been strong and had excellent coordination. True, she had never been in a "home" like this one, but still, she didn't like her momentary lack of physical control. She felt almost like she had as a young girl riding a Ferris wheel for the first time. She took a minute and drew a deep breath, her gaze traveling around the large gallery full of shadows created by the moon and streetlights. Mrs. Greene wasn't the nervous type, but to her surprise, she felt a tremor of unease pass through her like a cold wind.

"Oh, don't turn into a scared old woman at your age," she told herself sternly. "Sixty-three isn't old—it isn't even close to old." Her hand fumbled along the wall, searching for the light panel. "Now if you were *eighty-three*—"

Her sturdy, competent left hand had found the panel, and with a strong swipe upward she flipped every light switch. The room blazed as if on fire. For a moment, she was light blinded, raising her right arm to cover her eyes and stumbling to the edge of the last step. Her right hand still protecting her eyes, she fumbled with her left hand to find the panel and flip some of the switches to *Off*, but she kept missing most of them.

Slowly, she lowered her right arm, blinked away some of the tears, and barely opened her eyes. Turn off some more of these infernal lights, she thought, but for some reason she couldn't move. She stood rooted to the bottom step, her insides shaking, her eyes roving, roving—

Until she saw Ken Nordine propped beneath the portrait with the beautiful woman dressed in a ball gown and wearing a mask with a black star around the right eye—

Looking just like the hideous hole in Ken Nordine's face where his right eye should be.

2

"Should I take my child back to the hospital?" Dana Nordine looked at Chief Deputy Eric Montgomery with frantic eyes. "She had an appendectomy. I have a nurse here for her, but when Mary hears about this—"

Dana gestured in horror at the body of her husband.

"Does she know what's going on?" Eric asked.

"No. Only that there's some kind of ruckus. That nurse, Ms. Greene, found him and how she kept from screaming off her head I'll never know, but she just came after me and we called the police and here you are and here Mary is and I don't know what to do!"

Ms. Greene, who had been standing with forced calm beside Dana, looked at Eric. "Chief Deputy, I'm the nurse Mrs. Nordine hired to look after Mary for the next few days. You can certainly call a doctor for his opinion, but I believe it would be best for Mary not to be moved now. I just checked on her. She was just waking up and asking if something was wrong. I said there was just some minor trouble downstairs, checked her vitals, and she was drifting back to sleep when I came down. I think someone should stay with her and give her a story about what's going on down here—something that's not upsetting, of course—and we should see that she's kept calm and still. If we take her away, she'll know something bad is wrong. Also, it's supposed to be nippy today."

"Well, I don't think we need to call a doctor; then we won't," Eric said. "Is that all right with you, Mrs. Nordine?"

"Uh, yes. Yes. Thank you, Ms. Greene. I don't know what I would have done without you or what would have become of Mary or . . ."

"Just hush now, dear," Ms. Greene said gently. "I know this is awful, unbelievable, but the chief deputy and the rest of the police will get it all straightened out and everything will be fine. Isn't that right, Mr. Montgomery?"

Eric merely nodded. He could only wish he had Ms. Greene's confidence, because when little Mary learned her father had been brutally murdered he didn't know if everything would be fine for her again.

Eric and Deputy Jeff Beal stood side by side, staring. "I can't believe this," Jeff said. "On Tuesday we were looking at that Arcos fella with his right eye shot out and wearing strings of purple beads. Now here's Ken Nordine in what I'd swear is exactly the same position."

"The crime-scene photos will tell us, but I'd say you're right."

"But somehow, this looks creepier to me. I mean, Arcos wore all those strange clothes and had the long black hair and . . . well, he just didn't look like a regular person. Ken Nordine, though, was a different story. He was always dressed in those expensive suits and people said he had charm and kind of European manners and women were just crazy about him and . . . well . . . just look at him now."

Both men flinched at the sound of Dana Nordine's voice behind them. As his face reddened, Jeff's gaze remained fixed on Ken while Eric looked at Dana guiltily. "Sorry, Mrs. Nordine. We must have sounded unforgivably disrespectful."

"Not at all." Dana's eyes looked flat and emotionless in her pale, triangular face. She'd pushed her hair behind her ears, the lobes sparkling with small diamond studs. Her thin lips were colorless and her hands were clenched so tightly the knuckles had turned white. "I went upstairs with

Ms. Greene to check on Mary. She's asleep, thank God." Dana asked in a whispery voice, "Do you know what happened?"

"We know that your husband was shot. So far, we've only found one bullet, but there's a gash on the back of his head. I'd say he was bludgeoned before being shot." Dana cringed. Too much information, Eric thought. She didn't need to know everything right now. "Mrs. Nordine, can you describe your husband's evening? Did he get any calls, go anywhere?"

"Well, I'm not sure I can recall the whole sequence of the evening. I was distracted because of Mary," Dana said shakily, her gaze fixed on Ken.

"I need to ask you some questions. Would you like to go up to your living quarters?"

Dana hesitated, then shook her head. "I want to stay down here. I've already seen Ken. The hole where his beautiful eye should be, the blood, those horrible purple beads—those beads! Why in the name of God would someone hang those gaudy beads on him?"

She looked beseechingly at Eric, who took her arm. "You really need to sit down. You're a little shaky."

Dana covered her mouth as if she were going to burst into laughter. Then she slowly removed her hand. "Yeah, I'm shaky. This kind of thing doesn't happen to me every day."

Eric guided her to a pale leather couch and two-chair suite near the front of the gallery, as far away from Ken as he could get. Dana headed for the couch and positioned herself carefully, as if out of habit, tucking her long legs beneath her and placing her blue velour robe around them. Before her legs had disappeared beneath the robe, he'd noticed her bare feet and bloodred toenails.

"I saw the kitchenette. Do you need something to drink? Water? Coffee?"

"I need a tall glass of single-malt Scotch," she said tonelessly.

"I understand and you can have all the Scotch you want in a few minutes, but I need for your thoughts to be clear when I question you," Eric said gently.

"I know. I was only joking about the Scotch. I don't even like it." She drew in a shuddering breath. "Ken was the Scotch drinker. I don't want anything right now."

"All right." Eric sat down on one of the

chairs, withdrawing his notebook. "As I asked before, was Mr. Nordine acting differently this evening?"

"Differently? No. He was restless, but he was often restless in the evenings. He had so much energy he always wanted to be busy. Today wasn't a busy day at the gallery. Also, for some reason, Ms. Greene annoyed him, although he was hardly around her all day. I wanted her here. I'm afraid I'm not the most adept mother, especially of a child who's sick. Well, not sick, but recovering from an operation. Mary had an appendectomy on Wednesday."

"And your husband was worried about Mary?"

"Well, he was concerned, of course, but she seems to be doing well and we have Ms. Greene." Dana hesitated and then said a bit harshly, "Frankly, I don't think Ken was all that worried about Mary."

"I see. Any idea of what *was* worrying him?"

"Well, as I said, he's often restless and he doesn't sleep well. Sometimes he takes a sleeping pill. The last few days, though, he's been concerned about someone on our staff—Bridget Fenmore. She has the title of manager, but she really does the bookkeeping more than anything else and even Ken has to help her with that. Anyway, she didn't come to work yesterday or the day before and didn't call. Ken tried to reach her and couldn't. I can't say I was particularly impressed with Miss Fenmore's skills, but in the two months she's worked for us she's always been reliable and prompt."

"Does Miss Fenmore have family here?"

"I don't know. Ken hired her. When he was getting worried about her yesterday, I told him to look at her personnel folder and check on her family—maybe they would know something. He said he'd driven past her house and the newspapers and mail were piling up."

"He drove past her house?" Eric asked. "Did Mr. Nordine know Miss Fenmore well?"

Dana's eyes shifted away from his. "I'm not certain. Maybe."

He was having an affair with her, Eric thought. His girlfriend of not more than two months hadn't shown up for a couple of days and he was more worried about her than his own daughter, who'd just had surgery. "Do you know if he ever called her family or maybe contacted some of her friends?" Eric asked in a neutral voice.

"No. Frankly, I never thought about her again. I thought she'd show up on Monday with a good excuse—good enough to keep Ken from firing her. She's only twenty-six . . . and she looks a lot like Renée Eastman . . . did." Dana sighed. "If she hasn't come home yet, I'll look through her personnel papers today. Maybe I can locate her family and they'll know where she is."

"That's all right, Mrs. Nordine. We'll go through all your records if you don't mind."

"Not at all. Everything's in order and I'm not sure I could really concentrate today."

"No one would expect you to. It's really a police job, anyway." Eric cleared his throat. "Can you tell me about tonight? Was anything different than usual?"

Dana went silent for a minute. "I'm sorry. I'm trying to remember," she said. "Ms. Greene and I spent a lot of time with Mary early in the evening. Around eight o'clock, I came down to the main gallery. We usually have quite a few visitors at eight on a Saturday night, but there were only a few. I'd expected low business because of the Blakethorne wedding. Did you know?"

"I attended."

"Oh!" Dana must have realized she'd sounded unflatteringly surprised that a policeman had been invited to the wedding of the wealthiest man in town. "Was it nice?" she asked quickly.

"Very nice. My girlfriend's sister was Patrice Greenlee's maid of honor." Eric always avoided mentioning his personal life in an interview and could see the curiosity in Dana's eyes. Oh well, the damage is done, he thought. "I see Marissa Gray. Her sister is Dr. Catherine Gray."

"I know Catherine! Well, a little bit. Marissa did two very nice articles about the gallery. I didn't know there was a connection." Eric frowned and Dana added, "Between you and the Gray sisters."

I didn't mean for you to, Eric thought. "Our families were friends since the girls and I were children," he said more abruptly than he'd intended. "So around eight o'clock the gallery was nearly empty and your husband was surprised by that? Unhappy?"

"Both. We'd been invited to the wedding, although we don't really know either the bride or groom, but with Mary newly home and all, I'd said I absolutely wasn't attending. And Ken's heart didn't seem into going, either, which was odd for him. He loved to socialize." She tilted her head and looked at Eric ruefully. "To be honest, he wanted the chance to promote the gallery to Lawrence Blakethorne's wealthy friends."

"But not attending the wedding didn't seem to be what was bothering him."

"No. He was irritable. He said he had a headache. Well, actually he said he felt a migraine coming on. He's suffered from them for years. I told him to go upstairs, take some of his migraine medicine, and go to bed. He needed rest, quiet, complete darkness. That's why I often sleep in the guest room when he's having one of his headaches. That's where Ms. Greene found me after she found . . . Ken."

She drew another deep breath. "I told him I'd look after the gallery until about nine or nine thirty. We usually don't close until eleven, but as I said, it was obvious we weren't the biggest show in town last night. He refused and told me to go to bed because I've lost a lot of sleep because of Mary. He said he wanted stay up for a while. I didn't argue and went to bed after eleven."

"Sorry to interrupt," Eric said, "but do you know if he locked every door and turned on the security system?"

"He was always very careful about locking up." She paused. "But he was so distracted by his headache. . . . Why?"

"One of your back doors was unlocked and the security system was off."

"Oh. I shouldn't have left him alone!" Dana made a strangled noise between laughter and crying. "Oh God, I just can't believe this. I'm sorry. I'm usually controlled. Ken hated hysterics and here I am, acting like a fool. But then he wouldn't know about it, would he?"

"Mrs. Nordine—"

"Someone put him under *her* portrait!" Dana nearly choked. "I know their affair wasn't a secret, but someone punched or shot out his right eye and put him right under *Mardi Gras Lady.* Everyone knows it's a painting of Renée Eastman. It was valuable before, but after Arcos was murdered the price went through the roof. And someone bought it almost immediately."

"Who bought it?"

"I don't know. Ken said it was a surprise. He *said* he didn't want to tell me until I'd stopped worrying about Mary because I wouldn't really appreciate the surprise until then, but I had a feeling . . . no, I *knew* that wasn't the real reason."

"What other reason could he have had?"

"I don't know," Dana said slowly. "I honestly don't know. But there's one thing I feel like I do know." She paused as policemen and paramedics separated, making room for the gurney that would carry away the now-sheet-covered body of Ken Nordine. "The sale of that damned painting is responsible for the murder of my husband."

CHAPTER TWENTY-ONE

1

Catherine knocked on Marissa's closed bedroom door.

"Go 'way."

Catherine knocked louder. "Marissa, get up!"

"Never!"

Catherine sighed, opened the door, and began talking to the lump under the comforter on Marissa's bed. "I have to go to this wedding brunch. I'm the maid of honor. You said you'd go with me, but I know you're exhausted—"

"You're 'sausted, too."

"Yes, I am. Nevertheless, it's my duty to go. It's not yours. So I'm officially notifying you that you're off the hook. You can sleep away half the day if you like. After all, if it weren't for me, we would have gotten home at a decent hour."

"Decent hour?"

The lump moved and Catherine saw a mass of dark blond hair with golden highlights, then a slightly puffy-faced Marissa with a slight case of raccoon eyes. "Too sleepy to get off all your mascara last night?"

"What do you mean?"

"You'll know when you finally get up and look in the mirror. Go back to sleep now, though. I'm sorry I woke you."

"No, no, I'm going with you." Marissa clambered out of the bed, Lindsay coming to her side as if she might need help standing. "You can't go alone."

"Why not? Is there something dangerous about a wedding brunch?"

"Well, after last night . . ."

"You mean after I went into a tailspin because I thought I saw Renée's father."

Marissa plopped down on the side of her bed. "You don't know that you didn't."

Catherine rolled her eyes. "Why would Gaston Moreau be at Lawrence Blake-thorne's wedding?"

"Because he expected James to be there?"

"Why would he want to talk to James at a wedding? After all, they'd be talking about Renée's murder and the release of the body. A wedding doesn't seem like the proper place for that discussion, and from everything I've heard Gaston Moreau is *very* proper."

"From everything you heard. You only met the man once years ago at James's wedding. Needless to say, you weren't con-centrating on Gaston. Have you seen pic-tures from the wedding?"

"Some Dad took of us. A couple he took of James and Renée. I don't remember any of Renée's parents. I didn't really dwell over photos of that wedding, Marissa."

"I understand why. They're probably here in some of Mom's twenty albums, but neither of us wants to look for them now. Anyway, you've really heard very little about Gaston because James hardly knew him. James probably wouldn't say much about him if he did know Gaston—he avoids talking about anything or anyone having to do with Renée."

"That's true. And I understand it."

"Yeah, sure you do," Marissa said, half sarcastically, half sympathetically. "You know that James needs to talk about it. Also, the fact that he won't makes you feel shut out of the most traumatic part of his life."

"I thought *I* was the psychologist."

"You don't have to be a psychologist to see that you two have a problem. He was just getting over the shame she caused him when she turns up again, murdered, no less."

"What I'm worried about is when *Gaston* turned up," Catherine said. "I don't know if he saw Renée after she left here, but I know he only saw her two or three times after she got married. He had a problem with her—a big one."

Catherine hesitated, wondering if she should talk about the sexual abuse to Marissa. Then she saw from the expression on Marissa's face that she already suspected. Of course she would have, Catherine thought. Marissa was almost as good at analyzing people as a professional.

During the years of their marriage, she'd been around James and Renée more than Catherine. Marissa clearly had watched Renée and put the signs together.

"Anyway, I hope Gaston has just come back this week to take away his daughter's body," Catherine said. "But what if he came for a different reason?"

"Like tracking down who murdered her?" Marissa asked softly. Catherine raised her shoulders. "Oh. Like killing anyone he thinks might have murdered her. Good God, Catherine, if he's the kind of man I think he is, he's capable of anything."

"I know."

"Have you told James?"

"I don't want to while he's still in the hospital. He needs rest, not more worry." Marissa nodded. "I thought Eric was going to spend the night here?"

"As soon as we got to sleep, he had to go out. He said it wasn't serious—something at the Nordine Gallery. He was acting mysterious, though. I think it was something serious, but I don't want to know what just now. We have this damned brunch to attend."

Catherine smiled. "Admit it. You don't

want to miss one part of the city's biggest social event in ten years."

Marissa grinned mischievously. "Well, that might be part of my determination to go." She walked to her dresser mirror, peered closely, and let out a squeak. "I didn't know I could look this bad. I must have drunk too much."

"You didn't. You were too busy taking pictures and notes and looking around for Gaston Moreau. You work too hard, Marissa."

"I don't. How much time do I have to make myself presentable for the brunch?"

"Two hours."

"Thank God," Marissa breathed. "I'll need ever minute of it."

Fifteen minutes later Marissa appeared in the kitchen, her hair brushed and her face washed free of every trace of makeup and bearing a layer of light cream. "I know you said I didn't drink too much last night, but maybe I drank more than you thought or I should have. Alcohol dehydrates your skin," Marissa said. "Mom always warned us to be careful about putting on *extra* night cream after a dinner party."

"Or a keg party," Catherine said.

"I don't think our mother ever attended a keg party, Catherine."

"But we did."

"Maybe. I don't remember. College was so long ago. Umm, that coffee smells delicious."

"Caffeine is also dehydrating. Maybe you shouldn't have any without putting on another layer of cream first."

"Ha, ha. You are too funny in the mornings, Chatty Cathy."

"For using my favorite nickname you can make your own breakfast."

"No problem. I only want toast. We'll probably be having a feast in a couple of hours." Marissa pulled two pieces of wheat bread from the cellophane loaf and dropped them in the toaster. "We're not going back to the Larke Inn, are we? I mean, I love the place, but we've had two celebrations there in the last two days."

"Maybe you did have too much champagne last night. The brunch is at the Blakethorne house."

"Oh, sure. I remember now. I know it's considered traditional in formal weddings to have a brunch, but I wonder if the insistence on keeping with tradition was Lawrence's or Patrice's."

"Lawrence's." Catherine opened the refrigerator and took out the low-cholesterol butter container. "Patrice told me he thought it would be a good way to keep some of the Star executives here for most of another day for some face-to-face talk in a casual setting."

Marissa looked at Catherine in mock devastation. "You know what this means, don't you?"

"What?"

"Maud. Maud Webster, grand inquisitor, will be there to ask you more questions about finding Renée."

The toast popped up just as Catherine's mouth dropped. "Oh my God."

"We'll avoid her like we did at the reception," Marissa said, pulling out the toast, her expression growing more excited.

"There were more people at the reception than there will be today. And you're looking like this is going to be some childish adventure."

"It will be." Marissa slathered butter on her toast. "Don't worry. I'm already thinking up evasion tactics."

They heard a cell phone go off in the living room. "That's Eric's ringtone," Marissa said, jumping up from the table. "Maybe we'll finally find out what major catastrophe drove him out into the depths of night."

Catherine finished her toast, rinsed her plate, and poured another cup of coffee. She looked at Marissa's toast, now cold, with the butter congealed. Catherine was wondering whether or not to fix Marissa two fresh slices now or wait when she entered the kitchen, her face pale, her eyes disbelieving.

"What is it?" Catherine burst out. "Is Eric all right?"

"Eric is fine," Marissa said slowly. "But Ken Nordine is dead. He was murdered just like Nicolai Arcos."

2

"Remember, we're not to say a *word* about Nordine's murder."

Catherine looked at her sister sitting straight and tense behind the wheel of her red Mustang. "Marissa, you don't have to keep reminding me. You know someone is going to say something to us, though. Especially you, because you're involved with the chief deputy."

"Then I'll just say I haven't heard from Eric today."

"They'll ask why he didn't come with you."

"I'll say he must be busy, but I don't know with what. I'll act airy about it, like it's probably nothing important. I won't say anything about Ken Nordine, and if anyone asks me about him I'll say I don't know anything, either. I can pull it off. Can you?"

"Of course I can," Catherine returned, insulted.

"I'm just nervous. Eric is counting on me. He really shouldn't have told me anything, but he knows Patrice listens to the police scanner all the time and might have heard something to tip her off or maybe people have been driving through town and have seen the crime-scene tape around the gallery and will want to know what's going on. He didn't want us to be taken by surprise if anyone asked questions about Nordine."

"Well, thanks to him, we won't be. Maybe he shouldn't have told you, Marissa, but under the circumstances, I think he did the right thing."

"He usually does. It's infuriating sometimes, but we won't let him down, will we?"

"No, Marissa, we *won't.* I've said before you should have been an actress. Until we get through this brunch, you have to call on all your skills. Eric is counting on you."

Marissa slowed as they drew up to the large Blakethorne home where cars already lined the wide, circular driveway. To their surprise, as they neared the double front doors a valet rushed to help them out of their car.

"The brunch is being held in back, ladies," he said. "On the terrace and the back lawn. I'll park your car at the end of the drive. It's the last space!"

Catherine and Marissa each swept from the Mustang, smiling widely, then drew closer, their bright autumn outfits looking even cheerier in the gentle sun. As they rounded the house and saw the brunch area, Marissa's smile froze and she suddenly took Marissa's arm. "Let's try to forget all about Nordine and acting and actually *be* calm and happy."

"Okay, but I'd rather be invisible," Catherine said morosely. "I already see Maud Webster."

3

"Where's Daddy?"

Dana Nordine looked down at Mary lying restlessly on her bed. She'd wanted to get up at eight, but Dana and Ms. Greene had served her French toast and bacon and each had eaten with the child, drawing out the meal by telling stories. So far, Mary hadn't seemed aware of anything wrong—the police on the first floor were being extraordinarily quiet, for which Dana was grateful beyond words. But now it was noon, Mary didn't want to eat again, was obviously getting bored with Ms. Greene and Dana droning on and on, and was getting suspicious about her father's absence. Ken hadn't been a good father, but he had made a point of showing his little girl some attention on Sundays. Mostly, Dana thought, because he liked to look at the child's adoring face turned toward him.

"We could play some of those video gadgets you like," Ms. Greene offered, although they baffled her. She could not see the fun in them, but they seemed to obsess kids these days. If she was going to stay in this line of work, she might need to learn how to work a couple.

"I'm tired of my video toys," Mary said in a slightly whiny voice. "I want to see Daddy."

"Daddy had to go someplace today." Dana had startled herself with the statement and fumbled with the "where?" she knew would be following quickly. "He had to go to a town about two hours away from here. He didn't want to go, but he had to. He won't be back until tonight."

"Why didn't he kiss me before he left?"

"He did, but you were asleep. He left an angel's kiss on your forehead," Ms. Greene said.

"An angel like the one Bridget saw?"

Ms. Greene looked blank, but Dana said, "No, it was a *real* kiss from your daddy. A kiss from an angel wouldn't have been a kiss from him. Ms. Greene just meant it was as soft as an angel's kiss. That's why you didn't feel it."

Ms. Greene looked at Dana in gratitude, as if thinking the woman had warded off a terrible gaffe on her part. She'd seen the look on Mrs. Nordine's face when the child said "Bridget."

"How about watching a movie?" Dana suggested. "You haven't watched one of your movies for ages and I think we have a couple of new ones you haven't even seen."

"I don't feel like watchin' a movie," Mary said stubbornly.

Dana maintained a firm smile. "Let's go through some of your movie collection and see if something appeals to you. Let's see, here's *Finding Nemo*—"

"No. I've seen it a million times."

"All right. How about *The Lion King*?"

"Five million times."

"Not *that* many."

"Five million," Mary maintained.

"*Cars*?"

"Nope."

"*Over the Hedge*?"

"No way."

"Mary," Dana almost wailed.

Mary gave her mother a long, thoughtful look. Then she said, "*Cinderella*."

"Really?"

"You want me to watch a movie, don't you?"

"Well, yes, but one you want to see."

"I want to see something romantical like *Cinderella*."

"Romantical it is," Dana said, smiling for the first time that day. She looked at Ms. Greene. "Would you like to watch *Cinderella* with Mary?"

"I'd love to," Ms. Greene said enthusiastically. "In fact, I've never seen the movie before."

"You *haven't*?" Mary asked in disbelief.

"I truly have not."

"Oh well, that'll make watchin' it again lots more fun."

Dana slipped the movie into the player. "I *have* seen the movie a few times, so while you two are enjoying it I think I'll go downstairs and check around." She exchanged glances with Ms. Greene again. "Will that be all right with you two?"

"Yep," Mary said. "That way you won't tell what's gonna happen next and spoil it for Ms. Greene."

"A good thought, honey. Well, I'll see you two later."

Dana walked slowly down the three flights of stairs. Since the police had arrived, she had managed a shower, a shampoo, and some fresh clothes, but without her careful makeup job and hairstyling she knew she looked five years older than she had a week ago. Ten years older. Even the best cosmetics and plastic surgery could not always ward off time.

In the main gallery, Dana quickly looked away from the spot where Ken's body had lain in the early-morning hours, his legs splayed, his head tilted to one side, his mouth open, a hole where his beautiful blue right eye should have been, and those three strands of beads around his neck. Purple Mardi Gras beads. Dana had been to Mardi Gras many times. She'd thrown strands of beads just like those many times. Only she'd always preferred the gold beads, the gold symbolic of power. These had been purple—purple for justice.

"Mrs. Nordine?" A woman in uniform stood in the entrance to the hall leading to the offices. Dana went to her. "I've been going over your accounts for several hours now—"

"Our accounts?"

"Yes. Chief Deputy Montgomery said you'd given us permission."

"I did. I just didn't think you'd begin so promptly."

"Well, the chief had an idea he wanted me to check out and it does seem to me that there is a problem. I wonder if you might straighten it out for me."

"I'll do anything I can to help," Dana said, following the woman down the hall. "I used to manage all of our bookkeeping, but as the business grew, Ken took over more, and then two months ago we hired a bookkeeper, Bridget Fenmore."

"I see. Can we reach Ms. Fenmore today?"

"Well, she seems to be missing." The woman turned and looked at her. "Not missing. At least I don't think so. She just didn't turn up for work on Friday or Saturday and didn't call. She's very reliable—at least she has been since she's been employed here."

"Is she married?"

"No. I told Chief Deputy Montgomery about this. He said you'd check her personnel file to find the names of family."

"Yes, I believe the chief did mention

something about looking for a particular employee's file." The office was tiny and the policewoman motioned to the most comfortable chair. "Please sit, Mrs. Nordine. You look very tired."

"I am very tired. I don't think a whole bottle of sleeping pills could put me out right now, though." The woman's eyes widened. "Not that I'm thinking of overdosing!"

"I know you aren't. But this is a time of terrible strain. Maybe it would be best for you to call a doctor."

"I have a registered nurse. She's here for my daughter, who had an appendectomy last week. She'll get me through this. Physically, at least." She tried to smile. "Now, what do you need to know?"

"It concerns two sales that were made last week." Dana nodded. "The invoices caught my eye because they were sales for paintings by Nicolai Arcos. Naturally, because he was murdered this week, any movement of his work comes into question."

"I understand," Dana said slowly. "I saw the *Sold* sign on *Mardi Gras Lady.* I've been so distracted with my daughter's illness, though, and my husband has been handling everything himself with me or Bridget, that I didn't want to bother him with a lot of questions." Naturally, the woman looked at her oddly. Asking who bought a painting wasn't asking a lot of questions, but she couldn't say more without revealing where things stood with her and Ken, and just hours after his murder certainly wasn't the time to even hint at trouble between them. "What seems to be the problem?"

"Well, the name of your company is Nordine Galleries, Inc., correct?"

"Yes."

"This is the name on your company bank account and on your business license."

"Yes. Of course."

"Do you have a separate account?"

"We have a personal account in the name of Dana and Ken Nordine."

"Any other bank accounts?"

"No. We have had those two for years."

"You haven't opened another in the last two months?"

"No." Dana suddenly lost patience. "What are you getting at?"

"Is an account in the name KGN and Associates familiar to you?"

"KGN? Those are Ken's initials—Ken Guy Nordine." She paused. "Are you telling me my husband opened a new account two months ago?"

"Apparently. And it was more like six weeks ago. The first bank statement just arrived on Wednesday."

"May I see it?"

"Of course."

Dana took the statement with shaking hands and saw that on Wednesday the account had a balance of $25,000. Paper clipped to the balance statement was a deposit sheet dated Friday for $150,000. Written on the slip in Ken's hand was: "Thank you, Mardi Gras Lady!!!"

CHAPTER TWENTY-TWO

1

"Did you have nightmares about finding that dead body? Oh, I'm sure you do. Tell me about them!"

I knew it, Catherine thought as she looked down at her eggs Benedict. I knew I couldn't escape her. The woman had honed in on her as soon as Catherine set foot on the terrace. "I really haven't had any nightmares," she said.

"Oh, I don't believe that!" the little woman proclaimed. "You're trying to tell me a thing like what happened to you wouldn't give you nightmares? Why, I'd have nightmares for the rest of my life."

Which makes me even more happy that I'm not you, Catherine thought. "Maybe I've simply trained myself to shut out what frightens me during my sleep."

"Oh, that's not possible!" Maud exclaimed. "Fear and repulsion all have to do with the subconscious. I read that. You're a psychiatrist. You must have read it, too."

"I'm a *psychologist.* I don't have a medical degree."

"So psychologists don't believe in the subconscious? Well, that's a surprise!"

"Hello, Dr. Gray."

Catherine looked up to see the Blakethorne's housekeeper, Mrs. Frost. She liked the woman, although during the many times she'd stopped at the house to visit Ian over the years after his accident she and the woman had only spoken briefly and casually. "Mrs. Frost! How nice to see you. I haven't visited for months."

The sun shone on the woman's silver hair. "I know you've been busy setting up your new counseling practice. I only wanted to say hello."

"Well, we must say more than 'hello' at another time soon. You know, you're always welcome at my house."

"Oh, I don't leave here often, especially in the evenings, and during the day everyone is busy."

"Then I'll come here to visit. I know Ian doesn't live here anymore, but I can always visit with you and Lawrence." The woman smiled. "And Patrice, of course." The smile immediately vanished. "And maybe we can arrange a time for it to be just you and Ian and me. Or maybe some pretty Saturday afternoon we could go antiquing. . . ."

Catherine had never gone antiquing in her life, but Ian had once told her Mrs. Frost loved to visit antique shops and had even made some purchases over the years, which were kept safe and well preserved in a building at Blakethorne Charter. Occasionally, Ian or Lawrence drove her out to look at them.

"Well, I am glad to see you again. I saw you at the wedding and reception, but there were *so* many people, I stayed out of the general melee. I wanted to tell you how lovely you looked, though. That green gown fit you perfectly and the jewelry was beautiful."

"Thank you. The jewelry was my mother's."

"Bless her soul." Miss Frost looked around a bit anxiously. "I'd must be going now. There are a hundred things to do. . . ."

She took a few steps away before Maud burst out, "What's her story?"

Catherine noticed Miss Frost's slight head movement. She'd started to look back, then stopped herself.

"She is the Blakethornes' housekeeper. She's been here for many years."

"You must know her pretty well. You talked about coming here to visit."

"Yes, I've known the Blakethornes slightly since I was young. I became closer as I got older."

"There you are, Maud." Luckily, Patrice had come to Catherine's rescue once again, leaning over Maud. "I thought I might find you with Catherine, but there was another woman here looking for you—I can't remember her name—short, frosted-brown hair, blue eyes, just a bit taller than you."

"Oh, *her.*" Maud looked disdainful. "She's

such a gossip, I usually try to avoid her. Besides, Cathy and I are having a great conversation about the subconscious. She doesn't think it exists."

"That's not what I said," Catherine replied.

"Another mimosa, ma'am?" a waiter interrupted. Catherine felt like kissing him.

"Well, as a matter of fact, I love mimosas," Maud informed about ten people eating nearby. "I'd have mimosas every Sunday morning, but my husband Ed says we shouldn't have champagne on our breath when we go to church. After church, he says it's too late in the day. I say it's *never* too late in the day!" She turned to a slightly wilted-looking Patrice. "Lawrence must feel the same way about champagne, considering how he was carrying on last night. I think he would have whirled that pretty girl with the dark hair right through those windows if they hadn't bumped into Cathy and Ian first."

A short, embarrassed silence followed. Patrice's smile looked as if it had been set in concrete, and the little bit of natural color beneath her blush faded.

"Yes, Maud would like another mimosa,"

Catherine said gaily, and loudly to the waiter. "Maybe we should each have another one, Maud."

"I'm for that! Now where was I? Oh, Lawrence. Patrice, did your groom get drunk on you?" Maud asked coyly. "That couldn't have made for a great wedding night. But I know you two have been living together for a couple of months, so it probably didn't matter to you."

"Lawrence wasn't drunk. He didn't feel well," Patrice said stiffly.

"Okay, honey." She gave Catherine a conspiratorial wink. "We'll back up your story, won't we, Cathy?"

Exactly which level of hell have I reached? Catherine thought, by now too embarrassed to be embarrassed. But she felt bad for Patrice, whose lips looked thinner, her eyes narrower.

Then a woman with brown frosted hair and blue eyes walked by, tripped, and dumped a plate of Italian sausage and creamy scrambled eggs in Maud's lap. Maud squealed and leaped up, spilling the food mixture onto high heels dyed to match her hot pink suit. Her gaze clashed with the woman's—obviously the "gossip's." Amid

an arguing match, the two walked off together, Maud headed inside to clean off
the food clinging to her suit.

Patrice sat down beside Catherine. "I'm
so sorry about her. She's just awful, but
her husband is a dream and very important to Lawrence's negotiations with Star
Air. No matter how important he is, though,
I had to get her away from you."

"You don't know how much I appreciate
it," Catherine said. "I just hope Lawrence
doesn't suspect that you arranged the *accident.*"

"Oh, I'm sure he does, but as long as
Maud's husband isn't angry, he won't care.
And the two are talking seriously as we
speak, and I don't think it's about Maud's
embarrassment. I don't know how a nice
guy like Ed puts up with her. I guess he
spends a lot of time at the office."

Catherine laughed. Then she looked to
the head of the table where Lawrence sat.
Ed Webster had taken Patrice's vacated
chair on Lawrence's left.

Patrice looked for a moment at Lawrence. "Does he seem all right to you?" she
asked softly.

Catherine glanced at Lawrence, talking

animatedly with Ed Webster. He seemed steady, strong, and his color was good. "I think he seems fine."

"Well, I heard about the little incident last night. If I hadn't already heard about it, I would have from Maud talking to you."

"I think Lawrence just had a bit too much champagne," Catherine said carefully. Lately, though, he'd looked pale and strained and she planned on suggesting he get a complete checkup, but she wouldn't say so with the suddenly quiet people sitting near her and Patrice. "And he'd had two big nights in a row, plus a *wedding*!" She longed to ask Patrice how Lawrence had seemed when they got home, which she couldn't ask now or maybe ever. The question seemed too intimate. Perhaps she could put James up to the task. "After all, Lawrence has been a bachelor for a long time, Patrice. He was just excited, in high spirits."

"Yes. And he overestimates his dancing skills," Patrice said lightly. "I think he tried a tango move that didn't work out as planned."

When Catherine saw the smiles around her, she knew she'd been right about eavesdroppers. "Well, maybe one of the first things you can do together is take ballroom dancing lessons. I've always thought they'd be fun."

Patrice gave her a droll look. "He's taken them *twice*. You saw the results. No, I'd rather live at least through the first year of my marriage. No ballroom dancing with Lawrence for me!"

An hour later, as the brunch seemed to Catherine to be mercifully winding down—a few people began wandering over the grounds toward the hedge grouping and others went for that last cup of coffee and Danish—Lawrence stood up at the head of the table.

"Ladies and gentlemen!" he boomed, tapping a spoon against a china cup of coffee. "Ladies and gentlemen, may I please have your attention?"

The people walking over the grounds headed back for the table and the others drew nearer, all looking expectantly at Lawrence. All except Mrs. Frost, who caught Catherine's eye with what she thought was a bit of worry or even dread, which puzzled her. Lawrence seemed fine, if a bit louder than usual, and Catherine saw no sign of

Maud. Maybe she fell in the fishpond in the middle of the hedge fortress, she mused, wondering if anyone would try to save her.

"As you know, Star Air and Blakethorne Charter have been negotiating a merger for several months. Although we have a few things to iron out yet, things are looking very positive for the merger!"

Everyone clapped. Patrice stood beside Lawrence looking slightly wary, and Ed Webster's smile seemed false, a polite smile with no heart behind it. He's not glad about this announcement, Catherine thought suddenly. Lawrence has jumped the gun, assuming the merger is a done deal when it isn't.

"As I don't have to announce to any of you here, I am now a married man," Lawrence went on. "People have expected this for a long time, but I wanted to be sure that I was not making . . ." Oh God, don't say a *mistake,* Catherine thought, feeling her breath stop for an instant ". . . that I could make this wonderful woman beside me happy."

Catherine was certain she wasn't the only one whose breath had nearly stopped. Marissa caught her gaze and closed her own azure eyes as if in relief. It seemed that Patrice had gone even a shade paler, although her smile was wide and she drew closer to Lawrence, putting her arm around his waist.

"How about this, honey?" Lawrence blasted to Patrice. "I get you *and* Star within a matter of hours. Maybe we should show everyone we're not old fogies. We'll get you a star tattoo right here!" His right hand swept past Patrice's pubic area, hovered, then rose to her shoulder. "Oh, sorry, folks. I meant *here*!"

Weak laughter rippled through the crowd. People glanced at Patrice's crotch, then quickly looked away, many of them blushing. Patrice drew herself even taller, as if she was daring anyone to think she was embarrassed, humiliated, shocked. But she is, Catherine thought in sympathy. She is.

"I'm not done yet!" Lawrence nearly shouted as some people began to move around again. Or escape, Catherine thought. "I also want to take this opportunity to announce that my son, Ian, is an official member of Blakethorne Charter. He will be my second-in-command—my co-pilot." Lawrence laughed uproariously.

"And for his invaluable service, which has yet to begin, but I'm sure will soon, I would like to present him with a gift. Now, I've always been just a simple man with a middling education and a big idea. My son is different, though. He has big ideas, but he's not a simple man with a middling education. He's a *gentleman,* folks, a real gentleman who knows all about gourmet foods, and literature, and especially *art.* This young fella is an art aficionado. And that's why when he told me about a painting he loved, I decided to buy it. Ian, although I'll keep it safe for you in this house, any time you like you'll be able to look at Nicolai Arcos's *Mardi Gras Lady!*"

2

"You're *so* lucky you missed all the wedding events," Catherine said to James as she sat close beside him on the hospital bed. "Are you sure you didn't arrange to get shot?"

James laughed. "It sounds to me like I missed a fairly good time."

"Maybe it sounds good when I'm telling

you about it. Being in the middle of it was simply bizarre. I won't be the same for at least a month."

"Well, you came through it beautifully."

"I don't feel beautiful." Catherine leaned over and carefully hugged James. "I've missed you so much. I feel like you've been in here for a week."

"I feel like I've been in here for at least two. But tomorrow, I make my breakout."

"Yes, but you won't be going back to normal activities. I know you're a workaholic, James, but you won't be going into the office for a week."

"A week! That's ridiculous."

"Your father's orders. And Patrice's."

"What am I supposed to do for a whole week?"

"I could bring you to work with me."

"I thought your sessions with your patients were confidential."

"They are. You could sit in the lobby and talk to Beth. Oh, did I tell you Beth sang at the wedding?"

"Twice."

"I didn't know she had such a beautiful voice."

"If I come to work with you, she can sing

to me all day." James rubbed his hands up and down her arms. "Honey, I hate to break the happy mood, but something's been troubling me. I've always loved your patience, your optimism. Now I'm worried about what this last week has done to your view of the *true* world."

Catherine looked deep into James's dark brown eyes. "You sound as if this last week represents the *true* world. It doesn't. Not entirely. This week has been a nightmare, but we've been through a nightmare before, and you were in one before I came back to Aurora Falls. The nightmares weren't endless, though. You, we, came out of them. And compared to the rest of our lives, those terrible times have been brief—horrifying, but brief. You have to look at life as a whole, James, not just at the dark side. There *is* a bright side, a radiant side, and naïve as I might sound, I believe there is far more radiance than darkness if you only look for it."

"Your optimism is still intact," James said seriously.

"Yes, it is. But I've realized we've never talked as much about deeply personal things as we should have. Frankly, I think since we started seeing each other, we were both thinking of what happened between you and Renée. I understood why you didn't want to talk about her. The two of you didn't just have a bad marriage. You had a disastrous marriage ending with her disappearing and you being suspected of having murdered her. You underwent a police investigation, for God's sake. Who wouldn't have been traumatized? But, my darling, that's over."

"Is it? Renée *was* murdered and maybe you're the only person in town who doesn't believe I did it."

"I am *not* the only person who doesn't believe you did it! Don't even say such a thing."

"Then who did? And what about Arcos, Nordine, the attempt on my life?"

Catherine bent her head, pressing together her lips, and wondering if now was the time to tell him all she knew. After all, he would be out of the hospital tomorrow. Now, he might only lie awake all night and think about what she'd said.

"You're keeping something from me, Catherine. We're not going to do that anymore. No more silence because we think what we say might hurt the other. That's what has been keeping up apart, and I don't want us to be apart anymore. I want us to be together—mind, body, and soul. So tell me what's on your mind."

Had he actually said he wanted them to be together mind, body, and soul? Catherine could hardly believe it. She'd loved him dearly for years, but there had always been a barrier between them, even the last few months when there had really been nothing to keep them apart—nothing except their own silence. If she gave up this chance to truly reach James by withholding information because she thought it might upset him, she might never get another chance to reach him, she thought.

"It happened at the wedding reception," she began slowly. "I saw a man. He was leaning against a window and had been looking at the falls, but suddenly he turned and looked at me. Then he just stared at me." James remained silent. "He was about sixty, I'd guess, and very tall and slim. He had heavy black hair with just a sprinkling of silver. But it was his eyes that caught me. They were dark, sunk in hollows with deep lines. At first I didn't understand why he kept staring at me, even when he knew I was staring back. Then I got a feeling that there was something familiar about him. I was sort of overwhelmed with thoughts of the wedding and the humidity and . . . and a beautiful bride with dark eyes looking at me almost as if she were laughing at me." She paused. "James, I think the man was Gaston Moreau."

After a moment of silence, James asked, "Did you get a good enough look at him to make a fairly certain guess? You've only seen Gaston once."

"Once, yes, and it was a bad day for me. I was so unhappy about your marriage and most of my attention was on Renée, but I remember Gaston as an unusual-looking man. Not handsome, but striking—not the kind of man you forget seeing."

"Did he act like he wanted to talk to you?"

"No. He didn't motion for me to come to him or look as if he were going to walk toward me. He just stared with an almost scornful expression. Well, maybe it wasn't scornful, but it wasn't friendly or even . . . nice. I felt more as if he were sizing me up."

"Sizing you up? For what?"

"I don't know. That's what scared me so

much that I went tearing off, looking for Eric. James, you've been trying to talk to the man for a week to tell him that his daughter has been murdered. His wife always says he's out of town, she won't have him bothered; I don't know what all she's said. You told me she hates Renée. I can't guess how Gaston feels about her now, but he has to feel something. You sent him registered mail about the divorce and received acknowledgment of its delivery with his signature, so he had to know the marriage was over. And if he's here—which I'm certain he is—he has to know she's dead. Murdered."

James's gaze drifted out the window into the early night. The muscles around his eyes and his mouth tightened. He squeezed her hand so tightly, she almost shook it loose, but she knew James needed her right now, maybe more than he ever had. She was determined not to show the slightest sign of weakness.

"Does Eric still have a deputy following you all the time?"

"Yes. Tom right now. He's very diligent, James. He's standing outside the door.

He'll follow me home and sit outside the house until Jeff relieves him around three in the morning."

"Good. I don't want you to be alone, Catherine, not for a minute."

"I won't be."

"You'll go straight home after you leave the hospital, you'll lock all your doors and windows, and you'll stay inside. Don't go to work tomorrow."

"Well, I have to go to work. Dr. Hite won't be back to Aurora Falls until midweek and there's no time to cancel my appointments. But I won't be alone. Beth and Jeff will be there. Besides, I'm only keeping morning hours. I'm picking you up here at noon when you're released and we'll be together for the rest of the day."

"But you won't come here without sur-veillance. You promise me."

"I promise," Catherine said solemnly. "James, are you afraid of Gaston Moreau?"

"I'm afraid of what he's capable of. I used to just think he was odd. When I first married Renée, he gave me a bad feeling. And finally, she told me what he'd done to her for years. I never saw him after that, but I know he's a monster." He paused, looking intensely into her eyes again. "Catherine, I know in my gut that if Gaston Moreau is in Aurora Falls, it isn't just to claim the body of his daughter."

CHAPTER TWENTY-THREE

1

Catherine awakened with a dull headache and a sense of dread. The headache she understood—the recent events would give anyone a headache. The dread was a mystery. James would be released today and she'd planned a simple but intimate dinner and relaxing evening for them.

She ate a quick breakfast of toast, downed a mug of coffee, and looked out the front window to see Deputy Jeff Beal sitting in a patrol car. He saw her in the window and waved before Catherine went into the garage for her car. Marissa's was already gone, of course, and Catherine knew she was either tracking down a hot lead or looking for one.

To Catherine's disappointment, the day lay low and gray, as if the sky were pressing downward, closing in for winter. She had hoped for a beautiful mild, sunny day like yesterday. What a shame that day had been wasted on the brunch, she thought, when this was the day she would be bringing James out of the hospital and back into the world.

They pulled into the parking lot of the Aurora Falls Center, Jeff parking a few spaces toward the back and away from Catherine. She assumed Eric had given them instructions to not park at the front of the center or the parking lot because that might give patients a sense that something was wrong. Dr. Hite usually didn't arrive before 9:30, but Beth's small car was already parked at the very back of the lot. While Jeff sat in his patrol car, calling in to report that he was "on scene," Catherine looked at Beth's car, which bore dents, some rust, nearly bare tires, and about twelve years of bad care.

"All checked in," Jeff said brightly, jolting her from her study of the car. Either Tom or Jeff had entered the center with Catherine and looked around, said hello to Beth, then had a cup of coffee before they returned to a long day in their patrol car. "You okay there, Dr. Gray?"

"If you don't stop calling me Dr. Gray, I'm going to break the light on top of your car."

"Oh. Would that be a *no*?"

"That would be a *please* call me Catherine. After all, I call you Jeff. And if I seem a little draggy, it's because of the absolute blast I had this weekend."

Jeff started laughing. "Yeah, Tom told me about it. Actually, he said he'd been dreading the assignment—he's not big on weddings and social stuff—but it turned out sort of hilarious."

"I'm glad he had a good time," Catherine said, half seriously, half-laughing. "But I hope to go at least a year—make that ten—without another three-day gala like that one." They climbed the porch steps and she put her key in the door, which Beth kept locked until opening time at nine o'clock.

Catherine swung open the front door,

looking back at Jeff. She took several steps into the waiting room, Jeff close behind, and closed the door. She was still saying something about the wedding to him when she noticed the smell of good coffee didn't fill the waiting room and Beth wasn't sitting behind her desk.

Then from beside a tall bookshelf near the door stepped Ian Blakethorne. His face was smooth, handsome, untroubled, and before she realized what was happening he stuck a needle in Jeff's neck and pushed the plunger.

2

While Catherine stood frozen in shock, Jeff reeled slightly and reached for his gun. Ian's hand swept at Jeff's with more strength than Catherine could have imagined. Jeff stumbled and once again reached for the gun. This time Ian's leg shot out, his ankle crossing Jeff's and jerking the policeman to the floor. Jeff writhed, still fumbling for his gun, but this time Ian reached down, took the gun, and kicked

Jeff in the abdomen. Jeff grunted and curled into a ball, his eyes closed, his legs making rhythmic jerking movements that grew slower and slower.

"My God!" Catherine at last found her voice. "You didn't inject him with animal tranquilizer!"

"I used something almost as good," Ian said offhandedly.

"Where's Beth? What have you done with Beth?"

"I got here a little before Beth did. I was waiting for her—grabbed her on the porch. I'm afraid she's already asleep."

"*Asleep* or dead?"

"I'll keep you in suspense."

Catherine felt reality slip away from her for a moment. She thought she might faint. Then she saw Jeff twitch again. The dulled light from the front windows managed to pierce the fading light behind her eyes. She took a deep breath, waiting for Ian to come at her with the hypodermic needle, knowing she had no strength to fight him. Instead, they both stood still, him looking at her acutely, her looking at him with dim horror.

"Catherine, you're not going to swoon like some damsel in a romance novel, are you?"

"No," she said faintly. "No. I'm going to stand right here and ask you what's wrong."

"That's it? Nothing more clever? Just, 'What's wrong?'"

Catherine stood as straight and still as she could while gathering every bit of strength, of courage, of daring, she could muster.

"Yes." Her voice was steady, strong. "What did you want, Ian? Screaming? Crying? Begging?"

The controlled look on his face, the near-cocky tone of his voice, vanished. He looked at her in puzzlement and then shook his head before saying in a slow, mystified voice, "No. I thought that's what I wanted, but I didn't. If you'd acted that way, you wouldn't have been Catherine—my dearest Catherine—whom I've loved since I was ten."

"Loved?"

"Yes. Oh, not *that* way. I never thought of you sexually—I really didn't. No nasty fantasies. Only romantic ones. That was the kind of love I had for you." His forehead wrinkled as his eyes grew troubled. "I don't think she ever believed that, though. That's why she didn't like for me to talk about you. She didn't even want to hear your name." He looked at Catherine in a kind of wonder. "You're all that *ever* came between us."

"'Us'?" Catherine asked carefully. "Who is 'us'?"

"You know."

She started to deny it, then realized that was the wrong tack. "I want you to tell me. I want you to say it out loud. Who is 'us'?"

"Me and . . . Renée."

Catherine barely registered Ian pulling a gun, pointing it at her, and telling her in a courteous voice that he'd like to go into her office now. She nodded and led the way, trying not to flinch or give a sign he might mistake as an attempt to bolt away from him. She might have been escorting a regular patient in for a session.

God, what a session this would be, she thought as she sat down on her chair, crossing her legs and looking at handsome young Ian standing by her desk.

"So, what would you like to talk about today?" she asked, managing a small smile.

"Is that what you say to all your patients?"

"Yes."

"You're treating me like a patient?"

"I'm treating you like someone who acts as if they want to talk. Is that insulting to you?"

Ian appeared to think for a moment. "No, I guess not."

"You do want to talk to me, don't you? Otherwise, we wouldn't have come into my office."

"Yes, I suppose I want to talk." He glanced around, never moving the gun aimed at her chest. "I like the way you decorated your office."

"Thank you, but you helped. You brought me a gift when the redecoration was finished—the beautiful porcelain temple jar. I've had so many compliments on it."

"Who from?"

"Dana Nordine. And she knows art."

"Dana Nordine," Ian repeated in an almost whimsical voice. "Well, I guess she *would* need counseling, considering—"

Surprisingly, someone knocked loudly on the main office door. Please let that be the police, Catherine thought frantically;

then reason returned. The police wouldn't knock on the door.

"That's my father," Ian said calmly. "I called him before you got here. I told him to come alone." Ian's voice toughened. "He'd better have done what he was told."

"You told your father to come here?"

"Yes. Is it so unbelievable that someone can order around Lawrence Blakethorne? I suppose it is. But obviously, I've done it." He tilted the gun upward. "Stand up and walk to the door. Move calmly, naturally. I've locked the door. Unlock it and let him in. He'll be firing questions at you, but don't answer. Just say you needed to see him. Don't try to give him any secret signals or any of that silliness. He probably wouldn't notice anyway. After he's inside, lock the door behind him."

"And then?"

"And then he will get the shock of his life."

CHAPTER TWENTY-FOUR

Catherine opened the door to see Lawrence—tall, sturdy, and obviously annoyed. "Catherine," he said abruptly. "What's all this nonsense about? Be here precisely at eight forty. Don't tell anyone where I'm going. Is this a romantic tryst or a blackmail meet?"

"Neither, I'm afraid, but it is important. Please come in."

Lawrence stomped in as if he were wearing shoes covered with heavy snow. She closed the door behind him and locked it, as directed. Then she took a few steps back. What was she supposed to do now?

Invite him to have a seat while she put on a pot of coffee?

"Look, Catherine, I don't mean to be rude, but I'm a busy man. I'm always in my office by nine o'clock. I can't imagine what you have to see me about so early. And all this damned secrecy. Is this about some kind of surprise for Patrice? Because if it is, you could have had the courtesy to call me at my office at a decent hour."

"This is a decent hour, Father, but it isn't really Catherine who wanted to talk to you. It was I."

For a moment, Lawrence looked in bewilderment at Ian, who had appeared once again from his hiding place by the bookshelf. Then Lawrence started to laugh. "Good God, boy, what are you up to? And what's all this 'Father' business?"

"You are my father, aren't you?"

"What?" Lawrence's gaze shot to Catherine. "Have you been telling him something sick like you oddball psychologists come up with?"

"I haven't told him anything, Lawrence. Apparently, he has some things he wants to tell you. And me."

"Well . . . well, look, you two, I don't have

time for this. Neither do you, Ian. Work. Work comes first. Now come with me before we're late."

"Yes, work has always come first with you, hasn't it?" Ian asked calmly. "Building the business, building your *empire*."

"Stop being such a smart aleck. I've made a multimillion-dollar business out of nothing. Nothing, dammit! Now come with me!"

Lawrence reached for Ian, and in an instant Ian pointed the gun at Lawrence's face. "This time I don't take orders from you, Father, and this time work doesn't come first."

Lawrence staggered back a step, his mouth slightly open, his eyes wide. Then, for the first time, he gazed around the room and saw Jeff Beal lying on the floor, motionless. "What's this? Is he dead? Is someone holding you hostage?"

"*This* is a deputy who has been drugged into unconsciousness," Ian said calmly. "We are not hostages. Rather, I'm not a hostage. You and Catherine are a different matter. You're *my* hostages, and for once, Father, you will do what *I* say."

"Why are you calling me *Father*?"

"Because you are my *father,* but you've never been my *dad.*"

"I . . . I don't understand," Lawrence said, his voice weaker, almost shaking.

"You will," Ian returned. "Now let's go into Catherine's lovely office and have a talk."

Catherine preceded Lawrence, whose clumping steps seemed deafening even on the thick carpet. When they reached her office, she immediately went to her chair, whether out of habit or a sense of safety she wasn't sure. Ian motioned for his father to sit on the couch. Then Ian leaned against Catherine's desk, slowly swinging the gun from Catherine to his father and back. Moments of silence passed and Catherine saw the sweat popping out on Lawrence's forehead, although the room was on the cool side. But then, he hadn't removed his coat.

"Let's talk about Renée," Ian said calmly.

"Renée?" Lawrence asked incredulously. "Renée Eastman?"

"Of course," Ian replied. "You've known all along that's what everything has been about—everything."

"Everything?" Lawrence seemed bewildered. "Not just her murder?" Ian looked at him steadily. "Oh my God, you mean the other murders, too!"

"Yes. Don't pretend you didn't know they had a connection to Renée Eastman's murder."

"Well . . . well yes. Most people think so. Someone tried to kill her husband—"

"Her *ex*-husband."

"Okay, her ex-husband. It's been a helluva week for Aurora Falls. All this murder, mayhem . . ." Lawrence's concentration seemed to wander for a few moments. Then he snapped back. "But what does Renée Eastman have to do with any of us, Ian?"

"She was the woman I loved more than life itself," Ian said flatly. "And one of you murdered her."

Silence grew in the room until Catherine had a wild impulse to simply scream at the horrible, unbelievable scene unfolding in front of her. Was she having a dream? No, a nightmare. She must be having a nightmare and any second she'd wake up, heart pounding, breath heaving, but slowly realizing she was back to her blessedly ordinary reality.

Then Lawrence and Ian spoke again,

and she knew, unfortunately, this was no simple nightmare. "Are you out of your mind? You didn't even *know* her."

"We were lovers, Father. Renée Moreau was my lover, my love, since I was seventeen."

It's not true! a small, childish voice within Catherine cried. But a louder, more reasonable voice told her Ian was not lying. Renée taking a young, impressionable boy—an intelligent, sensitive, beautiful-souled boy who would see her as so much more than she really was—as a lover made perfect sense. He would have been what her own starving spirit wanted, craved, had no scruples about taking for her own needs, never considering what harm she might be inflicting on him.

"Seventeen! That whore took advantage of you when you were seventeen?" Lawrence burst out, making a clumsy effort to leap to his feet.

Ian stepped closer to his father, the gun pointed at his face. "Don't call her a whore."

"She *was* a whore! You're lying. You couldn't have let her put a hand on you, that bitch, that—"

As Lawrence made another unsteady,

enraged step closer to Ian, Ian came to within inches of his father's eyes, holding up the gun. "Sit down, Father, or I will shoot you right now."

The soft voice of Ian had turned to iron. He looked taller, stronger. And not quite sane. Fear rushed through Catherine like a fierce stream, and before she knew she was going to say a word she remarked, "Ian, no one is going to say anything else bad about Renée. This is my office and I will *not* allow it. Lawrence, sit down and shut your mouth for once. Ian, please tell us about you and Renée." Lawrence threw her a fierce look. Then, as if his legs had simply given way, he sank back on the couch. "Please, Ian, go ahead. I will *not* allow him to interrupt you."

Ian looked at her warily for a moment. Then, when neither she nor his father moved or said a word, Ian seemed to relax slightly.

"You didn't know Renée, Catherine."

"No, I didn't. I only met her at her wedding." She had to swallow before she could force out the next words in a calm voice. "Please tell me about her. How did you meet?"

"You might have killed her. Do you care?"

"Yes, Ian, I care," Catherine said solemnly. Denying that she might have killed Renée would be useless.

Ian looked around the room for a moment, as if considering whether or not to answer Catherine. Then he began to speak slowly. "I went to private school, away from Aurora Falls. It was summer, though, and I was home. I was restless, I had no friends here, so I decided to take an art course taught by some guy I'd heard was good—Nicolai Arcos. "Renée took the course, too. I was so shy. I didn't talk to anyone. But she introduced herself to me. She said it was her first summer in Aurora Falls and she didn't have any friends, either.

"Of course, Arcos was quick to have conversations with her—she'd studied in Europe, which he said fascinated him," Ian went on. "It was really her beauty that attracted him. I'm sure she realized that, but she didn't let that put her off. Nor did she push me away in favor of the exotic artist. Instead, she seemed to pull us into a threesome. I felt I had two friends. I didn't feel so alone anymore."

"You weren't alone, Ian. You were home, with me," Lawrence said.

"With you? When? You left early in the morning and came home no earlier than nine at night, when you said you had some business to finish in your office. You devoted weekends mostly to business on Saturdays, or luncheons or golf games or tennis or racquetball with business associates."

"And you were invited to participate in all of those things."

"Me? I hate golf, in case you forgot. And I may appear to have made a full physical recovery from the car wreck, but I cannot play tennis or racquetball. But I guess you forgot that, too."

Lawrence opened his mouth as if to make an excuse, then closed it again. He had no excuse, Catherine thought, except that Ian was right. Lawrence had forgotten his own son could not participate in rigorous athletics.

"So you, Arcos, and Renée became friends," Catherine said.

"In a way. It was like a play. Arcos wanted her. I loved her. Each knew how the other felt. Each pretended not to know."

"Did Renée know?"

"Renée was very unhappy and con-fused," Ian said brusquely. "I don't think she knew exactly how Arcos and I felt. Maybe she had a hint. Maybe not."

Like hell, Catherine thought. She knew exactly how the men felt. She enjoyed the attention, the competition for her affection.

"And then one day we began talking about how soon I'd have to go back to school. Renée started to cry." Ian went quiet, his gaze growing hazy, his expres-sion a mixture of sadness and wonder. "That's the first day she took me to the cot-tage."

Catherine expected an outburst from Lawrence, but none came. He simply sat, looking almost deflated, on the couch, his hands folded.

"The two of you made love," Catherine said.

"Yes! Yes! We made *love.* She told me she loved me and I said the same. We were together, one, from that day on."

"I see."

"No, no, you don't, because you're think-ing of her affair with Arcos!" Catherine looked at Ian in surprise. She had expected him to either deny it or not mention it. "When I went back to school, we kept in touch. She told me about their relationship. She said she didn't want it to hurt me, because it meant nothing. She was just so unhappy."

"Oh, Ian, how could you even think—," Lawrence began, but Catherine cut him short.

"If Renée was so unhappy with James, why didn't she go home to her parents?"

Ian looked at Catherine in surprise. "Why, her father molested her, didn't you guess? The only reason he wanted a child was so he could have sex with her, and he started when she was so young she can't really remember."

"And the mother did nothing?"

"Audrey, Renée's mother, is a lot younger than the father. And she didn't have any money. She and Gaston, Renée's father, had an agreement. She got to be Mrs. Moreau if she had a child. He'd wait if she had a boy first. He'd wait until she had a girl. And then the girl was his. It was a trade-off. Audrey has always known."

So Renée had told Ian quite a bit, Catherine thought. How much of it was true, though? "Why did she marry James of all people?" Catherine asked. "It seems to me she would have chosen someone a bit wilder. And he wasn't rich."

Ian gave Catherine an almost uncanny smile. "He found out things about Gaston. She wasn't in love with him, but she knew if she married him, he could protect her from Gaston. That's the *only* reason she married James Eastman. It's the reason she stayed with him even though she couldn't stand him. He could protect her from someone she feared more than anything—her own father."

"And what were these things James knew?"

"She'd never tell me. She said she was protecting me, too. Gaston might find out that I knew and if he did . . ."

"If he did?"

"He'd kill me."

Catherine stared at him. Renée had laid it on thick. Her story about James threatening Gaston was absurd, the stuff of movies and novels. Yet in spite of Ian's intelligence, he'd been willing to believe anything Renée told him. It's almost as if she bewitched him, Catherine thought with a giddy impulse to start giggling. She made a small choking sound to cover the nervous reaction, then looked seriously at Ian.

"What's wrong with you?" Ian asked.

"I swallowed wrong, that's all." Catherine cleared her throat again so he'd believe she'd genuinely gotten choked up and then asked, "What happened when you came home the next summer?"

"I was finished with school. I wanted us to go away together, but she said no. She said I had to go to college—I'd planned on it since I was young. She wouldn't take that chance away from me. We could wait, she said. We could wait a year or two, save money—neither of us had much of our own—and then we'd go away where neither Gaston nor James would find us."

"Gaston or James? What about your father? Didn't she think he'd come looking for you?"

"I knew he wouldn't. He'd be mad as hell, but he wouldn't take the time to look for me. He didn't think that much of me anyway."

"That's not true!" Lawrence burst out. "You're my son! I love you!"

"Actions *do* speak louder than words,

Father. You've given me elaborate gifts and bragged on me to your friends, but you've never spent any more time with me than you had to, especially after the car accident. Was that because I didn't act quite the way I did before?"

"You did!"

"I was physically injured, so I wasn't as strong as other boys my age—the sons of your friends. I had to spend months in a bed." Ian stopped for a moment, his mouth curling up in a snide grin. "And then there was that *head* injury. That's what you told people. 'Ian got a nasty bump on the head.' Nasty bump on the head? I had a *brain* injury. For a while, the doctors thought I'd be permanently brain impaired. That's what you really couldn't stand, was it? That you might have a son who wasn't mentally *normal*?"

Lawrence flinched and Catherine knew it was true. Any parent would have been distraught over the seriousness of Ian's injuries, but it was the assault on his brain that had worried Lawrence the most, and not for Ian's sake. For Lawrence's own pride. Hate flared through her for a moment and she almost said something vile, detestable, to Lawrence. Then she looked at him, sunken and pale on her couch, all of the old Lawrence Blakethorne bravado vanishing before her eyes, and she said nothing. She made herself look back at Ian.

"Did you talk with Renée when you were in college?"

"All the time. And she told me everything. I knew about Nordine and Arcos, but whenever I came home, it was like I'd never left."

"You were lovers again?"

"Oh yes."

"But you still didn't run away with her."

"We were still saving money—I wouldn't come into my inheritance until Grandmother died—and Renée said she wanted me to have another year to make up my mind that being with her was what I really wanted."

"She knew that your grandmother was going to leave you all her money?" Lawrence asked suddenly.

"Yes. I said we told each other *everything*. I know you think that's what she wanted. You think everyone wants money more than anything, but she didn't. She didn't care about the inheritance. She only cared about me."

Catherine saw some color come back into Lawrence's face. He was regaining a little strength. He was going to shout or even try to stand up again, maybe lunge at Ian.

Quickly Catherine bent over and let out a little cry of pain. Both Ian and Lawrence looked at her as she began vigorously rubbing her right calf. "Just a muscle spasm. They happen when I've held still too long or I'm nervous. It's nothing." And it really was nothing. "I'm sorry, Ian."

"I know about muscle spasms."

"I should think so! You had plenty of them in rehab."

"Hundreds, it seemed." Thank God he remembered, Catherine thought. "You always rubbed and rubbed until they began to ease or the doctor had to give me a shot of something to relax them."

"Yes. I remember. You had such a hard time in there for months."

"And I relied on you. Patrice came some, but she spent a lot of time with Grandmother or at work." He looked furiously at Lawrence. "And you hardly *ever* visited."

Catherine stayed in her bent position, rubbing her leg and glancing at her watch. Eight fifty-five. She'd been here for less than half an hour. It felt like she'd sat in this chair, listening to Ian, for a day.

"Is your leg better?" Ian asked in a concerned voice.

"A little. You see . . . I had a hard fall last year on my right hip. I didn't break it or anything, but it's caused problems with my leg ever since then."

Ian looked as if he was thinking things over. Then she saw decision in his eyes. "Stand up. Slowly flex your leg. That's how it's done. I remember. I don't want to see you in pain."

You don't want to see me in pain, but you're waving a gun in my face, Catherine thought. Ludicrous. But a chance was a chance.

"Well, okay." Catherine stood up slowly, wincing a bit as she leaned toward the right. "Oh, maybe this is a worse one than I thought."

"Keep rubbing it," Ian ordered. "You know how muscle spasms are. You remember how mine were."

"I felt so sorry for you. I wished I had

magic fingers that could massage away the pain. Then I'd have to admit defeat and call a doctor for an injection of muscle relaxer. You were afraid of needles."

"I wasn't afraid of them. I just hated them."

She took a small, staggering step to the right, then caught herself on the corner of the desk. "I'm all right. I just need to stand and flex it." Catherine flexed gently. "But about Renée—something changed between the two of you," she went on. "She left not long after you went back to the university for what would have been your—let's see—junior year. What changed?"

"Nothing! Not in our hearts. But after all Renée had been through in her life before Aurora Falls, after she'd come here and spent years with James, with Arcos and Nordine fighting over her when all she really wanted was me, she said she just couldn't take it anymore. She said she was leaving town. I begged her to come to me, but she said she wouldn't put me in danger." She was trying to escape you, too, Catherine thought in pity for the young, highly intelligent yet naïve Ian. "She said she would keep in touch. And she did. She didn't abandon me. I always knew where she was and if she was safe.

"Then she said things were getting shaky for her," Ian continued. "I wasn't certain what she meant. She began to sound frightened of what was going to become of her. She stopped telling me where she was. She didn't come home in June when I did. You can't imagine how frantic I was. And then, a month after the beginning of my senior year, my grandmother died. She left me a fortune. Well, maybe not what some people would call a fortune, but nearly twelve million dollars. There would be so much money, even after taxes, I could take Renée away and keep her safe. I was elated."

"But she didn't know your grandmother had died," Catherine said. Maybe it was hope or pure imagination, but she thought she'd caught a glance of a person through one of the windows in her office, someone who seemed to be walking slowly, carefully.

"Yes, she did. She'd been keeping up with me all along because she loved me." He smiled gently. "We talked about our plans. The will had to go through probate and that can take up to a year. I had an apartment at school, but she said she still didn't feel safe and she wouldn't feel safe until we could go away together. I understood. She *wouldn't* have been safe. My father started checking on me regularly." Ian's mouth pulled up slightly on one side, giving him a snide look. "I suddenly became more interesting when Grandmother had died and left me all that money. He always knew I was going to get it, but I believe he thought she might live another five or ten years."

"I finished my senior year; I came home; I acted as if I were going to invest all of the money in Blakethorne Charter. That made Father really happy, but it's what he'd been expecting all year. Actually, it's what he needed. I know more about business than he thinks I do. I secretly kept up with the books and I knew he'd overextended himself. What do you think all of this frenzied pursuit of a merger with Star Air has been about? Even all of my money wouldn't have been enough to bail him out."

"Merging with Star is a good business move!" Lawrence thundered.

"I agree. But I know you. You would

much rather have kept Blakethorne all to yourself, not merged with another company. My inheritance could help, but it couldn't save you. You *had* to have the resources of another company, even if it was one you hated as much as Star Air."

"I don't *need* Star Air," Lawrence thundered. "I'm giving Star Air the chance of a lifetime!"

"Save it, Father. I told you—I know all about your finances. Not everyone at Blakethorne Charter is a fan of yours. Some of your employees hate you and they don't have a lot of scruples about sharing information with your own son."

Lawrence made a low, grumbling sound, his fist clenching. He was furious, but for some reason he couldn't seem to act. Shock, perhaps, Catherine thought. But fear? She didn't think Lawrence was capable of a fear that would make him unable to act.

"When did Renée come back to Aurora Falls?" Catherine asked.

"I told you we kept in touch. All the legalities concerning Grandmother's will were finished in early September. Father expected me immediately to sink the money into Blakethorne, but I kept stalling. I was waiting for Renée. We texted and called, and set up a meeting for Saturday night, the first week of October at nine o'clock in the cottage. We still thought of the cottage as our place. My father was putting more and more pressure on me about giving him the money. He seemed to be getting suspicious, and every hour felt like a day to me until I'd meet up with Renée and get away from him. I'd withdrawn a lot of my money and getting the rest of it wouldn't be a problem for a long time. I figured that by then my father would have had a stroke or killed himself because of all his debt and not be able to give me any more trouble."

The two exchanged mutinous glances. "Anyway, Renée and I were going to leave town Saturday night," Ian went on. "No one would miss me until Monday morning, when we'd be long gone."

Catherine had heard no noises from the waiting room, and fear suddenly washed over her. She'd assumed Ian had injected Beth and Jeff with something to knock them unconscious, but what if he'd given them something fatal? She shuddered violently at the thought.

"What's *wrong* with you?" Ian flared in annoyance.

"My leg—"

"Your leg, your leg—that's a hell of a leg cramp, missy." Ian no longer sounded at all like himself. His voice had gotten deeper, rougher . . . angrier.

Catherine leaned a bit harder on her desk, pressed her fingers onto the wood until the knuckles stood out, and pretended to be quelling pain as she slid over one more small step. "So you went to meet Renée at the cottage on Saturday and what happened?"

Ian looked at her, his handsome young face wrecked by anguish. "She wasn't there. I waited for hours, but my Renée didn't come home to me."

CHAPTER TWENTY-FIVE

"What did you do then?" Catherine asked softly, compassionately, making certain Ian was looking at her when she winced slightly.

"What *could* I do? I went into the cottage. The place was old and crappy, but there weren't any signs of violence or any of Renée's things. I called her; I texted. Nothing. I was certain something awful had happened to her. I scanned the news, the Internet. I spent a hell of a week. I avoided Father as much as I could—he would see that something was wrong. But I had hope. Renée said we must always have hope and that we would be together someday.

Renée was always right. Most people only saw her beauty, her sexuality—they didn't see her wisdom." He paused. "She was the most amazing woman in the world."

She played mother to you, Catherine thought. You poor boy whose mother never acted like a mother and, finally, she almost killed you. And all those months, lying in rehab with hardly anyone coming to see you except me, you must have wondered if she would have cared that she almost killed you. And then came along beautiful, vivacious Renée who shared your interests, who took you to bed and at the same time acted like your mother with an unconditional love, both corporeal and spiritual.

Now Catherine was certain she'd seen someone at one of the windows behind her desk. She wouldn't give herself time to let her gaze focus on the person. She only knew the center was no longer in total isolation.

"You didn't think she was dead," Catherine said.

"No. I could not let myself believe that. Renée had said nothing would keep us apart."

"When did you find out she *was* dead?" Catherine almost whispered.

Ian's face crumpled. "Oh God. The next Saturday, Father had set me up with the daughter of a business associate. She was all right. She didn't want to go on the date any more than I did, which made things easier. We didn't have to pretend with each other. I took her to the Nordine Gallery."

"You were friends with the Nordines?"

"*Friends?* With Ken? God, Catherine, have you lost your mind? I went to the gallery to see the new art but mostly to see Mary . . . that poor little neglected girl. She reminded me of myself at her age. I loved her, Catherine. I don't usually take to children, but I honest-to-God loved that child. And she loved me. One time she told me I was her Prince Charming."

"I'm sure she did love you, Ian. You're handsome and gentle and I'm sure you gave her the attention she didn't get from her parents."

"I tried. Anyway, that Saturday night I introduced the girl to Arcos and everything was going okay, considering, when someone started talking about the body found at the Eastman cottage—the body found by you, Catherine."

"Yes. Finding it was horrible, Ian. But finding it is all I did. I did *not* kill Renée."

He gave her a dismissive glance. "My date wanted to go to a party her friends were having. By this time I could hardly even talk, and as soon as we got to her friend's house I headed straight for the bathroom and vomited. When I came out, she said she'd run into an old boyfriend, neither of us really wanted to be on this date, so why didn't I just leave and she'd stay with him? He'd take her home, but she'd tell her father I did, we had a wonderful time, et cetera. She wasn't mad. She really wasn't paying that much attention to me. The story of my life. So I was able to leave, thank God, without her running to her father with tales of my bad behavior. It was almost too perfect."

"You said that was Saturday night. James went to the cottage Saturday night and someone tried to blow it up using Molotov cocktails," Catherine said. "That couldn't have been you."

"Why not? Because of time? I went home around ten o'clock. Do you think a Molotov cocktail is hard to make? That it takes hours? It doesn't. I've become something of an expert. I practice in my apartment."

"You were such a strange kid," Lawrence suddenly rumbled from the couch. "When you were little, I'd take you to the terminal. I wanted to show off my son. But after the car wreck, you turned odd. You didn't act like other boys your age, like my friends' boys. You talked about things no eleven- or twelve-year-old would know. The doctors said there was no brain damage, but I didn't believe it."

"So that's why even our very few trips out stopped," Ian said, as if experiencing an epiphany. "You thought I was brain damaged. You were *ashamed* of me."

"Lawrence, Ian has a high IQ," Catherine said quickly, feeling hurt for Ian in spite of the position in which he'd put her. "His intelligence was above that of your friends' boys. And he'd had a whole year of recovery from the wreck—a year in which he'd read everything he could get his hands on and watched all the adult scientific and discovery shows. If he sounded different from other kids his age, it's because he was different—he was smarter."

"Humph," Lawrence managed, as if that single word were an effort. It was also a dismissal of everything she'd said.

Ian's gun steadied toward his father again, hatred sparking in those incredibly beautiful "Dreamy Eyes." Catherine was appalled at watching the destruction of a human being she'd loved like a brother for years.

"So everything that's happened this week has been an attempt to kill whoever murdered Renée," she said dully. "You were determined to avenge her."

"Of course I would avenge her! Did you expect me to just accept that someone had killed the most extraordinary woman I'd ever known?" His voice tightened. "My Renée."

"Ian, if I were in your position, the first person I would have thought of as Renée's killer was the man who'd used leverage for years to keep her, the man whose 'prize' had escaped him: James. Were you trying to kill him at the cottage with the Molotov cocktails?"

"Kill him with Molotov cocktails thrown from so far away?" Ian let out a small, soft giggle. "Oh, Catherine, you don't know anything. How clumsy, how inaccurate, that would have been! I just wanted to burn up the place, but I didn't want anyone to see me there, so I made the cocktails and threw them as hard as I could. I didn't even see James until after Patrice drove away.

"Besides, I always knew James didn't kill Renée," Ian said. "I was finally about to have her. I wanted to take every precaution. Patrice had told me James was going to a conference in Pittsburgh. I thought he might know Renée was coming back and the whole thing was a ruse, so I hired a private detective. He followed James to the convention and kept an eye on him the whole time. The police said Renée was probably killed on Friday. James left on Thursday and didn't come home until Sunday."

"But you tried to kill him!"

"With a .22 rifle from such a long distance away? I had three reasons for shooting him. One, to pay him back for all he'd done to Renée. Two, to make people think he was in as much danger as Arcos had been. And three—this is hard for me to believe now—to scare you away from him."

"To scare *me*?"

"I loved you, Catherine, like I would have loved a sister. For so long, you were so good to me. I hated hearing you were seeing him after Renée left. You deserved the best. Instead, you settled for *him.* In my eyes, he was little better than Gaston. I thought his 'near death' might scare you away. The phone call I'd made to Marissa the morning of Arcos's death didn't. I thought you'd see right away that anyone involved with Renée was in danger. I thought Marissa would convince you of it if she got to see Arcos up close, before the cops arrived and backed off the reporters. But it didn't work. Neither did Renée's lingerie I put in James's town house. I've kept that for two years, always sprinkling her perfume on it."

"But it didn't scare me away from him and neither did the mask you put in my car the night of the rehearsal dinner," Catherine said.

"I thought by that time you'd realize being with James was making you a walking target. But you're more stubborn than I ever thought, Catherine. You won't give up."

"Not when I believe in someone."

"And you believe in him?"

"Yes."

"Maybe you're right. He lacks the courage."

"You didn't think Arcos did, though?"

"Arcos is crazy, even when he's not on drugs. Mary told me she saw a woman who looked like the girl in *Mardi Gras Lady.* She told me she'd told Arcos, too. I didn't blame her—she's just a child. She thought Arcos would be pleased that there really was a woman who looked like 'my lady,' as he always called her." Ian drew a deep breath. "Arcos is big; he's volatile; he nearly went crazy when Renée left here. I knew he was just crazy enough to kill her for leaving him. So I waited and I planned. He stayed locked up in his warehouse for a couple of days after you found Renée's body.

"Then I heard about him coming after you. The police were after him. I drove for hours, even though I had a feeling he'd go to the morgue where her body was stored. It was like him to do something perverted like that. I waited and waited, and at last he showed up, high on something, trying to break into the morgue—God knows what he planned to do with her body if he found it. But he didn't get to her. I didn't let him. I don't think he even knew what hit him."

"You shot him in the right eye, just like Renée had been shot. How did you know she'd been shot there?"

"People talk."

"Robbie?"

"Robbie?" He looked bewildered. "Robbie wouldn't tell crime-scene details. At least I found that out. I guess it can't hurt to tell now. There was a paramedic. I'd run into him before when he came to an accident at the airlines. His hair was so red you couldn't forget him. He was a smarmy smart aleck and I knew he had no scruples. I also knew he wasn't going to be on the rescue team for long. I paid him for the information. It doesn't matter now. They fired him the next week. I have no idea where he is."

But Emergency Services might, Catherine thought, and if he's found, he'll be the one paying for what he did. "You put Mardi Gras beads on Arcos."

Ian smiled eerily. "Arcos liked jewelry. He never would have put on cheap stuff like those beads bought by the dozen. I picked purple—at Mardi Gras, purple symbolized justice. Justice is what I gave Arcos."

"You also put purple beads beside James's car."

"He didn't kill her, but he wasn't good to her."

"And Ken Nordine?"

"At least Arcos was passionate about Renée. When he heard about her death, he acted like a lunatic, but that was better than Nordine, going on with life as normal, still thinking first of himself." Ian's face turned hard. "And he'd already found a replacement for Renée. Not so intelligent, sensitive, beautiful, cultured, but a replacement."

"Bridget Fenmore." Ian nodded. "Ian, did you kill her, too?"

Silence spun out in the room as Ian looked downward, his eyes hooded. Just as Catherine thought she heard a slight, metallic noise in the other room, Ian said firmly, "No. But I took her away from Ken. I wanted him to spend a few days knowing what it felt like to have the woman you love missing. Not that I think he really loved her. I don't think he could love anyone. But he couldn't stand the thought of not being in control. He couldn't control Renée's disappearance, and he couldn't control Bridget's."

"What did you do with her, Ian?" Catherine asked softly, moving just a bit to the right. "Is she all right?"

"She would probably tell you she's not all right. She's weak, a whiner, disgustingly easy to frighten. She *is* all right, though. Police released Arcos's building on Thursday. I took her there after I'd finished with James. I've kept her warm, well fed, and in return, she placed a call for me to Ken. I made her tell him to come and get her in the fields of Arcos's warehouse. She told him she'd be killed if he brought the police, but I didn't trust him. I wanted to have room to get away if I saw anything suspicious. But Ken did as he was told. And Ken got what he deserved."

"And then you took him back to the gallery?"

"Yes. Dragging him around wasn't easy, even though I'd rolled him into a heavy blanket. I had Bridget's keys and she'd told me the security system code."

"So after you killed Ken, you were able

to put him under the painting of *Mardi Gras Lady.*"

"Yes. The placement of his body was an extra bonus." Ian sighed as if exhausted. "I thought I was finished. I thought I'd killed everyone who might have killed Renée. And then two things happened."

Ian's voice ran down like the sound of an old Victrola phonograph. Catherine felt as if even the air had stopped moving in the room—all except for Lawrence's heavy breathing as he looked downward, seemingly unable to stand the sight of his son. Catherine prayed no sound would come from the waiting room. She was certain help of some kind was coming. She just had to stall long enough for it to arrive.

"What two things happened, Ian?" Catherine asked.

"What?" he asked vaguely, as if he'd drifted away from the conversation. "Two things? Oh. The first concerned you."

"Me?"

Ian nodded. "I lose cell phones a lot. I lay them down and just forget about them. Then someone takes them." Catherine waited for him to go on. He looked back at the porcelain temple jar he'd brought her just over two weeks ago when she'd officially moved into her new office. "You remember when I brought you that."

"Of course, Ian. We've already mentioned the temple jar."

"At the reception, you rushed up to me and asked to use my cell phone. You said you'd forgotten yours or left it somewhere. It was like a light went off behind my eyes. When I brought you the jar, I was in close contact with Renée. I brought the jar on a Thursday and I was supposed to meet her Saturday night. I got a call when I was here—not from her, from Father—and when I finished, I laid my phone down on your desk. Later that evening, I wanted to use it to call Renée, but I didn't have it. I remembered I'd left it here." He looked at Catherine. "You used it to text Renée and tell her not to meet me on Friday night."

Catherine was flabbergasted. She felt her face slacken with surprise before she heard another, almost minuscule noise and burst into speech. "Ian, I didn't know you even had a relationship with Renée, much less that she was in town."

"Other people saw her."

"Or thought they saw her, but they didn't tell me. And what makes you think I had *any* idea that you were going to meet her at the cottage the next night?"

"Maybe James, maybe you, had someone watching her or. . . ."

"Or?"

Ian looked at his father. "The second thing happened yesterday at the brunch. You were toasting to a merger that obviously wasn't finalized. You were loud and obnoxious, talking about Patrice getting a star tattoo and pointing your glass right at her pubic area." He paused. "Renée had a pentagram tattoo right there. I knew that you'd seen it because at some time you'd forced yourself on her. She might have used Arcos and Nordine to ease her fear and loneliness, but *you*? Being with you would be like being with Gaston. You *raped* her. Then you had to kill her to keep her quiet."

"Rape her!" Lawrence exploded. "*No* one had to rape Renée!" Color flooded back into his face. "But I didn't rape her. I never touched her," he said loudly and unconvincingly. "I don't know anything about a pentagram tattoo. I only mentioned a star and swept my glass upward. Patrice was there and maybe my glass hovered in that area, but it was just a . . . a . . ."

"A what, Father?"

"An accident. Do you think I'd make a suggestion like that in front of all those people?"

"I think you'd do a lot of things you would have had better sense than to do a couple of years ago. You're different. I don't know if you're just in a frenzy over this merger or getting married freaked you out, but you are *different*."

"Goddammit, there is nothing wrong with me!" Lawrence shouted. "I'm the way I've always been. I'm *fine*!"

Another, louder sound came from the waiting room. Oh God, two or three more minutes, Catherine prayed. Just give me a little more time.

"Ian," she said sharply to get his attention, "why would I text Renée from your phone and tell her to meet you at the cottage on Friday night instead of Saturday?"

"You'd use my phone so she'd think it was me. And she'd be there on Friday night, but I wouldn't be the one meeting her—you would. You knew if James heard she was back, he'd probably be through with you. It was her that he wanted. It was always her, not you. I'd thought of that before, but I didn't believe you were capable of murder." Ian bent his head and said weakly, drearily, "But does anybody *really* know another person? Did I really know what you'd do to hold on to James?"

Ian looked as if he had no strength left, as if his muscles were weakening, his alertness diminishing. Catherine took a deep breath, pushed away all her fear, and made a leap for the porcelain temple jar. With a strong grunt, she picked up the fifteen-inch-tall jar, leaped forward, and crashed it over Ian's head just as grim Eric and a tragic-eyed Robbie, guns drawn, and a triumphantly smiling Mrs. Tate pushed through Catherine's office door.

Ian stood still for a moment, then slowly sank to the floor as Eric commanded, "Don't move." And in a second, "Catherine, kick that gun away from his hand."

She did as she was told, feeling nothing, not even relief, as she looked at the crumpled, unconscious body of Ian

Blakethorne. Then she saw the powerful Lawrence Blakethorne shaking, his majestic head bent forward, his big hands covering eyes streaming tears.

CHAPTER TWENTY-SIX

Five days later

"Maybe I expected too much of myself, but I really thought I'd be recovering from this horrible situation by now." Catherine sat beside James on the couch at the Gray home. He had his left arm wrapped tightly around her and her head lay on his shoulder.

"You've loved Ian Blakethorne since he was ten years old."

"But I'm trained to deal with situations like this," Catherine said.

"With patients. What you felt for Ian has been a mixture of sisterly-motherly love and it's been strong. How could you expect yourself to be recovering from his destruction in four days?"

"Oh, please don't say 'destruction,' James."

"What would you call it? A nervous breakdown? Do you think he'll be just fine and going on with his life in six months?"

"No. And don't be mean."

"I'm not trying to be mean. I'm only trying to make you accept what's happened. He killed two people, kidnapped one, shot me. Lawrence keeps insisting this is all the result of the brain injury he suffered in that car wreck. Maybe so, maybe not. Whichever, Ian will go to trial for Murder One and even if his lawyer tries to get him a not-guilty verdict by using the insanity defense, he'll either fail, which happens most of the time, or Ian will end up in an institution for God knows how long. And frankly, I think he needs to be put away somewhere. Don't look at me like that. Think of what he's done. Think of the fact that even though he supposedly loves you like a sister, he was ready to kill you. Thank *God* for Mrs. Tate!"

"Yes, she certainly was the heroine,

wasn't she, arriving right on time like that, knowing when the door was locked and she didn't see Beth when she looked through the windows that something was wrong, and calling nine-one-one."

"It helped that she saw a police car in the parking lot."

"Yes, I suppose that did give her another clue. Still, she's proud of herself and she needs some pride. I've thanked her a dozen times."

"And you have a friend for life."

"Oh dear. That might be as bad as having Maud as a friend for life." Catherine sighed. "I wish I could see Ian, talk to him. I know it wouldn't make me feel better, but I want—I need—to know if he killed Renée."

"Why would he have killed Renée?"

"Maybe he got there that night and after years of waiting, of promises from her, she rejected him. Someone 'better' had come along. He might have had a psychotic break and killed her. He might have done it and not even remembered."

"You know more about memory repression than I do," James said gently. "I still think you may wish you knew for certain, but if you did, you'd feel worse than ever."

He rubbed his chin against Catherine's hair. "Honey, I know this seems impossible, but you have to try to forget everything that happened. Dr. Hite is back, he closed the office this past week and he's given you next week off—"

"I'm not taking off next week. I can't just sit around here trying not to think about something. I have to keep busy."

"I completely understand because I'm the same way. We have a lot in common, Catherine, more than we've ever talked about. In fact, I think we understand each other amazingly well, considering how little we've really talked."

"Well, sometimes I think we do, too."

James bent his head lower and their lips were on the verge of meeting when his cell phone rang. He cussed so quietly he didn't think Catherine even noticed. In a moment, he heard an unfamiliar voice apologizing for bothering him, saying she was afraid something terrible was happening, begging him to help.

James placed his hand on Catherine's back and said, "This might be important.

I'm not sure who it is." Catherine immediately stopped laughing and shushed Lindsay, who hadn't made a noise. "Now, would you mind repeating all of that?" James asked, placing the phone close between him and Catherine so she could hear.

"This is Mrs. Frost, the Blakethorne housekeeper? Miss Catherine knows me."

"I'm here, Mrs. Frost," Catherine said. "What's wrong?"

"I really don't know." The woman's voice raced and shivered. In the twelve years Catherine had known Mrs. Frost, the woman had never spoken with anything but a calm, easeful English accent. "Things have been dreadful around here since all this business with Mr. Ian. It's so terrible. None of us can believe it. I still don't believe it. My dear little Ian." She made a choking sound and then drew a deep breath. "I shouldn't talk about household matters, but naturally there has been tension between Mr. Lawrence and Miss Patrice. I don't quite understand. I feel as if he blames her in some way. One night I heard him saying she should have seen this coming long ago."

"None of us saw it coming, Mrs. Frost."

"Oh, I know. Not even I. Mr. Blakethorne was gone so much of the time; now that I think about it, Ian was gone a good deal, too, although he claimed he had few friends. When he graduated from college he got his own apartment, and except for when he rented it in June he hadn't invited any of us over." She paused. "Well, this morning, Mr. Blakethorne was gone. Miss Patrice was in his office. Mr. Blakethorne doesn't like for people to be in his office, but what could I say to her? She's his wife now."

"Of course, I understand, Mrs. Frost. You couldn't tell her to leave her own husband's office."

"Well, I could tell she was getting into things—file cabinets, drawers, locked drawers—she was breaking the locks! I thought of calling Mr. Blakethorne but didn't really know what to do in this situation. Then he came home. He raced up to his office. They began to quarrel. They got louder and louder and finally Mr. Blakethorne left. Miss Patrice stayed in the office, making a dreadful fuss with more drawers, and then she got on the phone. I heard her say, 'He's doing *what*? Flying his damned plane around?' She came down the steps like a banshee, muttering about the airport. I asked where she was going, but she didn't answer. She was in a fury and she simply got into the Jaguar and drove off at *such* a speed. I hope the police stop her, but if they don't . . ."

"If they don't, she'll go straight to Blakethorne Charter."

"Yes. Oh, Miss Catherine, I know I should probably call the police, but this is a family matter. After everything that has happened, I can't make myself call them. I know Mr. Eastman is a friend of Mr. Blakethorne's. I thought maybe he could do something without causing a fuss, something that wouldn't bring even more unhappiness down on this family. Maybe I did wrong in calling, but—"

"You did exactly the right thing," James said. "I'm going to Blakethorne Charter immediately. I'll straighten this out, Mrs. Frost. You just try to calm down."

"Oh, thank you, sir. I know Mr. Blakethorne and Miss Patrice will be unhappy with me—"

"Don't worry about that now. They should be grateful. I'll call you just as soon as I find out what's going on. And once again, Mrs. Frost, please try to calm yourself. You've done nothing wrong. Fix a cup of tea of something. Talk to you soon."

"I'm going with you," Catherine said when James stood up.

"No, there might be trouble."

"I think I've proved I can handle myself when there's trouble." Catherine marched across the room and picked up her tote bag. "I'm going."

Twenty minutes later, James pulled into the parking lot of Blakethorne Charter and then pulled out again. "Where are you going?" Catherine asked.

"To the back. Lawrence's office faces the runways. Also, Mrs. Frost said he was flying. We'd just be wasting time wandering around the terminal."

They rounded the northern side of the terminal and, staying close to it, looked out at the two runways. A Learjet raced down one before lifting gracefully off the concrete into the light blue sky. Beyond it, sun shone through the rushing water of the Aurora waterfall.

"There they are," James said urgently.

"It looks like Lawrence has just come back from a flight. Patrice is with him."

Catherine peered at the two standing beside a small airplane, clearly arguing. Lawrence stood stalwart but tensed with anger while Patrice's voice rose so loudly they could hear it as soon as they opened their doors. Neither saw Catherine and James coming toward them.

"Lawrence!" James called. "What's going on?"

Both Lawrence and Patrice looked at them in complete surprise. They fell silent until Catherine and James stood beside them.

"I've been up today," Lawrence said casually. He turned to his plane. "Cessna Stationair. Only one engine, but one of my favorite planes for when you want to be alone, high above the little ants running around down here not knowing what's important."

"You bastard," Patrice snarled. "Little ants running around down here. That's all anyone has ever been to you, isn't it?"

"James, do you know this thing can rise at one thousand feet per minute?"

"No, I didn't."

"Did you know he's sick?" Patrice shrieked at James. "Were you in on this together? Did he promise you money, James? How much did you know?"

James looked at Patrice in shock. "I have no idea what you're talking about."

"Oh, don't you? What about you, Catherine? You're a doctor. You knew!"

"I'm not a medical doctor, Patrice, and I *don't* know. Calm down!"

"Calm down? After what I've just found out?"

Lawrence looked around the runways, toward the Orenda River, and up the crashing water to the top of the falls. "I think this will be the most beautiful airport in the world," he said dreamily. "People will come just to see it. In ten to fifteen years, the population of Aurora Falls will have nearly doubled. And it will all be because of Blakethorne Charter. I always knew it was destined to happen."

"Are you already losing your mind?" Patrice asked acidly. "Are your neurons already degenerating? Of course they are. I've seen the signs. I just didn't recognize them." She lunged at Lawrence so hard, she nearly knocked him off his substantial feet. "Now I know why you suddenly decided you wanted to marry me! You wanted a nurse!"

"Wait! Patrice, what do you mean about his neurons degenerating?" Catherine asked. "What are you talking about?"

"Oh, don't act so innocent, Catherine. You may not be a medical doctor, but don't tell me you didn't suspect something the night of the reception when he nearly knocked you down, then you pushed him into Ian's arms and told him to take his father someplace to rest." Patrice waved a handful of papers in Catherine's face. "ALS. Lou Gehrig's disease! Lawrence has it. Lawrence was diagnosed the first time two years ago and five times since then!"

Lawrence savagely grabbed Patrice's arm. "You've been in my office! You broke into locked files, drawers, my *safe.* How did you learn the combination? Secret cameras?"

"Exactly," Patrice hissed. Then she looked at James. "The early symptoms have been getting worse. The choking. The loss of muscle control and the muscle weakness. The slurring. All of his laughter at the wrong times. How much easier he gets tired than he did just a couple of years ago. I chalked it up to nerves over this Star merger, but he got too out-of-control even for that explanation. Then came the marriage proposal I've waited for ever since my sister killed herself. I was elated. *Elated!* How ridiculous. I should have *known.*"

Suddenly Lawrence looked at her, as alert as he'd ever been. "The proposal you waited for ever since your sister *killed* herself?"

"Maybe. She wanted to die. Did you even know that? I doubt it. You and Mother never knew anything you didn't want to know."

"You pushed her into killing herself."

"I didn't!"

"You visited. You stayed in her room and you talked and you talked and you talked. And whenever you left, she seemed sadder, even more withdrawn. Mrs. Frost told me."

"Oh, did she? That woman has always hated me. And if you did believe her, why didn't you do something about it? Why didn't you ban me from the house? I'll tell you why. Because I took up Abigail's time. She wouldn't come here looking for you, embarrassing you, making you come home. I babysat!"

"And that day of the wreck?"

"I'd had years of loving you, of seeing her with your wedding ring on her finger and doing nothing except drooping around her room in a fog of pills. She was worse that day than ever and I wanted to strangle her. Instead, I told her about your other women. I always kept track of you, Lawrence. I knew there were others. And she got more and more upset. And suddenly she ran out of her room with the keys to her car." At last tears shone in Patrice's eyes. "I didn't know she was going to grab Ian on her way out and take him on that nightmare ride with her. I didn't want anything to happen to Ian, I swear to you."

"But you pushed her over the edge!"

"You saw her going and you did nothing to help her!"

"I was building a business. I was putting in all my time and effort on building a good life for my family!"

"For yourself! And look how it turned out, Lawrence. You're dying and your son is a lunatic, a murderer. He killed Arcos and Nordine and he would have killed you and Catherine all because he thought you killed his precious Renée, the woman who'd preyed on an innocent teenage boy."

Catherine felt as if a gong had gone off in her head. "Patrice, how do you know Ian became involved with Renée when he was a teenager?"

"What? Oh, I don't remember. He told me, I guess."

"He . . . did . . . not . . . tell . . . you. He wouldn't have told anyone. You kept track of Lawrence. You kept track of Ian, too."

"I didn't. I'm too busy."

"I don't think you're ever too busy to do what you really want to do."

Lawrence was looking at Patrice, stunned. "You knew my son was with that whore?"

"Like you were? She probably had to keep track on a calendar—"

"I was with Renée *once.* Just once."

"But you didn't want it to be just once. I saw how you looked at her. You didn't care that James was your friend and she was his wife. And then you had the gall to buy that painting of her! You said it was for Ian, but it wasn't. It was for *you.*"

"As an investment, dammit!" Lawrence shouted. "Why didn't you tell me about Ian?" Patrice didn't answer. "Why didn't you tell me about Ian?" No answer. "You wanted to hurt me for never turning to you, didn't you? All those years after Abigail died, I never took you for my lover, much less my wife. So letting Renée have Ian, letting him get more and more involved with her, was my payback."

Lawrence's voice was growing deeper and grittier, the look in his eyes more venomous, the grip on Patrice's arm tighter.

"Let her go," James said. "Let her *go*."

"I only figured out lately they'd been lovers for a long time." Patrice began talking so quickly she was almost gibbering. "I just guessed about the teenage stuff."

"I doubt if you just *guessed* about anything," Catherine said. "I think you've been keeping track of them for years, especially after your mother died and left her money to Ian. You suspected Renée would be coming back for him. After all, he would be rich soon."

Patrice glared as Catherine continued. "Ian left his cell phone at my office a couple of days before he was supposed to meet Renée. I took the phone to the law office and gave it to Mitzi to give to you since you'd probably be seeing Ian that night."

"She didn't give it to me," Patrice said.

"I'm sure she did. Ian hadn't erased his recent texts. You read them and saw that he was supposed to meet Renée on Saturday night. You sent her a text from *his* phone changing the meeting to Friday night. Renée went to the cottage on Friday, thinking she was meeting Ian, but instead, she ended up having a fatal meeting with you. When Ian went to the cottage on Saturday night, Renée was already dead, but he didn't have a clue. There were no bullet holes in the wall for him to see. After you shot her, you must have dragged her out on that heavy hooked rug the police found in the cistern where you stuffed her until you could find a better place to hide her body, so you didn't even leave a trail of blood to clean up and maybe leave a streak for Ian to see. You cleared out anything she'd brought into the cottage, put it in her car, and hid the car in a neighbor's garage. By Saturday evening, there was no trace of her at the cottage."

"That's absurd!" Patrice shouted.

"You did kill her," Lawrence said, a sound of wonder in his voice. "By God, you *did* kill her." He shook her hard. "Admit it!"

"Okay! I did it for you. Ian's always leaving his cell phones around and it *has* been easy to keep up with his activities. I knew what he and Renée planned. You're in trouble, Lawrence. You spent too much money on Blakethorne. You're desperate. My mother's death was a godsend—you so desperately needed that money she left to Ian, and he was going to run off with and give it to *Renée.* I couldn't stand it. She was a blight, not just on him or you—on everyone. The world was better off without her. I had to do it. I had to get rid of her once and for all for everyone."

"For *you*," Lawrence said. "If my son had run off with her a week before our wedding, it would have been the end of us. It would have destroyed me and that would have destroyed all your plans. You'd waited twelve years to become Mrs. Lawrence Blakethorne, and Renée was going to ruin it all for you."

"She was going to ruin *you*."

"And that would have ruined *you*." His

eyes bored into hers. "Did you know who killed Arcos and Nordine?"

"Oh God, no!"

"You're lying."

"Lawrence, how could I have known?"

"It was obvious their killer and the person who shot James was trying to avenge Renée." He was silent for a moment. "Admit it, Patrice. You *knew*."

"I . . . I wondered. His brain injury. His passionate attachment to her . . ."

"But you didn't come to me with your wonderings. Instead, you let that boy go on killing and now," Lawrence choked, "and now he'll spend the rest of his life in a mental institution."

"Well, at least you won't have to watch it! You'll be dead in two years. The strong, successful, macho Lawrence Blakethorne will be a twitching, jittering, drooling hunched-up being who can't hold anything, who can't walk, who can't even *swallow*. That's the perfect end for a man like you. What will the women think of you then when you won't even be able to *swallow*!"

Suddenly Lawrence jerked Patrice's arm, pulling her closer to the plane. She began to shout, then suddenly to whimper as Lawrence's grip must have tightened. James rushed forward, but with an unexpectedly powerful thrust Lawrence pushed him backward, nearly knocking him down.

"James!" Catherine called helplessly as she stepped behind him, trying to steady him. "What's he doing?"

"Putting her on the plane."

"Patrice!" Catherine called, stunned by the brute force of Lawrence's movements, of slender Patrice's futile efforts to wriggle free of him to somehow break his grip. James started toward the couple again, but Lawrence kicked backward, this time connected with James's leg, and sent him stumbling back to the concrete.

By now, Lawrence had managed to literally stuff Patrice into the cabin of the plane. Just like Patrice must have stuffed Renée's body into that cistern, Catherine thought distantly. Lawrence slammed the door and began to start the plane.

"Oh no," Catherine said faintly. "What's he going to do?"

James simply stared as Lawrence, without looking at the instrument panel or picking up a microphone, took the plane to a runway, and began idling. Catherine could see Patrice struggling inside the cabin, but Lawrence held the back of her hair. She thought he might break Patrice's neck.

Abruptly Catherine remembered the women of the bridal party getting ready in the Larke Inn suite. "Lawrence has business to take care of now, but in two weeks we'll be walking on the Champs-Élysées," Patrice had said gaily. "Think of it—the specialty shops, the cafés, the cinemas . . ." Incredibly, Catherine felt pain at the memory. There would be no Champs-Élysées for Patrice now.

Lost in the recollection, Catherine didn't focus on the plane again until it began roaring down the runway. Around her, she saw workers gathering, stunned by Lawrence Blakethorne's behavior, the danger of taking off without clearance. Catherine grabbed James's hand, terrified to look at what might happen but unable to look away.

After what seemed an interminable time, the plane lifted and soared. The pale afternoon sun flashed on the wings and the plane circled and then headed straight ahead without gaining altitude. In one brilliant flash, sun sparkled on thundering water before Lawrence headed the Cessna straight into Aurora Falls, ending the whole tragedy in a giant ball of fire.

EPILOGUE

Two weeks later

"It's a beautiful day and we've been hermits for the last couple of weeks. That's not like a couple of workaholics like us," James said. "How about going for a drive to clear the cobwebs out of our heads?"

"Do you have cobwebs?" Catherine asked. "I feel like I just have sand. I'd love to go for a drive."

As they sped along, the seriousness gradually leaving their faces, James mentioned again how happy he was that Eric had won the election and was now Sheriff Montgomery. "I'll be getting out of parking tickets right and left."

"That's what you think. Eric isn't big on breaking the rules."

She seemed to drift away for a moment, then snapped back when James mentioned Gaston. "Eric had someone at the morgue call him when Gaston came to claim Renée's body. He cornered him and asked a few questions—there wasn't much else he could do because Gaston hadn't broken any laws. Anyway, the old pervert told Eric he'd come here to search for the person who'd killed his daughter. He told Eric if he'd found the person and had proof, he would have brought it straight to the sheriff." He paused. "Both Eric and I have doubts about that last statement."

"Well-founded doubts," Catherine said. "With a man like Gaston, you don't know if he just wanted to know who killed Renée, or if he would have murdered her killer. It's impossible to know how he felt about her. Probably just possessive. He wanted to avenge her death because she was his property, not because he loved her. He's incapable of love."

"Well, at least he's taken her home. And I think she'll be placed in the Moreau mausoleum, no matter what Audrey says."

They drove on in silence for a while. Then Catherine noticed they were traveling south, passing the Aurora Falls she hoped she would be able to look at again by spring without the dreadful memory of the explosion. On they drove, James slipping in a Tchaikovsky CD he knew she liked, until she began to recognize the remains of cornfields and remembered a bright October day when she'd traveled this way in Marissa's red convertible Mustang.

"James, where are we going?"

"It's a surprise."

"No, it isn't. James, I think you're taking me somewhere I *really* don't want to go."

"You can make up your mind when we get there. For now, just give me the benefit of the doubt."

Catherine sank unhappily in her seat, not at all surprised when James made a right turn just past the November ruins of cornfields. Finally they turned onto Perry Lane. Catherine remembered how annoyed Marissa had been that Catherine had yelled, "Turn right" and scared Marissa into slamming on the brakes in the middle of the highway, then tried to divert her anger by asking if the Beatles had done a song named "Perry Lane."

Finally they swung a wide circle in the road, and after passing distant lines of trees varying from dark red to yellow to orange James pulled to the side of the road. For a moment he didn't say anything. Then he asked, "Well?"

"This isn't the same place—I mean I know it must be—but it looks so different from where the cottage was."

"I had the cottage completely destroyed and all the trash hauled away along with the diseased evergreens. I had the land flattened and a big birdhouse put about a hundred yards north of where the cottage used to stand. I thought it could be sort of a focal point for what's now the center of the lot. It always was the center of the lot, actually. Grandpa put the cottage nearer to the dock."

"I see."

"In the spring, I plan to have the dock rebuilt, build a fabulous boathouse, have the riprap replaced on the riverbank, put in a sturdy fence to separate the level ground from the riverbank, and lots of trees and shrubs planted for color and . . . well, interest."

"What about the cistern?"

"It's been removed, Catherine. Every last trace of it." She stared at the spot where she remembered it being. "Your line of sight is off," James said. "That's quite a few feet from where it was. You see? You don't even remember it that well."

"Oh, I remember it. Maybe not the exact location, but I remember it."

"Okay, I stand corrected. Anyway, I'm going to hire a landscape artist to design and plant a big perennial garden with brick walkways. That will completely cover the area where the cistern was. And hey, look at my grandmother's apple orchard! The leaves on the trees are turning brown now. And to my way of thinking, it's pretty small to be an actual orchard. It could be expanded. Let's take a closer look."

Catherine got out of the car slowly and closed her door. She had to admit that without the shabby cottage, the overgrown, diseased evergreens, the fallen shutters, the pothole-filled gravel driveway, the place looked entirely different. Although some heavy clouds floated over now and then, a pale golden sun still shone through onto the turning leaves of the trees. Even a few birds were already investigating the big birdhouse.

"What do you think?" James asked.

"Well . . . I'd like to say it looks better than it did, but actually, it doesn't even look like the same place." After a moment of silence, she said, "It looks like it could be beautiful."

"*Could* be beautiful?"

"With the right house. Maybe a 'Cape Cod,'" they said at the same time, then broke into laughter. "I guess great minds run the same."

"Great taste runs the same." James stepped closer to Catherine, putting his left hand in his jacket pocket and his right arm around her neck. "Do you think you might like to live out here? I know it's farther from the center than you are now and there aren't many neighbors, although I've heard that a few folks are buying up land out here with plans to level the old fishing cottages and build nice houses."

"Are you telling me you're going to build a house out here, James?"

"I'm telling you that I've given it a lot of thought. It all depends on one thing."

"And what would that thing be?"

"On whether you think *you'd* like to live here." Catherine could do nothing but stare at him. "Catherine Gray, I love you more than I thought I could ever love anyone. When I was young, I was too stupid to know it, but I hope time has taught me a few lessons." Catherine felt her eyes fill up with tears. "My darling girl, will you at least think about marrying me?" Catherine burst into a hiccoughing sigh. "Good lord, is that a yes?" She nodded. "When you make up your mind, and if the answer is 'yes,' tell me when you're ready for me to propose. I'll get a ring."

"A *very* big one." She sniffled. "Yes. Ten carats at least."

"Twelve."

"Anything you say." James glanced over the land where the cottage had once stood. "We don't have to live here, you know. If you think you'd be the least bit unhappy, we can buy land at the other end of town."

Catherine gave the three-acre lot a long look, picturing a beautiful Cape Cod house, a multitude of flowers in the summer, lights on outside evergreens in the winter. "I'd like to live here and raise flower gardens and expand the apple orchard and add peach trees and have lots of cats and dogs."

"That's all?"

Catherine frowned as if lost in thought. Finally, she said, "Oh, and I'd like to have at least two kids. Maybe three, sir, if you don't think you'd mind."

"I don't think I'd mind at all." James beamed, then leaned over, gently pushing her long hair away from her face. Just before his lips met hers, he whispered, "Catherine, dreams do come true. I know, because at last I have mine."